The Cloud

by
Elmore Hammes

The Cloud

Copyright © 2008 by Elmore Hammes

All Rights Reserved.

* * *

ISBN-13: 978-0-6151-4715-4

ISBN-10: 0-615-14715-1

Library of Congress Control Number: 2008901428

FIRST EDITION, JUNE 2008

* * *

Published by
KANAPOLIS FOG PUBLISHING EMPORIUM
Anderson, Indiana

In memory of

Yvonne Louise Hammes,

through whom I learned

the unconditional nature

of a mother's love

Part One

The Cloud

Chapter One: Somewhere Outside the Milky Way

It looked like a gaseous cloud, like a thin mist of gossamer spanning hundreds of thousands of miles of space. It was beautiful, if you were a species that beheld such concepts as physical beauty. It was sentient, if you were a species that differentiated by levels of intelligence, one that defined sentience by willful acts, by knowledge or awareness of one's own being.

The cloud, for lack of a better term, was kept intact by innate cohesive properties of the fine particles that composed its being. It had the ability to essentially fly through the cold reaches of the universe by modifying the external shell of those particles to catch the solar winds. It would move from planet to planet, solar system to solar system, even galaxy to galaxy this way. The winds grew faint between galaxies, sometimes taking millennia to cross the silent void, but it did not matter to the cloud. It only knew more sustenance awaited it when this journey ended. It only knew that another journey would lie beyond this one.

As the cloud enveloped the planet, it had no idea of what life it was absorbing below. It knew there was energy: diverse, plentiful, satiating energy. The hundreds of billions of life forms that it consumed, that it absorbed to feed its trillions of particles, were not recognized by the cloud as anything but bits of energy, sustenance for it to continue its trek across the universe. The plant life, the animal life, the technologically advanced race of beings who had risen from crawling babies in the mud to space faring adults preparing their first interstellar flight, had no warning of the cloud's approach, no sensors that could register the cloud or the danger it brought. They had no means of communicating to it their own sense of being, their own right to exist. They had no chance as the cloud passed through their planet's atmosphere.

It was not a slow or painful death, just a complete and total one. Propelled by the inertia of the solar winds, the cloud passed out of the planet's atmosphere minutes after it had arrived, leaving a dry husk behind it. No life stirred on the once teeming orb. No flora, no fauna, no microorganisms to restart the biological wonder of life. The cloud did not recognize the desolation that remained in its wake. It only knew that the hunger would return soon, that the need for energy would resume. It had fed enough to undertake the next leg of its unceasing journey. It reoriented its particles and accelerated out of the solar system. Hundreds of millions of miles beyond the last planetary object in that system, it crashed through the termination shock where the force of the solar winds met their equal in the interstellar medium, the boundary edge of the heliosphere. These waves of the interstellar medium, stronger than a single star's solar winds, were the cloud's propulsion to the next system.

Chapter Two: Awareness

The cloud entered another solar system. This one seemed no different than the countless before: planets surrounding a sun, one or two in the narrow range that would support the types of energy that it fed on. The journey had taken longer, there had been a greater distance to travel this time as it had passed through countless systems without planets, without energy to feed it, and the speed it gathered from its trillion mini interstellar wind sails had almost dissipated as it entered the outer reaches of the solar system. It shifted properties of its particles, changing their attributes so they no longer rode the winds but let them pass through. It now let the gravitational forces at play in the solar system pull it in toward the life-sustaining planets.

It had no sensors to tell it which planet would offer it the appropriate energy fields to consume; it didn't target a specific solar system, rather it left the one it had consumed in a different direction than it came. It didn't matter whether it was centuries or millennia until it reached the next one, it didn't matter how many thousands of systems it passed through that were stale and lifeless; as long as winds pushed it and gravitational forces pulled it, it would eventually reach a viable energy source. When it arrived at a new system it would ride those gravitational forces from outer planet to inner on one side of the sun, and pass through the remaining planets on the way out of the system. Sometimes a planet might escape its feeding, if it was in an orbital pattern far enough out to one side or the other of its circling path through the system, but the cloud was wide enough that this rarely occurred. And it did not matter; if this system did not feed it, the next one, or the one after that, would do so.

The beings on the fifth planet of this particular system, unlike the previous inhabited worlds, did have sensors. Very advanced sensors, in fact, that had enabled them to see the aftermath of the cloud's passage through the previous solar system. They did not know what the cloud was, what composed it, what drove it; did not know anything about it other than the fact that it had left a decimated path of annihilation behind it. And they were certain that they wanted no part of it.

The beings on the fifth planet had their entire civilization working on a method to stop the cloud. It had taken the cloud four hundred years to cross the gulf from the previous solar system to their own, and it was amazing what a couple billion people working in harmony for four centuries could accomplish. War had been non-existent since the discovery of the cloud's approach. Various groups, long separated by geography, creed or history, reached across their hatreds and jealousies and banded together. The entire planet was unified in their desire to find a way to halt the coming doom. No approach was deemed too radical, no idea nonsensical; everything was weighed, all options considered. Children were encouraged to contribute their most outlandish schemes to stop the cloud; special schools were built to raise them as great thinkers, warriors, diplomats and theologians. No society had ever been so driven, so united, as the beings of the fifth planet in their quest to avoid the fate before them.

The greatest scientist of them all, the product of four hundred years of applied learning in astrophysics and ionic engineering, was Hugrant Thujalm. He (for this was a dual gender species, and he was male) alone of this entire species deserved nominal recognition, for he almost learned the weakness of the cloud. It was not intentional, nor applied in an effective manner for the sake of the beings of the fifth planet, but it was still notable for the effect produced as a result of it.

Hugrant Thujalm pounded his fist on the dais. "Confound it, listen to me! You are fools, all of you!" He stared out at the Inner Council, his face red with rage, spittle flying from the corners of his mouth. "I tell you, it's no use. We have tried our best, and we have failed. We cannot save ourselves. Let us at least save our race."

The Leader of the Council shook his head, his blue tendrils flopping below his double chin. "Hugrant, don't give up hope. The fleet is heading out even as we speak. They will meet the enemy within the hour. Surely one of the weapons will prove effective. Trust in our legacy."

"Our legacy." Hugrant spat out the words. "Our legacy is useless, can't you see that? We have no reason to believe anything we have developed will have any effect whatsoever on this alien force. No, I tell you, the only choice we have is to flee this planet. I told you, we should have put my ionic drive into production years ago."

The Leader did not react in anger, instead smiling at the scientist. "And what would that have done? Possibly a dozen ships fitted with your ionic drive, maybe a hundred passengers on each? And who would decide who would be saved? You? Me? No, better to stay and fight as a race, though we all perish, than to lose the unity we have gained over the past four centuries in a panic driven fight to be one of the precious few to flee our planet."

Hugrant stared at the Leader. "We could have continued the fight elsewhere. We could have avenged the rape of our planet."

"There is still the fleet," the Leader said.

"Bah! Your precious fleet, your cache of weapons, will prove useless. I should have been leading this Council. You have doomed our race, left it without even the chance of revenge."

The Leader's reply was interrupted by a shrill alarm. "The fleet is launching the attack!"

A large screen descended from the ceiling. Thirty silver ships floated near the eighth planet of their system. A vast cloud was before them, encompassing the entire view screen. Purple and pink hues, semi-transparent, with whorls of thicker vapor more opaque and almost deep red, caused the Leader to draw a quick breath.

"It's incredible," he said.

"It's death," Hugrant replied. He turned away from the screen and ran out of the Council room.

The Leader did not notice Hugrant's departure. His eyes were glued to the screen, where the lead ship separated itself from the fleet, moving closer to the cloud. He prayed as the communication satellites were launched. This was the way, he felt. Reach a peaceful accord with this alien force, if it was possible. Surely a being of such vast power had reached a level of compassion towards other life, if it was aware of it. They just had to communicate with it.

The communication satellite passed into the mists forming the cloud. It broadcast across every radiation band, every spectrum of sound, color, particle wave that their scientists had unearthed in four hundred years of research. It pulsated patterns, tones, numbers and pictures.

There was no response. The cloud continued its approach.

The Leader pressed his communicator. "Initiate Plan B."

The fleet spread out. The thirty ships formed a line, spreading across the path of the cloud. The ships fired the first round of missiles. The shells exploded in the midst of the cloud, nuclear forces unleashed, but to no avail. Particles were dispersed, but they rapidly regrouped. There was no lasting effect on the vapors.

"Plan B ineffective," came the report from the fleet commander. "Continuing attack."

The Leader sagged in his chair as he watched the thirty ships launch the end result of four hundred years of scientific research against the cloud. Salvo after salvo was fired, each round a different tactic, a different combination of chemicals or explosives, each round as ineffective as the first had been.

"Initiating Plan Omega," the fleet commander communicated. The Leader debated ordering a retreat, knowing in his heart that this attack would be just as ineffective. But where would they retreat? Those ships didn't have the range to escape; Hugrant was right, he realized. They were doomed, with no hope of even avenging themselves.

He watched the screen as Plan Omega was put into play. The fleet commander pressed the engage button, and vast energy fields sprang into place, reaching from wing tip to wing tip of each of the thirty ships, forming a vast net of energy that would be their planet's last line of defense.

He had a renewed sense of hope as the cloud entered the energy field. He thought it was slowing. Then all communications from the fleet ceased as the cloud continued past the net, leaving it glowing in space behind it, and the Leader knew they had failed.

"Fools!" Hugrant said, swearing at the view screen in his lab. "Well, this won't be the end of our race, despite the Council's idiocy." He activated the roof panel, exposing the night sky. He flipped a switch and a slender rocket tilted up from the floor until it pointed up to the opening. It was the prototype for his galaxy crossing ionic drive, the only one of its kind.

He double checked the readings on his terminal. "All is set, my son," he said. He walked over to the rocket, caressing the cool metal exterior. "Your long journey will be one of education, of learning our entire store of knowledge. I have programmed this vessel to teach you, to imbibe you with the tools to rule whatever world you reach. You will be a giant, a god among mortals. They will worship you, and you will rule them, will use them to continue the fight against this cloud of death."

He returned to the terminal. He made a final check on the readings. "It is time, my son." He launched the rocket.

It tore up through the opening in the roof. The cloud entered the atmosphere of the fifth planet, its vast particles absorbing energy as it passed over the inhabitant life forms The rocket soared through the air, picking up speed as the cloud drew nearer

The rocket reached the outer edge of the atmosphere just as the cloud enveloped it. The particles passed through metal, as they did brick or wood or glass, as easily as they did the vacuum of space. The mists approached the hibernating infant, seeking to absorb its energy, knowing no difference between it and the plankton it had absorbed from the planet's oceans, only sensing another source of energy to consume before it moved on in its journeys.

Just as the particles entered the infant's body, the ionic drive kicked in. The drive created an energy field unlike any the cloud had encountered before. An energy field that was not like metal, or wood, or glass. An energy field that it could not pass through.

The drive increased the speed of the rocket tremendously, sending it zooming away from the fifth planet, away from the cloud. Inside, the infant was no longer entirely a being of the fifth planet. Part of the cloud had been severed by the ionic field and had remained in the chamber with the infant. It was not enough to absorb the infant; instead it had merged with it. It was a new being now, part cloud, part infant; part mortal, part infinite.

The cloud passed through the fifth planet, leaving it a dry husk as it had left so many others before it, and continued on through the system, heading in the same direction as the rocket with its precious cargo. It knew something had happened to it; it had felt what another might call pain as the ionic field had removed some of its particles from its mass. But it was without curiosity, without awareness of what had really happened. It did not know what grew within the rocket ship. It only knew the energy was gone from this system, and it was time to go to the next.

Chapter Three: Forerunner

The rocket's ionic drive drove it away from its home world. It was a steady speed, increasing gradually, faster than the cloud. The onboard computer system monitored the infant, following its programming dutifully, feeding it as designed, running education modules, doing everything that Hugrant had designed it to.

The infant grew in body, increasing its mass as it absorbed the nutrients fed it by the computer. It had changed, however, the merging morphing its tissues, its internal organs, until they were a consistent substance, almost a gelatin form of the cloud's mists. The education modules were useless to it; it could not interface with the computer, with other beings, in any meaningful fashion. It simply absorbed the nutrients. It hungered, was sated, and hungered again.

As it developed, latent patterns from the original infant would resurface. Sensory organs formed and then were reabsorbed into the gelatin. Briefly, it listened to the sounds the computer produced, watched the videos it displayed on the terminal inside the rocket, felt the tactile sensations as needles pricked its thin skin. It started to form coherent thoughts, consistent feelings, a sense of awareness of itself. A cortex formed inside it, and this time it was not transformed back into gelatin, it was not absorbed; this time, it remained, solidified, grew. Each time a mutation occurred, however briefly, the new sensations were stored in this cortex. It began to differentiate the events occurring within the rocket. It recognized feeding from tubes as the source of energy, as sounds and video as the source of other sensations. Not food, not energy, but still something it could absorb. It began to learn.

At first, it was subject to its body's own mutations. It would form optical sensors at seemingly random, frustrating intervals. It howled, when it had an organ to do so, when the world turned dark again, when it was trapped within its own mind, when it could not see the terminal's screens. As it continued to grow, the continually looping education modules provided by the computer became more and more understandable to it. It developed knowledge bases in chemistry, biology, engineering. It learned all that Hugrant had wanted it to: it mastered the entire store of knowledge of the beings from the fifth planet. It took it decades to do so, but that was acceptable. The rocket was self-sustaining, the journey was long. It took decades, but it had decades. It learned it all.

It began to experiment. It found it was able to control its body, to mutate cells, to change their functions, to gather and group them and form entirely new organs within itself. Soon, it had created lasting visual, auditory, vocal and tactile organs. It modeled its shape after the images it saw in the videos, becoming virtually identical to the beings from the fifth planet. It watched the video of Hugrant time and time again. It was only after viewing much of the history of the planet that it realized their connection. That was when the infant realized its gender. That he was Hugrant's son.

He soon realized he was different from those beings, however. It was clear from the history presented to him by the education modules that they did not possess the same abilities to morph their bodies that he had. He watched the final video of the planet's destruction by the cloud over and over again. His father had been incapable of saving himself, he realized. But somehow he had granted his son the power to do so. Somehow he was special. He reviewed his father's final recording. He would avenge his father's death. That was his purpose. It was not just to feed, to consume energy from one place and then the next. It was revenge.

A warning bell chimed in the rocket. He looked at the terminal screen. The rocket was entering a solar system with inhabitable planets. He started as the background noise from the ionic engines faded. The blasters had turned off. The computer guided the rocket in toward the third planet from the sun.

He entered commands into the terminal, training long distance sensors on the destination planet. Various transmissions were captured, stored in the computer's data banks. He plugged into the terminal, began to translate, to understand, to absorb the knowledge cascading out from the planet in wave after wave of radio and electronic transmissions. He morphed his external appearance as he learned more about the inhabitants. Soon, he appeared as a being of the third planet of this system, not one from the fifth planet of a wasted system light years behind him. He tested their languages out, listened intently as the computer played his voice back. He shifted dialects, added idioms, facial gestures, mimicking actions and words, intonations, emotions, becoming a nearly perfect copy of an average everyday homo sapiens. He thought back on his father's last recording. He shifted more of his gelatin, forming larger muscles, increasing his height, altering his facial characteristics from average to divine, by the standards of the planet below him. A god among mortals, he thought. That was his father's plan for him. That was how he would defeat the cloud.

Chapter Four: Approaching

The cloud left the solar system, the rocket distancing itself before it. It headed in the same direction, not by deliberate choice, but because the rocket had been aimed away from it and it naturally left a system on the same path it had entered it. As it drew in the winds of the interstellar medium, its speed increased, until it was going faster than the fleeing rocket.

It closed the distance, until it approached the edge of the heliosphere. It shifted particles as it passed through the termination shock boundary. Now it allowed the solar winds of the new system to pass through it, so its forward progress toward the outer planets of the system could continue. It shifted its particles again, reducing speed so it would pass through the system at a slow enough rate that would allow it to absorb the energy it found within. Within days it would pass through the planets comprising this solar system. Within days it would feed again. It was in the outer regions of the system, beyond any system objects other than stray comets, none with energy that it could use. At its present speed of just over a million miles a second, it would take it a little more than two days to reach the center, another two to pass through the other side. In less than five days the cloud would be on its way to the next feeding ground.

Chapter Five: Planet Fall

The rocket approached faster than the sensors in various installations throughout the world could monitor. Scientists dismissed the few readings that were captured as anomalies, most likely glitches in the system. At best, a small meteor may have passed through, no doubt burning up completely upon atmospheric entry; nothing could have remained intact at the velocity that the instruments had recorded, they assured government leaders.

He guided the rocket down, flipping switches, external fins shifting to wings as it transformed its shape to that of a small glider with sensor-deflecting shields in place. He had continued to probe the planet as he approached. It had been easy to pull information from their data networks. He had mastered most of their technology; it had not been difficult to modify the rocket's shields to avoid detection.

He regretted that there would not be time to stop the cloud. Their technology was too backward; it would take too long to manufacture effective weaponry. He knew he had only days before he must leave. No, his mission here was to gather enough material to modify his rocket so it could outpace the cloud. The next system would be where the battle would be fought. This was simply a place to refuel, to upgrade his rocket, and move on.

He maneuvered the ship into a hay field. He reversed thrusters and landed softly on the ground. He checked the readings on the terminal. After analyzing the atmosphere, he made slight adjustments to his breathing organs, and exited the ship.

He had a communications unit strapped to his wrist. He entered a few commands, and the rocket slowly descended into the ground. There was barely a trace of disturbed earth where it had been, some faint ruts along the ground where it had rolled to a stop in the hay field. He concentrated on the cells forming his wrist. They softened, allowing the communicator to contract and descend below the outer layer of his skin, then solidified again, leaving no trace of the device.

Satisfied the ship would be hidden, he set off at a quick stride toward the farm house. He had the curiosity that was missing from half his heritage, and his quick stride turned into a slow walk as he drank in the natural wonders before him.

He had absorbed immense bits of knowledge about the plant and animal life of this hemisphere, yet as his nostrils breathed in the rich aromas of the farm - the turned over loam, the cut hay, the pungency of the animal droppings – his senses reeled. When he cautiously opened his ears, allowing the sounds to come through in addition to the smells, he stopped still. The birds, the wind through the trees, the insects – the noises enriched the aromas. The colors, so much clearer than those seen on his terminal screen, nearly blinded him in their vividness. He stood motionless, drinking it in with each of his senses, feeling the sun on his face, the wind across the small hairs he had grown on his arms in imitation of the images he had procured. He closed off the senses then opened them back up one by one, smelling, hearing, tasting, feeling the world around him, so different from the isolated chamber in his rocket ship. So much bigger, so intense, he could barely control himself.

He knelt down, sensing life near him, on the ground. He peered close, increasing his visual capacity until the beetle came sharply into focus. He watched it crawl along the meadow grass. It was the first living thing he had contacted. He felt a stirring within him, and reached out to the insect. His finger contacted the exoskeleton. He shuddered as he felt the life force within, minute though it was. The stirring strengthened, and he recognized it as hunger. Without thinking, he pulled the energy from the beetle. He felt a tiny surge of power as he bled its life force. He gasped as he realized what he had done, jerking his finger away from the beetle. It was too late. A dry shell remained where once a living creature had been.

He felt sick inside. Sick at what he had done, sick at how the life force, even as small as it was, had made him swell. The inner stirring had jumped at the energy the beetle had provided, had not settled down but had grown, demanding more. He felt the hunger, the energy from the beetle having activating the craving full force.

He didn't understand; this was not part of his education, he didn't know what was happening to him. He knew he was different – that his father had not had the abilities to manipulate his body as he could. But this bleeding of another's life force – it felt so wrong, it was against every principle he had learned when absorbing the morality, the theology of not only his culture but that of this new planet's. His father's legacy – that of his entire civilization's – had been one to stop the destroyer of life. He couldn't believe it was in his power to take life – to drain the very essence of another living creature.

But the hunger remained. It was strong, and new to him. It had taken him decades in the rocket ship to develop mastery over his senses. This feeling was primal, virile, consuming. It reached out, sensing more life forms nearby. Large life forms, full of energy. He looked up and saw cows on the other side of the meadow.

He rose to his feet. He stumbled across the meadow, unable to resist the hunger, the pull toward the energy in front of him. The cows stirred, uneasy at the shuffling creature approaching him, but they were too used to human shapes to do more than look warily.

He reached out to touch a cow, hand trembling, trying to fight the craving. It was no use; his hand pressed against the side of the cow, and his body shook as he bled its life force into his own. The energy filled him, the surge drawing him near to ecstasy as he drained the life force from the cow.

The power surged through his body. More, the stirring deep within him demanded. He was blind to morality, blind to thinking; all that existed was the hunger, the power, the need. He grabbed onto another cow, bleeding it in an instant. His ability to draw the life force in seemed to increase with each life he took. He bled another cow, and another, until he had fed a dozen times and nothing but lifeless carcasses remained of the herd.

He raised his hands in the air, drunk with power, overcome with the crescendos of ecstasy washing over him. He felt each life force in him, all twelve bovine, even the faint spark from the beetle. He staggered, catching himself on the trunk of the tree that had provided the cows shade from the hot afternoon sun. The life forces swarmed inside him, trying to maintain their uniqueness. They tried to preserve their characteristics, their previous lives, within his ambiguous form. He felt them attempting to modify his cells, trying to reestablish their prior forms through his mutating body. He struggled to regain control over his body. He forced the energies to comply with his demands. He divided their forces, spreading them thin within himself, then slowly attacked each one individually, transforming each individual cell, every aspect and attribute of the original host, until they had been completely and irrevocably assimilated.

He was tired when he was finished. Tired, but once again himself. The life forces had been taken in, but it had expended almost as much energy as he had absorbed. He had learned an important thing in the process. He might be able to take in another's life force, but only at a cost. If he wasn't careful, the new life force would take over and he would end up the one being assimilated. The thought quelled the hunger that was resurfacing. No, he would not risk feeding that way, not unless there was no other choice. He could absorb energy from less willful life forms with less concern for his safety. He had less fight from the beetle than the cows, he was sure that plant life would offer its energy at little or no risk, even if the quantity did not compare to that of warm blooded creatures. He would not absorb energy from live animals, but only plant life, for his own moral conscience. His father would not have condoned the actions he had taken. Not when other options were available. He was revolted at the thought of the beings he had destroyed; he was ashamed he had not been able to control the hunger. It was because he had been unprepared for it, he reasoned. He knew its flavor now, knew how it would come from within, knew how it would pull. He was certain he would control it next time. He would not take another higher life form. Never again, he swore.

He left the tree and resumed his previous path, heading to the weathered barn with peeling red paint. He felt faint stirrings as he approached, but pushed the thoughts of feeding aside. He entered the barn. There were two horses in stalls.

They neighed at the stranger. He took a deep breath, inhaling their odors, the smells of the barn, the sweat of the horses. He smiled, approached the first horse slowly, hand outstretched. "Be calm," he spoke, gently; it was his first vocalized speech. He touched the nose, stilling the inner pull, the demand for the horse's life force. He stroked it softly along the side of its head, taking joy in the control he had, in being able to hold back the hunger.

He was tired from the earlier struggle. Murmuring softly, keeping a steady hand on the horse, he entered the stall. He found by maintaining contact he was able to form a tenuous energy link. Not one to draw the life force from the horse, rather one to create an empathetic bond, a mutual sharing of force. The horse did not stir when he sat down in the corner of the stall and closed his eyes.

Chapter Six: Discovery

Char Amberson walked to the barn, irritated that she was going to have to fetch the cows in again. Couldn't they ever come in on their own? She brushed her long, brown bangs away from her eyes. She kept the back cut short, but the bangs seemed to grow out as fast as they could be shorn. It was still hot, though it was evening, and she was not in a good mood. Her shirt was damp with sweat from her chores, her muscles tired from doing the majority of the work since her father had strained his back. She didn't mind the work, not really – she had the brawn to do it, the smarts to know how to do it. She had been working the farm with her father for the past thirty years, ever since she was a little girl. Before she became what the kids at high school had called her before she dropped out - "big boned."

She stepped in the barn and sensed something wasn't right. Grey wasn't nickering at her in greeting. She looked over to his stall. The gelding was silent, standing quietly to the side of his stall, almost motionless, not like his normal antsy self. Her brow knitted in concern as she went to the stall, scared she would find her favorite horse sick with some illness that only very expensive medicine could cure.

Char entered the stall and put her head on the Grey's long face. "What's the matter, Grey? Not feeling good?" She felt along his sides, not feeling anything wrong. He was just too calm. She cocked her head, gave him a smile. "Well now, just what has gotten into you?"

The movement in the corner of the stall startled her. She turned to look and let out a small cry when she saw the naked man half covered in straw, curled up in the corner. He was just beginning to wake up. Char grabbed a pitchfork from the side of the stall, brandished it before her.

"Who are you and what are you doing in my barn?" she asked.

"Who – who am I?" He paused, thinking it over. "That is a very good question."

Char pointed the pitchfork at him. "Well, you better have a good answer."

He smiled at her and she felt her heart leap. His face was perfect: strong, rugged, handsome, with brilliant white teeth and deep blue eyes. She shook her head, trying to stay focused on the fact there was a naked man in Grey's stall.

"I never needed a name," he said. "I was just father's son. That's all. I was his son."

She kept the pitchfork pointed with one hand while she grabbed one of Grey's saddle blankets with the other. "Well, whoever you are, cover yourself up with this. Don't you know better than to go running around naked as a jay bird?"

He caught the blanket, inspected the rough fabric, turning it over, relishing the feel of it in his hands.

"Go on, wrap it around you!" Char said.

He held the blanket by the corners, stretched out his arms to get a good look at the whole of it. He nodded. "I understand," he said. He stood up and draped it over his shoulders, covering his back and chest, leaving his lower body visible.

Char blushed. "Around your waist," she clarified.

He thought about the recordings he had viewed. "Modesty. Local taboos." He lowered the blanket, covering his lower half. He paused a moment, considering language and customs. He bowed to Char. "I apologize if I have offended you. It was not intentional."

She looked at him, wondering what manner of man he was, how he had come here. How he could make her feel warm when she knew nothing about him. "So, you really don't have a name?"

"I am sorry. There was no one to name me." He looked into her eyes. "I have always been alone."

"You're an orphan? I'm sorry; I didn't mean to bring up any bad memories. It's just – surely the orphanage – or the State – I mean someone must have named you, somewhere along the line." Char smiled, trying to let him know she wasn't judging, was asking out of concern.

He thought about his first memories, of learning to interface with the computer. He remembered all the recordings, particularly those his father had made for him. In none of these had his father called him anything but son. The computer never talked to him, only at him, no personal address, no names. He shook his head. "I was never given a name," he repeated.

Char decided other issues were more important. "Okay, well don't worry about it; I am sure we can figure that out when we need to. How about the rest of it?"

"I do not have time to tell you everything," he said. "There are only days available, and it would take years."

"How about you just tell me the part where you end up naked in my barn?" By this time she had lowered the pitchfork. She kept hold of it, but with every word out of the man's mouth she felt safer and safer with him. She wanted to drop the pitchfork, wanted to rush forward, hold him tight and give him a name.

"I did not have clothing. I was walking and became tired. I saw the barn and thought it could provide shelter. The horse did not mind - I made sure it was not disturbed."

Char laughed. "I'll say. I've never seen Grey so settled down. He seems to like having you in here with him."

"It was pleasant for me, too," he said. "We calmed each other down, I think."

"You really are lost, aren't you? Wandering around, buck naked and nameless." She made up her mind, dropped the pitchfork. "Well, I figure if Grey thinks you're okay, that's good enough for me. Come on up to the house, we'll get you some real clothes."

When he hesitated, Char reached out and took a gentle but firm grip on his arm. She trembled a little at the contact, wondering at how perfect he seemed, physically, yet how lost he was at the same time. How vulnerable this strong looking man seemed.

At her touch, he gasped. The contact raised an almost uncontrollable stirring within him. It was the hunger again, seeking this life force more powerful, more vibrant than all the rest combined, but it was also something more, something different. It was like the empathy he had with the horse, but it was better – richer.

She kept her grip on his arm despite his reaction. "Hey, it's okay," she said, treating him as she had frightened farm animals in the past. "I'm not going to hurt you, we're just going to get you dressed, okay?"

He looked at her, drank in the touch on his arm, exalted in the knowledge that there was more depth in her simple contact than in all that he had experienced before. He was confused. At first, when she had awakened him, he was not sure what was going on. He was still somewhat dazed by the aftereffects of draining the cows, and then fighting for control. Now this new sensation, stronger than ever, diverse, complex, threatened to overwhelm him. He cleared his mind, refocused on what had brought him here. He forced the urges aside, quieted the monsters within him. He was to be a god among mortals, he remembered. These people were tools to the greater end of destroying the cloud.

"All right," he said.

She kept her grip on his arm as they walked up to the farm house. He tentatively investigated the sensations he was receiving where her skin contacted his own. He let a few of his cells merge into hers, tasting her in the most minute fashion, grabbing miniscule pieces of her essence. He told himself he was studying the tools available to him, learning more about the inhabitants of this planet so he would be able to better use them in his fight. It was perhaps the first lie he had ever told.

Char felt her hand tingling slightly where she grasped his forearm. She felt her face blushing. She hoped he would keep looking ahead, wouldn't see how he affected her. He was a man unlike any she had ever seen; not even on any of the three television channels their antenna picked up.

They entered the house and she led him to the kitchen table. "Have a seat. I'll go get some of my dad's clothes for you. They'll be a little tight but beggars can't be choosers."

He sat at the simple wood table, watched her leave. He glanced around at the trappings of a country kitchen. He recognized most of the items from recordings he watched on the journey. His memory retention was absolute; he had only to pause, to flip through the storage held in his cortex, to recover whatever knowledge he sought. But he had to consciously do so – he had absorbed so much information, that only what he needed for the current activities was immediately available. He used her absence to retrieve data more applicable to the setting he was in. But under all his cataloguing efforts, his attention to the mission he had undertaken, was a tingling along his forearm, where he had carefully isolated several of the woman's cells, holding them intact within his own.

Chapter Seven: Daddy's Girl

Char opened the bedroom door. She peeked in; her father was lying on his back, eyes closed, sleeping peacefully. She crept over to his dresser. She opened the top drawer, took out a pair of underwear and a pair of socks. She opened another drawer and retrieved a worn pair of jeans, the denim faded. She held them out, trying to determine whether they would fit the man.

"I don't think they're your size," Larry Amberson said.

She looked up into the mirror hanging over the dresser. She saw her father in the reflection, sitting up in bed, with a smile on his face, laughing at his own joke. "Dad! I didn't mean to wake you."

"Oh, you didn't, Char. I've been sleeping all day. I was just resting my eyes a little when you came in. Now what's so interesting about my blue jeans? I know they got some holes in them, but they still do all right. It's nothing that needs patched yet."

She turned around to face him. "I know, Dad." She walked over to the bed, sat on the edge beside him. "There's somebody that needs them more than you, Dad. He doesn't have anything. I was going to give him a set of clothes to help him out."

He raised an eyebrow. "And just who is this somebody?"

"I don't – he doesn't – know. His name – he doesn't remember it. I found him in the barn, Dad. He seems real nice, honest he does. I know what you're thinking, but I wasn't born yesterday. He's like a lost little boy. I just want to help him out a little, that's all."

"Well, Char, you know I trust you. You got a good – and a pretty – head on your shoulders. Just make sure you're using it." Larry smiled at her, ran his hand through her hair. "I suppose those jeans were about worn out, anyway. Why don't you get that red shirt out of the closet, the one with the collar – I wouldn't want to break up a good looking combination like that."

She gave him a kiss on the cheek. "Thanks, Dad."

She retrieved the shirt and walked to the door. "You need anything?"

"Well, my back isn't quite up to par yet. Come supper time, could you bring it in here for me?"

"Sure thing, Dad. About eight o'clock, okay? I still have a few chores to do."

"That's fine."

She started through the door when he called out to her. "Oh, Char? What exactly is he wearing now, if he needs all that?"

She blushed and turned away without answering.

Larry lay back down in the bed, laughing softly.

Chapter Eight: Kitchen Table Conversations

Char returned to the kitchen with clothes in hand. He looked up at her when she entered and she couldn't help but smile. "Here," she said, handing him the clothes. "I think these will be a little more comfortable than Grey's blanket."

He examined each of the articles of clothing, comparing them with images retrieved from his storehouse. He held the jeans out, fingering the denim, liking the feel of it against his finger tips. He poked a finger through one of the small holes in the pants.

"I know they aren't new, but they're better than what you got now," Char said.

"You wish me to wear these?" he asked.

"That's the idea," Char answered.

He reviewed the recordings a final time to verify he understood the function of each article of clothing before him. "I understand," he said. He stood up, removed the blanket from around his waist.

Char couldn't help but turn red as he was naked before her again. She knew she should turn away, should close her eyes, but he was so handsome, so physically attractive, that she just stood and watched as he put on the underwear, the socks, the shirt and lastly the jeans. She wasn't sure he was going to be able to pull the jeans on. He seemed to struggle with them initially, then he took a deep breath and suddenly they slid up, he buttoned and zipped them closed and everything just fit perfectly.

She shook her head. They were her father's clothes, faded, worn, but he made them look like a brand new suit. "I was going to suggest changing in the bathroom, but, well, I guess it isn't anything I haven't already seen."

He looked at her. "Did I violate your customs? I am sorry. It was not intentional."

"No, no, it's okay. I know you're a little confused right now." She sat down at the table, motioning for him to do the same. "How about we try to figure some things out?"

He sat down. "What do you want to know?"

She looked at him. She wanted to know everything about him, she thought. She wanted to know if he liked baling hay and riding horses and making love in the meadow. "Well, maybe if you tell me some of the things you do remember, you'll remember your name."

"But I told you, I do not have a name. I remember everything; there is no name to remember." He thought about the recordings he had reviewed. About local customs, traditions, etiquette of this region. Determined the appropriate action for this circumstance. "What is your name?" he asked.

Char blushed. "All this talk by me and I never introduced myself, did I? I'm Char Amberson," she said, extending her hand across the table.

He remembered this from the recordings. He met her hand with his. Although he was ready for it, the electric spark that ran up his arm from the contact still jolted him. He relished the sensation of riding just on the edge of feeding, just on the edge of empathy, interacting with the outermost layer of the woman but not drinking, just sensing the possibilities. Wanting to merge but needing to hold back.

She was lost in his touch. She stared at him, not understanding how a handshake could convey so much energy, so much passion that she wanted to rip the clothes off of him that he had put on moments earlier. She didn't know what was wrong with her. She had had crushes before, even been in what passed for love a couple of times. But nothing like this; nothing like this magnetic pull to a nameless stranger.

He released her hand, let the sensations fade. "You – burn things?"

She shook her head. "Ah, no. Char is short for Charlotte. I was named after my grandmother. Everybody just calls me Char."

"I will call you Charlotte," he said. "That is your name."

"I'd like that," she said. She drummed her fingers nervously on the tabletop in the silence that followed.

He looked around the kitchen, continuing to take in the items he saw, cataloguing everything that was visible. After a while his gaze returned to Char. He smiled at her. "Charlotte," he said. A simple statement. This was Charlotte. But the cataloguing was incomplete. "I need more information about Charlotte."

"There's not a whole lot to tell," she said. "I live here with my dad, Larry Amberson. Mom died when I was just a little girl; it's been the two of us on this farm for the past thirty years. We have a dozen cows, chickens, hay fields – we don't make much but we get by." She smiled, a look of pride evident on her face. "We never had to hire anyone; we always get the job done ourselves. Other than the note on the land, we don't owe anybody and nobody owes us."

"Your father is with you?" he asked.

"Yes. He's upstairs right now, resting. He hurt his back a couple days ago. I'll take you up to meet him a little later, when I bring him supper." The smile faded. "I'm not sure how long he's going to be laid up. I think it's pretty bad."

"I never had my father with me," he said. "He was killed."

She reached out, put her hand on top of his. Not thinking of electricity, not thinking of attraction, just in a sudden instinct to offer compassion. "I'm so sorry. How did it happen?"

He felt her sympathy, felt the warmth in her hand, in her life force as it reached into him, offering comfort. He thought of the cloud, approaching relentlessly, inevitably, the destroyer of worlds, the devourer of life. How it would leave this being an empty shell, devoid of spirit, bereft of the warmth which she so freely shared with him now.

She mistook his silence. "If you don't want to talk about him, I understand. I'm sure it's a painful memory."

He closed his eyes. He reviewed the medical data on this race. He shifted cells, needing to fully relate to them, to accept what was going to be erased when the cloud passed through this system. He molded his inner being to more closely match that of humans, modifying cell structures until his organs were nearly identical to a male human being. Only his cortex, the core of his knowledge, remained unchanged.

He opened his eyes, allowed a single tear to drop down from the newly formed tear duct. Char reached up, brushed it off his cheek, with a calloused hand, her rough skin scraping against his much softer surface. He reached up, captured her hand with his, squeezed it. He knew their customs thoroughly now, knew how males and females of this race interacted. And he knew how she had reached him, how he felt when they touched, when he allowed his cells to merge ever so slightly with hers. He regretted the forthcoming loss. This species, while technologically backward, held more warmth, more emotion – more love than his own race had. It was a shame it would all be gone in three days.

He was unsure what to tell her. He realized his father's concept of ruling over lesser creatures, of being a god among mortals, did not coincide with who he had become. He knew he was different from his father biologically; now he knew that difference ran deeper, included how he thought, how he acted, who he was. That didn't change his mission - the cloud still needed to be stopped; it was as much to prevent future civilizations destruction, though, as to revenge for his race's end. If only there was a way to stop it now, to save these people. Then he could tell her everything, if there was something to hope for. But it was futile, he thought. They didn't have the technology, or the time, to stop the cloud. Better to let her live her last few days without the knowledge that her entire civilization, that all the life on her planet, would vanish into the mists of the cloud.

"I was too young," he told her. "He died when I was still an infant. I've been away from home ever since. I have no family, there was no one else but father."

Char left her hand in his, prayed he would not disengage that warm grip, that touch that made her feel so alive. She blinked back her own tears. "It's been me and Dad for as long as I can remember. I don't know what I would do without him. I can't imagine how it must have been for you, having no family. No one to care for you, no one to talk to."

"I read a lot. I learned a lot. It was all right. It kept me focused," he said.

"Focused on what?" Char asked.

He released her hand. He felt their connection break, felt the snap inside him when her warmth was gone. He focused on the handful of cells of hers that he had encapsulated within his own, keeping them whole, entire – keeping her essence alive within his body. A bit of the warmth returned. He knew he could always rekindle the spark of her life force, could access a bit of her spirit when he needed to be reminded how special this race was. When he finally found a way to defeat the cloud, in whatever distant galaxy that might be, he would have her with him in this small way to witness the avenging of not only his race but hers.

"On growing up," he answered. "On keeping bad things from happening to other fathers." It was true, he felt, now that he had matured, had connected with other life forces; he knew he wanted to protect others so they would not have the losses he had suffered. So their fathers could live. He flashed back to when he drained the beetle and the cow herd. He shuddered. He had almost become a feeder himself. Had he found Charlotte first, before the cows – what would have happened? Would he have absorbed her, taken her life force? He probably would have, he conceded. He had not learned what it meant, did not know how to control the feeding, until after he had his episode with the herd. He was sad he had taken those lives, but grateful that their sacrifice had permitted him to meet Charlotte, and educated him so that he had not killed her.

"I don't even know you, but I can tell you mean it. I can sense you really care about… others." She had wanted to say 'me', but couldn't bridge that intimacy. No, that was too close, too open. She trusted him, she could already feel herself falling head over heels for him, but she wasn't going to be the one to say it. No, a guy like this wouldn't have any interest in a thirty-five year old big-boned farm girl. Her father might call her pretty but she had known the truth since the fifth grade, when Johnny Gardner had laughed in her face when she had said he was nice and asked if he would come to her birthday party. She wasn't going to be hurt. She would look at the pretty man, would help him out, and then he'd be out of her life and she would go on gathering eggs and milking cows. "The cows!" she said. "I still have to get them in before it gets so dark they all wander off again."

She went to the other side of the kitchen where the back door was. "I'll be back in a few minutes. Just stay put until I get back." She gave him a smile and went through the door.

Chapter Nine: Unexplained Phenomena

Major Clark Drake threw the report at the junior officer. "I don't care what the damn radar said, there was something there. Get Scott in here, now!"

After a "Yes, sir!" and a salute, the junior officer rushed out of the major's office, eager to be anywhere but in the presence of the major when he was in a foul mood. He ran down the corridor to the monitoring laboratory, looking for Doctor Scott. He found the doctor peering at the same report that the major had thrown at him.

"Doctor Scott? Major Drake wants to see you, ASAP," he said.

"I'll bet he does. Can't just accept the facts, can he? The old buzzard always thinks he knows things the sensors don't."

"Sir?" the junior officer asked, not sure he wanted to be part of this conversation.

The doctor laughed. "Oh, don't worry; I won't say that to his face. I'm not stupid, you know. Just old and tired. Go ahead, get out of here – no sense both of us listening to his bluster."

The junior officer left, relieved the doctor was going to see the major without him. He glanced down at the report lying open on the table. "Unidentified Flying Object Sector 45-12-104.4". UFO's, no wonder the doctor thought the major was half-crocked. Good luck, Doctor Scott, he wished the man as he watched him walk down the corridor.

Doctor Scott, in addition to feeling tired and old, felt angry as he entered the major's office. He frowned at the grizzled man with the salt and pepper mustache behind the desk. Thirty years behind that desk had done little to change the major's physique; he still ran five miles, did fifty push-ups and a hundred sit-ups, every morning before getting to work at six a.m. The doctor knew he was competent, just as sharp mentally today as when he had graduated at the top of the academy so many years ago. He knew the major well, had been part of his science team for two decades now, he knew him and he respected him. But the old salt sure could get under his skin.

"Scott!" Major Drake bellowed. "What kind of stunt are you trying to pull here?"

"Major, I don't know what you are referring to. I'm not trying to pull anything."

"Don't give me that. This report –" the major gestured at the papers scattered on the floor where they had remained after he had thrown them at the junior officer – "is full of crap. First you say the sensors had to be messed up, that nothing is capable of going through the atmosphere at the speeds that were recorded. Then you say whatever it was would have burned up due to the friction created under the suggested speed and trajectory. You can't have it both ways, Scott."

Doctor Scott removed his glasses, wiped them clean with a handkerchief, put them back on. He had a calm reply ready after this stalling tactic. "Sir, I stand by the first supposition. Nothing could have been moving that fast. But even if it could, it would have burned up. There would be nothing left to find."

The major slammed his hand flat against the desk. The doctor couldn't help but jump in reaction. The major smiled briefly. He lowered his voice from the booming yell that was his standard volume. "Come on, Scott. The report said all sensors checked out. There were no malfunctions, no missing relays, everything was operating correctly. Something was measured going faster than anything we have ever recorded. It blew away jets, meteors, hurricane gales – all speeds ever recorded, even theorized. Something that unknown, we can't just assume it would burn up. We don't know anything about it – what it was, what composed it, what its capabilities to withstand friction are. I think it far more likely something that can travel that fast would not burn up than that it couldn't handle a little friction!"

"I suppose it is possible," the doctor conceded. "But what of it? It either burned up, or it left as fast as it got here. It completely disappeared from the sensors, as you may have read in the report."

"But that's strange, too, don't you think? We didn't get any recordings from the other side of the country. Like you said, it just disappeared off the charts." The major shook his head. "There's something here, Scott, I know it. I can feel it, I tell you. I know it may not be as scientific as all your sensors, but it's not like they can make any sense of this either. I think whatever made these readings is still out there, Scott. I want you to figure out where."

"Sir, I really don't-" the doctor began.

"Doctor Scott, that was not a request. I want a new report on my desk by oh-six-hundred tomorrow. Understand?" The major rose to his feet, punching the air with an index finger on the last word.

"Understood, major," Doctor Scott replied.

Major Drake returned to his chair behind the desk. He tapped his index finger on the desk, trying to figure out just what about this unknown object was getting to him. It wasn't the first time unexplained sensor readings had come by his desk, that reports with no conclusive result had been given to him. But this one seemed different. His gut had gotten him through three wars; he trusted it far more than Doctor Scott's sensors. Scott was a good man; he knew he could depend on his brains. The guy just didn't have any guts.

Chapter Ten: Oops

It was new to him, obtaining information through the slow process of verbal communication. The interface with the computer had been so much more efficient. He had to eliminate the extraneous information, weigh the value of each word, each physical movement, each intonation, to get the true result. He had learned also, in analyzing the various transmissions he had culled from this planet on the journey in, that not all communication relayed here was accurate. Some of it was deliberately untrue.

He did not believe Charlotte would be deliberately untrue to him. There was too much warmth in her spirit. He did not know how he would react to others on this planet, yet somehow he was certain that this connection was special. That his link with Charlotte transcended normal interactions with other sentient beings.

He sat at the kitchen table, reassessing their conversation. He replayed her movements, how she drummed her fingers on the table top when she was thinking, how she had reached up and brushed the tear from his cheek. She felt it too, he decided. She cared for him like his father had.

He thought about how quickly she had changed the conversation. How it had shifted suddenly from talking about their pasts, to cows. He realized which cows she must have been referring to.

He was perplexed. She had told him to wait, to remain where he was, until she returned. But he had information about the cows. He needed to explain what had happened to them. He needed to let her know it was unintentional – no, that wasn't quite true. He had willfully bled them, he could not deny responsibility for the act. It wasn't the cows' fault that he had not learned yet how to control his inner hunger. No, it was his fault, his and his alone. He decided that the need to give Charlotte information outweighed her instruction that he remain in the kitchen.

He stood up and went out the back door. It was early evening, the hot sun had set and it was now a comfortably warm August evening. He shifted cells in his visual organs, increasing his sight range and clarity in the darkness. He walked to the meadow, knowing he would find Charlotte there.

He entered the meadow. He saw her under the tree. She was on her knees, stroking the emaciated side of what remained of one of the cows. Her body was shaking. He adjusted his ears and was able to pick up the sounds of her sobbing.

He walked across the meadow. He stood over the crying woman for a few moments, watching her body shake as she let out her grief. He bent over, placed a hand on her shoulder. She didn't realize it was him, didn't know anyone was there, so caught up in emotion that all she knew was her beloved animals had been killed. It wasn't until he poured some of his own life force through his hand and into her, trying to return some of the joy, some of the love, he had drawn from her earlier, that she became aware of his presence.

She suddenly felt warm, felt that the world had stopped spinning around so fast that she could hardly catch her breath. Could feel something other than the deaths of the herd. Her sobs lessened and she lifted her head up, brushing the bangs away from her forehead. She turned her head and saw the hand on her shoulder. She knew it to be the source of this comfort. She reached up and placed her own hand over the one on her shoulder. She opened her eyes wide as the warmth pulsed through her. She shuddered as her body fought the mixed emotions of pleasure and grief. It was too much, she couldn't feel this good and this bad at the same time. She jumped to her feet, stepped away from him. The warmth subsided, the grief remained. She felt a hollow pit in her stomach.

"I am sorry," he said.

She looked at him, then slowly looked over the fallen herd. He had come out here on purpose, she realized. He had known she was going to find them. Her grief turned to rage. "You bastard!" she screamed. She rushed at him, pushing him hard, knocking him off of his feet.

A hundred methods of self-defense ingrained through decades of martial education ran through his mind as she shoved him. He discarded them all; she was not an enemy. He was in the wrong here, and he would not defend himself against her. He remained on the ground, raising himself up on his elbows to look up at her. "I am sorry," he repeated.

She stood over him, wracked with rage, grief and humiliation. He had gotten to her; she had fallen for this creep. This beautiful, kind, son of a bitch who had reached into her heart and now was twisting it into a braid. She couldn't understand how someone who made her feel this way, who had such warmth and empathy emanating from him, could have done this. Could lay there and look up with those blue eyes and say 'I'm sorry' without blinking. As if this was something that could be forgiven. Her heartbeat quickened. He said it with such sincerity, as if there really was an explanation. As if there could be something after this discovery, as if this might not be the end of what had started today.

She gulped, took a deep breath, forced herself to calm down. She narrowed her gaze. Her tone was icy, firm, resolved, when she spoke. "What the hell did you do to my cows?"

He shook his head, not knowing how to respond. Tears formed, not intentionally, but he had mimicked the physical characteristics of the human body almost perfectly, and even prior to those changes he had been capable of emotional reaction. The tears were real, reflecting his sadness and frustration at the position he had put himself in. At what he had done to her cows.

Char felt her iciness dissolve at the sight of his tears. He was not denying responsibility, he had essentially admitted the killing by his silence, yet the expression on his face, the undeniable wetness falling down his cheeks, called out to her his innocence. Or at least his regret. She felt her own tears coming. No, she resolved. He did this. She would not cry for him.

"Answer me! What did you do?"

He pulled himself up into a sitting position, hands locked in front of knees and rocked back and forth, contemplating the question. Contemplating how he could answer. It was no use; he would have to tell her. He had obviously hurt her, there was no doubt about that. Hurt her worse than the herd of cows lifeless on the meadow grass. He had caused her pain, and he owed her the truth, at the least. Sparing her the knowledge of what was coming, of the impending doom to be brought by the cloud, was not acceptable to him anymore. She would be in pain, in sorrow, regardless of what he told her now. It might as well be the truth. He looked up into her brown eyes. He could see she was struggling, trying to maintain control.

"Okay, Charlotte. I will tell you – everything."

Chapter Eleven: Suppositions

Doctor Eugene Scott frowned at the readings. The old grizzly bear had a point, he conceded. They should have recorded additional data as it left the hemisphere. And at the speed it was going, it should have left a trail if it crashed. Unless it was vaporized by friction, like they had originally thought. But what if it wasn't?

He pulled up a modeling program on the computer. He entered data from the original readings, cursed when the numbers would not fit within the allowable parameters for the program. "Jenkins!" he called out to a man working at another terminal in the lab.

"Yes, Doctor Scott?" Jenkins replied.

"I need someone to reprogram the modeling software. I need to change the parameters."

Jenkins nodded. "I'll get Allan on it – he's our best programmer. Should have it ready for you by tomorrow afternoon."

"Make it four hours – I need it tonight to prepare a special report for the major," Doctor Scott said.

"Okay, I'll have him get right on it – he'll need to see you for the specifics," Jenkins said.

Doctor Scott laughed. "Oh, that's okay. I'll be right here. Doesn't look like I'm going anywhere before oh-six-hundred."

Chapter Twelve: The Truth

He got up slowly. He offered his hand to Char, wanting to lead her, to touch her, to comfort her. She pulled hers back and folded her arms, pulling them tight against her chest.

He sighed. "Follow me, Charlotte. It would be best to show you, first. Then I will explain it all." He started off across the meadow. He looked back and saw she had remained standing beside the tree, arms still crossed, swaying as if unsure which direction to take. "Please," he called to her. "It will all be clearer if you just let me show you."

She hesitated, then walked up beside him. "All right, but if this is some kind of trick, you'll regret it."

"I already have my regrets," he said.

He led her across the meadow to the spot where he had hidden the rocket ship. He held out his arm, concentrated on the cells, making them softer on top and firmer below, pushing the communicator up through layers of skin until it was completely exposed, then sealing the skin beneath it so it remained outside his body.

Char blinked, not sure what he was doing. It looked like the band around his wrist had emerged from his flesh, but she knew that couldn't be right. Maybe he was some kind of government man - that might explain the mystery about him. Might explain some things, she thought, but not her dead herd.

He noted the puzzled look on her face. It would only get stranger for her, he knew. He felt she was strong enough to handle the truth. It was the only way to explain things. It was the only way she might again look at him the way she had at the kitchen table, would connect with him, would link her life force with him. He entered the command in the communicator.

Char drew a breath in when the ground in front of them started to shift. She took a step back as a large metallic object rose from the earth, seeming to float on air before settling back down on the meadow grass. Settling down on grass and dirt that did not show the slightest trace that a large metal object – oh, admit it, she thought – did not show the slightest trace that a spaceship had just come out from it.

"Oh. My. God."

"No," he said. "I am not a god. That is what I learned – I am so sorry – from your cows."

She turned from the ship to look at him, then back to the ship. "Cows?" she asked, in shock.

He took her hands in his; Char offered no resistance. He felt her trembling, felt her heart pounding, her senses reeling. He let the cells in his hands intermingle with hers, creating a stronger connection than before. He drew her in to him, not merging but connected. He let his life force surround hers, nurture it and comfort it. He closed his eyes in the joy of being joined to her on so many levels. He kept her energy bathed in empathy until he felt her calming down. He slowly pulled back, releasing her life force, uncoupling their cells, until the only contact was the outermost layer of skin from where they still clasped hands. He opened his eyes and saw she was staring at him.

She couldn't believe what was happening. First the awful scene by the trees, with the desiccated remains of her herd, then the horrible awareness that he was responsible for it. She didn't know what was worse: the loss of her cows or the loss of the feeling of innocence she had felt for this man. And now – now? A spaceship coming out of the ground. She gripped his warm, strong hands. She somehow knew that he had returned her strength to her, that he had made her feel calm, feel safe and protected. She didn't know whether she wanted to shove him away or cling to him.

She looked into those bright blue eyes, saw the concern therein. She gripped his hands harder, wanting to squeeze the last half hour away, wishing to return to the kitchen table, where she had brushed his tear away. Wanting to forget about the cows and the spaceship. She closed her eyes, breathed deeply, opened them up. His gaze was unwavering; she knew he was waiting for her to decide it was time to continue. She wasn't so sure about moving forward. How could anything he say make this better? Either he was a sick whacko who slaughtered her sheep and had some illusion prepared to show a spaceship, or he was some secret agent government man in some complicated mysterious escapade involving cow sacrifices and invisible and then visible ships. Either way she was losing the man she thought she had discovered, the lost soul she thought she had sheltered and saved, the one who could have saved her in return. There was no winning, moving forward; there was no going back; she closed her eyes, deciding the warmth and succor she had obtained minutes earlier, though fading fast, barely kept alive by the hands she now gripped even harder, was all that she had left. She would just stay here with her eyes closed and his hands in hers forever, she thought. That was the best option she had.

He winced as her grip tightened. This body he had crafted was strong, but he had allowed it most of the same limitations that human beings had. It was not invulnerable; as he had made it match the medical information he had recorded, he had added all the nerve endings, all the pain receptors that a human male had in his body. His was in peak condition, but Char's hard labor on the farm had given her quite a grip and he was feeling it at its fullest intensity.

"Charlotte," he said softly. "Charlotte, it's time to explain everything. I know this is a lot to take in, but I really have no choice. I don't want you to think badly of me; I will understand if you do, but I don't wish it."

She opened her eyes at the sound of his soothing tones. She nodded, accepting that she could not remain in that moment forever. Whatever the future held, that was really the only option she had, in the end. She reluctantly loosened her grip on his hands. She felt cold when their hands no longer clasped, despite the warm summer night.

"All right," she said. "I'm ready to listen."

Chapter Thirteen: Edge of the Solar System

The cloud slowed momentarily as it passed near various comets. It expanded and contracted as it traveled, stretching out to investigate objects that were not in line with its direct path.

It encountered Pluto and its moons. Cold, lifeless orbs, offering it nothing for its efforts to shift its path to encompass them in its gaseous particles. It did not care; it did not know how to care. It learned there was no energy to be found here; it contracted and shifted particles, easily escaping the minimal gravitational forces of the dead planet. It was roughly three and a half billion miles from where there was life in this system. It did not know that, did not look forward to it. It simply moved on, seeking energy.

It wasn't capable of picking out the next system to journey to; it let the winds of the interstellar medium drive it to the next encounter. It could, however, detect the large planetary masses within a system, altering its course slightly to pass through as many of them as it could on its trek through the system.

The Kuiper belt, consisting mostly of countless pieces of ice and rock, its inner portion leading to Neptune and its moons, registered to it as the next potential feeding ground. It would be ten hours before it would reach them. It did not matter; time did not matter, not to the cloud.

Chapter Fourteen: Lessons from Spock

He reached for her hands again. "I think I know how to make this easier," he said. "A way to make you fully understand my story. To believe me."

She slowly uncrossed her arms, offered her hands to him. "All right, if it will help. I do want to understand. If there's any way for this to make sense, any chance at all, I want to hear it."

He pulled her close. His breath felt hot against her face. She stared into those pure eyes, wanting to believe anything he told her. Praying there was an answer to quell all the confusion, the fear, the pain inside her. It took all her willpower to keep herself from stepping on her toes and kissing him. She inhaled, drinking in the musky smell from his chest, letting go of the worries and tensions. Forgetting about the madness.

He smiled at her as he brushed her bangs away from her forehead. "I saw this in a recording," he said, releasing her hands and moving his hands to either side of her face. His fingers were splayed out and he lowered his forehead until it touched her own.

He shifted cellular structures, connecting himself to her at all points of contact. Each fingertip pulsed against her wind-weathered face, his brow tingled against the lines in her forehead. He created new patterns, new electromagnetic pulses, between her brain and his specially developed cortex. She slumped against him, his hands keeping their grip on either side of her face, preventing her from falling. She was physically inert, her body supported by his, as their chemical union intensified.

Cautiously, he let some of his life force flow through the connections. This was experimental - he was trying to meld with her in a manner he had learned from fictional stories. He gently probed her mind, memories and very being, until he finally reached the neurons he was seeking.

Suddenly, instantly, she was aware of his presence in her mind. He backed off, not wanting to frighten her. He slowly reasserted his presence, sending soothing messages to her cells, keeping her physical body calm until her mental presence had accepted his intrusion.

Direct conversation was not possible, not at this time, anyway. More experimentation, more cellular mutation, might enable a form of telepathy, but for now he had enough. He was able to share his memories with her; small segments of past experiences that ran almost like a series of short movie clips in her mind's eye.

He had hundreds of years of experiences; he had records of not only his civilization but hers. He showed her what he knew of his early years, locked in a rocket ship, learning about himself. He revealed what he had learned about his father, using images that had been recorded by the rocket as his home world was destroyed by the cloud. She cried over the billions of deaths, at the strange blue skinned, tentacled beings sucked lifeless as the vapors of the cloud passed over them. He showed her decades of research, centuries of learning his people had undertaken in order to fight against the cloud. She did not understand everything she viewed; he modified the visions, the dreams, into forms her mind could at least accept, if not comprehend. He showed her how he had learned about her planet, about her people – how he was still learning as he interpreted the vast amounts of information his sensors had been able to record from various transmissions.

Then, finally, he let her see how the hunger had consumed him initially, how he had succumbed to its will and had fed on the cows. He let her feel its passion, its insatiable appetite, let her feel as he had when he had first walked into the meadow and had been drawn to the life energies of the herd. It was too much for her human mind to take. He felt her panicking, more than he could safely control, and retreated from her mind. He maintained the physical connections long enough to ensure that she was not going to go into shock, and then he severed those connections as well. He lowered her to the ground and sat down cross-legged across from her as she recovered from the experience.

She blinked, rubbed a hand against her forehead, massaging the spot where he had touched his brow. "You're really from some other planet?"

"I am," he said.

"And this man sent you off in a rocket ship, before that – that thing came to your world?"

"Yes. Hugrant Thujaim was my father. He was a great scientist. But nothing he or any of the other scientists could do could stop the cloud. He tried to save some of our people, but they would not build the ships. They thought they could defeat the cloud." His face darkened at the memory. "They were wrong."

She looked at him in horror as the visions returned, as she saw him bleeding the life force from the herd. "It was you. You killed the cows. You were like a vampire, sucking the life out of them."

"I didn't know what I was doing. The hunger for their energy caught me unaware. I couldn't control it."

"And you can now?" Char asked.

"Yes. I tell you, I suffered, too. When I fed on the cows, their energy nearly overwhelmed me. It was all I could do to maintain my sanity, to keep my identity intact. And afterwards, when I saw what I had done to those poor creatures, I swore I would never repeat that action." He looked at her, pleading for her to believe him. "I won't, Charlotte. I won't take another life's energy ever again."

She remembered the final visions she had, before the connection had been broken. The attack on the cows with its voracious intensity had overwhelmed her, but just at the end, she had caught some of what he was telling her now. She caught a fringe memory of the remorse he claimed. She believed him, she realized. He had strange powers, unknown abilities even to himself; he couldn't help some things from happening. That he learned from them, that he intended to avoid repeating his mistakes, was something good to hold onto. But if those memories were true, if they explained what had happened to the cows, then the rest was also true. She felt the blood rush to her head.

She was shaking, from both the process she had been through and the knowledge she had been given. "Oh my God," she said. "It's coming here, isn't it?"

He could not lie to her. "I am sorry."

She leaned over and clutched at his arm. "But you can stop it, right? You're here to save the world, I know you are."

"You do not have the technology," he said. "At first, I had hoped that I could find something to improve my ship, but even that is doubtful. There isn't enough time."

Char's skin turned cold, clammy, as she felt a chill go down her back. She dug her nails into his arm. "How long until it gets here?"

"Approximately twenty-two hours, thirty-seven minutes and fourteen seconds," he answered.

She stared at him. "That – that thing is going to be here in less than a day? We've got to tell people, we have to warn them!"

He pried her fingers off his arm, held her hand. "Charlotte, there is no one to tell. Your people do not have the technology to stop the cloud. They can do nothing about it. Why make their last day painful? Why make it one of sorrow and fear?"

"People have a right to know! If they don't, why did you tell me? Why didn't you just leave me alone?"

Tears came out and her words changed to sobs. He held her in his arms, rocking her gently, rubbing the small of her back with one hand while the other encircled her shoulders. "I am sorry, Charlotte," he whispered into her ear. "I did not want to hurt you, but it was too late. I already did, through my own actions, through my own failure. I thought you deserved to know the whole story. I did not mean to hurt you any more than I already have. I am sorry."

Her tears dried up as she continued to assimilate the images he had shown her. It was like having an encyclopedia dumped into your brain all at once, she thought. She reviewed the most important episodes: the destruction of his home world, the cloud continuing in the direction of Earth. And his arrival, here to warn or to save us? Or just grab a tank of gas and get the hell out of Dodge?

"All that time you spent, haven't you figured out a way to stop it? A way to make it go somewhere else?"

He shook his head. "None of our weapons worked. It would not respond to any of our communication efforts. The only hope is to find some new technology, some advancement we had not reached." He sighed.

"Unfortunately, your world has nothing new to offer in the fight against the cloud."

"So that's it? Thanks for the cows but you're on your own?" She shoved him away from her, got to her feet, stared at him. "What kind of super man are you, running off at the first sign of trouble?"

"I am no super man. I am not a god. I am just a mortal being, doing his best to try to stop a galactic menace. I am sorry I have failed your people; they will not be the first to fall to the cloud; they will most likely not be the last. I cannot defeat the cloud here; there is nothing to fight it with. All I can do is flee before it arrives, hoping that one day I will find the means to destroy it. To someday avenge the loss of the people that I loved."

"No," Char said, "it can't be that futile. There's a reason you're here, I know there is. There's got to be a way. Please, let us try to stop it. At least talk to someone, to our scientists, to NASA – maybe there's something we have that you don't know about. Maybe there's still a chance."

He looked at her tear-filled eyes, felt her passion and strong will. He felt the life force pounding within her fragile body. "It is possible that I did not retrieve a complete technological profile," he conceded. "If you wish, I will talk with these people."

"Thank you," she said. "I know you'll find a way to help us."

"I have to depart in twenty-one hours, forty-seven minutes and twelve seconds in order to stay ahead of the cloud," he said.

"Then we better get back to the house and make some phone calls." She turned, beckoned him to follow her, and they went back up to the farm house.

Chapter Fifteen: Interpolations

"No, no, I need the velocity increased another factor of ten," Doctor Scott said. "You've got the other parameters set, we need to get the velocity up or the whole thing is pointless."

Allan Davis sighed in exasperation. "It just wasn't designed to model this scenario, Doctor Scott."

"Don't you think I know that? That's what you're here for, Davis. To modify it so it can handle the scenario! Now you think you can do that one thing for me, pretty please?" Doctor Scott finished his sentence with his face an inch from the other's nose, spittle flying as the doctor enunciated each word with a sharp staccato and a pointed finger thumping every syllable on the programmer's chest.

"Yes, sir," Davis replied. He backed his chair away, thankful it was on rollers and allowed him to move away from the irate scientist. He swiveled around to face his terminal and quickly began coding instructions. "I should have a new simulation in thirty minutes."

"Thank you, Davis. That's all I wanted. Call me as soon as it's ready."

Allan bit his lip as he typed the modifications into the computer. This was a waste of time, he thought. Nothing moved at those speeds. There wasn't a thing on Earth – wait a minute. He felt a rush of excitement. That was it – nothing on Earth. This was the big one – someone, or something, finally found Earth.

He finished his first set of changes, started the compilation process. While it ran, he opened a new explorer window and logged onto an external chat room. It was a private area on the internet, one that only a handful of his fellow Berkeley graduate students knew about; it was how they kept in touch, how they shared cutting edge technology and theorems with each other, believing that the pursuit of knowledge was a higher calling than that of corporate security or government privilege. They did not abuse the secrets they shared; it truly was a communal pool of knowledge, a way for each of them to learn more, to reach new plateaus of scientific achievements. He entered a special series of characters into the chat window and pressed the enter key to send a red alert message to his friends.

Chapter Sixteen: SOS

They sat down at the kitchen table. Char glanced at the clock. Going to have to get Dad his supper soon, she thought and laughed out loud. The world's coming to an end and she had to heat up dinner. It would wait a few more minutes. She flipped through the phone book. Who could she call? Sheriff Barnes wouldn't know what to do. He'd tell her to lay off the sauce and make sure her daddy knew where she was.

Aha, that's it, as she saw the entry. Department of Homeland Security. If this wasn't something threatening the homeland, then she didn't know what would be. She dialed the number.

An answering machine picked up on the other end of the line. "Hello, you have reached the Department of Homeland Security. Our normal business hours are eight a.m. to five p.m., Eastern Standard Time, Monday through Friday. If this is an emergency please press 1, otherwise please call back."

Char pressed 1.

"If this is a local emergency, please hang up and call 911 for immediate assistance. If this is a regional or national emergency, please press 1."

Char pressed 1.

"Thank you. Please select from the following list to indicate the specific emergency. If this is an act of terrorism involving explosives, please press 1. If this is an act of terrorism involving chemical or biological weapons, please press 2. If this is a direct threat of assassination or kidnapping toward a specific person, please press 3. If this is some other kind of emergency, please press 4."

No 'alien cloud approaching to decimate the entire planet' option, Char thought. She pressed 4.

"You selected option 4, other kind of emergency. If you would like to leave a message, an associate will return your call as soon as possible. If you need to speak with someone immediately, please press 0."

Char pressed 0. "Hello, Department of Homeland Security, Miscellaneous Threats Division, this is Linda, what is the nature of the emergency?"

Finally, a human voice, she thought. "Hello, my name is Char – Charlotte Amberson. I don't know quite how to explain it, but I need someone to come out here as soon as possible."

"Well, Charlotte, we are here to help. But we need to know the specific threat involved before we know the appropriate response."

Char paused. "I guess that would be the extermination of all life on the planet. Does that qualify for a response?"

"I see. Let me get your contact information, and one of our agents will get back in touch with you."

"Listen, lady, I've got a space man and his rocket ship in my back yard, and there's an enormous cloud that's going to suck the life force out of every living creature on Earth in less than a day." Char tried to hold her exasperation in, but she couldn't help yelling into the phone. "There isn't time for messages and getting back in touch with me!"

"Charlotte, please remain calm," Linda said. "I assure you that the Department of Homeland Security treats every call seriously. However, we receive hundreds of calls every day; sometimes thousands. We have specialized teams with qualified agents to scrutinize each and every potential threat. We have procedures in place that we must follow in order to efficiently handle the volume of calls that we receive."

"I'm telling you we don't have time for procedures! The whole planet is going to be consumed by a cloud from outer space, what part of that do you not understand?" Char slammed the phone down. "Stupid government!" she said, slumping down in her chair.

Linda recorded Char's name, added her phone number from the Caller ID to the log, and typed in the main details from their conversation. She tagged the entry to the recording that was kept automatically by their phone system. She closed the entry, releasing the information to their master database, and answered the next call. "Hello, Department of Homeland Security, Miscellaneous Threats Division, this is Linda, what is the nature of the emergency?"

Chapter Seventeen: Programming Complete

Allan Davis looked at the compilation results of his latest code modifications. That should do it, the programmer thought, double checking the new range of parameters allowed in the simulation model. He called Doctor Scott to inform him that the program was ready.

He opened a chat window while he was waiting for the scientist to join him. Two messages were waiting for him – Tia and Jeff had both responded to his red alert. They weren't online now, but each said they would check for an update as soon as they could. He posted a new note, letting them know that he would have additional information a little later. And reiterated that this could be big. Cosmic big, he wrote. He closed the chat window when he heard the door to the computer lab opening.

"Good news for me, I hope," Doctor Eugene Scott said as he entered the room.

"Looks like it, Doctor Scott," Allan answered. "The modifications are complete. We can model trajectories within the atmosphere up to the speed of light, practically." He laughed. "Of course, that isn't actually practical." He paused, but the scientist's face remained stone cold. "Get it? See, it isn't practical to move at the speed of light; Einstein proved—"

Doctor Scott cut him off. "Davis, I'm not here to listen to theoretical physics. Is the program ready or not?"

"It's ready, sir." Allan initiated the program on his terminal. "Here you go, just fill in the parameters and one super fast computer model will pop out."

"You know the numbers I want to run. Put in the data from the anomalous readings."

The programmer did as instructed. It took a few minutes of data entry to input the various sensor readings that had been captured. He looked up at the doctor. "All set, sir."

"Start the simulation," Doctor Scott said. "Let's see where our mysterious object landed."

Allan executed the program. Even with the powerful processing unit in his computer, it took a while to run through the computations. But before too long, a message appeared on his terminal: "Program Complete." He clicked on it and a three dimensional model was displayed. It was a computer model of the Earth. A bright red line intersected the planet, approaching from outer space and circling the globe several times as its path turned a tighter and tighter circle, breaching the upper atmosphere, creating almost a solid band of red as its many orbits blended together. An oval splash of green fell across a thousand mile stretch in the Midwest of the United States. Another bright blue line went off into space, in the opposite direction as the entry red line had come from.

"Why does it look like a ribbon?" Doctor Scott. "Is the thing that wide?"

Allan shook his head. "No, it's multiple orbits. The thing was going so fast, some of the sensor readings are from subsequent orbits."

"Christ, how fast was it going?"

"Based on the readings, and the model, just over two million miles a second," Allan answered. "I would say that's why it blew away the original version of the program."

"What else did we learn?" Doctor Scott asked.

Allan pointed at the bright blue line. "That's where it took off, if it left."

"And if it didn't?"

The programmer tapped the green oval on the screen. "That's the landing zone. Best guess, given what we could gather from the readings. It's assuming a lot: primarily that the thing didn't burn up, but also that it could stop on a dime - a thousand mile long dime, two hundred miles across, anyway. That's where it was angling down toward, based on the last four readings that we got."

Doctor Scott put a hand on Allan's shoulder. "Good work, Davis. Save that out to my file share on the network. I'm going to start on the report for Major Drake. I hope you didn't have any plans for tonight. I'm going to need you to stick around, in case I have any questions on the model, or I need any additional simulations executed. Better grab some coffee, Davis. It's going to be a long night."

"No sir, Doctor Scott. I mean I haven't got any plans, nothing that can't wait. I'll be here, as long as you need me." Allan watched the scientist leave. He copied the simulation model out to the file share as requested. He looked around, nervous; he knew he was the only one left in the computer lab, but he knew as well what he was about to do was in violation of his secrecy oath. This was too important, he thought. And he could trust the others; they'd never betrayed any of the shared confidences, not outside of their own group. He opened up a chat window and started copying information from the simulation model.

Chapter Eighteen: Supper

He rose from his chair and walked around the table. He bent his knees, putting his head level with Char's, and placed a hand just over her ear. He brushed the side of her head with his fingers, letting his hand travel from head to neck and down to her shoulder. She leaned her head against his shoulder.

"They did not believe you," he said.

She gave a thin smile and a brief snort. "Yeah, I don't know why. Surely I'm not the first person to call in a world devouring cloud that's going to destroy all life in less than a day."

"Perhaps if I talked to them; maybe they would believe me. I could show them the ship," he said.

"They'd probably just assume it was an optical illusion. No, the only way to convince them is for you to connect with someone, like you did with me. No one could deny you, could help but believe in you, if they saw you in their mind."

"Then," he said, lifting his hand from shoulder back to her head, brushing the bangs away from her forehead, gazing intensely at her, "you do believe in me?"

She looked away. She could not handle staring into those beautiful blue eyes; she did not want to lose her control, did not want to admit to herself that despite his alien nature, regardless of what he had done to the cows, that she still felt drawn to him like a moth to a flame. His spirit burned so bright, she felt pulled to him, even though she knew it could incinerate her in an instant. But what an instant. She moved his hand away from her, keeping contact to a minimum. "I believe your story," she said. "I believe there is a big cloud coming to destroy the Earth."

But not in him, he thought. He couldn't blame her; she had no reason to think good of him; he had done nothing but bring harm to her since he had arrived. He knew there was nothing he could do to change what had happened; he doubted there was anything to be done to prevent the annihilation coming. All he could do, all he could offer, was to comfort her in the short time remaining. To let her have whatever hope she was willing to have before he would be forced to abandon her to the approaching onslaught.

"What do you want to do?" he asked.

She laughed, pushing aside the fear. Ignoring her conflicting desires. "Well, for starters, can you cut up the carrots and green peppers for the salad? It's supper time."

He smiled as he saw her relax. "I have processed over twelve thousand hours of food preparation recordings," he said. "I believe I can cut up the vegetables for you."

Char hummed as she set about preparing supper. She had done what she could, she thought. She had contacted the authorities. If they were too stupid to believe her, it wasn't her fault. She turned around to check on the salad.

"Wow," was all she could say. He had carved intricate shapes out of the green peppers; they looked like models of an M. C. Escher drawing, in three dimensions. The carrots had been changed into spirals and multi-faceted diamond shapes, and a dozen other incredible works of art. "Wow," she repeated.

"Are these shapes acceptable?" he asked. "I could change them, if you want."

"They're perfect," she said. She added them to the lettuce she had cut up and tossed them in a large wooden bowl. She took the spaghetti from the boiling pot on the stove and drained it in a colander. She fixed a plate of pasta, pouring some homemade sauce on top of it, and a bowl of the salad. "Okay, you take the salad and bread; I've got the spaghetti and his drink. It's time to meet my father."

He followed her up the stairs and into her father's room. Larry Amberson was propped up in bed, two pillows supporting his back.

"I thought I heard some rumbling down there," Larry said. "I take it you're the cause for all the commotion?"

"Dad," Char said, "This is the man I was telling you about."

Larry extended a hand. "Larry Amberson, glad to meet you, son."

"I am glad to meet you, Larry Amberson," he said. "I wish to thank you for the use of your clothes."

"Don't sweat it, they look a damn site better on you than they ever did on me, isn't that right, Char?"

Char blushed. "Dad, I – we – have to tell you something. It's important."

Larry put the plate of spaghetti on his bedside table. "This is pretty sudden, Char. You just met this boy today; we don't even know his name."

"I am the son of Hugrant Thujalm," he said.

"Okay, but still," Larry said, "we don't know anything about this man, Char. You can't go off and –"

"Dad!" Char said, finally stopping him. "You don't understand! We aren't going off and doing anything!"

"You're not?" Larry asked.

"No, silly. What I've been trying to say is I do know something about him now. I've learned a lot, and I think you need to know it too. To know what's coming, what's going to happen." Char's expression turned from exasperation at her father's assumptions to a dark, sorrowful look as she explained the situation.

Her father sat motionless but for quick glances at the stranger in his bedroom as Char told him everything she had learned. His eyes grew angry at the fate of their herd, then wide with shock as she related the terrifying cloud and what it was capable of. "It's horrible, Dad," she said when she was done. "Homeland Security didn't believe me; I don't know what to do."

Larry stroked his chin, feeling the day old growth of grey hairs against his fingers. "Well, honey, that is quite a story. Quite a story indeed."

"You don't believe me," she said.

"Char, let's be serious. You come in here with a man you just met, obviously infatuated with him, and tell me he's from outer space and the harbinger of some space cloud that's going to eat us all up. What do you expect?"

Char frowned. "Okay, I was hoping it wouldn't come to this." She gestured at her father. "Go ahead, do your mind meld thing on him."

He looked at her, raised his eyebrows. "Are you sure? He is sick, Charlotte; I do not wish to harm him."

"I ain't sick, I just hurt my back," Larry said. "But wait a minute – what mind thing?"

"It's the only way, Dad. Trust me," Char said, pleading.

"I will be careful," he told Larry. He placed his hands on either temple, lowered his brow to connect it to Larry's forehead. "Just relax, Larry Amberson. You will soon understand."

He shifted cells, created the same neural and chemical linkages that he had when he had shared memories with Charlotte. It was different, he soon realized. In a way, it was easier; the link was not as intense, they did not share the same emotional connection. It was a purer communication, almost completely information filled, devoid of the nearly overwhelming passions from his earlier experience. It was more akin to showing Larry his memories, almost presenting a movie to him, rather than the mutual experience that he and Charlotte had shared.

Maybe he was learning to control these new processes better, to reduce the shock to the other's system. He thought it more likely that his connection with the father was simply less emotional than that with Charlotte. He held instant regard for the man, felt a kindred spirit in his warmth and liveliness, but there was not passion behind the bond, it was more of respect and kindliness, whereas Charlotte brought instant fire to his blood, immediate joy to their bond.

As he guided Larry's mind, he recalled the man's physical ailment. He tentatively sent cells to investigate his skeletal and muscular systems. He went through the numerous hours of medical recordings in his memory storehouse, compared the condition of Larry's vertebra, tendons, muscles in his lower back. He linked his cells with those areas, feeding them energy, giving them instructions, repairing damage and healing the ruptured tissue.

He carefully pulled his cells back, severing the connections, both physical and mental. He removed his hands from Larry's temple and stood back up.

The process in its less intense variation had likewise been less strenuous on Larry. He was still shaken by all the memories he had seen, by the horrors he had witnessed. He was tired, or he thought he should have been. Actually, he felt more energy. He realized with a start that the pain in his back was gone. He cautiously bent forward. Nothing, no pain at all. In fact, it felt better than it had in years.

He did not get as rich a sharing of visuals that his daughter had, but he had received enough. Both mentally, and it was clear to him, physically, this man had proved his story. He had given him enough to convince him that his daughter and this – this man from another planet – were telling him the truth.

"Well, I say again, that was quite a story. Even better in Technicolor," he added. "And my back – it's like I was twenty again!"

"So you believe me now, don't you? Believe both of us?"

Larry wiped the sweat from his forehead. He slowly nodded. "Yeah, Char, I guess I do." He looked at the two of them. "I believe you, and him – oh, we can't go on saying 'him' or 'the man from outer space', can we? What did you say your father's name was, son?"

"Hugrant Thujalm," he answered.

"Well, I hereby christen you 'Grant Thujalm,'" he said.

Char nodded, smiled at him. "It fits you," she said. "And it's part of your father's name."

He paused, considering the appellation. "Grant Thujalm," he echoed. "Yes, that is a good name. Thank you, Larry Amberson."

Larry chuckled. "You can just call me Larry."

Grant smiled at him. "Then you – and Charlotte – may call me Grant."

Larry nodded. "Okay, then, Grant it is. Now it's obvious no one is listening to us tonight. I've been sleeping almost all day; I want you two to get some rest while I work out a battle plan for the morning. I tell you, by sunrise we are going to be ready to tackle this thing."

"You really think we have a chance against the cloud?" Char asked.

"Oh, I don't know about that, honey," Larry said. "But this old veteran does know a thing or two about getting the government to listen. Go on, get some rest. It's going to be a busy morning."

Char smiled at her father. "You are amazing," she said. "Come on, Grant, we have some spaghetti to eat."

Larry let his plate go cold. He had no appetite. His calm appearance for his daughter notwithstanding, he was reeling at the story they had told him. He had to accept what he had been shown as the truth; the alternative was that he was crazy. He wished that were true; it would mean that they weren't all going to die in less then twenty-four hours. He smiled, despite what was coming. At least his daughter had found love. It had taken her long enough, he thought. Who cared what planet the guy was from, if he made her look at him the way she did. God bless them; God give them one night together. Nobody had called her Charlotte in over thirty years, not since Tommy Peterson in the fifth grade.

And Char had given Tommy a black eye. Grant must be something, all right, if she was letting him call her Charlotte.

He reached for a pad of paper from the bedside table. Might as well make some notes. Figure out who he wanted to wake up first thing in the morning. Going to be some ticked off people, might as well tick off the ones that could help.

Chapter Nineteen: Goodnights

Char heated up the spaghetti and sauce in the microwave, as it had grown cold during their visit with her father. She sat a plate down in front of Grant and another at the place setting beside him, where she sat down.

"Go on, eat," she said.

Grant looked at the food, watched her twirl the spaghetti around her fork and eat a bite, slurping in a stray strand of pasta with a swooping sound.

"I've never actually eaten this way," he said. "I had intravenous tubes in the ship, and well, you know about outside the ship."

She refused to recall those memories from their shared experience. "It's easy, just twirl your fork, put it in your mouth, chew and swallow. That is, if you can do that?"

He smiled. "I have mutated into a nearly identical physical form as a human being. All my organs function correctly."

"All of them?" Char asked. She blushed when she realized what she was asking.

"Yes," he answered, with no hint of embarrassment.

She resumed eating. He watched her, reviewed the processes from his recordings, and ate his first bite of spaghetti.

Char laughed at the expression of joy on his face.

"The sensations – the tastes – are incredible," he said. "I wondered at the purpose of the taste buds, at their connections to the sensory portions of the brain. But now I wonder no longer; it is astounding."

"You should try my pecan crusted chicken," Char said.

"I would... love to," he said.

She blushed deeper as he stared at her. He meant every word he said, she thought. No subterfuge, no lies, he was so unlike anyone she had ever met. Duh, he was from another planet. It figured, the perfect man wasn't even human.

He quickly finished his plate, and a second full helping of spaghetti as well. She smiled as she watched him enjoy the food. This could have worked, she thought wistfully. Despite their differences, there was a real connection between them. This could have worked. She pushed the thought out of her mind as she got up to put the dirty dishes in the sink. He rose to assist her.

"It is time to clean, correct? I can do that for you. I have watched approximately five thousand three hundred and eighty-seven hours of housecleaning programs."

"I appreciate the offer, Grant, but frankly, I don't care if there are dirty dishes in the sink. If somebody's around to wash them tomorrow night, then that's okay. If not, then I don't think I'll care about how clean the kitchen is." She turned on the faucet and squirted some dishwashing soap in the sink.

"Still," she said with a smile, showing hope was still in her heart, "there's no reason not to let them soak in the meantime."

She led him into the living room, pointed at the couch. "Here's your bed for the night. I'll get you a pillow and a blanket from the closet. It's not super comfy, but it's better than the floor."

"It will be fine," he said. "Thank you."

She got the pillow and blanket and handed them to him. "Well, I'm pretty tired, and like Dad said, we'll be starting first thing come sun up." She leaned in quickly, gave him a quick peck on the cheek. "Good night, Grant. Sweet dreams."

She ran off into her bedroom down the hall while he stood there silently. He reached up to his cheek, feeling the spot where her lips had kissed him good night. "Good night, Charlotte," Grant whispered.

Chapter Twenty: Narrowing the Splash

Doctor Scott shoved the door open. Allan Davis jumped up. The programmer had been half asleep at his cube. "Davis! I need some more data extractions."

"Sure thing, Doctor Scott," he replied. He noticed a flashing message in a chat window he had left open. He quickly minimized the window before the scientist reached his desk. He swiveled his chair around to face Doctor Scott. "What do you need, sir?"

"The splash area is too large," Doctor Scott said. "We need to reduce the search area." He paused. "There's no use being cute about it, Davis. I'm sure you figured out by now that we're looking for something extraordinary here. Something that originated outside the normal realm we deal in."

"Yes, sir," he said. "I kind of figured that, when you increased the speed thresholds a thousand-fold."

"Well, it should be equally obvious to you, then, that if this thing, assuming it exists, and assuming it did, in fact, land somewhere in the Midwest, must be found as soon as possible. It's in the interest of national security."

"Of course, sir," Allan answered. But wasn't it really in the interest of the world – of humanity? he thought, but chose not to say out loud.

"That's why we have to narrow the probable region. I need you to interface with the F.B.I., Homeland Security, Reuters – any electronic information source we have access to – to try to figure out if anyone has seen this thing. Check out UFO reports, strange lights, blackouts, anything you can think of that might lead us to it. I need an acceptable search radius for Major Drake's report. And by acceptable I mean no more than a dozen probable locations, no more than ten miles in diameter."

"I'll do my best, sir."

Doctor Scott rested his hand on the programmer's shoulder. "I know you will, son. We don't have a choice. You have to."

After the scientist left, Allan clicked on the chat window to bring it back into view on the terminal screen. He read the message flashing on the screen, "UNDERSTOOD, EN ROUTE TO HOME BASE, SEND UPDATE ASAP. TIA." He smiled at the thought of the beautiful woman behind the note, remembering the brief affair they had at school. Ah, fiery, voluptuous Tia. He shrugged – he knew even then she was not someone he was capable of holding onto. He was glad the group had remained intact, that they were still all friends, after the mixed relationships during their graduate days. She said home base – that meant they were meeting at Jeff's apartment in Berkeley. He would start the database searches for Doctor Scott and then send them the latest information. It was going to blow them away.

Chapter Twenty-One: Restlessness

Char turned over again. She tried pulling the covers over her head, she tried muffling the night time creaks of the house with a pillow, but it was no use. She couldn't sleep. She kept thinking of what was going to happen tomorrow. She knew her Dad still had some connections with people he had been in the army with; she hoped he could make them listen. And then what? She was supposed to think that the army had something that could stop the cloud? When Grant's people couldn't, not even with all their advanced technology and rocket ships and abilities to do whatever they wanted, it seemed? When they were so… perfect?

She let out a heavy sigh. They weren't perfect – she knew that from the memories Grant had shared with her. He was different from his father, from the rest of his people. He was the perfect one. And not just on the outside, she felt. No, when he touched her, when he connected with her, however he did it, she felt like they really were merging, were inside each other's body, inside each other's mind and heart. It was the most intense, most passionate experience she had ever had. And he was so sincere! There was no faking, no lying, nothing but what was really there with him. She had never met anyone remotely like him. Never would again, she thought. Not after tomorrow. Not when there aren't any more tomorrows.

She shut her eyes, tried to relax. It was pointless. Suddenly she sat upright in the bed. No tomorrows. No more feeding the chickens. No more cooking supper. No more fishing in the stream with Dad. No more Dad.

Oh God, it's really the end, she thought. She started quivering. She grabbed her pillow and put her face in it as the sobs came out. She could hardly breath as they wracked her body, as she let the grief, the fright, the sorrow, the rage she had held in explode out in violent cries into the muffling softness of the pillow.

Grant had been engrossed in the biological process of digestion within his human mimicked body, fascinated as the digestive juices broke down the food he had eaten. He shifted cells to process what would have become waste in a genuine human body and converted it into energy. After a while, he let his enhanced senses investigate his surroundings, giving it the same scrutiny he had given the kitchen earlier.

He could hear Larry Amberson scratching on paper in the room above him. He listened to the shutters on the house as a mild breeze stirred them. Then he detected the muffled cries in the room down the hall.

Grant frowned. He was concerned about Charlotte, but knew from his recordings that walking into someone's sleeping quarters uninvited was not an acceptable act. He walked down the hall, stood outside her door, and listened carefully.

Eavesdropping was also impolite, he remembered, but he decided that his intentions were not devious, that he was not trying to procure information in order to do Charlotte harm. He listened as she cried into her pillow. There were no coherent words that he could hear. All he could sense was her grief. He felt her pain and tears began falling down his cheek. He did not care about customs. He did not care about socially accepted practices on this world or any other. He cared about Charlotte.

He opened the door of her bedroom and went over to her bed. She was on her side, clutching a pillow to her face, heavy sobs shaking her body. He sat down on the bed.

Char turned over when she felt his weight beside her. She lowered the pillow, her face red and wet with tears. She looked at him, so beautiful in the moonlight coming in through the large bay window, and she stopped crying.

He brushed her hair away from her face. "I heard you crying, Charlotte. I'm sorry if I shouldn't be here, but I couldn't help it. I didn't want you to hurt anymore."

She sat up. She leaned against his chest, breathed his musky scent in. "It's okay, Grant. I'm glad you're here. I don't want to be alone. Not tonight."

He held her, one hand massaging the nape of her neck. He nestled his nose in the hair just above her ear, breathing in her smells, feeling his human body tremble, feeling hers do the same.

She lifted her head off his chest. She put a hand behind his head, drew him down to her, and kissed him. Thousands of hours of recordings on relationships and sexual habits of the inhabitants of this planet had not prepared him for the sensation of being kissed on the lips by a woman in love, of being kissed by one he loved. It was far more interesting, far more sensational, than digesting spaghetti.

He drew back, gasped for air.

She smiled at him, rubbing her hand on his chest, relishing the feel of him, the warmth that emanated through his shirt. "I need you, Grant," she said. "I need you to be with me tonight."

She unbuttoned the flannel shirt he was wearing and pulled it off of his arms, throwing it on the floor. She lifted her night shirt over her head and tossed it on top of his shirt. Suddenly shy, she knew he could see her naked body in the moonlight. She realized she was not the perfect physical specimen that he was, that she was not the woman he deserved. She crossed her arms over her breasts, not sure that he wanted to proceed.

He gently pulled them down. He looked her over – not clinically, not judgingly, but with love and passion in his eyes. She felt her pulse quicken when he smiled at her and said, "I have seen hundreds of thousands of recordings, Charlotte, but nothing compares to what I see now. You are beautiful."

She lay down, pulled him on top of her. He spread his body over hers, wanting to maximize the contact between their flesh. He shifted cells, merging their outer layers, becoming one with her in a million places. Each point was shared warmth, shared life energy, shared essence.

He had not misled her when he told her his body was almost perfectly human, Char thought. Thank God, this would have been awkward if his parts didn't fit hers. But he had been faithful in his physical modifications, and his parts did fit, and they made love as two people in love do: wild, joyfully, with tears of joy, with cries of ecstasy. Their union was more complete than the mind meld that had joined them before; it was all that the mind meld had been, coupled with the physical joining of their bodies, on the cellular level, as their cells intertwined, and on the human level, as they coupled as man and woman. It was more than she had ever dreamed was possible: physical bonding, emotional linking, with a man she loved. With a man who loved her. She knew that no matter what the next day would bring, she had these last moments of happiness. This last true, joyful experience.

Afterwards, she fell asleep. He lay there the rest of the night, holding her in his arms, thinking what a wonderful thing love was. Trying not to think how soon he would be losing it.

Chapter Twenty-Two: Berkeley Reunion

Jeff Stanton opened his apartment door. He instantly smiled at the raven haired beauty before him. "Tia Montoni, how are you?" he asked.

She leaned in and gave him a peck on either cheek. "I'm marvelous, darling, as always." She entered the apartment, gave a glance around the stark interior, bereft of decoration, empty but for a sofa, a card table with chairs, and a large computer desk with various technical manuals on the shelves above the desk. "Nice place," she said.

"Oh, you know me, I never did care much for superfluous knick knacks," Jeff said. "You want anything to drink? I've got beer, juice, pop. Bottled water, too – can't tell what they're putting in the city stuff."

She smiled. "Always the conspiracy theorist. You haven't changed a bit."

Jeff closed the distance between them. He looked at her sincerely. "Neither have you."

Tia placed a hand on his arm. "Oh, darling, let's not go there. You know how life works; it was time to move on. Let's not spoil things."

Jeff turned away. "Of course. I merely meant that you still looked as beautiful as ever. On the outside, that is." He smiled. "Just kidding. Come on, let's get that drink."

She smiled back. It was just like the old days. Once Allan and Becky got here, it would be complete.

"So, any updates?" Tia asked.

"Last message had some prime locations for the landing site. Allan said he would send us the most likely spot as soon as the simulations were finished. He thinks the military will be moving in this morning. We'll have to be ready to head out as soon as he gets us the data."

She raised an eyebrow. "He's not going to join us?"

Jeff shook his head. "He doesn't think he'll be able to get away in time. He said it was best if the two of us check it out."

"What about Becky?" Tia asked.

"She hasn't been on-line. I think she's still in South America; she probably hasn't been able to get a clear signal to log on."

"Well, okay, I guess it's up to us."

Jeff raised his beer can to hers. "Here's to us. Cheers."

She smiled, clinked her can against his. "Cheers." She warmed to the excitement of the adventure that was beginning. Well, maybe old flames could be rekindled, for a weekend anyway. It would make it more satisfying, to be with someone, if this was as big as Allan had indicated. She let her gaze meet Jeff's for a trifle longer than was necessary, just long enough to get him thinking she might be flirting. But not enough to make him confident of her meaning. No, that wouldn't be as much fun, if he got too sure of himself.

Chapter Twenty-Three: Likely Candidates

Allan spread the large printout on the work table beside his cube. It was a map of the Midwest states, with hundreds of colored lines leading to thousands of green ovals. "Okay, Doctor Scott, this is what we came up with. I cross-referenced all the key words – you know: aliens, weird lights, sonic booms, UFO's etc. – against the national databases. I got a couple thousand hits."

"Allan, we don't have time or manpower to go to all these places."

Allan smiled. "I know. That's why I added the expected time frames into the criteria for those hits and reduced it to less than a hundred." He unfurled another sheet and rolled it out flat on top of the first map. Now there were a couple dozen colored lines with just over eighty green ovals. It was far less cluttered than the first one, and the green ovals covered half as much geographical territory as the first set of ovals had.

"Well, that's obviously improved, but it's still not good enough. We just can't cover that much ground. I thought I made it clear, we can't handle more than a dozen sites, and they need to be within a couple hundred miles of each other, not across six states!"

"And that's why we have map number three." Allan held up a hand to prevent the scientist's interruption. "Hey, last one – I promise. And this one will make you happy."

The third map covered the upper half of Indiana and Illinois. Three thick red lines crossed into the map from the left side, heading east across the states. Each line branched into three lines, with each branch ending in a big red arrow pointing to a small green oval. "Down to nine highly probable sites, based on cross checking the key words with most likely trajectory scenarios."

Doctor Scott clapped his hands, rubbed them together. "This is what I can bring Major Drake," he said. "Now why didn't you just show me this one at the start?"

Allan shrugged. "I guess I wanted to show you how I got there. I didn't want you to think I spent the last six hours goofing off."

"Davis, I understand it takes time to sift through all this information. You don't have to show me all the middle steps, I trust that you went through them. I'm a scientist myself – not a computer scientist, but believe me, I've been through more multi-step processes than I would have preferred. I know how it works." He looked at his watch. "Four o'clock. We've got two hours to get the presentation ready for the major. Are you up for it?"

"Yes sir," Allan replied. He wasn't going to miss out on this, not for the world.

"Great. I'm going to need the full file on each of the database reports for the nine target zones. I want pictures, text, audio – whatever we can get. We need to rank them from least to most likely, based on all the data we can get." Doctor Scott smiled at the programmer. "Allan, I've got a good feeling about this. This is going to be something big, something we will never forget." He pointed at the map. "And your work will have been instrumental in us finding it. I appreciate your working all night with me on this. I won't forget it."

"Thank you, Doctor Scott. I kind of have the same feeling. I copied the maps out to your file share. That should let you get started on the report. I'll come over to see if you need any assistance as soon as I get the rest of the supporting data files moved over."

"Very good. I'll expect you shortly."

Allan opened a chat window as soon as the scientist had left the room. He had listened to the audio files already; he was pretty sure he knew what was going to be number one on the list. "KANAPOLIS, INDIANA" he entered into the chat screen. He attached the audio file from Homeland Security that had matched the green zone and hit send. He closed the window and proceeded to copy all the target zone files to Doctor Scott's file share server.

Chapter Twenty-Four: Trans-Neptunian Region

The cloud expanded to its greatest width as it passed through the Kuiper belt. It found no life energy within the frozen rocks. It contracted again as it let the gravity of Neptune draw it near, slowing its speed slightly as it neared the largest object it had detected since the last planetary system. Again, its quest for energy was fruitless.

It shifted direction and widened its scope in order to encompass all of Neptune's moons in its path as it left the planet. It shifted particles, easily escaping the planet's gravitational forces.

It continued its journey to the center of the solar system, orbiting the sun, letting its gravitational forces pull it in tighter and tighter circles, so it would intersect as many planetary objects as possible on its journey toward the sun. It would then use the great speed built up by the gravity of the sun to slingshot out of the system. It was within the boundaries of the outer planets now, having passed through the first of the four gas giants. Uranus, approximately the same size as Neptune but with three times as many moons, would be next in line. It would take just over three hours for the cloud's circular orbits to cross the void to reach Uranus, where it would probe for life energies again. It would take another three hours for it to pass through Saturn and the colossal Jupiter. After that, less than an hour to go through the asteroid belt and Mars. From there minutes to the only planet in the system that harbored the life energy it sought. Only minutes to the planet called Earth.

Chapter Twenty-Five: Slideshow

Doctor Scott knocked on Major Drake's door.

"Come in," the major instructed. "Ah, Scott. You have the report for me?"

"Yes sir," Doctor Scott said. "It's actually more of a presentation. I have the conference room set up, whenever you are ready."

"Well, let's go then. It's oh-six-hundred, we're burning daylight."

Doctor Scott struggled to keep pace with Major Drake as he strode quickly down the hall and to the main conference room. Allan Davis was already there, connecting a projection screen to his laptop. He and Doctor Scott had spent the last two hours preparing the presentation. He was tired, running on adrenaline and caffeine. He stood up and saluted the major when he walked in.

"At ease, Davis," Major Drake barked at him. "Just get that thing hooked up and show me my movie."

"Yes sir, Major Drake," Allan said, and resumed hooking up the projection screen.

"Allan worked all night on this," Doctor Scott said. "I could not have done it without him."

"Save it, Scott. I'll let you know if we're going to pin any medals on the boy after I see it."

"Better get the polish out sir," Doctor Scott said. "Okay, Allan, start the show."

Major Drake was impressed. The two had done a good job, he admitted. The simulations were very clear; they had removed all the superfluous information, making it easy to see the relevant trajectories, the reasons they had selected the final nine target zones.

"Okay, Allan, go to the summary page." Doctor Scott paused while the programmer displayed the requested page on the screen. "Major Drake, we figured you wanted to start at the top. We can go into details on the other eight sites if you want, but this is the highest probability of landing site based on our computer models. And heavily reinforced by this." He signaled to Allan to play the audio file of Char Amberson's phone call to Homeland Security.

After the audio file was finished playing, Doctor Scott grinned at the major. "This could be the real deal, sir. This woman has no history, no suspect affiliations – there's no reason to think she doesn't personally believe this. And she's located almost in the heart of the prime target zone. Little town in Indiana called Kanapolis, about a hundred miles north of Indianapolis."

Major Drake sat back in the conference room chair, rocking slightly as he considered the information presented. "The other eight sites – how likely are they, compared to Kanapolis?"

"Well, I couldn't say, exactly," Doctor Scott said.

"Damn it man, I don't want exact. Just tell me whether they are worth my time or not."

Doctor Scott bit his lower lip. "Kanapolis is it, sir, in my opinion. It's either going to be there, or there's nothing to find."

Major Drake looked over at Allan Davis. "You agree, son?"

Allan nodded. "Yes, sir. I would bet on it."

"That's that then. Scott, I want you and Davis with me on this. If there's a biologist in the lab, bring him along too, but that's it. I'll get the military transport set up. We're in the air in fifteen minutes. Oh, and keep this low key. Nobody but us needs to know what we're going out there for. They'll figure it out soon enough if we're right."

Chapter Twenty-Six: Road Trip

Jeff and Tia got off the plane in Indianapolis and headed for the car rental booths. "Do you have anything in a convertible?" Tia asked the clerk behind the counter.

"Let's see. I have something in four cylinders with four doors and an engine," the clerk said.

"Not funny," Jeff said. "Is that the best you can do?"

"Sorry, the Amateur Track championships are this weekend. All I have is an economy model."

"We'll take it," Jeff said, passing the clerk his credit card. He looked at Tia, gave her a roguish smile. "Nothing but the best for you, baby."

She laughed, letting him enjoy the remark. He was cute when he clowned for her, she thought. Always was the funny one in the group. "Do you have any maps for north of the city?" she asked.

"Aw, don't worry about it, Tia – I've got everything downloaded on my PDA." Jeff patted his pocket. "All set with the latest and greatest – construction, detours, speed traps – clear sailing ahead."

"If you say so, captain," Tia said. "I guess we're off then."

"Thank you, have a pleasant trip," the clerk said after handing Jeff the keys.

Jeff raised his eyebrows. "How could we not, in the cornfields of Indiana?"

"Hey, there's more than corn in Indiana."

"There is? What?" Jeff asked.

The clerk stammered. "Heck, I don't know. That was the slogan a couple years ago, there must be something. I came from Florida. I'm just here on a temporary assignment."

"We'll let you know what we find," Tia said. "Who knows, it might be interesting."

She got in the passenger side of their boxy little compact car. "I don't know why they bothered putting in four doors," she said. "There's no way two people could fit in that back seat."

Jeff licked his lips, gave her a quick, nervous glance. "Well, maybe we could test that theory later."

"You scoundrel," Tia said, giving him a playful sock on the shoulder.

He grinned, glad she hadn't gotten upset, hadn't mentioned again that theirs was an affair in the past, not the present. Maybe, just maybe, this trip would be productive in more ways than one. Regardless of whatever Allan got them out here for. Who cared if it was a wild goose chase if it got him back together with Tia!

He pulled out of the rental car lot and onto the local expressway. He reached into his pocket, retrieved his PDA and handed it to Tia. "Here," he said, "open up the 'Road Trip' folder."

Tia turned it on and found the indicated folder. "Okay, I'm guessing we want the 'directions' file." She opened that file up and read the contents. "All right, stay on the expressway until you see Interstate 65 North. That will get us out of Indy and headed in the right direction."

"Roger, co-captain," Jeff said. He gave her a grin and settled into driving the car. It was a pleasant morning, just before sunrise, and traffic was light. He rubbed his eyes; it had been a day and a half since he had any real sleep. He had tried to get a nap on the plane flight but could do nothing except daydream about Tia, about their times together. She had been nothing short of a tornado at Berkeley. How she had ended up in their group, he had no idea. It seemed she just showed up, and there was no way Allan or he were going to tell the hottest girl on campus to get away from them. Even Becky seemed more surprised at her interest in their group, than jealous of the sultry newcomer. Actually, from some of the hints Becky had been dropping in their last couple chat sessions, maybe she had as many reasons as he and Allan had in welcoming Tia into their small circle. Becky never had shown much interest in the guys she knew. Yeah, that made sense, now that he thought about it.

His thoughts returned to his daydreams. It was like it was yesterday, though he knew almost six years had passed. Tia was so beautiful. When she had made the move on Allan, he sincerely wished his best friend all the luck in the world with her. Hey, he didn't ever expect to be with a woman like Tia; it was enough to have her around. That's what he told himself, anyway. But he did feel jealous, he had to admit, when she was clinging to him and kissing him and spending the night in his room. When she came out for breakfast wearing nothing but a stretched t-shirt it nearly drove him insane.

Their breakup had gone surprisingly well. One day Tia was sleeping with Allan, the next it was hands off. Allan seemed to accept it; he never believed he could hold onto her, and he let her go as easily as he had taken her in. What was unexpected was when a week later she followed Jeff to his room and spent the night with him.

Their affair was even briefer than the time she was with Allan. It lasted twelve days, Jeff remembered. He remembered every one of those days, each of those dozen nights of heaven. He had never been with anyone like her before or since. Every time he thought he might have met someone, the woman failed when he invariably drew her up against the Holy Grail that was forever etched in his mind. The Tia Test was impossible to pass for any of the women he had encountered.

He shook his head, trying to clear the memories from his mind. Sure, she was letting him tease her, even flirting with him a little. But he couldn't take that seriously. No, if he fell for her again, if he even entertained the thought of getting back together, he knew he would end up facing the breakup again. And his and Tia's breakup was nothing like the simple acceptance that Alan had shown.

He was depressed for months, bringing Allan, Becky, even the indomitable life of the party Tia down to his level. He would barely eat, rarely bathed, and almost flunked out of the graduate program. It finally took an intervention by his friends, where they sat him down and one by one launched into him, verbally knocking the sense back into him.

He gave a sideways glance at the lovely woman in the passenger seat. She was so beautiful, he thought. So beautiful.

"Take the next exit," Tia said.

He shook his head, again focusing on the road. "Next exit. Gotcha."

He pulled off the interstate and onto a county road. "Left or right?"

"Right. We take this for about twenty miles before the next turn."

Jeff checked the gas tank. They had used less then an eighth of a tank since leaving the airport. "Well, I'll say one thing, it gets good gas mileage. We won't have to fill up until we're ready to return it."

"I'd still rather be in a Porsche," Tia said, pretending to pout.

Jeff smiled at her, drinking in the site of her full lips pursed out, wishing he could pull the car over and take her in his arms. "Sorry, the Escort will have to do. There's an Amateur Corn Husking Tournament in town, you know."

She giggled. "Oh, Jeff, you always could make me laugh. That's what I always loved about you."

His heart beat faster. He continued to alternate between thinking about Tia and telling himself not to think about her. This occupied most of his time. There was a comfortable silence in the car. Tia checked their progress against the directions and maps that Jeff had downloaded on to his PDA, letting Jeff know as they passed milestones along the route.

"Okay, we take the next left. We want to head north on county road 300 East."

Jeff slowed down as they came near the next intersection. It was a narrow paved road with faded yellow lines separating the two lanes, one in each direction. He spied a small green sign at the corner. "This is it," he said, turning left and heading north on the road.

"All right, this one is going to wind a little bit. We'll go through two stop signs before we have to worry about turning again."

Jeff slowed the car as the road turned left and then right before straightening out again. It was getting brighter. The corn fields on either side of them, tall stalks reaching six or seven feet high, made it seem like they were driving through a tunnel. "Well, so far the clerk was wrong."

"About what?" Tia asked.

He gestured to either side of the road. "So far, there isn't more than corn here."

She laughed, placed a hand on his forearm. "Oh, Jeff, sometimes you're just too much." She let the hand trail slowly off his forearm. She could feel him tremble slightly. She looked out the passenger window, smiling at her faint reflection in the glass. Still putty in her hands, she thought.

Jeff did rolling stops at the next two intersections. "Okay, what are we looking for now?"

Tia consulted the PDA. "This is where it gets interesting. A small dirt road, 725 North. It might not be marked."

Jeff slowed down, keeping his eyes forward, trying to spot the road.

"There!" Tia said. "Turn left, just up there."

"Where?" Jeff asked. "There's no road."

"Sure there is. Look over there, between those two corn fields."

Jeff looked at her questioningly. "That's not a road. That's a drainage ditch."

"We're not in LA, darling. That is what passes for a road out here."

He kept his foot on the brake.

"Just turn," Tia said.

"Fine, but when we're late for the big welcoming bash for E.T., don't blame me." He lifted his foot off the brake and turned off the road between the two corn fields.

Fifteen minutes later, Tia was in the driver's seat, pressing on the gas, as Jeff was up to his ankles in mud behind the car, attempting to push it free. Only after placing the car's floor mats under the front wheels were they able to extricate the rental car from the mud.

He got in the passenger side, slamming the door shut. He was covered in mud thrown by the spinning tires when he had been pushing from behind.

"Not one word," he warned Tia.

She leaned over, pulled his head close to hers, stared at him with her big brown eyes. She gave a sorrowful pout, then raised her head to give him a kiss on the lips. She was careful not to get the mud on her.

She shifted back to the driver's side of the car. "I'm sorry, darling, truly I am. Do you forgive me?" She resumed her sorrowful pout, bright red lips sticking out, head tilted to one side.

He touched his fingers to his lips, where he swore they still felt like they burned. His scowl slowly turned upwards until he couldn't help but laugh. "Not exactly the Hollywood Expressway, is it?"

"No," she said, laughing with him. "Not exactly."

She drove back to the road they had turned off of and continued east. A half a mile later, Tia spotted a one lane dirt road on the left side. A small green sign indicated that this was 725 North.

"Not much wider," Jeff noted. "The ditches are pretty deep, you better stay close to the middle. I don't think we'd be able to get out of them."

Tia raised her eyebrows. "This road is so narrow, all I can do is stay in the middle. There aren't any lanes."

"Well, just drive slowly," Jeff said. "The house we're looking for is on this road. A couple more miles and we'll be at Charlotte Amberson's."

Chapter Twenty-Seven: Sunrise

Larry stretched, trying to get the kinks out of his body. He smiled. His back still felt great. He had fallen asleep after an hour or so of jotting down notes on his pad. The four hours had been the best sleep he had received in years. He reached over from a habit unbroken after thirty years of disappointment, his arm falling against the unoccupied side of the bed. The smile faded as the old heartache returned. He looked at his alarm clock. It was almost six o'clock. Time to get up and make some phone calls. He got up out of bed and took a quick shower to finish waking up. He pulled on a pair of jeans, as worn as the ones lent to Grant, and a t-shirt and headed downstairs.

He noticed the blanket and pillow on the empty couch. Good for them, he thought. He had hoped for love to come to his daughter for so long; he had almost given up on her ever finding someone to share with, someone to care about the way he had cared about her mother. Amy had been the love of his life. He still missed her every day, his heart suffered each morning when he reached over and found the bed empty beside him. He lived for Char, had done his best to remain joyful in life for her sake. And it was a good life, he reflected. They had had good times together, had enjoyed the labor of the land as they worked the farm, as they drew its fruitful harvest from the rich earth. But when they sat down at the supper table, they both knew pieces were missing. His Amy, her unfound partner, neither were there. They talked freely in the fields, their conversation light, but at the table they mostly just ate, too aware of the absence.

His smile was slightly bitter as he continued past the sofa and into the kitchen. Pity it had to come now, he thought. A shame that she would find someone to love for just a single night. He sat down at the table with the pad of paper before him. In the end, he had crossed every option but one. Some of his names were inaccessible; he had lost track of them. Some were unlikely to believe him, or would take too long to react. One name remained who he felt would not only believe him but had the authority to do something about it. There was still a chance, he reminded himself, as he picked up the phone and dialed the number.

It took a bit of yelling and cajoling, working his way through secretaries and junior officers, but he finally got his army buddy on the line.

"Larry Amberson, you old saw horse, how the hell are you?" General Adam Crowell said.

"Not good, to be honest, Adam. I need some help," Larry answered.

"Hey, anything I can do for the man who pulled my butt out of enemy fire. What's the problem?"

Larry explained the situation. Adam didn't say a word throughout the entire story. "So that's it, Adam. We need someone over here, ASAP, or we're all going to end up dead."

There was silence on the line as Adam weighed his friend's words. Larry had not misjudged the faith Adam placed in him, but they were tense moments until Adam broke the silence.

"Larry, I got to hand it to you. You sure came up with a doozy this time."

"It's true, Adam. You've got to believe me."

"You don't have to convince me, Larry," Adam said. "Your word is good as gold with me. If you say you have a space man in your house, you have a space man in your house. Let me make a couple calls and get the ball rolling."

"Thanks, Adam. I owe you for this."

"You don't owe me squat. If this is happening like you say, then we are all going to owe you big time, for giving us a chance to fight back. I'll be in touch."

Larry put the phone down. Well, that's all he could do. It was in Adam's hands now. All they could do was wait for him to call back. He got up from the table and went to the refrigerator. He might as well get breakfast started. Smell of bacon always woke Char up.

Char was already up. She lay in bed beside Grant, running her hand over his chest, staring into his blue eyes. It was growing lighter in the room as the sun's rays brushed the top of the corn stalks and illuminated the room where they shone through the half closed curtain. She wanted to remain here forever, to freeze this moment of complete contentment in her mind. She had never felt so at peace with another person, certainly not with someone she was laying naked next to. He didn't mind her bland features, her coarse skin, her big bones layered with thick muscles from years of hard labor. He didn't care if her hair wasn't long and soft and she had freckles on her face from hours in the sun. He accepted everything about her, he loved her. She was as sure of those things as of the sun rising in the east and setting in the west. She gave a wry smile at the thought that even after the cloud had passed, that would still be true. That gave her a strange calmness, a feeling of security that if the cloud could not affect that truism, then neither could it dampen their love. That regardless of the outcome of this day's events, their love would remain unscathed.

The clattering in the kitchen was soon followed by the enticing aroma of bacon cooking on the stove. She debated stalling longer, but accepted that it was time to get up. They had shared their passions last night. Today was about the rest of the world. If they survived, there would be future nights for love making.

She turned her back to him as she dressed, still shy despite her knowledge of his love for her. He smiled, realizing she was still following her people's customs, still inhibited by her years of feeling inadequate, by their standards of beauty. He came up behind her, put his arms around her, nuzzled her neck. "You are beautiful, Charlotte," he whispered.

She leaned back against him, tempted to reward him – herself, she admitted – by returning to the bed. "Hmmm," she sighed. "You are crazy. I love you, but you're crazy."

He turned her around and kissed her. "I love you, too, Charlotte. If that is what passes for madness then I am insane."

She smiled at him. Perhaps breakfast could wait fifteen minutes. She kissed him, leaning against him, pushing him toward the bed. They fell on it and soon the clothes they had just adorned were tossed back onto the floor.

Chapter Twenty-Eight: Destination Kanapolis

There were six of them in the army helicopter: Major Drake, Doctor Scott, Allan Davis, biologist Sid Eckham from the lab, pilot Scott Wolf and co-pilot Stephanie Jackson. They had departed the base in the fifteen minute time limit the major had stated. They carried Allan's laptop and a couple cases from the lab with them. It was not a highly equipped mission. That would come afterwards; if they found what they were looking for, it would be a matter of hours before they had half the specialized equipment in the country set up in the corn fields outside Kanapolis. This trip was to see if that was necessary. Major Drake felt in his gut that it would be. This was it, he thought. All these years chasing phantoms, this one was going to be real.

Sid Eckham looked nervously around the interior of the chopper. He barely knew anyone else other than Doctor Scott. He had been at the lab for less than a month. He had never been on a mission - he had signed up for the military because he wanted access to their laboratories, to their vast funding for his research. He wasn't a soldier by any stretch of the imagination. He looked at the rifles clamped against the interior wall. He had passed basic training but could he actually fire a gun at someone? He was more likely to shoot himself.

"Doctor Scott?" he whispered to the man sitting beside him. "Are we going to be fighting?"

Doctor Scott could see the fear in the other's eyes. "Well, Sid, I don't think so, but I'm not really at liberty to say. To be honest, though, I don't really know what we're going to do."

Major Drake noticed the two talking. The topic was obvious, given the situation. He cleared his throat. "It's all right, Doctor. He has a right to know." He tossed a folder over to the biologist. "Go on, read that. It should make things as clear as they are for any of us."

Sid opened the folder. He sifted through the contents, looking at the maps, before arriving at the concluding summarization. He read it quickly, his eyes widening as he grasped the nature of their mission. He looked up at the major, his voice rising with excitement. "This could really be – alien life?"

"That's why you're with us," Major Drake said. "Whatever we find – and I honestly believe we're going to find something – you're going to have to figure out just what it is, and where it came from."

"What then? What if it is from another planet?" Sid asked.

"Well, then everything changes, son," Major Drake replied.

Chapter Twenty-Nine: Breakfast

Char finished dressing, less self-conscious now, accepting that he watched her as she put on her clothes. It was okay; she welcomed his look, knowing he appreciated her for who she was. It was difficult to put aside old feelings about her body, about her appearance, but there could be no doubt that he loved her unconditionally, without reservations.

He put on the same clothes he had borrowed the day before. He reached for her hand, enjoying the contact with her flesh, feeling the bond between them grow by the moment. Every touch was sacred to him, each contact enhanced his awareness of her life energy, reinforced his love for her.

They held hands as they walked from the bedroom, down the hall past the sofa, and into the kitchen. Char's face turned red as they entered the kitchen. She had never slept with a man in her father's house before, and she knew he had to have seen the empty sofa, had to know where Grant had spent the night. But she felt the strength, the support, in the hand she held, and she forced a nervous smile as her father turned from the stove to look at them. "Good morning, Dad," she said. Please, please accept this, she willed, as she saw him glance down at their clasped hands.

He smiled, and she beamed brighter. He nodded his greeting at the two. "Bacon will be done in a minute. I suspect you two have an appetite this morning."

"Dad!" she said, blushing, but happy, so happy he was joking, that he wasn't hurt or angry at her.

"Just kidding, honey. Go on, have a seat. I'm waiting for a call; we might as well get some food in our bellies now. I have a feeling we're not going to have much time for eating once the circus starts."

Grant and Char sat down at the table. Char couldn't help looking at him. He never blinked, she realized. She would hold her stare forever. He reached over, put his hand on top of hers.

"I am glad to be with you, Charlotte," he said. "And with you, Larry Amberson."

Larry brought a plate of bacon to the table. "Well, I'm glad you're here, Grant. Anyone that can make my girl smile like that is welcome at my kitchen table."

He went back to the stove, scooped the scrambled eggs into a large bowl and joined the two at the table. Char put eggs and bacon on plates and passed them around.

Grant ate the food with relish. Each new sensation was a wonder to him, every taste an experience to savor, to catalogue with the millions of other memories he had stored. But the experiences since he had left the ship were more complete than what he had learned by interfacing with the computer.

They contained sounds, aromas, tactile sensations that enriched them beyond anything he could take in remotely. "This is very good, Larry. Thank you for the nourishment."

"As I said, you're welcome. I'm glad you are enjoying it. I wasn't sure if you could, you know, eat our food."

"My body is almost an exact duplicate of yours, physically," Grant told him. "All my organs, with the exception of my brain, operate within normal human parameters."

"Oh, that's… interesting," Larry said.

Char could see the wheels turning as he mulled over those words. What had been implied before, what her father had sort of assumed by the empty sofa and their clasped hands, was brought into the foreground as he thought about what Grant's human parameters might include. She couldn't help it. She had to blurt out, "Some are even beyond normal human parameters!"

She burst out laughing, turning red but enjoying the look on her father's face as he, too, started laughing. Grant smiled bemusedly at them, not quite sure what was funny about the remark but was heartened to see father and daughter laughing together.

The ringing of the phone cut their laughter short. Larry reached for it. He gave a solemn look at Char and Grant before picking it up. "Hello?"

"Looks like somebody believed your story," General Adam Crowell said.

"That's great, Adam. I can't thank you enough."

"Don't thank me, I had nothing to do with it. I made some calls, and before I knew it I was getting the run around. It took a lot of brow beating, had to remind them how many stars are sitting on this shoulder, but I finally got the dirt. I guess Char's phone call must have reached the right people. There's already someone on the way to see you guys."

"Do you know who it is?" Larry asked.

"I just know it's being kept low profile. Someone out of Norfolk, I think. I don't have a name. All I could find out was it was happening – I wish I could tell you more."

"That's okay, Adam. I'm just glad they're on their way. Listen, can you do me one more favor? This will be the last, I promise."

"Name it, Larry."

"If these guys start raising the flag – if they come up with a plan to fight this thing, can you support it? Can you make sure we can get it put into place while there's still time?"

"You can count on me," the general said. "After all, if this all goes down like you say, we don't have a choice."

Larry hung up the phone. "They're on their way. Best finish up."

Their appetite, however, was gone, and they did little but push the remaining food around on their plates. Eventually, Larry picked the dishes up and scraped the leftovers into the garbage, putting the plates in the sink with the previous night's dirty dishes. He returned to the table and sat down.

He held out his hands, and Char and Grant met them with their own. He looked at Grant. "I don't know about your religious views, son, but I think a prayer wouldn't hurt, right now."

Grant nodded. "I believe in life, Larry."

"Good enough, so do I." He bent his head and closed his eyes, holding tightly onto their hands, and prayed. "Heavenly Father, please guide us and protect us in our hour of need. Please let wisdom prevail, let your grace fall onto us, let your love fill our hearts. Please spare us from this cloud of annihilation, if that is your will. And Father, I ask you, please let your grace fall on Char and Grant, please bless their union and watch over them. In Jesus' name, we pray. Amen."

Char blinked the tears back as she squeezed her father's hand before releasing it. "Thank you, Dad." Thank you for understanding, she thought. For blessing them, for accepting and loving them without prejudice.

Grant looked at Larry thoughtfully. "That was beautiful, Larry. I have learned many things in my journey. I have expanded that knowledge in so many ways in the short time I have been here. I now begin to comprehend the concept of faith – of blind trust beyond the sure knowledge that fact gives. I have learned what love is, and some of this faith was present in the experience, but I did not know how to understand it. The way you care for your daughter, the way you accept what will happen, that your life will go one way or the other, as it will, opens new paths for me. Thank you for this sharing."

Larry rose to get another cup of coffee. He had no way to respond to that kind of talk. He was a pretty open man, he considered, willing to talk about emotions, not afraid to cry if it was warranted. But this was a little too Dr. Phil. He poured the coffee and sat back down at the table.

Char saw his discomfort and smiled. "So, how about those Bears?"

Larry laughed. It was a comment they had used to breach awkward moments in the past. "Yeah, how about those Bears?" he repeated.

Grant looked around confusedly. Char leaned over and gave him a peck on the cheek. "It's okay, Grant. Everything's okay."

Grant cocked his head to one side. His enhanced senses picked up the whirring blades as the helicopter descended. "I believe they have arrived."

Chapter Thirty: Meetings

"Okay, cut the blades," Major Drake ordered. He addressed the team as the loud roar of the spinning rotors lessened to a quieter thwipping sound. "We're going in easy. Remember, this woman called for help. She wants us here. We're going to assume that has not changed. Captain Wolf, you and Jackson are to remain in the helicopter. Maintain visual contact. Radio for assistance at the first sign of trouble."

"Yes, sir," Captain Wolf said. "You sure you don't want one of us with you?"

"No offense, Captain, but if they can take me out you don't stand a chance." He slapped Wolf on the back and gestured to the rest of the team. "Come on, let's go say hello."

He got out of the helicopter. Doctor Scott, Allan Davis and Sid Eckham followed the major out onto the yard. The group walked up to the front door and Major Drake knocked loudly.

Larry Amberson opened the door. "Good morning. We've been expecting you. Come on in."

Major Drake gave a sideways glance to Doctor Scott, who shrugged in return. The major gave a chuckle, and entered the house with his team close on his heels.

They followed Larry into the kitchen. Char and Grant were sitting at the table. Larry counted the newcomers. "I'll grab a couple more chairs and we can get started."

"Look here, Mister Amberson, I presume – I think it would be best if we cleared the air a little first. We haven't even introduced ourselves," Doctor Scott said.

Larry laughed. "I'm Larry Amberson, this is my daughter Char, and that's Grant. He's from outer space. Now, can I go get the chairs or do you guys want to stand the whole time?"

Major Drake let out a guffaw. "You served, I can tell. Army?"

"Twelve years and two campaigns," Larry answered.

"I thought so. Okay, get the chairs. We'll get started when you're ready."

Larry looked at his uniform. "Thank you, Major. I'll be right back." He nodded at Allan Davis. "Son, could you help me with the chairs, please?"

Allan went with Larry to the living room where they each took a couple chairs and returned with them to the kitchen table. They spaced them among the three that were already around the table and all seven people sat down.

"Well now, Larry – can I call you that? – good, we don't need to stand on formality here. I am Major Clark Drake out of Norfolk. I'm in charge here, obviously. Along with me we have Doctor Eugene Scott, my chief scientist,

Allan Davis, lead programmer, and Sid Eckham, a biologist. We're here in response to your daughter's phone call to Homeland Security."

"Thank God you came," Char blurted out. "Listen, we don't have much time – the cloud is almost here!"

"The cloud? Oh yes, there was mention of something along those lines in your call," Doctor Scott said. "But we're really here for him," he added, pointing at Grant. "At least, I hope we are."

Grant shifted in his seat. These people were different; there were too many new things all at once and he was not sure he felt the same about them as he did about Larry and Char. The older man, Major Clark, seemed sincere, but he could not tell about the rest. "I am sorry, Doctor Scott. But I am not what matters, here. Charlotte speaks the truth - the cloud is the imminent concern, I am a mere messenger."

Sid leaned across the table, trying to detect any trace of the alien about Grant. "I'm sorry, but you appear to be human." He looked over at the major. "I don't think this man is any different than you or I, Major Drake."

Larry slammed a hand on the table, causing the group to jump. "Listen here, we don't have time for this. Let me put it straight to you. Grant here is in fact from outer space. He came here in a spaceship that I am sure he would be happy to show you. But as Char said, there is a cloud of alien origin approaching this planet and within a matter of hours it will consume every living thing on it unless we find a way to stop it! Now does that help you set your priorities?"

Major Drake rubbed his forehead with the flat of his hand. "I'm sorry if we seem a bit inquisitive, Larry. But you should understand that the United States government can't just assume that every alien invasion story someone tells it is the truth. To be frank, every other one that has come to my attention has been patently false. So if you want us to take this seriously – and believe me, we are willing to, or we wouldn't be here – then we're going to need to see the alleged flying saucer, and some proof that Grant here didn't pop out of the local asylum."

"Everyone, please join hands," Grant said.

His team looked at Major Drake for direction. He nodded his assent, and the seven people linked hands where they sat around the table. Grant closed his eyes, commanding his cells to shift, to travel into the bodies of Char and Larry, whose hands he held. He sent more of his life energy out, extending his connections from his body to theirs, and then traversing beyond their bodies to the people holding their opposite hands. He strained, he had never pushed his energy this thin, over this many people. It was similar to his struggle when he had absorbed the herd of cows; he had to keep his own identity intact as he stretched it through the other six people, yet needed to merge enough of his energy with them to communicate, to send the memories and visual images to their minds.

It was a much shallower connection than when he bonded with either Char or Larry; it had to be, from necessity of keeping his own self whole, to be able to control each of his connections without harm to himself or the others. It was still quite effective in conveying his memories, however, and after a rapid succession of transfers he drew his energy back, leaving the others with the impressions of the dangers of the cloud, with its awesome capabilities, with the nearness and immediacy of the danger. He collapsed in his chair, slumped over, drained from the effort.

"Grant!" Char cried, jumping out of her chair and cradling his head against her chest.

He looked up at her, smiled briefly. "I'm all right. Just tired. Did it work?" he asked.

Char looked at the stunned faces of their visitors. "Yeah, I think it did."

Chapter Thirty-One: End of the Road

"I think we found it," Jeff said.

"What gave you the first clue – the huge military helicopter in the middle of the yard?"

Tia and Jeff had stopped on the dirt road just short of the gravel driveway that led up to the Amberson's house. She had turned off the engine, hoping their approach had gone unnoticed. The car would be barely visible from the house, she thought – the driveway curved slightly and there were a few trees along its path to serve as windbreaks that would serve as additional cover for the small vehicle.

"Try calling Allan," Tia suggested. "Maybe he can give us a heads up as to what's going on."

Jeff flipped his cell phone open. "No signal. Stupid corn fields."

"Well, nothing ventured, nothing gained," Tia said, opening the car door.

"What are you doing? That's an army helicopter out there!" Jeff said, grabbing on to her arm to prevent her from exiting the vehicle. "You can't go waltzing in!"

She shrugged her arm loose. "Let go – of course I can. What are they going to do, shoot me? This is America. There's no law against a couple of people having car trouble walking up to a farm house is there? We're just looking for a phone to call a tow truck, okay?"

Jeff looked worried. "I don't know, Tia. If this is as big as Allan was suggesting – if this is really proof of alien life – then maybe they would shoot us."

"Quit being so paranoid," Tia said. She put a hand on his, gave him her best coquettish smile. "If this was that big, this place would be swarming with g-men. Anyway, Jeff, I've got you to look out for me."

He had no choice but to hurry out of the passenger side and follow her as she sashayed up the driveway. She sure knew how to work it, he thought, debating whether to catch up immediately or enjoy the view from behind. He decided the part of knight in shining armor, which he could only hope was his role in her eyes, demanded he jog up until he was walking beside her. He gingerly took her arm in his, his mood lifting when she did not pull free.

They slowed their pace as they approached the house. Jeff looked around the front yard, tried to see if he could spy anyone standing watch or sitting in the silent helicopter. The windshield was smoky from the outside, and he could not see if it was still occupied. He nervously looked up near the barn, wondering if he would see the glint of sunlight off of rifle barrels if there were snipers up there, training their sites on him and Tia. What if there were, he thought. Nothing they could do about it. Tia's plan was the only viable option in the situation, once they had decided to become involved. Walk in open handed, pretend they just happened to be in the neighborhood and needed some help. Oh, and excuse me, was that E.T.? Sure, the plan had a couple holes in it, but what could you expect from a couple of Berkeley grads wandering the corn fields of Indiana?

"This is Captain Scott Wolf of the United States Army. Stop and identify yourselves," a voice boomed out from speakers on the outside of the helicopter.

Tia and Jeff halted. Jeff started to put up his hands. Tia gave him a look of disgust and he lowered them.

"Sorry," he whispered, "thought that was standard procedure."

Tia shook her head and then spoke loudly so her voice would be picked up. "I'm Tia Montoni, this is Jeff Stanton. Our car broke down - we're just looking for a phone."

"Please standby," Captain Wolf told them through the speakers.

"Want me to go check them out?" Stephanie Jackson asked the pilot.

"No, I want us both in here. Major Drake would not want us to compromise our position. I think discretion would be the proper move."

Captain Wolf clicked the microphone back on. "I'm sorry, folks, but you're going to have to leave the premises. This property is currently under military jurisdiction."

Tia put her hands on her hips. "There's nowhere to go! This is the only house for ten miles!"

"I'm sorry, ma'am, you'll have to leave. This is a restricted area."

"Can't you at least call us a tow truck?" Jeff yelled.

Tia turned to him. "We don't want to really get out of here, Jeff," she whispered.

"I know, but it might buy us some time. And anyway, the more witnesses the better, in case they do decide to shoot at us," he whispered back.

"Standby," Captain Wolf replied.

Stephanie Jackson shrugged. "It couldn't hurt. We can get the local police, have them send a truck. Just make them head back and wait in their car – that should keep them out of the way."

Captain Wolf nodded. "Okay, folks, we'll call for a tow truck. But we need you to return to your vehicle immediately. You need to remain out of this area, understand?"

"Yes, we understand," Tia said. She waved at the helicopter. "Thanks for calling the tow truck – you're a lifesaver!"

Tia took Jeff's arm and spun him around, leading him back down the driveway.

"You took that defeat rather well," Jeff said when they got back to the car.

"Are you kidding?" Tia said. "That was just working your little delay angle. It's obvious they don't have a lot of people out there, or they would have taken us in somewhere, or at least sent someone out here with us. We're going back, just not by the front gate."

"I thought you acquiesced too easily," Jeff said. He shook his head. "Tia, it's one thing to try to bluff our way in — at least we weren't hiding anything or surprising them. They catch us sneaking up there and who knows what they'll charge us with."

She came in close to him, encircled his waist with her arms and pressed her chest against his. "Aw, come on, Jeff, it will be fun. Exciting." She tilted her head, licked her lips. "Don't you want to go on a little adventure with me?"

She felt so good against him. He knew it wasn't his brain making the decision, but there were enough other parts flush with emotion that it was outvoted anyway. "Well, I guess we could go around back, through that corn field. We should at least be able to look at the back yard."

"That's my boy," she purred. She ran her fingers through his hair, sending an electric shock through him. Putty in her hands, she thought. It would be such a shame if she had to kill him.

Chapter Thirty-Two: Battle Plan

"Jesus H. Christ," Major Drake said. "This is really it." He looked at Grant. "We get visited by a man from another world, and he's here to tell us the world is coming to an end."

"We're not dead, yet," Char said. "That's why I made that phone call. There's still hope, we can still try to stop the cloud."

"Char's right, Major. We can't just throw in the towel," Larry said. "Don't you boys have anything we can throw at this thing? Surely those billions of tax dollars we spend on defense have produced some kind of weapon we can shoot at it."

Major Drake shook his head. "We've got nukes, of course, but from the show we just watched it looked like bombs had no effect on it."

"Your bombs might be more effective," Grant said. They all turned to him at his words. "My people were not very aggressive. Our world had been at relative peace for centuries. Our offensive weapons were limited. Perhaps yours might have an effect on the cloud." He paused. "If you were able to strike across its entire width, the force might disperse it - might prevent it from becoming cohesive again. It may be possible, if the strike force is sufficient and comprehensive, that you could destroy the cloud."

Their faces shifted from fear, from anguish, to looks of nervous hopefulness. Doctor Scott leaned forward. "You really think that would work?"

"It's worth a shot," Char said. "It's not like they're going to do us any good sitting in silos after the cloud gets here."

"Girl's got a point." Major Drake stood up, started pacing across the kitchen floor. "Okay, say we go forward with this. How much time do we have before the cloud gets here?"

"A little less than six hours," Grant said. "I could give you more precise data as to the probable orbital vectors and velocity, if that would be helpful."

"It would," Major Drake said. "Give that information to Allan here, and he can plug it into his modeling simulations. And any other information that might help us hit it. We don't want to be missing the target."

Char realized their shared visions hadn't been as clear as her experience had been, did not let them see the cloud as detailed, as gargantuan, as she had. "Sir, I don't think hitting it is going to be a problem. You won't be able to miss it. This cloud – it's enormous. It engulfs entire planets as it feeds on them."

"I was hoping that was an exaggeration. Well, then, we still need some real data on how wide the thing is, so we can space the impact zones. We don't want to blow it in two, we need to scatter it all into little pieces." Major Drake stopped his pacing behind Doctor Scott's chair. "Scott, I'm going to need you to get a report ready for the Pentagon. Use Eckham to help you."

"Me, sir?" Sid Eckham asked. "I don't know anything about nuclear missiles."

"We don't have time to wait for the experts, and as excited as you must be to have an alien being in the room with you, we can't afford to compare blood samples. Just help out Doctor Scott however you can, even if it's bringing him coffee." Major Drake turned to face Larry Amberson. "Larry, I'm afraid we're going to have to make this Home Base. It would take two hours to get back to Norfolk, and I'm afraid we can't spare that time."

"No problem, Major Drake. We expected it would get crazy around here, once you arrived. Just let us know what we can do to help."

"I'd say keep the coffee brewing for now. I need to start making calls; it will go quicker on the dedicated radio in the chopper. Okay, everybody, let's get cracking. Time to save the world." He gave them all a confident smile and left the kitchen.

Larry hurriedly got out of his chair and followed the major. He caught up to him at the front door. "Major Drake? One more thing, in case it will help. If you start running into red tape, give General Adam Crowell a call. He already knows what's happening; I spoke with him this morning and he said he would support us."

Major Drake looked at Larry with increased respect. The farmer had already impressed him, but this was a totally unexpected bonus. "Larry, you must have been a hell of a soldier, when you can call in favors from four star generals! God, we might even be able to get this done, if you brought Crowell to the table. This really gives us a chance to get the Pentagon to act in time." He slapped Larry on the back and trotted out to the helicopter to get on the radio.

Larry returned to the kitchen and started a fresh pot of coffee brewing. Grant was sitting next to Allan. The programmer was typing data into his laptop keyboard as fast as Grant could feed it to him. Char sat on the other side of Grant, her chair close to his. She had her head leaning against his shoulder, half watching the laptop display, but mostly just being there with Grant. Larry smiled as he watched the two lovers, as he spied Char sneaking glances up at Grant, as he saw Grant squeeze her hand gently even as he dictated reams of data to Allan.

Doctor Scott and Sid Eckham were huddled at the other end of the table. "Excuse me," Doctor Scott said. "Did I see a table in the entrance room? Next to the sofa? It's a little crowded here, between our papers and Allan's laptop."

"Yes" Larry answered. "There's a coffee table in there you can use."

"Ah, that would be better. We need to spread out a little. Come on, Sid," he told the biologist, "we're moving into the front room." The two of them gathered their papers and went into the other room.

Larry sat down at the table, pulling a chair over next to Char. He placed a hand on her shoulder, patted it a few times. "Major Drake thinks he can get through to the Pentagon, with General Crowell's help. I really think they're going to listen to us, Char."

She smiled at her father. "Thanks, Dad. I knew you could help us."

"What's the use of fighting in a couple wars if it doesn't get you some connections?" He grinned at her, mussed her short hair, and got up to check on the coffee.

"Is that all the information you need?" Grant asked.

Allan shrugged. "I don't even have parameters for half the data you were giving me; our computer model isn't that sophisticated. I'm not sure our mathematical theory is, to tell you the truth. But you gave me everything that I can model. Now let's run the simulation." He entered a few commands into the program and clicked the button to initiate the program's execution. "It'll be ready in a minute," he said. "Then we'll have a pretty good picture of where and when this cloud is going."

Larry brought over the coffee pot and filled up cups for Char and Allan. Grant sniffed Char's coffee and politely declined a cup. They sat staring at the laptop screen, waiting for the program to finish. It seemed eons but in reality only seconds passed before a window popped up with the message that the program had completed. The simulation model was ready.

Allen clicked on the button to display the target zone for the cloud. The entire screen went bright green.

"What happened?" Char asked.

Allan grinned sheepishly. "It was still set to display at the same level as our projected paths for Grant's ship. Guess this whole area is part of the target area for the cloud." He modified the settings and reset the model. This time, when he clicked, it was a spatial view, with the Earth centered on the screen, filling about a third of the viewing area. A very wide line entered the screen from the bottom and intersected the planet. A large green oval, translucent, was layered over the spinning orb, wider than the diameter by a good measure, leaving little doubt that the cloud would pass over every bit of the planet. The thick blue line continued on the opposite side, heading away from the planet after the fateful pass.

Larry gasped at the display. "I knew it was big, but this really puts it in perspective. God, it's really heading dead center for Earth."

"Actually," Allan corrected, "it's not. But based on all the information that Grant has supplied, we know that it adjusts it course as it approaches planetary objects. There's no reason to think it won't hit dead center, not on a planet our size."

Grant nodded. "Allan is correct. He has reduced its current width, in fact, to match the history that has been recorded of its activities as it approaches objects. It tends to widen out half again the diameter of the object as it nears it. It would be more than eleven times this width as it passes through the gas giant you name Jupiter. This is a reasonable model of the cloud's dimensions as it approaches Earth."

"So why'd we bother to model it, if we know it will change course and size so it hits dead center?" Char asked. "What's the point?"

"We needed to do this to get the most likely orbital paths," Allan explained. "If we are going to send rockets up there, we need to be able to plan the best trajectories, as well as programming their firing mechanisms to initiate at the appropriate time, for maximum effect. Even when this thing is as wide as Jupiter, it's still sitting out there in empty space, which there's a whole lot more of than occupied space. We're guessing it will contract from about fifty thousand miles across as it goes through the asteroid belt to just about seven thousand miles to pass through Mars. From there, it will expand to about ten thousand miles wide to engulf Earth. Right after it comes out of Mars, that's our best shot at hitting it, when it is most compact, and our nukes have to disperse their detonation effect over the least amount of coverage area."

Allan paused, making sure the rest were following him. He saw from their nods of understanding that they were. "Okay, as I mentioned, this data will help us figure out where and when this maximum density opportunity will be. That will let us program the rockets' targeting mechanisms and their firing sequence so they hit it at the same time. It is imperative that the explosions occur within microseconds of each other, or there will be a strong possibility that the remaining pieces are large enough to bond together, to reform the cloud. And since this is all going to be happening at incredibly fast speeds, we're going to have to cross our fingers after we launch. We won't be able to modify a thing, once they're airborne. And the time from detonation to when the cloud hits us, if it survives, will be less than the time a successful radio transmission will reach us."

Char grimaced. "So, we launch, pray, and then we either get consumed by the cloud or we don't."

"That's what I'm – well, what the computer model is showing."

"So we can do this? The simulation says it's possible?" Larry asked.

Allen shrugged, a gesture he was getting too used to doing. "Well, it's got a lot of assumptions I had to build in." He ticked them off on his fingers. "One, that the cloud will be vulnerable to the nukes. Two, that the targeting and firing mechanisms of the rockets can be synchronized properly. And three, that we have enough missiles to cover almost 50 million square miles of surface area on the target."

"When will we know?" Char asked.

"We won't, on the first point. That's the praying part you mentioned earlier. I should be able to find out about the other two when Major Drake gets back – I need to set up a satellite link to connect to the Defense network."

"I feel my ears burning," Major Drake said as he walked into the kitchen. Doctor Scott and Sid Eckham entered behind him. "Well, thanks to Larry's contacts, and a little bit of swearing on my part, we have a meeting scheduled with the Pentagon in ten minutes. Eckham, Davis – I need you two to get the equipment out of the chopper and get us ready for the video conference. Scott and I will finish prepping the report. Once the equipment is up we'll need to add your computer models to it, Davis."

"Sir," Allan said, hesitating to interrupt.

"Yes, what is it?"

"I need to check some figures before we start. It could be critical."

"Well you better get it set up pronto. But in ten minutes we go live with the Pentagon, with or without your figure checking," Major Drake said.

"Yes, sir," Allan said. He and Sid rushed out to the helicopter.

Larry pointed after the two and looked at Major Drake. "All right if I lend them a hand hauling stuff in?"

"Have at it, Larry. Okay, Scott, let's take a look at the model."

The setup crew brought in a digital video camera on a tripod and linked it to Allan's laptop, then connected a projection unit to the laptop. This would show the conference room at the Pentagon, and allow those in D.C. to view the group surrounding the kitchen table in the farm house just outside Kanapolis, Indiana. Allan connected a cable to the laptop that led outside to a satellite receiver and transponder. This would be the connection that all the video, audio and data files would be transmitted from and received into. He hooked up a duel-directional speaker and microphone unit and placed it in the center of the table, where it could pick up all of their voices and broadcast the incoming audio from the Pentagon conference room.

While the others were setting up the equipment, Char did her best to relate Allan's findings from the computer model simulation to Major Drake and Doctor Scott. Grant corrected her on some of the terminology and statistics, but let her inform them of the essential details of the situation.

Allan hooked the final cable into the back of his laptop. "Okay, we're set in here. Go ahead and flip the satellite switch I showed you earlier," he told Sid.

The biologist-turned-gopher ran out to the yard and flipped the designated switch. Power hummed in the unit and indicator lights turned green. Everything was working; they had satellite linkage.

Back in the kitchen, Allan grinned as his network connection status changed from 'Network Unavailable' to 'Secure Connection Enabled.'

"We have connectivity!" he cried out. He quickly launched several sessions on his screen, initiating multiple queries into the Defense systems databases. He knew he had only minutes before the video conference call would start.

"Okay, I have those started. That will take a minute or two. We have three minutes before we do video and audio test with the Pentagon conference room controller; five minutes until the conference starts."

Major Drake gave him a hearty slap on the back, almost knocking the younger man down. "Thatta boy, Davis. Doctor Scott, are you ready with the report?"

"Yes sir," Doctor Scott replied. "It's sitting in Allan's work folder – ready for the final numbers based on his last minute queries. Once those finish, we'll send the report to the Pentagon."

Larry filled everyone's coffee cup a last time as they waited impatiently for Allan's queries to run. Major Drake paced, the rest sat nervously in their chairs around the kitchen table.

Allan typed rapidly on his keyboard. He had tilted the screen slightly, and his position at a corner of the table hid the majority of the display screen from the rest of group. He opened a chat window, reduced it so it took up only a small portion of the screen in an area not visible to the others. He typed a short message and sent it as a text message to Tia's and Jeff's cell phone numbers. It was all he could do, all he could risk in this situation. He closed the chat window and went back to monitoring his queries.

The first query result came back. "I've got the information on the targeting and firing systems," Allan announced. He smiled. "They're up to the task!"

Everyone cheered at the information. Doctor Scott came up to the laptop and directed Allan to his report. The two of them worked together to add the new information, removing the concern from the assumptions caveat at the end of the report.

"Time to test communications," Sid Eckham informed them. "One minute until we have to send the final report."

Allan initiated test signals for data, audio and video. He told everyone to wave at the camera so the operator in the Pentagon conference room could verify the video feed, and that they were all in range of the lens. They looked at the projection screen and saw a junior lieutenant waving back at them.

"All good here," Allan said.

"Roger, broadcast begins in two minutes, data files must be received in one minute" came the response, heard through the unit in the center of the table.

Major Drake pressed the mute button, cutting off their sound from transmission. "We'll turn sound back on when we start. There might be a few last minute words we have here that are better kept among ourselves. How's that last query going? We have less than a minute to send that report."

Allan clicked on the query, urging it to finish. He shook his head. "Not finished, yet."

"Doctor Scott, what do you think? Do we have enough –will they cover it?" Major Drake asked.

Doctor Scott held up his hands. "Sir, I just don't know."

"There has to be enough," Char said. Everyone looked at her. She was fighting tears as she spoke, trying to get the words out, trying to keep from crying. "Don't you see? We have to tell them it will work! If we don't they'll spend the next six hours debating it and we'll all end up dead. It's got to work, because we have no other choice!"

Grant reached for her, pulled her to his chest as she released a few quick, violent sobs. "That's enough," Char said. "Thanks, Grant, but I'm okay now, I can make it through the call."

Major Drake nodded his head. "Scott, make the changes. Plug it in so it works."

"What numbers should we use? How many missiles do we send up?" Doctor Scott asked.

"You heard her, Scott – we really have no choice. There's no point holding anything back. Use them all. Send up every warhead we have against that thing."

They modified the report and transmitted it through the satellite link. No turning back now, Allan thought. He briefly wondered if his friends had received his last text message. He stopped himself from shrugging, but inwardly his mind gave the mental equivalent. He couldn't talk to them now; they were on their own, wherever they were, just like everybody else on the planet would be.

Major Drake checked his watch. "Thirty seconds until we go live. I'm turning sound back on. Behave yourselves," he added with a smile, "they can hear us now."

Chapter Thirty-Three: Reconnaissance

Jeff Stanton and Tia Montoni peered through the crisscrossing leaves of the cornstalks they hid behind. They had crept along the corn field on the opposite side of the farm house, as far from the helicopter as possible. It had taken them a while to skulk through the fields, but they finally worked their way around until they were behind the farm house.

"I was hoping the corn field went right up to the back yard," Jeff said. He looked at the much more open meadow between them and the house. There was little to hide them there, certainly not as well as the corn had shielded them. "Not much to see from here."

Tia pointed to the tall tree halfway across the meadow. "Let's head for that tree. That should give us some cover. But move slowly – we don't want to wake up those cows sleeping under it."

Jeff nodded and the two crept on hands and knees to the tree. "Oh my God," Jeff said, when they had reached the spot. "These cows aren't asleep – they're dead! What happened to them? They look like they've been freeze dried."

Tia shook her head. "I have no idea. I've never seen anything like it. There are no marks on them, they're just shriveled, dried-up – I can't imagine what could have done it."

"Alien vampires," Jeff said, only half joking. "If Allan was right about this being the real thing…"

"It's not alien vampires," Tia said. "Some local strain of mad cow disease, probably, or mange – I think that's a farm animal sickness. Whatever, we need to focus on the house Think we can get to that back porch?"

"I don't know. There's no real cover. If anyone's watching, we're dead meat."

Tia glared at him. "Come on, Jeff. This is huge. We're talking E.T. in the flesh! If we don't make our move now, this place is going to become a military camp and we'll never get in."

"That's still assuming it's the real deal. If it isn't we're risking everything on a National Enquirer headline. It's not worth it, Tia. Not until we get confirmation from Allan."

Tia frowned. She had to admit he had a point. He was worried about jail, maybe losing his job; she was concerned with whether it was worth blowing her cover. She had spent years creating the Tia Montoni persona; had spent much of that time fostering relationships and forming cliques like the one she shared with Jeff, Allan and Becky. If this really was extraterrestrial in nature, the choice was clear. But she couldn't risk her cover on what might be a hoax. If she was wrong, it was more than a few days in jail and the unemployment line for her. It'd be a permanent vacation six feet under the ground.

They were laying chest down on the ground, staying flat in an effort to avoid detection, their elbows tilted below them, chins in their hands. She shifted her weight so she pressed against Jeff's side with her own. She felt him startle a little at the contact, then adjust his own balance so he leaned slightly into her. She rolled over onto her side, facing him, one arm crooked under to support her head, her other hand rubbing his back. "You're right, darling. It would be best to wait until we hear from Allan. To make sure before we do anything rash. We'll just have to keep each other company until then."

He smiled at her, enjoying the feel of her hand making small circles on his back. He wanted Allan to confirm that this was the real deal so that he could share such a mind-boggling experience with Tia. People that share life-altering events often form bonds, he thought. Often fall in love. As Tia's hand pressed against him, as he looked into those wild, gorgeous eyes, he thought this was going to be the best day of his life. Give them confirmation, Allan, he pled, but not just yet. Let him soak this in for a little while longer.

Chapter Thirty-Four: Jupiter

The cloud expanded to its widest area as it neared the largest planet in the system. It had left Saturn behind almost two hours ago, had contracted after it had passed through the gas giant and its rings, but when it detected the colossal Jupiter as the next planet in its wake it reversed its particles, thinning its mass until it encompassed a swath of space covering a hundred thousand miles across, its vaporous mist forming a rolling fog of energy that drank all life energy it found in its ten billion square miles of frontage.

It modified the properties of its components, plying the magnetic and gravitational forces to align its center with that of Jupiter's as it passed into the gas giant. It enveloped many of the over sixty satellites orbiting the king of planets; it did not regret, or even recognize, those that passed just out of reach. It had no concept of opportunities won or lost, of victory or failure. It knew as it completed its search for life energy on the planet that it did not find any. There was no sadness, just the awareness that energy was still needed. The knowledge that the journey continued as it left the planet behind it.

It modified its properties to decrease the pull of Jupiter's gravity and its prior momentum carried it away. The orbit angle altered as it continued to circle in toward the heart of the solar system. It would be almost three hours before the next noticeable objects would appear to its senses, until it reached the Asteroid Belt just outside the planet Mars.

Chapter Thirty-Five: Video Conference

The video conference was underway. The group in the Amberson kitchen had been introduced to those present in the Pentagon conference room and vice versa. General Adam Crowell, Secretary of Defense Jacob Burns, Admiral Norm Mathis and the Vice President of the United States, Martin Timmons, had just finished reviewing the report that had been transmitted minutes earlier through the satellite link.

Major Drake addressed the Pentagon leaders. "As you can see, we don't a have a minute to waste. Based on the projections that Scott and Davis put together, we have less than thirty minutes to launch the attack, in order to hit the cloud at the optimum moment, when it is most compact. If we don't strike it then, it will be too dispersed for our warheads to have the desired effect."

Burns looked up from his report. "Major Drake, I'm sure you understand our reluctance to send our entire nuclear arsenal off into space without any concrete evidence there is something out there. We don't even know this threat is real."

"I assure you it is," Major Drake said. "You have my word on it."

"And mine," General Crowell said. "I trust Larry Amberson with my life, Secretary Burns. If he says this cloud is out there then it's out there."

Mathis raised his hand to add his input. "But that's the problem, Adam. It's not your life we're risking here. It's the security of the whole nation. Once we launch, our ability to defend ourselves will be seriously compromised."

"Not to mention how this is going to look to the rest of the world," Timmons said. "They already think we do whatever we want, without consultation – they are going to assume we have ulterior motives, that we're trying to pull a fast one on them."

"If we don't stop the cloud there won't be any nation, anywhere," Char shouted at them. "Can't you get it through your thick skulls that this isn't about security or politics or what anyone is going to think of us? We're all dead if we don't stop the cloud, end of story!"

She waited nervously, trembling, clutching Grant's arm tightly as the silence deepened in the aftermath of her explosion.

Major Drake broke it with a hand slap against the kitchen table. "She's right, boys, you know she is. There won't be a United States if we don't launch those missiles."

"Give us a moment," Burns said. The speakers went silent and the project screen went blank.

Major Drake leaned back in his chair. "We did what we could; it's up to them, now."

Allan glanced down at his laptop screen. A window popped up, alerting him that his other query had finally completed execution. He opened up the results and his face went pale as the blood rushed from it. "Major Drake," he said, his voice quaking, "we have a problem."

"What is it, Davis?" Major Drake asked.

"The last query finished. The one to show effective coverage area, based on warhead capacity and maximum disbursement. It's not enough. Even if we get all the missiles launched in time, and they hit the cloud at maximum density, we can only cover seventy-three percent of the front surface area."

"You mean after all this, is doesn't even matter what they come back with? Whether they agree to launch or not, we're still dead?" Sid asked.

Allan looked at the biologist. "Yeah. Numbers don't lie – we don't have enough warheads to complete the pattern. They'll be spaced too far apart."

"We don't know that, not for a fact," Larry said. His voice was strong, reassuring, confident. "This whole plan was based on assumptions. We don't know the effect of our nukes on this cloud anyway; we're hoping that by blowing it apart it won't be able to come together. There's no reason to quit hoping now. For all we know, a wider pattern will work. We're going into this fight on a wing and a prayer. Don't lose faith now; it's our best weapon."

Major Drake stood up, commanding their attention. "Larry's right. This nation was built on faith. I, for one, would rather die by it than live without it."

Grant reached out for Larry's hand; he already had Char's in his other. Larry nodded at him, then reached for Allan's. The circle continued to form, hand to hand, until Sid clasped Char's hand, completing the loop.

Grant considered linking them with his energies, thought about bringing them together in shared vision as he had before. No, he decided, it was better this way. The human way, on faith alone, would keep them united.

The projection screen turned back on and the speakers crackled as the connection between the two sites was resumed. Secretary of Defense Jacob Burns faced into the camera. "We've spoken with the President," he said. "We're going to launch."

Relief ran through the group in the kitchen. They wanted to clap, to applaud the decision, but they knew their fate was not yet resolved. "Should we tell them?" Allan whispered across the table to Major Drake.

The audio equipment was very sophisticated, and his whisper, while low, was picked up by the microphone and broadcast to the Pentagon conference room.

"Tell us what?" Admiral Mathis asked.

Major Drake sighed. "Well, sir, some of the projections in the report were based on various assumptions we had to make at the last moment."

"We are aware of that, Major," Mathis said. "It's unavoidable due to the time available. This is a calculated risk, but we really have no choice, as the young woman so diplomatically pointed out to us earlier."

"Yes, well, while we were waiting some additional calculations finished. If our other assumptions still hold, then this new information is… well, it suggests the plan might not work. We can only cover seventy-three percent of the cloud's front at maximum effectiveness."

The Pentagon group sat back, stunned. Burns stood up, enraged. "You mean after all this, after all the hoops we just jumped through, after getting the President to authorize us to launch our entire arsenal into space, it won't even blow the damn thing up?"

Major Drake held his ground. "Sir, we really don't have a choice. We're guessing on this thing, we admit it. But it's our best – our only chance. We've got to try it."

General Crowell cleared his throat. "It might not be our very best chance," he said.

Everyone looked at him expectantly, hope rising in their hearts at his calm words.

"This isn't just our problem, it's the world's. Yes, that same world that is always yelling at us for going off half-cocked and trying to do everything on our own. My recollection of other countries' stockpiles is a little rough, but I would say that if we can cover roughly seventy percent of the target, the rest of the world ought to be able to cover the other thirty percent." General Crowell smiled.

Burns rubbed his chin, thinking the idea over. "It could work, if we can convince them fast enough."

Vice President Timmons shook his head. "There's no way we are going to convince the rest of the world to fire their entire stockpile on our word. They will think it's a trick. They won't want to launch until after we do, at the best, and then it will be too late. We need simultaneous detonation for this plan to work."

"Why don't you guys get started on getting everyone lined up," Larry said. "We have to go ahead with the plan assuming they will join us; it's not like we're going to hold back if they don't. We'll work on something to help convince them."

Burns raised an eyebrow. "What do you have in mind?"

Larry laughed, a joyful sound in the tense atmosphere. "Let us worry about that. Get everyone lined up; tell them we will give them visual proof that we're not blowing smoke here. Just make sure they have everything coordinated with our target and firing program."

The Pentagon group looked around their conference table, getting a quick visual read on the consensus opinion of Larry's proposal. "Okay," Burns said. "You've got fifteen minutes. We'll be back in touch."

The screen went blank and the speakers silent as the connection was shut down. Larry looked around the kitchen table. "It will be okay," he assured them. "We'll get them all to believe."

Char squeezed Grant's hand, prayed her father was right. She couldn't accept the fact that this could all be gone in an hour, that she might never wake up next to him. That she had been given a single night with the love of her life, and that would be the end of it. The end of everything.

Chapter Thirty-Six: Confirmation

Jeff lay flat on his stomach, concentrating on the feel of Tia's palm as she caressed the small of his back. His eyes were closed; he was lost in her touch. The twin chirps interrupted his pleasantness.

He rolled on to his side and dug the cell phone out of his front pocket. "Finally picked up a signal," he said. He looked at the readout, saw there was a text message in his inbox. He entered his password and retrieved the message.

"Allan texted me," he told Tia.

"What'd he say?" she asked. She pulled herself close to him so she could see the small display on his phone.

Jeff clicked on the message to display the text. "E.T. CONFIRMED. DEATH STAR APPROACHING ONE HOUR. LOVE YOU GUYS."

"Christ, this is really it," Jeff said.

Tia's mind raced. This was the big moment, she realized. She had been preparing for this all her life. She had never known what the exact culmination of her career as a sleeper agent would be; she had never known when it would be time to break her cover, what secret technology would prove worth it. She certainly never guessed it would be the first encounter with life from another planet. She fingered the intricate ring on her right hand, twisting the faceted stone until she felt it click into place.

"I'm scared, Jeff," she said, letting her voice tremble, dropping it to a deep, husky sound. "What does he mean by Death Star – what's going to happen?"

He reached to hold her, pulled her against him, wanting to protect her against whatever Allan was warning them about. Knowing that there was little that he could do, but also feeling there was no other place he wanted to be than in the meadow grass outside Kanapolis, Indiana, with Tia Montoni in his arms.

He pulled his head away from her shoulder, looked into those beautiful brown eyes. He blinked away tears - it was hard to see her clearly. He started to tell her he loved her, that he would keep her safe, but he couldn't get the words out. He felt tired, dizzy, and then everything went black.

Tia shifted her hand away from his neck and reset her ring so the tiny needle would not accidentally administer the same narcotic to herself. "Sorry, darling," Tia said. "If it all goes well, you'll wake up with no worse than a headache. If it doesn't, well I suppose none of us will be waking up. Not with the Death Star approaching." She looked around to see if anyone was in sight. Everything looked clear. She dragged his comatose body to the corn field and left him several rows in, where he could not be easily seen from the meadow. She looked across and saw no one watching, so she ran through the meadow and up the back porch steps.

She peered through the window of the back door. She saw the group sitting around the kitchen table, noted the various equipment and cables in the room. The projection screen was at an angle to her current position, and she could not see the image on it.

A couple civilians, some military – no guards, other than the two she presumed were still in the helicopter out front. E.T. must be hiding somewhere, she thought. She pulled back as the people around the table stood up and started heading for the back door. She dove behind a bush close by the house and hunkered down against the ground.

Chapter Thirty-Seven: Convincing Display

"That ship of yours still working?" Larry asked Grant.

"Yes, Larry. It is fully operational. But it has no weaponry."

"I don't want to shoot anyone, Grant. I just want to put on a little show for our friends around the world. Let them know you're the real deal." Larry stood up. "Come on, let's get a look at it. I always wanted to see a flying saucer."

"It is more of a tubular shape, Larry, not unlike your own country's rockets. But I can alter its appearance somewhat, if you would like."

"Just a figure of speech," Larry said.

The rest of them stood up and followed Larry out through the back door. Char and Grant walked arm in arm. She avoided looking at the fallen herd as they passed by. Larry held his hand up to silence Sid's questions. The biologist let the others go ahead for a moment as he looked at the desiccated carcasses, before trotting to catch up with them.

"This the spot?" Larry asked when they had arrived at the edge of the meadow.

"Yes," Grant said. He motioned for Davis and Doctor Scott to move a few feet away, to clear the spot the craft would ascend to. He concentrated on his wrist, shifting densities and pushing the communicator up to the top layer.

"Could you do that again?" Sid asked.

"Later," Major Drake said. "There'll be time for that later."

Grant nodded. He signaled his ship. Char had seen this before, but it was still amazing to watch as the rocket ship rose from out of the meadow grass, rising until it rested completely above the ground, with no trace of its path left underneath it.

"Christ," Major Drake said, "we should have telecast that. They'd believe us in a heartbeat."

Larry shook his head. "They'd just assume it was digitally created. No, we're going to show them live and in person. That will shake them out of their political grandstanding."

Char held onto Grant's arm. "You want him to leave?"

Larry walked over to her, put a hand on her shoulder. "Just for a few minutes, honey. We need him to do this. If Grant jets this ship around the world, buzzes all the capitols, they'll have to believe us. They know we don't have anything that could do this; heck, even if they don't believe us, even if they think we built this ship, they'll know they don't have anything to compete with it. They'll come on board, whether through belief or fear, I don't care."

Major Drake clapped his hands. "By Jove, I think that might do it. What do you say, son, are you willing to give them a show?"

Grant gently removed Char's arm from his. "It will be all right," he told her. "I will be back before... well, in time." He took Char's hand and placed it in her father's hand. He looked at Major Drake and nodded. "I will give them a show."

Grant pressed a button on his communicator and a hatch opened up on the ship. He got in and closed the hatch behind him. The group stepped back as he activated the engines. He flipped several switches, issued commands to his ship's control computer, turning off all of the sensor blocking technology. He wanted them to detect the ship on this trip.

Larry held onto Char tightly as they watched the ship hover a few feet off the ground. Then, suddenly, there was a whoosh and it was gone.

Char turned around and nestled her face in Larry's shoulder. "He'll be back," he told her. "Don't you worry, he'll be back."

Tia blinked. It was everything Allan had hinted at, and more. That guy didn't look like E.T., but he sure had one fine rocket ship. She reached down to her ankles, felt under her jeans. The slender pistol was there, she knew it was, but it wasn't time for that. She thought about Allan's message. That had to be E.T. who took off in the ship, but she was pretty sure that the Death Star was something else. Something bigger, deadlier. She felt mixed emotions; if the E.T. was real, then so might the Death Star be. What did she really want to happen?

For so long, life had been nothing but a big game, an adventure where she hid herself in false identities, where she played her part and reaped the rewards of confidences, stolen technology and secrets. She had passed enough information on, in discrete fashion, so she was allowed her freedom, to work how she wanted and with who she wanted. She was always able to get her job done using her charm, sexuality or mind; never had she been forced to kill. She had been trained in those arts, had thought she would have no qualms about it, should it be necessary, but now she hesitated. There were three choices here, she thought. Kill them now, while E.T. was still flying around - well, leave the geeky one alive, he'd be easy to coerce information from. Or she could walk away, get out of here while the getting was good, they'd never know she was here, what she had let slip through her hands. Or, finally, she could jump feet first and join them, blowing her cover and turning double agent, in order to see what this whole thing was all about. Three seconds to decide, she thought, three seconds before they start heading back this way.

She bolted from the tree, running across the meadow and to the back porch steps. She gave a quick glance back. No one had seen her. She opened the door and walked into the kitchen, careful not to let the door slam behind her.

Tia quickly scanned the room. She peered down the hall. She was alone. She walked over to Allan's laptop and started opening up the recent documents. She sat back in the chair. If this report was to be believed – and after seeing that spaceship, why wouldn't she believe it – the Death Star that Allan had texted them about was all too real. Not mechanical, but just as deadly. This cloud – it was going to kill them all if this attack didn't work. She looked up as the projection screen turned on. She froze as she recognized the people in the video display. It was clear that they did not recognize her.

"Who are you?" Burns asked. "Where's Major Drake?"

"I was just passing by. I had some car trouble; I was looking for – oh, screw it." She faced the camera directly, all pretense vanished from her expression. "My name is unimportant. What matters is that I'm a sleeper agent for the KGB. Well, what used to be the KGB. I report to, and get paid by, their legacy now."

"Contact Captain Wolf," Burns told General Crowell.

"That isn't necessary," Tia said. "I assure you, I have not harmed anyone. I haven't had any contact with the others. They're outside; they just sent your alien off in his ship."

"We have confirmation the alien vessel has flown through every major capitol, Secretary Burns," Admiral Mathis said. "He not only buzzed their capitols, he flew the ship right through their walls and into their war rooms. We're getting buy-ins from most of the Western states – the Eastern block has been silent. We're going to need some of them to make this work. There's nobody else left that has the technology and the missiles to help."

"I can get through to them," Tia said. "I need an access code for your satellite link. I can send confirmation - I have the codes that will reach them. I can get at least twenty more missiles added to the attack." She paused. "I'd rather take my chances with what happens to me tomorrow on the run than let this cloud suck the life out of me."

Major Crowell felt it in his guts. "We're going on faith, why not go all the way? Alpha Nine Zero Zero Beta Three Zulu Zulu Four."

"Thanks," Tia said, and rapidly activated an external link through the laptop. She logged onto a secured network, entering additional commands and passwords. She sent the messages off to her operatives.

"Okay, try contacting them again," Tia told the Pentagon officers. "I've sent verification protocols."

Admiral Mathis smiled as he checked the readouts. "Three more missile bays have accepted launch and targeting information. Each has ten to twelve missiles. We have enough missiles online now to cover the entire surface area at maximum force!"

The conference room erupted in cheers, with military and governmental big wigs high-fiving each other as if they had just scored the winning touch down. When they looked back to their projection screen to thank Tia, they saw an empty kitchen.

Chapter Thirty-Eight: Showtime is Over

Tense minutes passed as the group in the meadow awaited Grant's return. Larry held Char in his arms, comforting her as best he could. Doctor Scott and Allan Davis quietly discussed the simulation, second guessing their assumptions, the trajectories they had selected as optimal for the attack, wondering what they could have done differently to increase the chances of success.

Sid Eckham wandered back to the tree; even under these circumstances, he could not help but examine the bodies of the herd. He marveled at the change, at the unknown forces capable of performing such a complete draining of energy. It was strange, how human Grant seemed, yet he had done this to the cows. The biologist wondered at what he would find, were he allowed to dissect the alien. He trembled as he realized how slender the chance of that happening, of him ever dissecting another specimen again, was.

Major Drake stood still, arms crossed, gazing up at the sky. This was going to be a new world, he thought. If this – no, when this succeeded, the technology that Grant could teach them was mind blowing. He glanced at Char. She would be the key. If they convinced her it was for the best, she would lead Grant wherever they wanted. He was pretty sure they could do that; her father was an army man. He would help his daughter realize it was for the good of the world that the United States held onto the advantage the space man would give them. They were the only ones that could be trusted to do what was best for everyone.

Larry Amberson held his daughter. He prayed that Grant would return safely, prayed that this demonstration of speed, of heretofore unknown technology, would sway the world's leaders to follow their plan. He prayed there would be a tomorrow for his daughter.

Char took comfort in her father's arms. She kept her eyes closed, swore not to open them until Grant returned. She didn't want to look out in the meadow and see it empty. She didn't want to look anywhere but into his blue eyes. God, how long since he had left, since that miraculous ship hovered and sped away in the blink of an eye? It seemed hours, but she knew it was not. Hours meant they were dead, victims of the cloud.

She heard the engines above them and opened her eyes. The spaceship was hovering twenty feet above the meadow grass. It slowly descended. The hatch opened and Grant came out. Char ran to meet him, threw herself into his arms and pressed her lips against his.

Major Drake laughed. "Hey, let's find out whether it worked before we go rewarding him!"

Char looked over her shoulder, smiled, happy for the moment, glad she had at least one more kiss to share with Grant.

Larry smiled at the two of them. "Let's go check with the Pentagon."

They walked back across the meadow. When they got to the tree, Sid Eckham was still examining the dead cows. "I think I would rather stay out here", the biologist said. "If this doesn't work, I'd rather be outdoors, studying, doing what I love."

"I understand," Major Drake said. "I'm sure whatever you learn will be useful. We have whole new worlds opening up for us, Sid, and you're going to be at the forefront."

Sid nodded, smiled hopefully as if there would be a tomorrow. He watched the group walk on, staring at the alien among them. He softly spoke, wondering aloud, "What is your true nature, Grant, that you could do this? Are you man or monster?"

Grant's acute ears alone picked these remarks up. He half-stumbled, catching himself before he fell, as he heard them. He gave a quick smile to Char to reassure her that he was okay. But the words remained, the thoughts behind them churning in his mind. He was so different from his father. He had wondered how his father, great scientist though he was, had been able to make such an incredible advance in genetics, had transfigured his son's genetics light years beyond any research in his home world's knowledge base. It didn't matter how, he supposed – he should just be grateful it had occurred and he had the abilities he did so he could live among these people. So he could be with Char.

They went through the back door and entered the kitchen. They took their seats around the kitchen table. They looked up at the projection screen and saw it was already turned on, showing the group in the Pentagon conference room busily checking readouts and talking on phones.

"Did they like the air show?" Major Drake boomed out.

Their heads all swiveled to face the screen on their end. "They sure did," Burns told him. "That zipping around the globe got almost everybody on board."

"Almost?" Allan asked. "How many warheads? Did we get full coverage?"

"Between the allies who came on board after Grant's demonstration, and a couple last minute additions in the Eastern Block, we made it. We wouldn't have, if not for some unexpected help. You haven't seen another woman out there, have you?"

They looked at each other, shaking their heads.

"I'd keep your eyes open. I'm pretty sure she's long gone, but stay alert. She was able to bring the last couple missile bays to the launch, the ones that will allow us to completely saturate the target zone. But now that they are with us, I think she's going back to the other side."

"We'll keep watch for her. But frankly, we're a little more concerned about larger matters," Major Drake said. "Is the launch on?"

"Affirmative," Burns answered. "We launch in nine minutes. Everything is locked in." He paused a moment. "Char, Larry – I can't thank you enough. Your country – the world – owes you a debt it can never repay. If you hadn't had the courage, the perseverance, to make us listen, well, we all know what would have happened."

Char smiled, still happy to be clinging to Grant.

"It was what we had to do," Larry said. "Anyway, without Grant we wouldn't even have known about the cloud. He's the one who saved our bacon."

Burns nodded. "Yes, Grant, we are in your debt as well. I look forward to getting to know you better, when this is all over. But for now, we have to finish coordinating things on this end. With God's blessing, we'll talk to you in a couple hours."

The screen went blank as the link was cut. The group around the kitchen table was silent, thinking about what was coming. Wondering if they would still be alive to make the next video conference call.

Char leaned against Grant, smiling and crying at the same time It was blissful to be with him, to feel his cheek against hers, to sense his vibrant energy pulsing below his skin. Her father had spoken truthfully when he said that Grant was the one they owed this chance to. He had given them hope, however slim. Because of him, she had experienced true love, even if only for a night and a day.

Char tensed, clutched at his skin, pinching it unintentionally with her fingernails. He was going to die, too, she thought. They would all be dead, no matter what, if he hadn't come. If the bombs worked, if they defeated the cloud, it would be because he had given them the opportunity to fight. But if they failed, then he would die; their love would die. And that damn cloud would keep on going. The next world wouldn't even have the chance they had. She suddenly realized what she had to do. For Grant and for their love.

"Come with me," she whispered in his ear. "I want to be alone with you."

The others watched as she led Grant by the hand out through the back door. Larry put a hand out in warning, just in case anyone considered joining them. "They deserve some privacy," he said, and no one could argue with that.

Chapter Thirty-Nine: True Nature

Char and Grant walked hand in hand across the meadow. They met Sid walking toward the farm house. "I've got to write some of this down," he said as they crossed paths, and then he hurried on into the house. They smiled their understanding and continued walking through the meadow. They stopped when they got to the rocket ship, still above ground.

A pair of sultry dark eyes peered between tattered corn stalks in the field at the edge of the meadow. Tia waited to see if the rest of the group were going to join them. She couldn't hear what the two near the ship were saying, but she recognized the man as the one who had flown it earlier. She started to think of contingency plans, in case the world wasn't going to end in an hour.

Char was smiling as they held hands, but her eyes were wet, and she kept wiping the tears away with her free hand. This had to be done, she thought. Better to give up her last hour with him, so that he could live. If by some miracle the plan worked, he could turn around. If you loved something, set it free; if it loved you, it would come back. That trite cliché summed up the whole situation, she thought. She put her arms around his waist and hugged him as tight as she could, wanting to imprint his body into hers, wanting to remember every point of contact, to feel his solid chest against hers even when he was gone. She wanted to be able to recall this, wanted to be able to draw on this memory as she prayed for his safety, as she hoped for the impossible dream of their being reunited.

Grant breathed her scent in, the smell of hay and sweat and love. His tears ran down his cheek, dampening her hair. If his existence were to end, then this was how he wanted the finish to be. An hour with Char was worth sacrificing centuries of isolation. He thought of how she had helped him, trusted him despite his origin. How it had felt to bond with her emotionally, physically, psychically. How it had felt to connect with her on every level possible. He remembered their love making, an experience more intense than anything he had been through. A love so complete, so pure, that its power rivaled that of the cloud, he thought.

Char breathed in deeply, slowly exhaled her warm breath against his neck. She drew back slightly, enough so she could look up in his face. "I love you, Grant."

He kissed her, his lips telling her of his own love. Their eyes met unblinkingly as they shared what they each feared would be their last moments together.

"Grant," Char said, doing her best to keep her voice steady, "I need you to do something for me."

"Anything, Charlotte," Grant said.

Char put a hand behind his neck, looked him in the eyes. "This is very important. You have to promise, Grant, that you'll do it, no matter what. You have to promise."

Grant met her gaze, his blue eyes showing no distrust, no fear of whatever she would ask. "Anything, love. I promise."

Char bit her lip. Tears welled in her eyes, and she was unable to keep her voice from quaking, but she managed to get the words out. "You have to go. You have to get in this rocket ship and fly away from here, as far and as fast as you can."

"Char, I can't leave you. I love you!" He tried to kiss her but Char held his face away from hers with her hands.

"No, Grant. You promised, you have to do this. Listen to me," she cried, as he shook his head in denial, tears streaming down his face. "If you love me, you will do this for me. For our love. I'm sorry, Grant, but we both know the chances of this plan working are slim, regardless of how much faith Dad has in it. If this cloud destroys the Earth, if it kills us all, well you're still the only chance to stop it. I'm not saying I want to die, I'm not saying I don't want to spend every last second with you. But you have to go. If we fail, then maybe you can reach the next civilization in time to make another stand. One that will destroy the cloud. I can't take an hour with you and remove any future hope of stopping it, as much as I want to. You have to leave now, to stay ahead of the cloud. If we wait until after the attack, it could overtake you."

"Maybe the bombs will work," Grant said.

"God I hope so," she replied. She wiped the tears from his cheeks, loving the feel of his soft skin, loving everything about him. "And if it does, you come flying back here as fast as that ship will go, you hear me?"

"I hear you, Charlotte."

"So you'll go?"

"One more kiss, and I will go." He bent his head down and Char did not push away, rather she kept her hands around his head, holding on for an eternity, it seemed. They left the world for a moment, as their life energies mingled, as they linked cells and hearts and souls.

"Isn't that the sweetest thing," Tia said. She had her gun out and pointed at them. "Nobody get excited, and this will all go nice and easy."

"Who are you?" Grant asked.

"You're the woman the Pentagon warned us about," Char said.

"Smart girl. For your own sake, I hope you stay that way." Tia looked at the rocket ship. "Okay, space man, how many does that thing seat?"

"The ship? There is only room for me. It is designed to interface with my body alone."

"Ooh, wrong answer." Tia said. She had debated her options, tried to figure a way out of this mess, just in case this missile attack worked. She hadn't wanted to be killed by a nameless cloud from outer space; she had no choice in assisting them with the attack. But assuming it worked, she didn't like what the life of Tia Montoni will have turned into. She had compromised her sleeper status – the United States government had her on video now. Worse, they would trace most of what she had done through their network. Her codes and her operatives, all her key contacts, were just as compromised. And those people knew she was the one who had revealed them. It wouldn't matter that she was saving their hides too – not when it was over. The only way she could get out of this alive was to capture the prize herself. She had wanted to escape in the spaceship with the alien. Two bargaining chips and a way out of here would have been ideal. But if she couldn't fit in it with him, and she couldn't fly it without him, there was only one positive gain scenario left. She would have to sacrifice the ship and take the one bargaining chip that could travel with her.

She fired the gun and hit Char in the leg. The small amount of noise due to the silencer belied the effectiveness of the bullet as it lodged in her thigh bone.

Char collapsed to the ground, grabbing her leg where the bullet had hit her. A small red spot of blood seeped through her jeans, rapidly growing larger.

Grant gasped in shock, knelt down beside Char. He looked up at Tia, an expression of disbelief on his face. "Why did you hurt her? She did nothing to you."

"I had to show you I mean business, space man. I don't have time for games. You are my meal ticket, my way to fame and fortune and getting out of here alive. So, right now, you are going to come with me or I swear to God the next bullet goes through her brain." Tia pointed the gun at Char's head menacingly.

His look of disbelief changed to rage. Grant's blood boiled. This woman, no, this evil creature, had hurt Charlotte. After everything they had been through, after all the sacrifices they were forced to make, this vile person had cause his Charlotte pain. And she threatened to kill her! To deprive her of her life, to take that precious energy, her vital spirit, and throw it away.

The hunger, kept at bay through self-control, through the love that had developed within his heart, rose up like a phoenix. It raged through his body, swelled to a thunderhead that could not be contained. He extended an arm toward Tia, reaching out with his fingers pointed straight at her.

Tia panicked, realized she had miscalculated, that this being was capable of doing her harm, with or without a gun. She emptied her gun into his chest, firing five bullets at Grant, each one hitting the mark, ripping into his lungs and heart, passing through the other side, leaving entry and exit wounds that blood gushed from.

He felt the pain as the bullets tore into him, but the hunger was not affected. The hunger continued to surge, and even as his body was falling it struck, latching on to Tia's life force. He hit the meadow grass hard, his body convulsing in reaction to the shattered ribs and critically wounded organs.

Tia felt the hunger attack her, felt an energy unlike any she had ever known pull at her very essence. She screamed as it drained her, as her life force poured out as rapidly as the blood was gushing from Grant's body. She felt so empty, so cold and yet burning at the same time. Then she didn't feel anything at all as her emaciated, empty corpse lay still on the meadow grass, so thoroughly drained that it was unrecognizable as the woman who had masqueraded as Tia Montoni.

Char crawled over to Grant, ignoring the pain in her leg. She cradled his bullet-ridden body in her arms, rocking back and forth, sobbing, crying, unable to accept that he was dying, that this was how it would end.

She felt his body shudder and she let out a howl, certain that this was his death cry. She looked down at him, wiping his face clean of tears and blood with the front of her shirt.

He opened his eyes, still blue, still full of life. "Do not cry, Charlotte," he whispered. "My father made me a god among mortals. I will not die."

She let out a choked cry, a mixture of grief and joy, as she saw the blood had stopped flowing from his wounds. He was going to live, she realized. "Thank God," she said, kissing him, holding his head against her chest and rocking back and forth in joyful thanks.

Grant closed his eyes and concentrated on repairing his internal damage. He used the life energy he had absorbed from Tia to reconstruct tissues, nerves and bone. The memory of what he had done played again and again in his mind. He had taken another life. He had let the hunger out again. He knew it had been done to protect Charlotte, but that did not alter the fact that it had occurred. He recalled the biologist's remarks. He recalled his own questions about his father's abilities to endow him with these powers. Recalled how the people on his planet had looked after the cloud had passed through. Recalled how the herd of cows, how the body of their attacker laying five feet from him, looked now. What was his true nature, Sid had asked, as Grant had asked himself? He could not avoid the conclusion he reached. Somehow, the cloud was not just his enemy, but his heritage.

He sat up, calming Char's protests with a gentle smile. "It is okay – I have healed the injuries." He examined her leg, probing the wound. It was simple for him to link with her cells, to direct their properties, to shift the bullet up and out of the wound. He sent some of his energy into the injury, speeding the process, repeating the healing that he had performed on his own wounds.

Charlotte tentatively stood up. It felt sore, but that was all. She hugged him again, wanting to hold on forever, but knowing it was not an option. "I'll miss you."

"And I you," he said, giving her hand a final squeeze. He opened the hatch on his ship and entered it.

Char watched, tears rolling down her cheeks, as the ship hovered for a few seconds, and then it was gone.

Chapter Forty: The Hardest Part

Allan was busy connecting to the Defense system targeting systems. He entered commands and security codes to let him tie into the master control system that would handle the launch sequences.   He reactivated the projection screen. It showed a grid map of outer space, with the Earth, Mars and a broad band representing the tens of thousands of asteroids and meteoroids comprising the Asteroid Belt's prominent features. "I have this tied into the Defense system now. We'll see the path of the missiles after they're launched. There's going to be a twenty-three second delay in the data the sensor missiles transmit back to us."

Allan entered a command into the computer and a small digital clock appeared in the upper left corner of the screen. Its bright green digits were counting down. It showed three minutes until launch. He added a second countdown clock in red digits below the first. This one was set at fifty-eight minutes. It had not started counting down. "The green is time until launch," Allan told the group in the kitchen. "The red will be time from launch until the missiles reach the cloud. It will start counting down once launch has occurred."

"What will we see when they get there?" Doctor Scott asked.

"I don't know. When they get close, maybe fifteen minutes away, we're hoping their internal sensors will pick up energy traces of the cloud, to enable last minute course adjustment. We have a dozen unarmed missiles trailing the warheads by two minutes – they'll provide sensor readings on the other missiles and hopefully the cloud. They should be operational for ten to fifteen seconds before the backlash from the detonations hits them. We're hoping that will give us time to confirm a successful attack."

Doctor Scott looked down at his hands, wrung them, afraid to ask. Major Drake saw his hesitation and asked what they were all wondering. "If it fails. How long – how long until the cloud gets here?"

Allan shrugged. "From what Grant taught us, it varies its speed slightly as it encounters mass, so we can't be precise. But based on its average speed, it will take it about sixty seconds to travel from the target zone to Earth."

"Good God, a minute! We'll have a minute from the time we know the result before it could hit us."

Allan cleared his throat. "Actually, sir, because of the lag in transmission, it will be more like forty seconds."

The green digits hit zero. On the projection screen, hundreds of yellow arrows pushed out from the Earth, curving beyond the atmosphere and forming a moving phalanx of nuclear missiles heading out to intercept the cloud. A smaller group of a dozen light blue arrows – the unarmed rockets – trailed the yellow armada, spaced out across the hundreds of armed missiles, already sending back data on the flight. The red countdown clock started running down. Fifty-seven minutes remained until the missiles would reach the cloud.

"God be with us," Larry said.

Sid looked up from his notebook. "Can you e-mail a report to Scientific American, Allan? I'd like to think I contributed one article of significance, just in case this doesn't work out."

"No problem, Sid," Allan said. "Just give it to me when you're ready."

"Thanks," the biologist answered. "I'll have it finished in a few minutes."

The back door opened. Char stood there alone, tears running down her face, meadow grass and dirt on her clothes and hair, a dark red spot on her thigh. Larry rushed to her side.

"Char, what's happened? Are you okay?"

"Oh, Dad, he's gone. Grant's gone. I sent him away." She sobbed against his chest, deep wracking sobs that shook him as deeply as they did her. He let his tears join hers. He didn't know the whole story, but he knew his daughter had lost the love of her life. He held onto her, offering all the comfort a father could, wishing he could take the pain from her, knowing it was hers alone to bear.

Four minutes had passed on the countdown clock before Char had calmed down enough to explain what had happened outside. She stopped several times to catch her breath, to keep from collapsing as she related the story. No one spoke, their attention riveted as she told them about the woman spy, how Grant had saved her and finally Grant's departure. She looked up at her father when she was done. "I had to make him go, Dad. It was the only way to keep this from happening to some other world, if the missiles don't work."

He pulled her head to his shoulder. "I know, Char; you did what you had to do. You acted out of love, as hard as it was. I'm so proud of you, baby."

Major Drake sighed heavily. Char had done the right thing, he was all too aware of that. But to lose that technology! With Grant on their side, the United States would have started to get back some of the respect that they deserved. No one would have stepped out of line after they had a fleet of ships that could traverse the globe in seconds. Still, maybe the alien would be back for the girl. He resolved to keep constant surveillance on her when this was over.

Char sat down, head in her hands. Larry talked quietly to her, giving her reassurance, letting her know he loved her, reminding her that it was better that they had shared some time together.

She looked up at him, tried her first smile since Grant had left. It didn't kill her, she decided. "Thanks, Dad. I am glad I met Grant. It hurts like hell knowing he's gone, but I'd rather hurt than just be empty."

He tussled her short hair, picked out the loose pieces of grass that were stuck in it. "I'm glad you met him, too, Char. Glad for all of us, but especially for you." He got up and opened the cabinet over the coffee pot. He took down a bottle of whiskey and placed it on the table. He got out six glasses and placed them on the table and then filled them from the whiskey bottle.

Major Drake reached for his glass.

"Uh-uh," Larry said. "These are for when those red digits all show zero."

The major laughed. "I like your style, Larry."

They watched the countdown spin ever closer to zero. Fifty-two minutes. Forty-seven minutes. Sid finished his report, handed it to Allan. The programmer copied it over to his e-mail server and sent it off. The biologist then huddled in his chair, staring at the red digits, watching the trace of the rockets' paths as they crossed the void between Earth and Mars.

Allan opened up a chat window. "BUTTON PUSHED. FORTY MINUTES. WISH YOU WERE HERE." He sent the text message to Tia and Jeff and closed the chat window.

Char breathed in deeply, exhaled slowly. That's all there was to it, she thought. Just take the air in, let the air out. Again and again and he was never coming back. No, don't think that, never think that. He was going to get out of here, find out that cloud wasn't pursuing him and turn his butt right around and come back. Come back? For her? A big-boned, plain-Jane, thirty-five year old farmer? When he could have the universe? She dug her fingernails into her palms, focusing on the pain, trying to drive the doubting thoughts from her head. Don't think that, Char, she told herself. Don't pretend the love wasn't there. That wouldn't make it better, it would only make it worse. He loved her as much as she had loved – no, as much as she still loved him. That was why this cloud was going to fall apart into a billion pieces and he would see that and come back. They'd have not just one more night but thousands of them together. She looked at her father and repeated the small smile she had given him in response to his comfort earlier. Dad, have faith for all of them, she wished. Please have enough.

Grant had to go, Larry knew, as he looked at his little girl – ha! How long since he had thought of her as his little girl. He'd counted on her for so long to help with the farm. She had done as much as two sons, carrying the heaviest burdens, especially the last few years when his back had started acting up. He was the helper, she the farmer, he thought. Had he kept her from being happy? Sure, they had good times, enjoyed each other's company whether in the fields or at the fishing pond, but had he kept true happiness – kept love – from her? He shook his head. No, she had been out a few times. He knew about the few crushes she had had. But this with Grant – this was real love. This was love like he had with Char's mother.

Thirty-six minutes. Thirty-two. Twenty-five. The countdown continued its march to zero. Less than half an hour until human destiny would be cut off in its infancy, or allowed to continue.

Doctor Scott thought of the opportunities he had missed over the years. He wondered about the choices he had made: career versus family, army versus business, research versus private practice. Had anything he had accomplished really changed anything for the better? And even if it had, what would that have mattered, if the cloud prevailed and annihilated their entire world? What would be the difference if he had been a murderer instead of a scientist, what difference had any of his choices made?

Fifteen minutes. On the projection screen, a vast expanse of light green dots appeared. "The sensors have picked up the energy from the cloud," Allan said. It was huge, covering slightly more width than the planet Mars did on the screen. "Thank God, it contracted like we had hoped. The missiles can cover that much surface area."

Larry Amberson reached for the hands of those sitting next to him, Char and Major Drake. He nodded and they reached out to those next to them until they had once again closed the circle of hands.

"Heavenly Father, you find us in our gravest hour. Please give courage to us. Please provide comfort as we await the coming events. It is only through you that we have been given life; it is only through you that it can end. Whether it is on this Earth or in Heaven above, please be with us. Love us and help us love you and one another. In Jesus' name we pray, Amen."

"And may those missiles blow the hell out of the cloud," Major Drake added. Larry smiled at him, and added an "Amen to that."

Ten minutes Suddenly on the projection screen, another object appeared. A flashing green arrow came from the opposite side of the Earth, headed across the planet and out onto the trail of the missiles, rapidly closing the distance.

"What is that?" Major Drake asked.

"An unidentified object," Allan said. "That's why it's flashing. Sensors just picked it up – it's moving incredibly fast. At its present rate it will catch up to the target zone just seconds after the detonation is triggered."

"It's Grant," Char said, her face pale. "Oh God, he's going to try and stop it. He must know the bombs won't work." She clutched her father's hand. "Dad, why is he doing this? He can't stop it, his world tried and failed! He's just going to die like the rest of us."

"Maybe he can," Sid Eckham said.

Char turned to him. "What do you mean? What can Grant do against the cloud?"

"He's not like the rest of his people," Sid said. "What he did to those cows, the absorption of energy – to be frank, it's exactly what he showed us the cloud doing on his world."

"What are you saying?" Larry asked. "That Grant is another cloud?"

Char leapt from her chair and attacked the biologist. "He's not a monster, you take that back!" she screamed as she hammered blows on his chest, knocking them both from his chair and onto the floor. It took Major Drake and Larry Amberson working together to drag her off of Sid.

Larry closed his arms around Char, stilling her rage, calming her down until he was able to get her to return to her chair.

Sid was wide-eyed and shaking his head frantically. "She didn't have to do that, she didn't have to attack me," he mumbled. Major Drake had a hand on his shoulder, trying to reassure him that he was safe now.

Sid looked at Char. "I'm sorry, I didn't mean to hurt you, or insult him. I'm not saying he is a cloud, just that he has some of the same abilities. And maybe, just maybe, he's figured that out – figured out a way to use that against it. I don't think he's on a suicide mission, Char. I think he believes he can win."

She nodded, her face still flushed, her eyes red and moist. "I'm sorry, Sid, I shouldn't have hit you. It's not your fault."

A chime sounded and they looked at the project screen. The red digits had crossed the one minute barrier. They felt each second as their hearts pounded. Char held Larry's hand, praying as she had never prayed before. Let it work, God, please let it work. Bring Grant back to her.

Zeroes were displayed across the countdown clock. The yellow arrows brightened, and then were gone. They stared at the expanse of light green dots representing the cloud on the screen. It did not even pause as it continued to travel through space, heading for Earth.

They watched on the projection screen as the cloud approached the light blue arrows transmitting to them, with the flashing green arrow close behind them, getting nearer by the second. The flashing green light overtook the light blue arrows and headed straight ahead to intercept the cloud.

Chapter Forty-One: Awareness

Grant had directed the rocket ship away, slinging around the Earth to pick up speed and heading as he had before: away from the cloud. He would go as far as he could and still pick up the cloud on his sensors, far enough so he would be able to stay ahead of the cloud on the journey to the next system.

The hunger that Tia had wakened slumbered restlessly under his surface. He knew that it lusted after more energy – that it could strike without a moment's notice. Even miles above the atmosphere, as he continued his flight from the farm, he could feel thousands of life energies below him.

Once clear of the atmosphere, he ignited the ionic drive and sped away. He rode in silence, his inner turmoil quieted, his hunger dormant. He must be too far to sense the life forms, he thought.

He sat silently, monitoring his sensor readings. He saw the armada of missiles heading the opposite direction on their futile mission. He did not belittle the faith of the Ambersons, but he knew all too clearly the strengths of the cloud. He knew to the exact degree the power that his home world had assaulted it with, and it had emerged unscathed. He had no doubt that the cloud would pass through the nuclear assault of the Earth's rockets as easily as it crossed the vacuum of space.

But still he slowed his engines, coasting until the fateful moment when he would have to bring them back to full power and leave the Earth and his love to their fates. As the ionic drives shut down, he became aware again of the teeming masses on the planet he had left. Though millions of miles away, he sensed the life energy of Earth. His hunger awakened.

He watched his sensor readings as the missiles closed the distance, as they raced to meet the oncoming cloud. He reached up and wiped the dampness from his cheeks. His sorrow lessened the intensity of the hunger, the conflicting emotions broiling within his body. The hunger - he considered it anew. He had seen the similarity between the body of the woman who had attacked them and the bodies lying in waste on his home world. He was aware that the cloud was a part of him, although he still did not know how. The hunger continued to pull at the edge of his thoughts, coaxing him, urging him to head toward the life energies it sensed. It pulled at him, so many million miles away. Yet, he realized, it had quieted when he had been closer. Had been silent, undemanding, dormant – until he had turned the ionic drive off!

He fired the ionic engines, his theory confirmed when the hunger ebbed, no longer able to sense the life energies beyond the field generated by the drive. He adjusted his course, turning about face and heading back to Earth, and then beyond, continuing on toward the red planet and the approaching cloud.

He was there in minutes. He saw the armed missiles on his readouts a few hundred thousand miles ahead of him. He cut the ionic drives, letting his momentum carry him forward. He would stay far enough back to avoid the backlash from the explosions. While he could conceivably survive it, knowing his true nature, he needed the ship, particularly its ionic drive, to remain intact. And despite his awareness of the cloud's apparent invulnerability to physical assault, he still owed it to the Ambersons to allow the missiles to strike before he acted. He owed it to their faith.

He maintained position. He pushed the renewed hunger aside, tried to use its awareness of the life energies of the distant planet as reminder of his purpose. He adjusted the recording controls to allow it to display and store the upcoming attack properly, allowing for the expected levels of light and radiation from the nuclear explosions. He checked the readouts again. Ten seconds until the missiles would reach the front edge of the cloud. Eight seconds. Five seconds. Four. Three. Two. One.

The missiles hit the target zone, a broad phalanx of the Earth's most powerful weapons spread over a million square miles of frontage. The timing mechanisms went off in almost perfect synchronization, well within the microseconds variance allowed for in the battle plan.

In the vacuum of space, the explosions looked quite different than if detonation had occurred in the atmosphere of Earth. Additionally, they had been spaced apart so as to overlay their concussive effects, and the ripples of their explosive force crossed each other on all sides, forming a tight weave of interlaced force. It was the largest release of force ever produced by man. It was all-powerful, irresistible, completely saturating the target zone with a shock wave of incredible strength.

Hundreds of thousands of miles away, Grant still felt the aftershocks of the attack. The ship automatically shifted power and used minor engine thrusts to ride the wave out. He looked at his readouts, hoping despite his knowledge of the cloud's composition that the attack had succeeded. It was several times greater than the force of their own strongest attempt, he reflected, as the sensors fed him data on what had occurred. Maybe, just maybe there was a chance that it had been strong enough to break the cohesiveness of the cloud's particles, that it was able to disperse the cloud into a billion harmless, separated pieces.

He hung his head as the sensors let him know how complete the failure was. The cloud continued its course toward the Earth, without measurable difference in its speed, direction or size. Complete and utter failure. Well, he knew it would come to this. This was why he had turned around.

He maintained normal thrusters. As the cloud approached, he felt the incredible energy within it. His hunger threatened to rise up and consume him, to completely take over. He fought to keep it in check. Not yet, he said to himself. He remembered Charlotte, remembered lying beside her, their legs intertwined, her hand running across his chest. He remembered making love to her, emotionally and physically bonding with her. He remembered their love, and was able to quell the stirring monster within his body. Not yet, he repeated.

The cloud sensed the life energy in the object before it. The missiles had been nothing but metallic meteoroids to its senses, with no life energies contained within. But this object was different. There was strong life energy within, so strong it burned bright, brighter than any it had ever encountered before.

There was something different about the energy. The cloud shifted its particles, slowing its speed until it drew to an even pace with Grant's ship. It contracted swiftly, pulling its vaporous mists from either side until it covered dozens of miles rather than the hundred thousand it had before. This life energy drew it in, called to it. It seemed familiar, but it was new as well. For the first time in its existence, the cloud was unsure whether this was energy to consume, or to share.

Grant trembled in his ship. He felt the pull of the cloud's energies, struggled to maintain control over his hunger. He did not know what kept the cloud at bay, why it hadn't rushed over his ship and tried to drain his life energy. He was glad for the time it gave him to collect himself.

The cloud expanded tentatively toward the ship. It shifted particles and sent an amorphous tendril of mist to surround the ship. It slowly contracted the tendril around it, getting closer and closer to the hull. It breeched the hull and sought the life energy within the metallic container.

Grant gasped as he saw the cloud penetrating his ship. He steeled his nerves, forcing himself to wait as long as possible. The mist of the cloud touched his hand. An electric shock went through him as he was connected to the cloud. Unwillingly on either Grant's part or the cloud's, their life energies intermingled, cascading waves of energy passing back and forth between them.

The cloud's natural instincts guided its reaction. It shifted its particles, trying to drain the energy, attempting to alter the dual nature of the exchange into a one way flow that would feed all the life energy back into its mass. Grant struggled to maintain control. He had less total life energy to fight with, but his was of a higher nature. His willpower, his sentience, was greater than the primal nature of the cloud. He let his hunger feed, but kept it reined with purpose. He bled the life energy of the creature, not out of lust for energy, but out of love for Charlotte. He did what he had to do to save others, to prevent this monster from ravaging endless successions of worlds.

He pulled the life energy into his body, compacting it, keeping it from escaping back to the cloud. The energy swelled within him, he felt his body burning white hot, felt the power crackling in his finger tips. Felt he could do anything, could move worlds, create universes; that nothing could stand against him.

The cloud had never experienced a life energy that could not be consumed, let alone one that was consuming it. It tried to pull away from Grant, to separate and flee, but it did not know how to break apart. Its energy continued to flow into him, until there was nothing left outside the ship but lifeless particles, dust motes floating in the vacuum of space.

Grant reveled in the feeling of absolute omnipotence. The life energy of the cloud flowed through his body, swirling in bursts of energy, leaving him drunk with ecstasy. He shifted cells, modified particles, altering his body chemistry in order to contain the incredible power. It threatened to burn him out; it was almost more than he could stand.

The essence of the cloud rebelled against its absorption. Grant felt it welling against him, collecting itself inside his body, trying to reestablish its identity, as the cows had fought for control when they had been absorbed. It lashed out, trying to dominate his mind, seeking to return to its known self, to rule the body they now shared.

Grant fought desperately, trying to isolate the cloud's energies, trying to compact it down into miniscule particles and surround it with impenetrable shields of his own cells. Every partition he made, the cloud's energies found a way around. He slammed barriers around it, but it broke them down. The cloud had been sucked in by Grant's initial attack, but its instinct for self-preservation, its millennia of being the aggressor, of taking others' life energies, kept it on the offensive and Grant found himself retreating within his own body, trying to erect mental and physical walls within his body to slow the progress of the cloud as it began to win the fight.

It could not succeed, he thought. After all this, after coming back here and taking it in to protect Earth, to save Charlotte, it could not end like this. He seized on memories of Charlotte, her warm flesh, her wind-roughened skin, her hard muscles, her soft lips. He pictured her in his mind, and drew upon the strength of her love. He expanded his energy within his body, catapulting his force forward and swarming back over the life energy of the cloud. He gave no quarter; this was his last battle with the cloud, and there would be no second chance. He was relentless, assaulting the remnants of the cloud's essence with his new found resolve, barricading it with the power fueled by his love. He assaulted it again and again, cutting it into millions of particles until nothing was left that was identifiable as belonging to the cloud. Until its essence had been completely assimilated. Until he had finally, and utterly, defeated the cloud.

He lay back, breathing hard, tired but victorious. He still felt power crackling within him; even after the battle he had just fought, there was power beyond mortal imagination coursing through his body. He controlled the flow, passing it through his cells, repairing damage, strengthening bonds, until his physical condition matched the feeling of euphoria at his success.

His senses were heightened exponentially by the ten-thousand-fold increase in his life energy. His hunger had been fed the meal of its life, but this only served to increase its lust. More, it demanded, it must have more, and it latched onto the energies it sensed from the green-blue spinning planet. It craved more life energies; he suddenly realized its hunger would never be satisfied. There was still so much power that the hunger seemed to have a better connection with it than his own willpower did. He did not know if he could control it. He knew one little slip and it would leap beyond his control, draining whatever – or whoever – was in range. He remembered the dried husk of the woman who had attacked Charlotte. He remembered the lifeless planet that had been his home world. He knew that he held the power now to repeat the annihilation that the cloud had performed. He, too, could drain the life out of an entire planet.

A single tear rolled down his cheek as he made his decision. His love for Charlotte could only be proved in one way. He tightened his control, altering cells and locking the core energy from the cloud away, keeping himself from accessing it. His hunger lessened and his awareness of the life forms of Earth dimmed as he cut himself off from the majority of his power.

He engaged the ionic drive and his senses were completely cut off from anything outside the field generated by the engines. He shifted his course, using the gravity of the sun to slingshot the spaceship away from the Earth, away from his love.

Chapter Forty-Two: Faith

They sat around the kitchen table. The whiskey glasses remained untouched, the final toast forgotten as they watched in rapt attention. The flashing green light intercepted the countless green dots. It was enveloped by the vague shape representing the cloud on the projection screen.

Char let out a cry. "Oh, God, Grant, get out of there!" What was he doing? He should be millions of miles away from here; he should be heading to the next solar system. He wasn't supposed to die today. He had to save lives, to keep this monster from repeating the horrors again and again and again. Oh God, why had he come back?

Larry kept his arm around his daughter, trying to lend her comfort as they watched the events occurring fifty million miles away, just outside of Mars.

"It stopped," Allan said. He was right; on the screen the green dots contracted, pulling in from all sides to surround the flashing green arrow that represented Grant's ship. He looked at the clock. Ten seconds had passed since the attack. At best they had five more seconds of visual transmission before the backlash from the explosion took the sensor missiles out of commission. The cloud stopping would buy them a few more seconds, he thought. But once it resumed its trek it would take less than a minute to arrive at Earth.

"It recognizes him," Sid said. "That's why it stopped."

"We have to have faith," Larry said. "Come on everybody, join hands. One last time, for Grant."

They linked hands and prayed internally, the deepest, most fervent prayer they had ever pled. They stared at the merged green lights on the screen.

The green dots disappeared. A flashing green arrow remained, for just a moment, before the projection screen turned blue. Thick white letters reading "NO SIGNAL" were displayed in place of the map.

"Did you see—" Allan started to say.

They looked around, not sure what the last image had meant. The green dots had rushed in toward the ship, they thought the green arrow remained but weren't sure.

Major Drake released the hands of those sitting next to him. He reached for his glass of whiskey, raised it up in the air. "We've either won or lost. We'll know in a minute or two. To life," he toasted.

The rest of the group reached for their glasses and echoed his toast. "To life," they said in unison. "To Grant," Char added, and the others nodded. They drank the whiskey down and slammed the glasses onto the table.

They sat, each silently counting to sixty, each wondering if they would complete the count.

Forty-five seconds. The cloud just traveled fifteen million miles, Allan Davis thought. Thirty seconds. Doctor Scott recalled that first report he had filed, dismissing Grant's appearance as an unexplained phenomenon, most likely aberrant readings. Twenty seconds. Sid Eckham wistfully regretted his final article would never see print. Fifteen seconds. Major Drake imagined a world with the United States as its rightful leader, the technology that could have assured the fight for freedom would be victorious. Ten seconds. Larry Amberson prayed, his faith intact through it all. Five seconds. Char Amberson blew a kiss upward, imagining it pass through the ceiling, through the sky, beyond the Earth and through space until it found her lover.

Zero. Zero. Zero. They looked at each other, confirming that the minute had passed. Disbelieving at first, unsure whether ten seconds or ten minutes had passed. "It's been a minute," Allan confirmed after checking the clock. "It's been a minute!" he shouted.

He adjusted the settings on his laptop, changing the source of the feed. After a second, the projection screen showed the view of space again. "This is from the Defense satellites," he said. "It can't detect as far out as the missiles, but it can pick up about halfway to Mars, if it's big enough."

"You mean big like the cloud, don't you?" Doctor Scott asked.

"Yeah," Allan confirmed.

They watched in trepidation. The screen remained constant, showing the moon, the Earth and Mars, with nothing between the two planets: no flashing arrows, no green dots.

"It's not coming," Major Drake said. "He must have found a way to stop it!"

Char stared at the screen, her heart pounding. She smiled and cried simultaneously. He beat it – he really had! Somehow Grant had overcome the cloud. God, she had felt worse when he had returned to save them than when she thought he would be fleeing, not with her but alive – but now that the cloud had been defeated! Now, it was going to be perfect again. Now, he could come back to her; they could be together. No cloud, no death, no being apart ever again. She knew his love was genuine, that what they had shared could not have been illusion. There were no lies when you were merged body and soul, flesh to flesh, skin intermingling as thoughts and dreams coalesced.

Larry didn't want to ask, but had to. He was overjoyed the cloud was absent, that it had apparently been defeated. But the cloud wasn't the only thing missing from their screen. "Where's the ship?"

Char blinked. Oh God, where was it? Where was Grant? Where was the green flashing arrow, why wasn't there a trail showing his ship on the screen?

"Don't panic," Allan said. "His ship is tiny compared to the cloud; we won't be able to pick it up until it is much closer."

Char leaned against her father. "Dad, it's not fair – he has to come back. He saved us. He saved us so we could be together."

Larry held her tightly. "It's okay, honey. Have faith. Allan said it will take longer to pick his ship up. Just wait – any second now we will see that flashing green arrow, letting us know he's coming back. He's coming back for you, Char, just have faith."

She closed her eyes, prayed for his return. When her eyes opened, there would be a green arrow on the screen, she prayed. There would be a green arrow because he loved her and he beat the damn cloud and they're supposed to be together and live happily ever after. The hero got the girl, it was his reward, there would be a flashing green arrow when her eyes opened.

She opened her eyes. A green arrow flashed on the screen. "Oh, thank you, God," she cried. "Thank you."

The rest of the group shouted in joy.

"I told you, Char, have a little faith in him. Grant loves you too much to let some interstellar monstrosity stand between you and him." Larry didn't care how corny it sounded. His future son-in-law was coming home to his little girl.

The flashing green arrow raced through space. It had been picked up by the satellites and displayed on the screen when it was roughly twenty-million miles away from Earth.

The group watched as the arrow flashed closer and closer to their world. In ten seconds it had closed half the distance from where it had first been picked up. In another five it started arcing slightly off course, angling toward the edge of the planet rather than dead center. As it got nearer its course shifted again, sliding in toward the planet and then away as it performed the slingshot maneuver, using the Earth's gravity to increase its momentum.

"What's he doing?" Char asked.

No one had words to comfort her as they watched the ship shoot away, faster than it had arrived, the flashing green arrow leaving a trail on the screen until it reached the limit of the satellite's sensors. Seconds after it had appeared, it was gone.

Char stared in disbelief, the shock numbing her body. After all she had gone through, she was beyond tears, beyond sobbing – beyond anything but staring blankly at the projection screen that was absent the flashing green arrow.

"He's gone." Her words were stoic, emotionless. "The cloud's gone, Grant's gone. It's like it never happened."

Larry hugged her. "It happened, Char. No matter how it ended, it happened. You had love, whether he ever returns, you had love. Don't ever forget that."

She pushed him away. "If you love something, set it free. I set him free, Dad. I set Grant free, and he didn't come back. That's not love. It never was." She got up from the kitchen and went to her bedroom, closing the door quietly behind her.

Larry looked around the table. The rest of the group was torn between celebrating the escape from the cloud, and empathizing with Char for her loss.

Major Drake put a hand on Larry's shoulder. "I don't know exactly what in the hell happened here, today, Larry. But I have no doubts that you and your daughter did a great service for your country. For the world."

"Somehow, I don't really feel that great about it," Larry said.

"I know. I'm sorry for your daughter, truly I am. But I can't help but think that maybe this was for the best." Major Drake paused a moment. "I mean, even when that cloud was wrapping around his ship, I was thinking about what it would mean to have Grant fighting on our side. I can't deny I'd give my right arm for that ship of his – for any of the technology he could have given us. I thought it would make us invincible, that the rest of the world would have to toe the line."

"You don't think that anymore?" Larry asked.

"No. Now I realize all that would have done was given them another reason to envy us. Another rallying cry to band them together against us. No, being the biggest and baddest isn't necessarily the best. We've got to let freedom win the right way. It's got to be the people's choice."

"So what happens now?" Doctor Scott asked. "Can we really go back to business as usual, after this?"

"Oh, killer clouds and space men and ships won't change us that much," Major Drake said. "Give us a couple years, and we'll have prototypes doing some of the stuff Grant's ship did. Mankind is always up for a challenge, especially if it gives us an edge on the other guy."

"The status quo has changed," Sid piped in, "besides whatever scientific breakthroughs this inspires us to."

"How so?" Major Drake asked.

"He just disarmed the entire world. There isn't a nuclear missile left on the planet."

"By God, he's right," Doctor Scott said. "Grant not only saved us today, but he gave us a chance to make it through the next generation, if we take advantage of this."

"Let's all have a little faith, and a whole lot of prayers, that we do," Larry said.

Chapter Forty-Three: Banishment is not Enough

Grant sped through the solar system. He had passed the inner planets, was orbiting back around the sun and settling into an orbit just beyond Neptune. The hunger remained dormant, thanks to the ionic drives, but his thoughts were heavy on it, filled with worry over what he was capable of. Scared that he would become as energy dependent as the cloud had been, that he would turn into an overwhelming force that had no purpose other than to feed off of the life energies of helpless victims.

Was he just postponing the inevitable? Did it matter that he spared one planet, that the people of Earth would live? Did Charlotte's spirit surviving count enough against what he feared he would one day do? He knew that a single momentary lapse of restraint would unleash the monster within – that the hunger would only be kept in check with unrelenting control. He knew the ionic drive could shelter him from the burden for awhile, but he could not simply rocket through space for all eternity. The ionic drive would eventually fail, and he did not think his current being, composed of energy, mutated beyond mere physical limitations, would die before then. He wasn't sure he could die.

The ionic drives. He had to use their power; their energy field alone could strike against what he had become. The longer he waited, the more likely that the hunger would awaken, that the cravings for life energy would take over. He considered the problem. He altered cellular structures, shifting his form until he had a thin tendril, similar to the one the cloud had used to investigate his body. He reached out with it, nearing the edge of the energy field created by the ionic drive. He phased through the hull with the tendril until he contacted the field.

He pulled back, pain searing through his body. He investigated the outer layers of his membrane, ascertaining the level of damage caused to his cells by the ionic energy field. He smiled, despite the pain, rather because of the pain and what it reflected. The field had destroyed those cells it contacted with, severing them from the living tissue, leaving them inert. He shed those cells, and shifted more of his body, extended the tendril. He thought about adjusting his structures, dampening or even removing pain centers. He decided against it, wanting to feel it burning. Wanting the pain to remind him why he was doing this. Needing to focus on the pain so he could override the sense of self-preservation that was trying to stop him from completing his sacrifice.

He shifted more and more of his life force through his tendril. He abandoned the human form, transforming into a gaseous shape not unlike the cloud's form. He did not have enough mass left to form skeletal structures or organs. It was easier to float in the cockpit of the spaceship than maintain solid shape.

He struggled to retain enough of his mental cortex to finish the process. He gathered all that was left of his essence and phased through the hull, sending his final life energy directly into the ionic engines.

Dry cells filled the spaceship, infinitesimal specks of a once vibrant being. His shift to gaseous form had precluded the presence of even an emaciated corpse that other victims of the cloud had left. No other sign that a once near-omnipotent being had piloted the craft. No sign of what had become of Grant Thujalm, or why he was no longer there. No sign, but for a tiny protective sphere of solid but inanimate matter, holding the few living cells he had captured from Char; small reminders of a once perfect love, the only essence that he had not sacrificed to the ionic drive.

The computer had been given no last minute commands. It continued its orbit around the sun, one small object among the thousands of frozen ice and rock meteoroids of the Kuiper belt.

Chapter Forty-Four: Cleaning Up

Major Drake looked around the living room of the Amberson farm house. He was ready to leave. It was strange how attached he had come to the place in just a few days. His men had bagged up the unrecognizable body of Tia Montoni, along with the carcasses of the cattle. Sid Eckham had taken hundreds of samples from the grounds, capturing soil, blades of meadow grass, fragments of anything that might have been touched by Grant or his spacecraft. There was nothing else to do for now. They would know more once they had a chance to examine all the samples back in the laboratory at the base.

"There will need to be follow-up investigations, of course," Major Drake said to Larry. "Don't be surprised if an offer to buy this place comes up. I'm sure it will be a seven figure proposal."

Larry smiled and shook his head before replying. "Thanks, but no thanks. Char and I have lived here all our lives, we couldn't imagine living anywhere else."

Major Drake nodded. "Yeah, that's what I figured. I just thought I would give you the heads up, let you think about it for awhile. Who knows, after what your daughter's been through, maybe a change of scenery would be a good thing."

"Well, we'll talk about it whenever it comes up. Not sure what this place would do for you, but if there's an offer I promise to discuss it with Char."

Major Drake shook Larry's hand. "That's all we can ask. I'll be seeing you, Larry. Say goodbye to Char for me."

Larry watched the officer walk out the door and get into the military helicopter that had been waiting for him. The chopper took off and the house was empty save for Larry and Char.

Larry sat down in his easy chair. He glanced down the hall where Char's bedroom was, wondering how things were going to be now. She had hardly spoken, barely eaten, since Grant had left. He could not blame her; he remembered how he had felt when he lost Amy.

Out in the corn field behind the Amberson house, Jeff stood up groggily. He watched the chopper fly away. He looked around, could not see Tia anywhere. The last thing he remembered, he had been laying beside her on the ground, her hand rubbing his back, her deep, dark eyes looking into his as if she could read his mind. Now there was nothing. Nobody around the house, no beautiful girl beside him. He realized with a sinking feeling that she had left him, again. Years after she had left him the first time, he felt the old pain rip through his chest. He rubbed his eyes as he fought against the feeling of loneliness and despair that threatened to crush him.

He bit his lip, trying to drive out the memory of her raven black hair, her smell, her chest pressed against his. She's gone, he told himself, she'd left him again, so quit thinking about her. He brushed the dirt from his clothes and dejectedly walked back around the house through the corn fields. He found the rental car undisturbed by the side of the road where they had left it.

Jeff got in the car, quickly started the engine and drove away from the Amberson farm, away from the memory of Tia Montoni and her luscious, red, deceiving lips.

Chapter Forty-Five: If You Love Someone…

Char lay on her bed, watching the blades of the ceiling fan revolve. It wasn't fair. Regardless of what she had told Dad, Grant had loved her. She knew that, deep in her heart and soul, she knew that he had loved her.

Why? Why had he left? She knew it would have been difficult for the two of them to live any kind of normal life. Everybody would have wanted a piece of him, but they could have handled that. He could have created some sort of force field to keep them out, or they could have gone into the mountains. He could have built another ship, big enough for both of them, and they could have gone out there somewhere. They could have found some deserted planet and walked hand in hand together as a purple sun set in the North. She didn't care where they would have gone, what they would have done. They would have been together. They should have been together.

The tears would not come. Her eyes were dry. Whether it was shock, numbness, or a fatal acceptance of how cruel life was, she did not know. She wished she could pray, but she couldn't handle another joke like the one God had just played. Her father's faith – her father's, no longer hers. How strong he was. How sure of himself, of his God. As sure as she thought she was. She had not asked for this love. She had given up on the idea of Prince Charming sweeping her off of her feet. She had been content to work the land, to share the labor and the fruits with her father. To accept the love of his companionship versus the passion of a lover.

But Grant, Grant was everything any woman could ever have wanted, more than she had a right to expect. She thought of her father's last words to her: was she better off having loved him, and then lost him? Was such a cliché true? Would she rather have had the cloud wipe away the whole human race instead of feeling her heart shattered like it was? She didn't know. She really didn't know.

There was a knock on her door. She didn't answer. She had nothing for anyone else. She just wanted to lie there and die.

"Char?" Larry opened the door, walked over to the bed and sat on the edge. "Do you want to talk about it?"

She shook her head.

He brushed the bangs from her forehead. The soft touch, the gentle motion, made her remember Grant doing the same thing. The tears welled up and she reached up for her father. He held her, rocking her gently, until she had let it all out.

"I love him so much," she said, after he had wiped the tears from her cheek.

"I know you do, Char. And baby, he loves you. He did what he did because he loved you so much. We'd all be dead without him. I know right now you're probably thinking that doesn't sound so bad, and I'll let you feel that way for a day or two if you want, but that's when it ends."

She looked up at him questioningly.

"I mean it. After a couple days, you're going to get out of this bed and help me feed the chickens and rake hay and go on living. You owe that to Grant. He came back and saved us all, and it would be a dishonor to him – to the love that you shared – to throw his sacrifice in the mud. Now, I can't explain why he took off like he did, but I do know that Grant loved you, and he would never have done that unless he thought he was doing what was best for you. Maybe the cloud injured him, and he was heading off to the stars to make his peace. Maybe he detected another cloud and he's off to save some other world. But wherever he is, whatever he is doing, I know in my heart that he is doing it because he loves you."

He kissed her good night and pulled the blankets up over her. "Sleep tight, Char. I love you."

Char watched him stand up and walk to her door. He turned off the light. Before he closed the door, she called out to him. "Dad? I love you, too. And I'll be ready to feed the chickens. Just not tomorrow. But I'll make it."

"I know you will, honey. Good night," he said, and closed the bedroom door.

Char lay back. The room was dark, little light getting through the drapes that she had closed earlier. She heard the hum of the ceiling fan but could barely make out the circling blades. She thought about her father's words. Thought about sleeping in a couple of days, and then going back to life on the farm. Feeding chickens, raking hay – could she really do that again? She smiled as she thought about how it would have been, had Grant lived on the farm with them. How he would have relished each new experience, found delight in discovering how warm eggs were when you pulled them out of a nest, or the smell of fresh-cut hay, or the sounds of cornstalks rustling in a summer breeze.

She could do this, she thought. She could live each day with him, through his eyes. That was how she could honor him. By enjoying life, by cherishing each moment that he had given them.

She smiled at the thought of being with him, even as he traveled throughout the galaxies. She curled up, hugged the pillow beside her, smelling his musky scent on it. She would never wash that pillow case, she swore. She held it against her, thinking of him, until she fell asleep.

Part Two

Rain Drops

Chapter One: Germination

It was eight weeks after the alien cloud had been defeated. Eight weeks had passed since Grant had flown off in his spaceship. Char had taken the several days her father had allowed to rest, cry herself dry and let the scar tissue form over the tear in her heart. Since then, she had gotten out of bed, done her share of the farm work, but she was really just going through the motions. She was more of an automaton than a human being. She still missed Grant with all her heart, still ached for his touch. Though she had known him but a day, she knew it would take the rest of her life to forget him.

Eight weeks, Char realized, as she lay in bed, staring at the ceiling. The fan blades circled six times a second, she estimated. She watched them spin, wondering if getting out of bed was ever going to become easy again.

Suddenly, she was overcome with nausea. Her stomach did back flips and somersaults. She ran for the bathroom, flipped up the lid to the toilet and hunched over the bowl.

Char rested her weight against the side of the tub. Her throat felt raw from the bile she had thrown up. She got up slowly, still feeling queasy, and washed her mouth out several times in the bathroom sink. She wet a wash cloth and cleaned the sweat from her face; the cool wetness gave her mild relief.

She hoped she wasn't coming down with something. It was November, and while there were some chores that lessened as fall turned into winter, there was always something to be done on the farm. No more milking, since they had not replaced the cows that Grant had killed, but still plenty of work for her and her father.

She brushed her teeth twice, finally satisfied the taste of vomit was eradicated. She checked herself in the mirror. Good enough, she thought. No noticeable after effects of the throwing up episode.

Larry Amberson was already in the kitchen when Char entered. She smelled the usual aromas present at their breakfasts: bacon, hash browns, and fried eggs. Breakfast was one of her favorite meals. Her father normally cooked breakfast, lunch was a do-it-yourself sandwich affair, and Char performed the honors come supper time. She loved starting off the day with a hearty meal, especially one prepared by her father.

This morning, however, the smell of the eggs did not sit well with her. She ate a piece of toast and a couple pieces of bacon, leaving the eggs untouched on her plate.

"What's the matter, Char?" Larry asked. "Did I overcook them?"

She shook her head. "No, just not real hungry today. I think I might be coming down with something. Maybe just a forty-eight hour flu. I'm a little tired, that's all."

"I'm sorry, Char. Maybe you should head back to bed, see if some rest will nip it in the bud."

"That's okay. I think a little work might sweat it out. I'm sure I'll be fine."

Larry picked up their plates and put them in the sink to soak. "Okay, if you say so. I figured we'd fix that fence out back today, before it gets too cold."

By lunch time Char was feeling pretty good. She was finishing her second sandwich when she looked at her father and said, "See, told you I just needed to sweat it out. I feel good as new."

Larry smiled at her. "We'll see if you still feel that way after we tackle that hay field this afternoon."

The rest of the day went smoothly for the two Ambersons. They caught up on some of their winter preparations as well as finishing their daily chores. Larry and Char were both tired and sweaty by the time the sun dipped below the horizon, signaling the end of their day's work.

They cleaned up and met back in the kitchen. Larry went through the mail while Char prepared supper. "Got a letter from Major Drake," he said.

Char stopped in the middle of peeling the potato. She didn't dislike the major, but it was another tug on the myriad strings that pulled her back to what happened that day. "What's he want?" she asked.

"Says he can never get a hold of us on the phone, so he wrote to tell us he's coming by on the twenty-fourth. Say, that's day after tomorrow," Larry realized.

"Does he say why he's coming?"

"Nothing specific – you know, it's probably another offer to buy the farm." Larry shook his head. "You'd think by now he would have figured it out that I'm not selling."

"Maybe… maybe it would be best if you did sell," Char said. "It's not like we're doing anything more than making ends meet here. And you know you'll never get a better price – they're offering ten times what this place is worth."

Larry looked at her in surprise. "This land has been farmed by Ambersons for a hundred and fifty years. It's not going to be turned over to a bunch of military scientists so they can try to recreate a spaceship from a bunch of soil samples. I don't care how much money they're offering."

Char bit her lip. She felt tears coming to her eyes, fought to keep them at bay. He didn't understand, she thought. How could he? His love had lived here, had died here; it was her love that had run away. He looked around the farm, at the meadow and the corn fields and the barn, and remembered sharing that view with her mother. He walked from room to room in this house and saw pleasant visions of the past. Her every step was filled with pain and sorrow. She remembered Grant kissing her goodbye and not returning. She remembered making love to him in her bedroom on that magical night, and all the nights since she had slept alone.

She wanted to wait to speak, to give her emotions a chance to settle down. She didn't want to be a burden on him; her father had shown nothing but kindness to her all her life, and she would not have made it through the last eight weeks without his shoulder to cry on. But she couldn't help it; the anguish was too strong to hold back. She felt hot tears run down her cheeks. She let the potato drop onto the kitchen counter, placed the knife beside it. She turned to her father, wanting to lash out, yet at the same time wanting to curl into a ball and shut the world out. "Don't you get it? There won't be any more Ambersons," she cried. "I'm the last. Grant left, and he's not coming back, and there won't be anyone left to farm this damn place."

She rushed out of the kitchen and into her bedroom, slamming the door behind her. Larry Amberson sat still from shock at the table. He had known Char was taking it hard, that hadn't been unexpected at all. He knew that the love she had for Grant was as real, as deep, as if they had been together for years. But it seemed like she was giving up on the future completely. He got up, started to walk down the hall after Char.

He stopped outside her door. No, he thought – she needed to do this for herself. She had to be the one to decide to live again. He couldn't do that for her.

Chapter Two: Fool Me Once...

Morning found Char in a similar state as the day before. She tried to forget the harsh words she had spoken to her father. She had tried to forget them all night long as she tossed and turned, getting little sleep in the process. She sighed. Didn't matter how she felt, didn't matter if she and her father went through the day pretending those words had not been said. None of that mattered, on a farm – she still had to get up. The chickens wouldn't wait, the hay wouldn't wait. Time didn't stop just because your world had no meaning.

She could smell breakfast cooking in the kitchen. The smell of bacon crisping in the pan, the aroma of eggs frying – she bolted for the bathroom. The nausea had returned.

Char had her arm across the top of the open toilet bowl, her head face down, forehead pressed against her forearm, trying not to breath in the noxious vapors of what she had just vomited into the toilet. She reached up blindly, feeling for the handle to flush it away, not wanting to lift her head for fear she would trigger another upheaval.

This wasn't the flu, she thought. No fever, no aching, just a really weird feeling and throwing up over the smell of eggs. She slowly pushed herself upright, repeating the washing, rinsing and brushing from the morning before until she felt somewhat human again.

Char stared at her reflection. She pulled her t-shirt up, revealing her abdomen. Didn't look different. Same thick waist, same muscles, nothing new there. But she knew looks could be deceiving. She knew that in a few more weeks the difference would be noticeable. The swelling would start.

She started to cry, a mixture of fear, sadness, joy and hope. She was going to have a baby. More specifically, she was going to have Grant's baby. She let the t-shirt fall back down as she hugged her arms close to her chest, no longer able to see her reflection as her vision was blurred by the tears running down her cheeks. She stumbled out of the bathroom, went down the hall past the living room and to the kitchen.

She stood in the archway between the kitchen and living room, leaned against the wall, letting it support her weight as the strength seemed to flow out of her legs. "Dad," she cried softly.

Larry dropped the spatula onto the kitchen counter and rushed to her side, holding her with his strong arms, keeping her from falling down. He helped her to a chair.

"Char, what's wrong, honey? Tell me what's wrong."

She looked up at him, blinked the tears away until she could see his face. "I'm pregnant."

He didn't know what to say. He was all too aware of his daughter's lack of social activity the last couple years – it was clear there was only one man she had been with recently. But how could Grant have impregnated her? He was from another world, for God's sake! It didn't matter how, he realized. He had been witness enough to the miraculous abilities that Grant had demonstrated, had been told of the mutating, shape-shifting powers that bordered on the impossible. Yet, it was not just two species, but two entirely different worlds involved.

He hugged her, reminding her that he was here for her. Letting her know he loved her, would take care of her. He considered that this might not be a real pregnancy. He had read of phantom symptoms, where the woman wanted a child so badly that she experienced morning sickness. Could this be Char's way of trying to hold on to Grant?

"Are you sure, Char?" he finally got the courage to ask.

She stiffened in his embrace.

"I'm sorry, Char, I have to ask. It's been rough on you – real rough, I know. It seems pretty far fetched that you and Grant – well, that two people from different galaxies could – well, you know what I mean."

She dropped her head, and started shaking.

He felt horrible. Shouldn't have said anything, he thought. Should have just played along with it; she would have come around eventually, would have accepted the truth. "I'm sorry, Char. I'm so sorry."

She shook harder, sniffling sounds growing in volume until they turned into snorts. Larry was dumbfounded when she looked up and he saw she was laughing. A big smile was on her face and she was shaking with mirth.

He couldn't help but laugh with her, smiling and rocking her in his arms. It was several minutes before they had calmed down enough to talk.

"I don't think I understand what we were laughing about, Char, but that's the best I've felt in eight weeks."

"Me too, Dad," Char agreed. She wiped the wet trails from her cheeks, remainders from first tears of sadness and then of joy. "Dad, don't you see? This is Grant's gift to me. I know it's crazy, but I swear to God I'm pregnant. He could do anything to his cells that he wanted. He shifted his whole body to a near duplicate of the human form. Believe me, it was a man I spent that night with."

"Too much information for your father," Larry said, his weathered old face turning red.

"Sorry, Dad. I just want you to know I'm not making this up. Trust me. Have faith," she said. She gave him a kiss on the cheek.

"I'll always have faith in you, Char," he said. If this was what it took to get her out of her funk, then let it be true, he prayed. God help her if she found out she wasn't really pregnant. Another crash and Lord only knows if she'd get back up.

Chapter Three: Major Drake

The next day Char felt better than she had since Grant had left. Her stomach still gurgled slightly when she got up from bed, but she did so slowly and was able to keep the contents inside her. It was almost as if now that she knew the cause, had accepted the signals, her body was content to let her have some peace.

She washed up and went into the kitchen. "Good morning, Dad." Her father was sitting at the table with a bowl of cereal in front of him.

"Morning, Char. You feel up to breakfast? I didn't want to cook anything that was going to upset your stomach."

"I think I'll stick with toast and juice."

"Everything the same?" he asked.

"If you mean am I still pregnant, the answer is yes. It's okay, Dad. Wait a couple weeks and it will be clear I'm not crazy." She leaned over and kissed him before sitting down at the table. "Don't worry; I'm not holding it against you. I know it seems impossible. Just take it easy on the eggs, give me a little room and we'll get through this okay."

"Sounds fair enough."

Larry watched his daughter eat her breakfast, his cereal growing soft from the absorbed milk. He imagined how it might have been, had Grant returned from the meeting with the cloud. Grant would have been sitting in the third chair at the table. The alien – ah, he considered him a man, after all he had done for them, after all he meant to Char, he couldn't deny that Grant was as human as any of them in the ways that mattered – would have been helping around the farm, would have completed their little family. His little girl would have been happy.

If this pregnancy was genuine, if Char carried the child to term, what would happen then? He supposed they could explain it as a child from a distant relative, orphaned by some tragic event. They were fairly isolated on the farm; it would not be that unlikely that Char's absence from local events would go completely unnoticed. She had no suitors, no close friends in the area. He would be able to manage the chores as she became unable to help; his back had been restored better than ever by Grant's wondrous healing powers, he felt he could do the work of ten men now, it felt so strong.

There would be time for that later, he supposed. She wouldn't show for several weeks, would probably be able to do her part on the farm until the last couple months. He had witnessed and aided hundreds of live births over the decades working the farm; he could handle that without difficulty. No, they could discuss the explanations, the subterfuge necessary for her safety and the child's, when the time drew nearer. When the pregnancy was a certainty, for one thing; no use planning until they were sure of that, regardless of Char's own conviction.

Of more immediate concern was Major Drake's visit this afternoon. "Char, I would suggest we keep this just between us. I don't think it would be wise to mention it to Major Drake. I know he's been very understanding, but –"

She cut him off. "Dad, I may get a little irrational – given the situation, I don't think that's unexpected – but I'm not stupid. Major Drake definitely helped us; he was the first to really believe my story, enough to come check it out, anyway. But he's still a government man, and I know what will happen if he finds out I'm pregnant. I'll be taken away to some cold, sterile military hospital and kept there until I give birth. And then they'll take my baby – Grant's and my baby – away. They'll poke and prod and study and it won't know anything about its momma and daddy and won't be loved and that's not going to happen. Not to my baby."

Larry laughed. "I couldn't agree with you more. Ambersons were meant to be raised outdoors, where they can feel the sun on their face and the wind in their hair."

He face turned somber. "He'll still be coming, though. It's all well and good to keep mum about your condition, but he's going to want to talk about the farm. He's going to pressure us quite a bit to sell it. Maybe we should go ahead and give in to him."

"What? You can't be serious, Dad. You love this place – you can't sell it to them!"

"I love you more, Char. If selling them the farm gets us a nest egg that will let us set up someplace else, someplace far away from here and from everyone else, then maybe it would be for the best." He paused. "Char, I have to admit I had some doubts about this pregnancy. About whether it was something you were just dreaming about, or praying for so hard you convinced yourself it was happening. But I know you, I have faith in you, and I believe you. Grant loved you so much; it doesn't really surprise me to know he found a way to give this gift of life to you. It was as if he knew what he had to do to get you to come out of your shell, to get you to go back to living after he was gone. And I know what I need to do to help that remain true. In the end, this is just a rickety old house that needs paint and a whole lot of fixing up. If selling it gets us someplace safe, where we can raise your child without worrying the government is keeping watch on us and is going to take everything away from us, well then by God I'll sell it."

She used her napkin to wipe away the tears from her eyes. "Dad, I love you so much. I don't know what I'd do without you."

"You'd do just fine, Char. You're an Amberson, and by hook or by crook we always get by. Never quite prosper, but we get by." He rose from his chair and placed his dishes in the sink. "Finish up now, we have a lot to get done this morning before Major Drake gets here."

The morning went quickly as they rushed through the chores. The mundane tasks of cleaning up after their animals, feeding them, checking fences – it all seemed to go smoothly, a welcome release from their trials and tribulations. The simple yet necessary tasks let their bodies work out the kinks while their conscious concerns simmered in the background. It was better still since the tension that had been just below the surface most times, with the occasional boiling over, was gone. Char was alive again, her smile illuminating her face, turning a dour, sad woman into a vibrant, joyful work companion.

Larry found himself whistling as he mucked the stalls. It had been so long since she had been happy. Even before Grant, he thought. She had been content, living with him, working the farm with her father, but he knew she had not been truly happy. Love had changed that. The burst of life within her had fired that change, smelted it into a glow that shone from her otherwise ordinary visage. She looked good, he thought.

They finished the chores that could not wait until evening, working a little longer since they would be busy in the afternoon. They returned to the house and cleaned the morning's sweat and dirt from their tired but gladdened bodies.

Char took longer in the shower than Larry, letting the hot water wash away not just the morning's labors but most of the anguish and sorrow from the past eight weeks. She was going to make it; she had a reason to get up, to embrace the rising sun, to breathe. Dad would help; they'd have a good life, this baby, her and Dad. And maybe someday his daddy would come home. She cut the thought off. No, it was enough that she was having their baby. She couldn't think about Grant coming back; not now, not tomorrow, not ever. She had to live her own life – they would have to live their lives – as if he never would. This baby was not going to be a victim of her pining for Grant; this baby would not even notice that his father was missing – she was going to love this baby so much it wouldn't matter.

She toweled off and dressed in a flannel shirt and jeans. She brushed her short hair a few times to appear somewhat less disheveled and went out into the living room.

Larry was sitting in an easy chair, reading a book. He looked up at his daughter's entrance. "Major Drake should be here in a half hour or so, I would guess."

"Okay. I'm going to go clean up in the kitchen."

He put the book down, started to get up.

"No," she said, "you go ahead and read. I can handle it."

"You sure?"

"Yeah, I haven't been much help lately. You deserve a little break."

"Well, I am in the middle of a chapter. Thanks, honey."

He sat back down and retrieved his book. Char went into the kitchen and started washing dishes. Even after the morning's efforts, her body felt good. She didn't mind the normal aches and pains from the fast-paced chores today. She embraced every bit of the awakened awareness of life that had come to her since she realized she was carrying Grant's child. For eight weeks she had been numb to the world. She was fine if it bumped and bruised her a little as she came back to it.

She thought about what her father had said. She knew he meant it, that he would actually sell the family farm if it would keep her and the unborn child safe. She was so blessed to have a father who cared for her like he did, who would sacrifice his life, his way of living, to protect her.

She finished the dishes and wiped off the counters and the table. She looked around. Good enough, she thought. She returned to the living room and walked behind the chair Larry was sitting in. She leaned over him from behind, draping her arms over his head and shoulders and giving him a hug.

"Hey, Char, that didn't take too long." He put the book down. "I just finished the chapter."

"We didn't dirty very many dishes for breakfast," she said. "Say, Dad, I've been thinking about what you said – about selling the farm."

He watched as she circled around the chair and sat on the edge of the sofa nearest him.

"I think maybe you should hold on to the place. I know, Major Drake will be hanging around and checking up on us, but seriously, wherever we go he's going to keep an eye on us. We're the big connection to the space man; there's no way he's going to let us slip out of sight. Besides, we're Ambersons. This is the Amberson family farm. I want my child to grow up in the same place that I did. I want him to go fishing down at the pond and chase the chickens around the yard."

Larry smiled at his daughter. "Well, Char, I can't say I'm disappointed. You know how I feel about this place. I just wanted you to know that you mean more to me than any old house ever could. If you think it's best to stay, then we'll stay."

"I do, Dad. We'll figure something out to tell Major Drake later – we don't have to worry about that today."

The sound of a helicopter descending and then landing in their front yard let them know that Major Drake had arrived. They got up and went to the front door to greet him.

Major Drake walked up to the door alone. He shook their hands and followed the Ambersons into the living room where they all sat down, Larry in the easy chair and Char and Major Drake on the sofa.

"It's good to see you two again," Major Drake said. The grizzled war veteran had genuine affection for the Ambersons. He had been impressed with their character, their actions and their words in the encounter with the cloud. He understood their reluctance to part with the family farm, but he still had to do his job.

"Larry, Char, I have to ask you again. I know the answer, but I still have to ask. Would you please reconsider selling the place? It's important, you know I wouldn't ask if it wasn't."

Larry gave Char a quick glance. He could see she had not changed her mind. "I'm sorry, Major Drake, but the answer is still no. We both grew up here; it's where we want to stay. We let the government have the remains of the cow herd, Sid Eckham took several soil samples with him before he left – I don't think there's anything else here that's of any value to the government. And I know it means the world to us."

"They've doubled the offer," Major Drake said. He knew it wasn't a matter of money, but again, he had to let them know.

"They could offer us Fort Knox and we wouldn't sell, Major. I think you know that."

Major Drake sighed. "Yes, I know it, and I told them so. But I had to ask you."

"I understand," Larry said. "No harm done. He reached for the bottle of whiskey sitting on the coffee table and poured out three glasses. "How about we have a drink and get to swapping war stories?"

Major Drake took the offered glass, drained it in a single motion, throwing the fiery liquor down his throat. "God I needed that." He put the glass down on the coffee table. He placed his hands on his knees, leaned forward and stood up from the couch. "I'm sorry, Larry, I can't stay. I had to come out here, try one more time. I felt I owed that to you."

Larry walked with him to the front door. Major Drake shook his hand. "Let me know if you change your mind."

"We won't," Larry told him.

"I know. Goodbye, Char," he called out from the door. "Take care of your old man, would you?"

"Sure thing, Major Drake."

Major Drake got into the military helicopter. Larry watched until the chopper had risen from the yard and flew off. He closed the door and returned to his easy chair. He sipped at his whiskey.

"That was a pretty short visit," Char said. "What do you think he meant when he said he owed it to you?"

Larry shook his head, took another sip of the whiskey. "I'm not sure. I'm afraid it might mean the government won't be asking us politely, the next time they come knocking."

She passed her glass to her father. "I'll let you drink this, Dad. I'm on the wagon."

He smiled. "I know. I just figured the Major would think it strange if I didn't pour you a shot, too. Believe me, you were going to hear about it if I saw you drink it!"

"Well, now, how about we get some lunch? There's more work to be done today. I'm sure Major Drake will let us know if someone's going to ambush us about this place."

"I hope so. I know he's been fair with us. That's all we can expect from him." She got up from the couch. Larry stood up as well and they went into the kitchen to have their late lunch before finishing the day's chores.

Chapter Four: The Pentagon

Secretary of Defense Jacob Burns was not pleased. He had sent Major Drake with an ultimatum to be delivered to the Ambersons: sell or have the land possessed in the interest of national security. Play it smart and take the lottery windfall or be stubborn and get stuck with what the tax assessor valued the place at. It didn't make any difference to Burns. All that mattered was that they got control of that property. If there was any chance of acquiring alien technology, they would pursue it.

The playing field had been leveled in the aftermath of the battle against the cloud. Virtually every nuclear warhead on the planet had been fired off into space in their attempt to destroy the cloud before it could annihilate their planet. In an unprecedented display of world unity, countries from both hemispheres, from all forms of government, had launched the joint assault on the cloud. It had been unsuccessful, but the space man had come through, had somehow defeated the cloud before flying away in his rocket ship.

That rocket ship had been instrumental in convincing the rest of the world of the veracity of the United State's claim that the cloud was coming for them. When it had appeared throughout the world in a matter of seconds, materializing within the very chambers the military and civic leaders met in, it had been undeniable evidence of technology beyond anything this world had ever produced.

Alien technology was what Burns was after. He imagined a fleet of those rocket ships, able to travel at incredible speeds, impervious to any Earth-made weapons; it would give the United States the military superiority that it had not held since the end of World War II. The studies made on the remains of the bodies affected by the space man's life draining powers had not yielded anything of significance to their scientists yet. The soil samples likewise had been uninformative. He wanted to blockade the entire farm off, to unleash scores of scientists and technicians to examine every grain of dirt, every blade of grass, until they found some trace that would lead them to the secrets of the alien rocket ship. There had to be something there. There had to be.

He looked up from his desk. Major Drake was still standing before him, cooling his heels, pretending he wasn't getting ready to blow a gasket from being ignored. Burns decided he had waited long enough.

"So, Drake, would you mind explaining to me what in the hell you did out in Kanapolis, Indiana? Because I know what you didn't do. I know you didn't follow the express orders you were given, to come back with the deed to that farm."

Major Drake took a deep breath, let it out slowly. "Sir, the Ambersons have lived on that farm for five generations. We already took the soil samples; there's nothing else there for us to find. There's no reason to kick them off the only home they ever had."

"That's not your decision, Major! Until our scientists have gone through every clod of dirt on that farm with a fine-toothed comb, we won't know what is or isn't there to be found. The security of the United States is at stake here, Major. In case you've forgotten, we no longer have a dominating military advantage. We blew our stockpile outside of Mars, and unless we do something to change the status quo we are going to quickly become the world's red-headed step-child."

"I know that, sir. It's just—"

"It's just nothing, Major Drake. I gave you a job and you failed to do it. We tried to be nice about it – the Ambersons wouldn't listen to reason. Play time's over."

"What do you mean? What's going to happen to them?" Major Drake asked.

Burns waved at him in dismissal. "That's no longer your concern. I'm assigning someone else to this matter. You're on leave until you receive your new assignment."

"Sir, please. I think I can help with this. I know the Ambersons. Please give me another chance to work it out."

"You're dismissed, Major Drake." Burns began to shuffle through the papers on his desk.

Major Drake stood still for a moment. His shoulders sagged. He turned away, the resignation clear on his face.

Burns reached for the phone after the major had left his office. "Get me Major Atkins."

Chapter Five: Colored Lines

Char checked her watch. Thirty seconds had passed. God, she had another two and a half minutes to wait. She had sworn ten minutes had gone by. She closed her eyes, tried to count the seconds one by one. This was stupid, she thought. She knew she was pregnant. She had missed her period; that had never happened to her. Still, she knew her father would like to know for sure, that the test result would reassure him that Char wasn't going crazy. He believed her, he had faith in her, she knew that – but sometimes even faith could use a little evidence to shore it up.

She opened her eyes. Two minutes had elapsed. That wasn't so bad, she thought; it only seemed like hours, not days. Maybe the last minute would pass before the baby was born, grew up, went to college, got married. Maybe it wouldn't take a hundred years for the next sixty seconds to tick by on her watch.

She knew this would be a big change for both of them, her being a mother, her father serving as both grandfather and father for the child. But she also knew how much love they had to give, that no baby could ask for more than what they would give to it. She would always miss Grant; there wouldn't be a day or night that he didn't enter her thoughts and dreams. But this child, this being created by their love, would let her live. This child would be her life, her joy, her heart.

Three minutes. She bit her lip, suddenly nervous. Suddenly scared that this test would be negative, that she was crazy, that it was all made up and she wasn't pregnant. She shook as she leaned over the bathroom sink.

She forced herself to look at the test strip. The two little windows, one square and one round, showed two nearly matching vertical lines, each a shade of pink. Two lines, she saw, filling her heart with joy. She had a momentary panic attack, thinking she was remembering the instructions incorrectly. She grabbed the box from the top of the bathroom counter. She sighed in relief. Two vertical lines: positive, pregnant. She was pregnant. She had known it, had felt it in her heart, her soul, her body - but this was something concrete. This was a physical result that offered evidence that her union with a hybrid alien from another planet had in fact produced a viable embryo in her womb. She was going to have Grant's child.

She tossed the box and test strip into the trash can beside the toilet. She washed the nervous tears from her face. She smiled at her reflection. A mother's reflection, she thought. She ran from the bathroom and into the living room to tell her father the test results.

Chapter Six: Storm Troopers

A couple days after Char had shared the good news with Larry, the two Ambersons were working in the yard. It was getting colder, and despite the exertion heating their bodies they were bundled up against the early November chill.

Chickens scattered, running out of the yard as a large black military helicopter descended from the sky. Larry held his hand up to shield his eyes from the glare of the sun as he watched the rotors slow after the engine was cut.

Larry walked over toward the helicopter, Char following close behind. It hadn't been that long since Major Drake had visited, and there had been no letter or phone call informing them of a return visit; Larry felt a knot form in his stomach, a tightness warning of bad times ahead, when it was not Major Drake but an unknown military officer who got out of the helicopter.

The man was flanked by two armed soldiers. The trio marched up to Larry. "Mr. Amberson?" At Larry's nod, the officer continued, "I'm Major Frank Atkins."

"Well, Major Atkins, pleased to meet you," Larry said. "This is my daughter, Char."

"Ma'am," Major Atkins said, nodding at Char.

"What can we do for you, Major?"

"Sir, perhaps we could talk inside."

Larry's smile remained on his face, but his tone was as icy as the November breeze. "How about you tell me what this is about, and then we can decide if we're going to have a nice chat inside or not."

"If that's how you want it." Major Atkins reached inside his coat and removed a thick white envelope. He handed it to Larry. "Here. These papers explain everything. You have until noon tomorrow to clear the premises."

Larry's smile vanished. "What the hell do you mean, clear the premises? I told Major Drake, and I'll tell you: we aren't selling!"

The soldiers took a step forward at Larry's outburst. Major Atkins held up a hand, letting them know it was okay. "Mr. Amberson, I'm afraid this isn't a request. This property has been seized in the interest of national security. There's a check in there for fair market value, less liens on the place, plus an allowance for all equipment, material and furnishings on the property. You can pack up your personal items – clothes, photographs – but everything else is the property of the United States Government, effective immediately."

"You can't do this," Larry cried. "This is our home – you can't just throw us out of here."

"Mr. Amberson, if you are not off the premises by noon tomorrow, that is precisely what we will do. Oh, and don't get any bright ideas about removing any unauthorized items. All boxes will be searched before being allowed off site. We'll have a moving van and some men to assist you in the morning."

Char put a hand on Larry's arm. "Come on, Dad. Let's look at the papers inside. He's not going to listen to us."

Larry gave a hard glare at Major Atkins and then allowed Char to lead him into the house. Major Atkins watched them go. "I want two men out front and two in back for the next twenty-four hours," he told the soldiers. "Nothing goes in or out of that house without getting checked."

"Yes, sir," they answered, and set off to follow his orders.

Major Atkins looked at the farm house. What a place to set up command, he thought. Stuck in the middle of a corn field in Kanapolis, Indiana. He spat on the ground and returned to the helicopter. He would fly back to base tonight, and return tomorrow to his new headquarters. He was already making lists in his mind. Half of them were for equipment, personnel, specialists – everything needed to turn the farm house into a scientific research center. The others were more personal in nature, involving items needed to turn a rustic hundred year old house into acceptable accommodations for an officer of the United States military.

Chapter Seven: No Choice

Larry unfolded the contents of the envelope on the kitchen table. There were several different documents with various official seals and stamps and assignments from one government agency to another. He looked at the two checks, one for the house and land and one for the miscellaneous items that were being seized. He held his head in his hands and stared miserably at the papers.

Char sat across from him. It tore her up to see him like this. She was so used to her father being the strong one. A solid rock, always there when you needed a shoulder to cry one, an arm to hold you up – that was Dad. He had been so understanding and supporting with everything that happened with Grant. He hadn't blinked an eye at her falling in love with a man from another planet. Sure, he had doubts about the legitimacy of her pregnancy, but after she had talked to him, even before he saw the test results, he had shown faith in her, had been willing to support her through it all. He had been willing to sell the homestead, when he thought it would help her and the baby. But she wanted her child raised on the family farm, and he wanted the same thing. It was so stupid. There wasn't anything for them to find here. Grant hadn't buried a second rocket ship or left hidden instructions on how to contact him. She should know; she had searched every inch of her bedroom, hoping there was some secret beacon or super galaxy-spanning communicator that would let her hear his voice once more. She had dreamed several times that he had appeared as a hologram in the middle of her bedroom and spoken those magic words: "Prepare to beam up." But she knew those were dreams, not visions. That was part of how she knew she was still sane; she could still tell the difference between her hopes and reality.

She leaned over the table to look at the papers that Larry was studying. "How's it look, Dad?"

Larry shook his head. "Well, it seems the Homeland Security Act, coupled with existing eminent domain law, gives them pretty much all the power they need. And because of the national security concerns, we can't even sue to block the action in open court. Our only recourse is a military hearing with the Department of Defense."

"Huh. Since they're the ones taking the farm, it doesn't seem like our chances are very good." Char reached out, squeezed his hand. "I'm sorry, Dad. I wish there was something I could do to help."

"Well, maybe it's better this way. I know we talked about raising the baby on the farm, but we couldn't have gotten away with it, not really. They would have found out, and no matter what cover story we came up with, they wouldn't have believed us. And if we had taken their offer earlier, they would have been suspicious as to why we changed our minds. Not the top brass, they would have assumed we were money grubbers, but Major Drake would have known something was up." He smiled at Char, returning the squeeze. "By them kicking us out, with enough to live on, but not enough to go crazy with, maybe they'll leave us alone. We can go somewhere up in the hills, get away from everyone for a while. They'll be so busy tearing up this place they won't care if we go off the radar for a little bit."

Char nodded. "Maybe so. I still think it stinks, them just showing up like this and telling us to be out by noon. It's like some bad western."

"I would have expected Major Drake to give us a heads up. But in the end, he has to do what's best for the country, as he sees it. I suppose he felt he gave us enough chances to take the money and run. It probably would have been as hard on him as on us to come and deliver the bad news."

Char looked around the kitchen. "I'm going to miss this place."

"Me too," Larry said. "Let's go through these papers and see what we're allowed to take with us. I want to get out of here first thing in the morning so we can get to the bank and settle accounts in town."

They started going through the list of seized items. It was amazing how detailed the inventory was. "They know more about what we have here than we do," Larry muttered. He read further down the list, past the farm machinery and buildings. "Hmmm, as I expected, they're claiming all the animals. It's a shame, they're probably just going to cut them up and examine them. Waste of food."

Char read the list alongside her father. "Doesn't look like much left for us to take."

"No, not that there was much here worth bringing along anyway." He gave a small laugh. "Nothing in this house to excite the boys on the Antiques Road Show, that's for sure."

"Well, I'll pack up the pictures and photo albums, and Granny's china. Who knows, maybe someday we'll set the table with it." She grinned at her father at the longstanding joke about all that nice china that they never ever used at dinner.

"Okay, Char, thanks. I'm going to make a couple phone calls, let folks know we're heading out of town."

Larry picked up the phone. The line was dead. Major Atkins, he thought. Couldn't even let the place grow cold before he took over. Fine. He could just as easily make a few stops tomorrow morning in town and handle things in person. That was more his style anyway.

He placed the handset back on the base. He gathered up the papers from the kitchen table and returned them to the envelope. He went into the living room and sat down before an old wooden desk that had various papers strewn over its top. He went through them and created three piles: one to throw away, one for papers with personal information to burn in the fireplace, and a much smaller stack to take with them, containing birth certificates and bank books and other vital information.

It did not take him very long. Char joined him in the living room with three boxes containing framed pictures and loose photographs. "I think I got most of them," Char said. "Are there still some old boxes up in the attic?"

Larry nodded. "No, most of those got ruined when we had that roof leak, remember? The ones that were salvageable should be in with the rest of them."

"That's right, I forgot about the roof leak." She smiled. "They may not have paid a premium for this place, but they'll find out it wasn't a steal either, won't they?"

Larry grinned. "Yeah, between the roof, the toilet handle you have to jiggle to get it to stop and the squeaks in the floors – they're going to have quite a time in their country retreat."

Char placed the boxes she had packed down next to the small shoe box that Larry had filled with important documents and papers. She brought him a trash bag for the majority of what he had cleaned out from the desk. Larry burned the rest in the fireplace.

They walked through the house, pausing in each room to reminisce about family gatherings, silly arguments, places they had hidden when Char was a little girl playing hide and seek. Each room held a hundred memories, not just of the two of them but of five generations of Ambersons. Larry had been accurate in his description of the furnishings; most of it could be replaced at local rummage sales or thrift shops for very little money. The Amberson money, whenever the fields returned more than they took to plant and harvest, was invested in their basic necessities. Generally, a windfall harvest meant that the loan was caught up on, that a tractor was repaired, perhaps a splurge of new clothes for the winter instead of patched up hand-me-downs.

They took a few small knickknacks as keepsakes of their years in the house. In the end, a small pile of items was in the center of the living room. Char and Larry packed them up in boxes. It would easily fit in the back of their ten-year old pick-up truck. At least the truck hadn't been on the list, Larry thought. Must know better than to mess with a farmer and his truck.

"I think that's it, Char," he said. "Let's call it an early night. I know we're not going to get much sleep, but I don't think I want to hang around this living room. With all the pictures off the wall it already looks like someone else's house."

"I know what you mean." Char hugged Larry. "I'm scared of what we're going to do, where we're going to go, Dad, but I know as long as I'm with you, everything will turn out all right."

"Thanks, Char," he said, returning the hug. "We're going to get though this together. Good night. I love you."

"I love you," she said.

They went to their respective bedrooms. Larry sat up late, thinking about his wife, Char's mother, and how they had spent so many happy years in this home. It would be turning into a house again: no longer a home, no longer the Amberson family farm, just a heartless building. Char sat up just as late; while she was sad at departing the only home she had ever lived in, she was more worried over what was to become of them. She was frightened for the future of her unborn child. It was a long, sleepless night for the Ambersons.

Chapter Eight: Final Goodbyes

By six a.m. Larry had given up on sleep. He rolled out of bed and knelt down. He leaned over and peered beneath it. He reached under and pulled out a dust-covered suitcase. He wiped off the dust with one hand, leaving a small pile of clotted-together dust bunnies on the carpet beside the suitcase. Something for the scientists to analyze, he thought with a tight smile. He rose, placed the suitcase on the bed, and went through his dresser and closet to fill it with clothes.

The contents were pretty basic, when he had finished: underwear, three pairs of faded jeans, a half dozen t-shirts and four flannel shirts. He looked it over. Socks. He needed socks. He added several pairs of socks to the suitcase, went into his bathroom and returned with his toilet kit and packed it. He took the picture of his wife from his nightstand, wrapped it in a towel, and placed it in the suitcase before closing it. He gave his bedroom a final glance. Nothing else that mattered, he thought. Everything else was either here – he touched his temple – or here – he touched his chest over his heart. He carried the suitcase into the living room and placed it beside the boxes they had packed the night before.

Char was performing similar tasks in her bedroom. Once the dawn started to peek through the curtains in her bedroom, she realized the wait was over. She knew her father would be up soon, if he wasn't already. No sense delaying it. She would rather leave early than have the soldiers pushing them out at noon. They didn't need to wait for the moving van; she knew they didn't have that much stuff to take with them. She checked her profile in the bathroom mirror. No more tummy than normal, she thought. Not showing yet – but she would. She smiled at the thought of her belly growing larger, when the baby would be obvious to others. She wondered how it would feel the first time someone asked her when the baby was due. Her smile faded as she thought about the inevitable questions about the father. She shook her head. No sad thoughts, she ordered herself. Just happy, 'going to have Grant's baby and Dad was going to help' thoughts. Happy, happy thoughts, she repeated. That was the order of the day.

She dragged her suitcase out from under her bed and loaded it up. As she packed it full she grabbed another smaller suitcase to finish putting her items in. She added her toiletry items to the smaller suitcase, gave a final assessment of her room. She looked wistfully at the bed where Grant and she had shared their brief passions. That was where it happened. That was where the baby had happened, she thought, looking down at her belly. On a sudden impulse she grabbed the pillow case from the pillow Grant had used and added it to her suitcase. She smiled again at the memories, then picked up her suitcases and carried them out into the living room.

She found Larry in the kitchen. He was frying up bacon. He looked up when she came in. "Just bacon, Char – I skipped the eggs. Figured you wouldn't want to start out feeling sick this morning."

"Thanks, Dad. Bacon sounds good." She sat down while he finished cooking. "Saw your bag; it looks like you packed pretty light."

He brought the bacon over on a plate and split it up between them. "Well, there's really not much an old man like me needs. Couple pair of jeans, some shirts, a tooth brush: it's a simple life I lead."

Char laughed. "I filled up a small one just with my bathroom stuff. But don't worry - I limited myself to two suitcases. It will all fit in the truck."

"That's good, because as good as my back feels since Grant fixed it, I don't want to give it an excuse to act up again."

"No worries, there's nothing I can't carry." He gave her a questioning look. "Oh, stop it. I'm pregnant, not helpless. I can carry a couple suitcases. Believe me, you'll know it when I decide I can't lift a finger. I'm kind of looking forward to it."

He grinned. "I bet you are. There hasn't been a whole lot of lying around on the farm, has there?" He sighed. "I know it's been hard some times, Char, but I've done the best I could for you. Maybe I should have encouraged you to go off to school, to get out of here."

Char gave him a stern look. "Now don't get me started, Dad. We've been through this before. I loved it here on the farm; I wouldn't have traded it for anything. This is what I wanted. Besides, if I hadn't been here, I wouldn't have met Grant. I wouldn't be having this baby. Nothing could make me happier than to be having Grant's baby, Dad. I'm just glad you're here to help me."

He picked up the dishes, quickly turning away, but not before Char caught the tears in his eyes. He cleared his throat. "Well, best get the things loaded. I want to stop by a few places in town, then we'll be on our way."

She got up from the table and walked up behind him at the kitchen sink. She hugged him, put her head on his shoulder. "Thanks, Dad. Thanks for everything."

She went into the living room to check the bags and boxes a final time. Larry started to wash the dishes, years of routine directing his movements. He chuckled, left them in the sink to soak. "They're the government's dishes now; let them wash them." He dried his hands off and joined Char in the living room.

They each picked up a suitcase and went to the front door. Larry opened the door and was startled by the soldier standing guard just outside the house. "Good morning, son," Larry said. "I would have slept a little sounder had I known we were so well protected."

"Good morning, sir. Just following orders."

"I understand. We're just going to load up and you can have the run of the place."

The soldier put a hand out to halt them from walking out to the truck. "I'm sorry, sir. But we have to check the bags."

Larry started to protest, but Char put a hand on his shoulder to stop him. "It's okay, Dad. We don't have anything to hide." She put her suitcase down and after a momentary pause he followed suit. "Let's get the rest of the stuff out here so they can check it."

They brought the other bags and boxes out in a couple trips between the living room and the front porch. Two soldiers were already going through the bags by the time they put down the last boxes.

The Ambersons stood quietly as the soldiers went through their belongings. The soldiers were careful not to damage anything, and repacked the bags when they were finished. "You're good to go, sir, ma'am. Nothing personal."

Larry grimaced at him. "Yeah, I know - just following orders. Hope that lets you look in the mirror without blinking, son."

"Come on, Char. Let's get out of here before they reconsider and confiscate our underwear."

They loaded the boxes and bags in the bed of the truck, glaring their refusal at the soldier's offer to help. Larry started the truck up, turned it around and headed down their driveway.

"Shouldn't have snapped at the soldier," Larry said. "I would have done the same thing, in his shoes."

"Hey, this is hard, Dad. I'm sure he understands how we feel, getting kicked out of our home."

"Doesn't excuse my rudeness, Char. He's doing his job, protecting the country, possibly risking his life – no justification for me jumping down his throat, when it's the brass that I'm mad at."

"Well, say a Pledge of Allegiance and a Yankee Doodle Dandy for penance, and he'll be okay."

Larry smiled. "What's done is done. Let's head into Kanapolis and finish up business there. Then we're on the open road. You, me and baby to be."

She rubbed her belly. "Wherever we end up, it will be home, with you there, Dad."

Larry drove down the dirt roads that led into the small town of Kanapolis, Indiana. He pulled into the brick building that served as a combination courthouse, police station and jail. "Just going to let Sheriff Barnes know we're going out of town for awhile."

"What are you going to tell him about the army being on the farm? You know he'll check the place at least once a week."

"I thought about that. I'll tell him they're doing soil samples, testing to see if chemicals have been carried by wind or rain out of Indianapolis. It's close enough to the truth, as far as testing goes. Less he knows the better for him, I figure."

"I'll walk down to the post office and have Betty hold our mail until we send for it."

"Sounds good. I'll meet you back here in a couple minutes."

They accomplished their errands without incident. Larry drove the truck a block and a half further down Main Street to park at the bank. Char waited while her father went in to cash the checks from the government.

He came out and got in the truck, shutting the door a little harder than he intended.

"What's wrong?"

"Oh, I should have known they wouldn't have much cash on hand. I got two thousand dollars out. Joe gave me a certified check for another five thousand. We'll have to stop at a larger branch to get it cashed. The rest will have to sit in our savings account for now. It makes things a little tighter. I was hoping to avoid writing checks – didn't want to leave any kind of a trail."

"You think we have to worry about that?"

He shrugged. "I guess not. I just figured the sooner we fell off the radar screen the better. It doesn't really matter; it's not like they couldn't find us if they really wanted to. We'll cash the certified check on our way through Indianapolis. That will cover us; we can always have Joe wire us some more later, if we need it."

He put the truck in gear and headed out of town. Char looked in the passenger side mirror as they left Kanapolis. She wondered if she would ever see her home town again.

Chapter Nine: On the Road

It was late afternoon. Larry had driven until noon, with a short stop in Indianapolis to cash the check. They stopped for lunch in southern Indiana, and Char had taken the wheel. They had crossed into Kentucky after seven hours on the road.

They took turns at driving and napping, making up for the last night's lost sleep. Each was caught up in their thoughts: memories of the farm, the few friends in town, their beloved animals. When bittersweet memories weren't filling their heads, concerns over the path ahead weighed heavy on them. Where they would end up, how they could raise the child to come, what life without the farm would be like for them. It was the only way they had ever known, until Grant had turned their lives upside down.

Larry suddenly laughed out loud. Char looked at him quizzically. "What's so funny, Dad?"

"Oh, I was just thinking of those military scientists getting all excited when they see burned papers in the fireplace. They're going to think I was destroying the plans to build a rocket ship or something. I can only imagine the look on their face when they find out the ashes are from old bank statements "

She laughed with him. "They'll probably send all the numbers to some code cracking unit. You think they'll figure out that forty-five dollar check was for the gas bill?"

He slapped his knee. "No, they'll think it's the combination to the safe where I hid the plutonium to power our space tractor!"

"Oh, I think we're getting a little punch-drunk from driving so much, Dad. How about we take a break at the next gas station? We're down to a quarter of a tank."

"Sure, Char. That'll give me a chance to make a phone call. I want to see if I can get through to Major Drake. I'd feel better if I let him know we don't take it personally, not from him anyway."

"I think that'd he'd like to hear that, Dad," she said.

A short while later they pulled into a gas station. Char got out to fill the truck up with gas while Larry walked over to the pay phone near the air pump.

He dialed the number. "Major Drake, please. Tell him Larry Amberson is calling."

"I'm sorry, Mr. Amberson, Major Drake is currently unavailable."

"Do you know when he will be back?"

"I'm sorry, I don't have that information. If you would like, I can take a message, or put you into his voice mail."

"No thank you," Larry said. "How about Doctor Eugene Scott? Is he in?"

"I'm sorry, Doctor Scott is currently unavailable. If you would like, I can take a message, or put you into his voice mail."

"Sid Eckham?"

"I'm sorry, Sid Eckham is —"

Larry cut the receptionist off. "I know, he's currently unavailable. And no, I don't want to leave a message. Thanks, goodbye."

"Goodbye."

Larry hung up the phone. Nobody from the original team was there. They were cutting him off, he thought. He shook his head. Don't be silly, you old fool. Of course they're not available. Those are probably the first people in line to get back to the farm. They're not in the office because they're sitting around your own kitchen table. No point in apologizing; they're going to be so caught up in trying to find traces of alien spores in the dirt clods of the farm they wouldn't even remember why he was saying he was sorry.

He started to leave the phone booth, then reconsidered. Wouldn't hurt to check up with an old friend, he thought. He dialed another number. "General Crowell, please. It's Larry Amberson."

"Please hold, I'll see if he is available."

After a minute, the gruff voice of his war buddy came on the line. "Larry, good to hear from you."

"Adam, good to hear a friendly voice. Sorry I haven't called you lately, but it's been pretty tough the last couple weeks."

"Char still taking it hard? Poor girl, she never had much luck with men before, did she?"

"No, Adam, she didn't. And Grant — God, I know it's crazy, him being from another world — but I swear, I couldn't have asked for a better man for her. He was solid, Adam. It tore her up to lose him."

"Well, who knows, Larry? Maybe the space man will come back. I tell you, all the battles, all the crap we've been through and seen, there's no power on Earth like a woman, once she gets her heart set on something."

Larry sighed. "Yeah, I wish he would come back, but my gut just doesn't feel it."

"Well, that gut of yours has saved my butt a dozen times, I wouldn't bet against it."

"Listen, Adam, I don't know if you've heard anything yet, but I wanted to let you know what's going on. Just in case I need some help later."

"I'm not aware of anything, Larry. Are you okay?"

"For now, we are. But a Major Atkins just took over the farm. He showed up last night and gave us walking papers."

"Jesus, Larry, that's terrible." General Crowell paused. "Hmmm, I take it they threw the national security line at you."

"Yeah, and a little eminent domain to make sure they were covered. I can't say it's completely unexpected, just a pain. They're not going to find anything. But I guess with what the potential is, they felt it was worth it."

"I'm sorry, Larry. There's really nothing I can do about it. If I had known earlier, I might have gotten it delayed, but I couldn't have stopped it. Not with alien technology at stake."

"I know, Adam – I'm not trying to get the farm back. Like you said, the stakes were too high for them not to do it. I just wanted you in the loop, in case anything else comes up. I'll feel a lot better if you have my back."

"You know I do, Larry," General Crowell said. "I'll check around a little, see what this Major Atkins has in his closet. Where can I reach you?"

"I'll have to get back with you on that. I'm not sure where we are going to end up."

"Okay, Larry. Give me a call tomorrow."

"Thanks, Adam. I knew I could count on you."

Larry hung up the phone. He felt better, knowing Adam would be looking out for them from his end of things. A little heads up the next time the government planned something for them would help.

Char was sitting in the passenger side of the pick-up when he returned to it. "Your turn to drive," she said, smiling. "Oh, I picked up some provisions." She handed him a pop and placed an open bag of pretzel rods between them on the seat.

"Not quite the same as a home cooked meal, but it will do," he said, returning the smile. He leaned back in the seat, feeling the weight of the world that had been sitting on his shoulders reduced to no more than the weight of the moon, he estimated. Still rough waters ahead, but he thought there might be a tinge of silver lining on that storm cloud.

Chapter Ten: Sifting Through the Ashes

The military scientists were indeed going through the Amberson home with a fine-toothed comb. Each and every room was being taken apart, thoroughly inspected for any possible trace of alien presence. Forensic specialists operated multi-spectrum lights over carpets and bedspreads. The traps under the sinks were removed and the gunk within analyzed. The ashes in the fireplace were sifted carefully. Half the livestock had been immediately harvested for dissection and examination. The other half had been caged or penned and would be studied as living specimens.

"The main problem, sir," biologist Sid Eckham said, "is that Grant had modified his body to a nearly perfect duplicate of a human body. Whatever particles we pick up may be indistinguishable from any of the normal ones left by Larry or Char."

"I don't want to hear excuses, Eckham," Major Atkins said. He did not bellow, like Major Drake would have. It was a quiet, calm, icy tone that sent chills down the biologist's spine.

"It's not an excuse, sir. I'm just telling you the facts. I'm a scientist; I'm here to record the data and present conclusions."

"You're here to find the secret to the space man's technology, Eckham. First, last and in between, understand? Now go do it. I don't want to see you again until you have something positive to report."

Sid gulped. "Yes, sir." He walked away, wondering how he was going to find something that in all likelihood wasn't there to be found.

Major Atkins leafed through the thin sheet of reports that had been prepared so far on the contents of the house. So far, nothing of any use had been uncovered. The household contents had been mundane. Generations of cheap clutter, second hand shop quality furniture, worthless paintings – not a hint of alien artifacts or technology. So far not a trace of the space man, organic or inorganic. He stared at the list. All basic items, nothing extraordinary, nothing that would be unexpected in a farm house in the middle of nowhere.

He flipped the page and looked at the inventory from the kitchen.

Chipped dishes, mismatched glassware, basic food stuffs. A couple bottles of whiskey, he noted with a slight lift in enthusiasm. At least those would be of use.

He looked at the next page. It detailed the items that had been identified in the barrels to the side of the house, where the Ambersons burned their trash. Again, normal household waste appeared on the list. Suddenly, he gripped the paper tightly. Jesus, he thought, as he read the line item again. A partially burned box from a pregnancy test kit had been recovered from a trash barrel.

He yelled at a soldier standing guard at the front door. "Get me the file on Char Amberson."

He paced while he waited for the file to arrive. He had only had a chance to glance through the data they had collected on the Ambersons. His mission had not been to get chummy with them, merely to get them off the property so they could start their investigation. But he was pretty confident there had been no mention of Char being pregnant before the cloud incident. There had been no known associations listed, if he recalled correctly.

A soldier arrived with the file. He went through it closely. He had been right. No close relationships in the past couple years, no traveling, her last medical checkup had been a routine check up three months earlier with no notable changes in her health. Good God, if this ended up being what he thought it was – he could hardly contain the idea. They had to find Char Amberson. They had to bring her in. All this scraping and dusting and sifting through dirt to try to get a sample of alien DNA, and they had let her walk right out the door carrying the biggest sample on the planet in her womb. His mind raced, weighing the options, oscillating between drawing the fetus out from the woman or having her bring it to term. Short term studies versus the potential of his very own alien-human hybrid. Who was he kidding? A live hybrid would guarantee all the funding, all the control, he could ever dream of. Assuming it would live, gestating in her human body. Well, if it didn't then they could analyze the remains. The best way to give it a chance would be to put her under the care of their medical team. First things first, though – he had to get the woman. Then he could worry about setting up a maternity ward.

He walked out into the front yard to the communications trailer that had been set up that afternoon. He looked around and found Allan Davis, the computer programmer for the site.

"Davis, I need you to initiate tracking on the Ambersons. I want credit card hits, phone records, banking transactions – everything. I want to know where they are going and what they are doing, twenty-four seven."

"Didn't we check them on the way out, Major Atkins?"

Major Atkins stared at the young programmer. "Let's get something straight, Davis. Just because you've been here before, that you were here when the whole thing went down, doesn't mean your position is any different. I'm the commanding officer here, and when I give an order I expect it to be followed, not questioned. I don't know how Major Drake handled things, but I use this little thing we like to call chain of command."

"Yes, sir. I'll get right on it," Allan said, his face flushed with embarrassment. He had had it easy under Major Drake, he realized. He had gotten used to less formal work arrangement. They had almost become friends, their entire work group, during the brief but intense episode with the cloud. Events like that changed people, regardless of rank or position. He sat down at his terminal and started the tracking requests for Major Atkins. It was still worth it, he thought. There was no place he'd rather be, than in the thick of this. He just wished his friends were here with him. He missed them, but Tia had vanished again, as she was apt to do occasionally, and Jeff had been bummed out because of it. He hadn't heard from either of them in the past couple months. Well, with or without them, he couldn't deny the excitement of working on the grounds of the only verified contact with an alien being.

He finished his tracking requests. It would take a while for the information to come back. He opened up a chat window on his laptop, connecting to the secure external server that he and his friends had set up. "GETTING FRESH AIR AGAIN" he typed into his keyboard, and pressed the enter key to post the message. Just in case any of them checked in, he wanted them to know he was working at the site again. He closed the chat window and went back to his programming tasks.

Chapter Eleven: First Night Out

Larry pulled into a motel in southern Kentucky. It was late evening, and after twelve hours on the road they were ready to stop for the night. He told Char to wait in the truck while he got the room.

He walked into the lobby and up to the desk. He rang the bell and a young man in need of a shave came out from the back room. "I'd like a room. Non-smoking, two beds, please."

"No problem," the clerk said. "That will be $49.99 for the night. I need a driver's license and a credit card."

Might as well start the blank trail now, Larry thought. No more credit cards unless it's an emergency. He handed the clerk a hundred dollar bill. "How about Ben Franklin here vouching for me?"

The clerk took the bill without hesitation, slipping it in the front pocket of his jeans. "Any friend of Ben is a friend of mine. Room 114, it's on the other side of the parking lot, halfway down the building." He handed Larry a key. "Check out is eleven o'clock, free doughnuts, juice and coffee in the lobby until ten-thirty. Have a good night, Mr. Smith."

Larry started to correct him then realized what the clerk meant. "Oh, yeah, sure. You too."

He returned to the truck and pulled it around the side of the building. He parked just outside room 114. He and Char took their bags and boxes from the bed of the pick-up and carried them into the room.

"Here you go, Miss Smith," Larry said, extending his hand to show off the not-so-luxurious room.

She cocked an eyebrow at him. "Smith? Did I miss something?"

"Oh, I figured it would be a good time to start our life of anonymity, so I paid a little extra cash when I got the room so I didn't have to show identification. The clerk called me 'Mr. Smith.'"

"So am I your niece or your illicit affair?"

"You're still my daughter, Char. He didn't actually ask any questions, once I gave him the hundred."

"I'm glad we got the check cashed at Indianapolis. We're going to have to be careful with it, if we want to keep from using credit cards," she said. "For that matter, this 'Smith' stuff has some merit. I'm not so sure that's the right name for us, but we probably should come up with aliases. No sense making it any easier, if they do come looking for us."

"I agree. I tell you what – your choice: decide what kind of pizza you want to order, or pick our new names."

Char laughed "I'll figure out supper. You figure out our new names "

Larry picked up the phone book by the bed and leafed through it until he got to the pizza delivery section. "Chain or local?"

"Definitely local," Char replied. "Chain tastes like cardboard. Local at least gives us a fifty-fifty chance of hitting a place that uses fresh ingredients."

"Okay, here's one: Annabelle's Authentic Italian Pizzeria. They deliver. What do you want on it?"

Char consulted her stomach. "Pepperoni and olives seems to be the urge of the moment."

"Sounds good to me." Larry dialed the number and placed the order. He told them the motel and room number. "The name? Uh, Jones. Okay, thanks."

He looked at Char. "Forty-five minutes."

She frowned. "Jones? Might as well leave it as 'Smith.' Come on Dad, think Bonnie and Clyde, Thelma and Louise, something with a little character. If we're going on the lam, we need something more exciting than 'Jones.'"

"Sorry, Char. She asked me for a name and I realized I didn't have one yet. I'll come up with something better."

She patted him on the shoulder. "It's okay, Dad. Maybe Jones is best. We try for something original and we'd probably stick out like a sore thumb."

Larry turned on the television set while they waited for the pizza to arrive. "Nothing much happening," he noted. "No stories about the fugitives from Kanapolis."

Char shrugged. "What do you expect? The whole cloud thing got passed off as an international nuclear disarmament treaty. Nobody outside the government knows the whole planet almost got wiped out by a huge energy absorbing cloud from another galaxy. Why would they put a little thing like a couple of farmers getting evicted from their land for soil studies on the news?"

"Yeah, I suppose so. It just seems like the guys on the run in the movies always get to watch TV stories about themselves."

She laughed. "Quite the headline story we would make. Probably interview Sheriff Barnes to find out we were always quiet folk, kept to ourselves."

He grinned. "Maybe you're right. We're not exactly front page news."

They watched the local news and weather report. A little over half an hour later, they both jumped at the loud knocking on their door.

"Pizza," Larry said, grinning sheepishly.

He opened the door. The delivery boy handed him the pizza. "Fifteen dollars."

Larry handed him a twenty. "Keep the change," he said, and closed the door.

They ate dinner with relish, enjoying the fresh food. It was obvious that Annabelle knew her pizza. They finished most of the pie as they continued to watch the news.

They watched television for another hour before the yawns became the dominant element to their conversation. They washed up for the night and went to bed.

Chapter Twelve: The Jones' New Home

The next morning, Larry had Char stay in the room while he went into the lobby to get breakfast. Better to not be seen together, he thought, regardless of whether or not anyone was looking for them. He nodded at the young clerk, filled two cups with coffee, grabbed a couple doughnuts and returned to the room.

"Thanks," Char said, taking her cup of coffee from her father. She sniffed the glazed doughnut, tapped it with one finger. "I take it these aren't straight from the oven."

"Sorry, it was all they had." Larry bit into his doughnut. "Not too bad, maybe a day old. Nothing growing on them that wasn't intended."

She tried her doughnut. "I've had worse."

They finished eating and double checked the room. Everything had been packed up again. They loaded the truck bed and resumed their journey south.

They stopped for lunch near the southern border of Kentucky. They sat down in a booth at a small roadside diner.

Larry smiled when the waitress put the blue plate special down in front of him. "Now that's what I call a meal." The plate held generous portions of green beans, mashed potatoes and roast beef slices, all covered with thick brown gravy. "Beats the heck out of stale doughnuts."

"Enjoy it, honey," the waitress said. She placed a lighter plate in front of Char; her stomach hadn't reacted well to the doughnut so she had ordered a side salad and a bowl of tomato soup.

After a few bites, Larry glanced around, saw no one was near their booth, and spoke in a quiet voice. "Another couple hours, Char, and we'll turn off the main roads. There's a place in Tennessee I used to hunt, back when I was on leave from the army. A little cottage in the hills, a place to lay low for as long as we need to. They're good people, and not too curious, if you know what I mean."

Char nodded. "Tennessee sounds nice. I always wondered what it would be like to live somewhere with hills and trees. Somewhere that wasn't one corn field after another."

"You know you always could have left, Char. I never wanted you to feel like you had to stay on the farm on my account."

She reached across, clasped his hand. "That's not what I meant, Dad. I loved the farm. I never wanted to go anywhere else. Like I said, I just wondered – no more than I wonder what it's like by the ocean or in Alaska."

He gripped her hand once in affection and then released it and resumed eating. Char smiled as she watched him polish off the plate with gusto. It would be nice in Tennessee, she thought. She imagined huddling by the fire as the snow came down in winter, for once not having to worry about taking care of the animals, just snuggling under blankets and drinking hot chocolate and doing her best to take care of her body for her baby. It was going to be wonderful, she thought. Tennessee would be perfect.

Larry left a couple dollars for the waitress under his empty coffee cup and went up to the cash register to pay their bill. Char watched him flirt with the girl at the register. She laughed softly, enjoying how he could still have so much fun with life. How he could instantly make people feel happy and glad to know him – treat him like a neighbor they've known for fifteen years. He always had that way with people. Especially young women, she thought. He never felt the way he did about Mom with anyone else, but he still loved to flirt with a pretty girl. She understood; she knew there would never be anyone like Grant again in her life. Obviously no more men from other planets, but more to the point no one that she would ever feel that in tune with. No one she could love with every ounce of her being, with all her heart, mind and soul. She sighed, forced a smile as Larry returned to their booth.

"All set?" he asked.

"Yes, let's go find that cottage."

They got back on the highway, Char taking her turn behind the wheel. They headed south for two and a half hours before Larry saw the exit he was looking for. Char turned off the highway and pulled into a gas station.

"I'm going to give Adam a call," Larry said.

"Okay, I'll gas her up and check the oil."

He walked over to the phone booth. He pulled out his calling card. He shook his head, put it back in his wallet. He went into the station and got change instead. He returned to the pay phone and made his call using coins.

"Larry, I was hoping you would get back to me today." The familiar voice warmed Larry's heart, reminding him there was still one friend he could count on.

"Well, we're going to be out of reach in a little while. I probably won't be able to check in but once a week, if that often, so I figured I'd better give you a call today."

"I did a little snooping around for you." Major Crowell paused. "It's pretty much what we thought – there's nothing I can do for you, as far as the farm goes. Even if we tried they could tie it up with injunctions and sealed court orders for years."

"That's what I expected, Adam. It's okay. We're a family, with or without the farm. We'll be all right."

"Listen, Larry, I'm a little concerned. I know you two are persons of interest with this whole thing, but it seems that somebody is trying pretty hard to keep tabs on you. They have ongoing alerts on all your accounts. Anything you do that hits an electronic network gets fed to them. Is there something they're after, Larry?"

Larry considered telling Adam about Char, but decided against it. It would only put his friend in an awkward position; what he didn't know he could plausibly deny. "I think they're still hoping that Grant is going to come back to us. I'm sure they realize it's a long shot, but they sure don't want to miss out if it does."

"And I assume your gut is still saying that isn't going to happen?"

"I promise I'll be on the horn to you faster than greased lightning, the second a spaceship lands in my front yard."

General Crowell laughed. "Well, I can't ask for more than that. I can't keep them from running these alerts, Larry. If you want to stay low, well, you know how."

"Understood, Adam. I'll give you a call in about a week. Thanks for everything, Adam."

"No problem. I still owe you another half dozen saves, by my count. Take care and be safe."

Larry hung up and returned to the truck. Char closed the hood. "Everything checks out, oil is up to the line."

Larry nodded. "Good. Nothing much new from Adam. He says they're keeping tabs on our accounts, but we had figured that much. As long as we use cash and stay in the country, we should be fine."

They got in the truck with Larry in the driver's seat for the final leg of their journey. They headed away from the urban areas and were soon driving along country roads in the hills of Tennessee.

Toward late afternoon Larry turned onto a dirt road, not much wider than the one their farm was off of back in Indiana. He followed this for a quarter of a mile, driving slow to avoid the numerous rough patches and outright holes in the road. They crested a small hill and arrived at the Shenandoah Acres Estate. That was what was printed in faded, peeling white paint on a three foot by four foot cracked wooden sign posted at the entry drive.

"Doesn't look like it has changed in twenty years," Larry said. He idled the truck down the driveway. It curved around a stand of trees for a hundred yards before opening into a large dirt parking area. A half dozen dilapidated shacks were spaced out in thirty foot intervals along the outside edge of the parking lot.

Larry smiled as he saw his daughter's crestfallen reaction to the falling down buildings. "Don't worry, Char. These are the old guest cabins, haven't been used in decades. We're walking up that little trail to the manager's cabin. Trust me, it will look like the Taj Mahal compared to these shacks."

She breathed a sigh of relief. "I was imagining trying to survive the winter in one of those."

"Let's go check it out. We can come back for the bags."

They walked along the path beyond the guest cabins. It ran up the hill that overlooked the back of the driveway. At the top of the hill the path led them to the manager's cabin.

"What did I tell you?"

Char laughed as she skipped ahead to the cabin. It was not the Taj Mahal, but after seeing the run-down shacks below, it did make her feel a lot better. It was a solid log cabin, with sturdy walls and the roof appeared to be in good shape. "It looks wonderful from the outside, Dad."

He walked over to the front door and leaned down. He retrieved a key from underneath a rock beside the door. "Same place as always," he said. He unlocked the door and the Ambersons – now the Jones – went into their new home.

It was small but cozy. The front room served as dining area and living room, boasting a fireplace, a comfortable couch, a couple chairs and a square wooden table for meals. It opened into a small kitchen area with a sink, small refrigerator and electric stove. There were two bedrooms and a single bathroom to complete the layout of the cabin.

"It's perfect, Dad." She hugged him tight, squeezing her eyes shut and enjoying the warmth and security of his embrace.

Chapter Thirteen: The Trans-Neptunian Region

Just outside the orbit of Neptune, amid the tens of thousands of asteroids and meteoroids comprising the Kuiper belt, a solitary spacecraft collided with one of the large masses of ice and rock. The ship had been in an elliptical orbit for months, the computer's guidance system successfully navigating safe passage through the mostly empty reaches of space within the solar system, but a sudden shift in the objects around it caused by their own collision proved more than the automatic system could compensate for.

The craft was mostly empty. The only life inside was a tiny sphere surrounding a small collection of cells. The sphere had been dormant, but the force of the blow threw it against the interior hull of the ship, and that broke the layer of cells between the protective coating and the cells at the center of the sphere.

That layer had been the barrier keeping the cells of the protective shell from interacting with the pure human essence in the center. The outer shell had been composed of the last living particles of Grant. His final act had been to surround the small clutch of cells he had captured from his bonding with Char. He had been unable to destroy them; his love for Char was too great to harm even these remnants from their bonding. To protect them, he had created the inert barrier to keep his own cells from feeding on their life essence, and then surrounded that barrier with his living cells, necessary to keep the inner core safe. His cells could mutate as needed, protecting the essence of his love from harm of whatever would threaten it.

When the barrier cracked, the result was instantaneous. The alien hybrid cells woke from their dormancy, sensing the life energies that the inert layer had hidden from them. They flowed through the crack in the protective shell and latched on to the essence within, merging with the human cells, assimilating the energy and particles into their own.

The united cells pulsed within the broken sphere. Latent memory cells activated; it reached a thin tendril through the crack, seeking the feeding tube within the cockpit of the spaceship. It connected to the tube, drawing on the rich nutrients, absorbing vital proteins to sustain its rekindled birth.

Chapter Fourteen: Still Searching

Major Atkins threw down the report on Allan Davis' desk. "It's been six months, Davis. Where the hell are they?"

Allan raised his hands, palms up. "I wish I knew, sir. I can't find them if they don't do anything that shows up on our servers. They're not using any of their accounts, so there's nothing to trace. They haven't sent for their mail, they haven't made any phone calls on their cards, their plates haven't shown up in any motor vehicle records – they're staying completely off our radar."

"So what can we do? There has to be something. You can't tell me the United States government can't find two farmers on its own soil."

"I'm a programmer, Major Atkins," Allan said. "I work with databases and numbers and web trafficking. I can't perform miracles; if the data isn't there, I can't do anything. Maybe if I had more to work with I could try broadening the search."

Major Atkins turned away from Allan, crossed his arms in front of his chest. He had kept the information concerning Char's possible pregnancy out of his reports. He wasn't sure how he would play that card, had wanted to wait until the woman was in custody before deciding. Well, six months had passed and the search had not ended. Assuming she hadn't miscarried, then the baby would be delivered soon. Or if she had miscarried then they had to recover the tissue remains. Either way, he needed to find Char Amberson soon. He turned around and bent over close to the other's face. "Davis, what I'm about to tell you is strictly confidential. You're not to disclose it to anyone without my permission. Understand?"

"Yes, sir," Allan said.

"Good. It might be helpful if you started checking hospital records. Specifically maternity wards. Also any prenatal specialists."

Allan sat confused for a moment. Then it hit him. "She's pregnant? And you think it is Grant's baby!"

Major Atkins nodded. "I believe she may be. That's why it is vital – not just for national security, but for her own health – that we bring her in as soon as possible. We have the finest doctors in the country on staff. I'm very concerned that there could be difficulties in the delivery, considering the identity of the father. There could also be dangers associated with the baby, if that's what we can call it."

Allan tapped his fingers, thinking of the ramifications of Char's pregnancy, what it could mean if she delivered an alien-human hybrid. What if the offspring took after the alien more than the human? What if it inherited Grant's powers, could feed off of their life forces? He didn't like Major Atkins, but he knew the risks to Char and Larry Amberson were real. "I can try some additional searches using that information," he said. "I'll get right on it."

Major Atkins nodded. "Fine. Let me know if anything comes up."

Allan watched his commanding officer walk briskly away. There had to be another way, he thought. Obviously the Ambersons were doing their best to keep from being found. They might not know the government was actively looking for them, but after being evicted from their home they probably assumed the worst. He doubted the new searches would be any more effective than the others. He didn't grow up on a farm, but he was pretty sure that with their rural background the Ambersons would be delivering this child at home, wherever that was, if Char really was pregnant.

He typed the queries in anyway, knowing he had to try, but doubting the use of it. He tapped his fingers after he submitted the searches, trying to come up with another method to find the Ambersons. Trying to think where they could have messed up in their efforts to remain hidden.

That's when it hit him. He remembered the conference call with the Pentagon when Major Drake and the Ambersons had convinced the government that the threat from the cloud was real. One of the deciding factors in even getting the conference call to occur was General Crowell. Crowell and Larry Amberson had been war buddies, Allan recalled. If there was anyone at all Larry had remained in contact with, he was willing to bet it was General Crowell.

He started new queries, checking the General's itineraries from the last six months, his inter-department report requests, everything that he could access through the various networks available to him under his high security access status.

He drummed his fingers nervously as the queries ran. He could feel the excitement that came to him when he was getting wrapped up in a new project. He felt this was what he had been looking for, that this was the new line of attack that would succeed in uncovering the hideout of the Ambersons.

He paged through the various screens of information as the multiple searches concluded. He frowned as they offered no support to his hypothesis. Then the inter-department requests came back – this was what he was looking for. General Crowell had not tapped into information on the Ambersons directly – he had nested his query by actually keeping tabs on Allan's own requests. He was checking the status to see what Allan had been checking on. It didn't tell him where the Ambersons were holed up, but it made him pretty confident that General Crowell had at minimum been in contact with them.

With this information, he had enough justification to request phone records from General Crowell's office. He ran matching routines against all incoming and outgoing calls from the last six months, eliminating all numbers that were also present in the six months prior. He then screened official numbers from the military directory. This reduced the list to less than a hundred. He checked each number individually, crossing them off his list one by one as he determined the nature of the phone number. After official calls, family calls and other identifiable numbers were removed, there were a dozen unknown phone numbers left on his list.

He checked the listings for each number. Further research yielded his final list – five incoming calls in the last six months that matched up to pay phones in Tennessee. He plotted the locations on a map. He had just narrowed the search to a hundred mile radius in rural Tennessee. He sat back, smiled, happy with his detective work. Once Major Atkins let loose the hounds, Char Amberson and her little package would be brought in. He tried to reassure himself that it was for her own good, that the risks from what she carried were real, but the elation at his successful sleuthing faded and he suddenly felt hollow inside.

He shook his head. She could die, trying to do this on her own, he thought. He put the information together into a small report, including the numbers and the map with the pay phone locations marked on it. He printed off a copy and took it to Major Atkins.

Chapter Fifteen: Closing In

Major Atkins had his hand-picked crew in Tennessee by midmorning the next day. They were soldiers and officers that he had groomed for this detail. These twenty men had sworn oaths to him, owed their careers, their lives to him. They would be the first members of his new organization. It was time to go independent, he had decided, assuming they found Char Amberson and she was still pregnant. With an alien child in his possession, there was no limit to what he could do. Even if it was stillborn, the tissue samples alone would be worth hundreds of millions of dollars, enough to keep him and his men in comfort on some tropical island. If it lived then the entire spectrum of alien technology would be within his reach. He could develop and control the most powerful weapons on Earth. Nothing would stand in his way, if it was a live birth.

He was tired of the rules and regulations forced on him by the military. The government was worse; they passed laws to protect the terrorists, made him fight his battles with one hand tied behind his back. The hell with them, the hell with all of them, he thought. He would clean the whole world up once he was in charge. There'd be no coddling of criminals on his watch. That's why he was here in Tennessee. To get the power so he could make them do the right thing.

They had canvassed each of the locations that the phone calls had originated from, interviewing the gas station attendants and the waitresses in the diners. They confiscated the security tapes from the places that had cameras operating, and had taken them back to the hotel room to view. It was not until the fifth location's security camera tapes were played that he recognized the weathered face wearing a brown jacket and a baseball hat.

Major Atkins paused the video tape player. "Larry Amberson," he said, pointing at the older man in a baseball hat shown on the screen. "This seals it; go ahead and finish reviewing the tapes from the other cameras and see if Charlotte is on any of them. See what she looks like these days, in case she's cut her hair or dyed it."

He left the video screening to two of his men. He walked over to the map hung on the wall of the hotel room they had set up base in. It was a topographical display of the hundred miles surrounding them, with each pay phone location marked with a large blue star. Even with the dozen vehicles he had commandeered for the search, it would take weeks to cover all the ground. There were just too many back roads, old barns, abandoned houses and thick woods.

He paced back and forth, trying to come up with a better solution, some way to ferret the Ambersons out of their hiding place. It was no good; they had gone over it on the trip out this morning. They were going to have to post stake-outs at each of the target locations, and they were going to have to search a whole lot of ground. It was going to take routine drudgery, covering mile after mile of dirt roads through the hills of Tennessee, and spending hour after hour monitoring the pay phones.

He split the men into two groups. The first would take rotations on the target locations. The second group would continue to travel throughout the search area, trying to find someone in a grocery store, gas station or local watering hole that recognized either of the Ambersons.

Major Atkins cursed softly. To have them, to know they were somewhere in that big circle, but be unable to close the knot. It ate at him, leaving his stomach a roiling mess of nerves. If only there was a way to flush them out, to make the Ambersons come scurrying out from under their cover.

Well, he would keep thinking about it. For now, he dispatched his crews to their tasks. Maybe they'd get lucky, he thought. Maybe Larry and Char were careless after six months, had gotten too close to someone that would remember their faces.

He paced back and forth in the hotel room. Should have brought Davis here, he thought. Have him run some more searches, circle in on any Tennessee connections. He shook his head. Davis wasn't loyal to him personally. He knew he was going to have to bring the programmer into the organization, along with the biologist Eckham and their department head Scott. Those three were the closest things to experts on the alien that existed on this planet. But he couldn't bring them in until he had made his move. He couldn't risk them blowing the whistle. No, when they were brought in it would be for good. There would be no turning back by then; not for them, not for him, not for anybody. His vision would come to fruition. A feeling of absolute power filled his body as he envisioned the days to come. The days when he would control it all.

Chapter Sixteen: Just Another Day

Char breathed deeply. She felt like an elephant, a big lumbering pachyderm that crashed into everything because it couldn't see beyond its huge mass, letting her bulk clear the way of incidental items like lamps and end tables. She steadied the lamp she had bumped into, catching it before it crashed to the floor. They were running out of bulbs, so many had been broken due to her mishaps.

She felt her swollen belly. Despite how uncomfortable she had become, despite the ache in her lower back, despite all the usual changes in body and mind from the pregnancy, she still smiled whenever she felt her stomach. The life growing within her made up for whatever fatigue or pains befell her.

She hummed gentle lullabies as she finished straightening up the living room in their small log cabin. They had settled into a routine as the months went by. Char would spend the morning doing light housework while Larry worked on outdoor tasks – chopping firewood, setting traps, fishing on the nicer days. He would come back for lunch and visit for an hour or so before heading back out while it was still light. She would spend most afternoons reading or napping, as her pregnancy took more and more out of her. In the evening they sat and talked, sometimes reminiscing about the farm, just as often dreaming about the future with her child.

It had been pleasant. The log cabin was in good condition, and even on the harshest winter days they had been comfortable, between the electric heat and the fireplace. She had never felt so relaxed. Every day seemed a blessing, filled with joyful anticipation of the baby, with the companionship of her father, surrounded by the beautiful countryside of Tennessee.

Char and Larry were used to spending the majority of their time by themselves. Other than a few trips into one of the nearby towns to get some bulk supplies, they had limited their contact with the outside world. Larry had checked in with Adam a few times on those trips with little new information to exchange. He had also contacted the owner of the cabin they were staying in. True to his recollection, no questions were asked after he gave him most of their remaining cash, paying the rent in advance through May. They still had about eight hundred dollars left. It would be enough to get them through the winter, past the end of the pregnancy. Later in the spring they would need to wire Joe at the Kanapolis Savings and Loan for the rest of their savings. They didn't want to risk that until they were ready to make another move.

She finished washing the morning dishes in the small stainless steel sink. She left them to air dry and waddled across the open space and plumped down on the couch. She wiped the sweat from her brow with her sleeve. Again, the image of a lumbering elephant came to her mind. She reached for the romance novel she was in the middle of and settled back against the cushions of the couch to read.

Twenty minutes later a knocking on the door brought her out of the impassioned scene between the single mother and the fireman. She pushed against the arm of the sofa to help herself to her feet and went to the door. She peered through the glass window. A man she did not recognize was standing outside.

She bit her lip. Dad was outside somewhere, but might be too far to hear her if she called for him. She didn't want to be a frightened little girl, but it wasn't just herself that she was worried for, it was her baby, too. She stood still, debating whether to open the door or just wait for the stranger to leave.

She let out a little cry when she heard the key slide into the lock. She watched, stock still from fright, as the door knob turned and the door opened.

The man let out his own cry as he saw Char standing before him. "Oh! I'm sorry, I didn't mean to scare you. I'm Reed Saginaw. I rented this cabin to you and your Pa."

Char let out the breath she had been holding with relief. "Mr. Saginaw, I would have let you in but I didn't know where Dad was and –"

He cut her off with a wave of his hand. "Don't you apologize, young lady. You shouldn't answer the door when you're by yourself. And please, call me Reed. I'm not so old that hearing 'mister' from pretty young ladies doesn't cause a little heart ache."

Char held out her hand. "Well, Reed, I'm Char. It's nice to meet you. I can't tell you how much we appreciate staying here. It's been wonderful."

Reed looked around the interior of the cabin. "I'd say you have this place looking better than it ever has. You done real nice with it."

"Thanks," Char said. She put a hand on her belly. "It got where I couldn't really help much outside, so I spend a lot of time doing little things in here."

Reed smiled. "Pretty far along, aren't you? When is the baby due?"

"Next week, if things go on schedule. It's my first, so I'm not really sure if it will be early or late."

Reed noted the absence of a ring on her finger, coupled with the fact it was Char and Larry out here, no one else. Not the first time a woman had a baby out in the woods, away from prying eyes, he thought. Won't be the last, either. She seemed like a good person; he knew Larry was, had known him for years, although it had been more than a decade since he had hunted with her father. He wondered what exactly they were running from, why they were hiding out here in the hills. It was more than old fashioned banishment of a young woman pregnant without a husband, he felt.

"Char, do you expect your father back soon? As you might guess, I had a reason for coming out here – I don't normally let myself in a place I've rented out, but I wanted to make sure everything was okay. When no one answered, I got a little nervous."

She felt a chill down her back. "Why wouldn't everything be okay?" The room seemed to begin spinning, blood drained from her face and she stumbled.

Reed rushed to her side and steadied her. He helped her to the couch. "Char, are you okay?"

She breathed heavily in and out several times. "Yeah, I think so. I just got a little dizzy there for a minute. I feel better now."

"I didn't mean to frighten you," Reed said. "Why don't you sit down and rest a bit? I'm going to go find Larry. I'd like to share my news with both of you."

"I think he's at the lake," Char said. "He said he was going to try to catch some bluegill for lunch."

"Okay. You stay here; I'll be back in a jiffy."

Reed left the log cabin and walked a brisk pace along the narrow dirt trail leading to the small lake beyond the nearest stand of trees. He quickly found the elder Amberson sitting on the end of a short pier in sore need of repairs.

Reed cautiously stepped past broken planks and out to the edge of the pier. Larry turned to look back over his shoulder as Reed approached him.

"Reed! Good to see you," Larry said. He smiled at the man. "What brings you out here?"

"Hello, Larry," Reed responded. They shook hands, warm friendly grips of men who had not been together in years, but had changed so little in all that time they still knew the nature of each other. "Saw your little girl up at the cabin. I'm afraid I spooked her a bit when I came in."

Larry noted his question had gone unanswered. All in due time, he thought. "Yeah, she's a little gun-shy, with the baby coming soon. She's a good woman, Reed. Going to be a wonderful mother."

"If she is anything like your Amy, she will be."

Larry put his hand on the other's arm. "You know, Reed, Char looks just like Amy did when she was pregnant. That same glow about them, that look of peace - I swear I thought I was looking at Amy this morning at breakfast when Char turned around and smiled at me."

"Can I ask where the daddy is?"

Larry frowned. He didn't want to lie to Reed, but sometimes that was what you had to do. "He's dead. He was a good man, he really was. It's been hard on Char. I'd appreciate it if you would keep it out of the conversation."

"Of course," Reed said. "I can understand why coming out here might make it easier on her – on both of you." He looked out over the dark water of the lake, at the woods surrounding it. "This country sure makes a lot of things go down softer."

Larry nodded. "It's beautiful out here. Beautiful and peaceful. Lets a body figure things out, appreciate life no matter what's been thrown at you."

"Now, how about we head up and clean those fish in your basket? I haven't had fresh pan fried bluegill in months. Give us a chance to talk, you and Char and me, over lunch."

Larry pulled the line up attached to the basket in the lake. He opened the lid for Reed to see his catch. "Not bad for an hour's fishing, huh?"

Reed whistled. "I tell you, Larry, for a farmer you sure know how to reel them in."

They walked back up to the cabin in silence. When they got there Char was in the kitchen, cutting up vegetables for a salad. "I figured you'd be back for lunch," she said.

"Heard Reed gave you a scare," Larry said, putting the basket of fish in the sink.

"Oh, I just got a little dizzy, that's all." She looked over at Reed. "He said he was checking up on us, and I started to wonder what there was to worry about, and about fell down before he helped me to the couch."

The concern was evident on Larry's face as he left the sink and went to her side. He brushed her bangs back from her forehead. "Now, Char, you better start taking it easy. I don't want anything to happen to you. You need to get more rest." He took the paring knife from her and handed it to Reed. "You go lay down on the sofa. We'll call you when lunch is ready."

She started to protest but Larry shushed her and led her by the arm over to the couch. She gave up and sat down. "Go ahead, lay back and get a cat nap. It'll be a good half-hour or forty-five minutes before lunch, by the time I clean the fish and fry them up."

She decided after the dizzy spell a nap might be in order after all. She lay back and closed her eyes, just to rest a minute. The familiar drone of her father's voice in the kitchen was soothing to her. The crackling of the logs in the fireplace was a sound equally familiar, and soon she fell asleep.

Larry cleaned the fish while Reed took over the salad preparation. They talked idly for awhile, catching up on what had happened the years since they had last hunted and fished together on this land. Larry talked about the life Char and he had shared on the farm; Reed recalled the years he had spent in these hills doing much what the Ambersons had done the past six months.

Larry threw the bluegill fillets into the pan with a half a cup of vegetable oil. As the oil spit and spattered he occasionally flipped the pieces of fish to cook them evenly. He glanced across the open room and saw that Char was sound asleep.

"Reed, I know you were planning on talking to us together, but I think in her present condition it might be best if we chatted first. I'm guessing it isn't casual gossip that brought you out here, and I don't want Char to worry about anything but taking care of herself."

"I suppose that would be best. I don't know how serious it is, Larry, but I figured it was best to come out and let you know, so you could judge for yourself." Reed paused as he scooped the vegetables into a large bowl and mixed them together with the lettuce that he had already placed there "There have been some men in town, asking questions. They had pictures of you and Char, wanted to know if anyone had seen either of you."

"Did they say who they were? Why they were looking for us?"

"They were a little vague on that. They implied they were Homeland Security, but I'm not so sure. They seemed military to me. Maybe special ops, I don't know for sure. They just said you were persons of interest, that they needed to talk to you."

"Yeah, I bet talking was what they were interested in." Larry ran a hand through his hair. "Did anyone say anything to them?"

"No, not that I know of. I'm pretty sure I'm the only one who knows you're out here. From the look on your face this isn't entirely unexpected, so I assume you've done your shopping elsewhere."

Larry nodded. "Always at least an hour away. Never the same place twice. Listen, Reed, I appreciate your telling me this, especially your letting us stay here."

"Hey, you paid me twice what anyone else would, it's not charity."

"It's because I trust you. I know we haven't spent time together in recent years, but I know the kind of man you are. I don't want to go into the details about why we are hiding, that information would give you nothing but trouble. But it probably is military, and I'm not sure what they will do to find us. Say the word and we'll clear out of here."

Reed laughed. "Are you kidding me? Char is going to pop any day now! You can't go on the run with her in that condition. Now, if you need to go solo, I can stay here and take care of her. I'm no farmer, but I've delivered my share of babies into this world."

Larry smiled. "No, she's as caught up in this as I am, maybe more. I'm glad you're okay with us staying here; that was as much a bluff as anything else – I don't know where we would have gone."

Reed clapped him on the back. "Don't worry about it. How about we get this food on the table and have us a good meal?"

They brought the food over to the table and sat down. "Does she have a name picked out?"

Larry nodded. "Two, actually, since we don't know the sex. If it's a boy, Hugh Grant Amberson. Hugh is for her other grandfather, Grant is for the father. If it's a girl, Amy Grace Amberson. Amy after my Amy; Grace was just a name she liked."

"Sounds like good, solid names to me." Reed glanced over at the sofa. "Looks like someone's waking up just in time for lunch."

Char stretched out on the couch. The nap had helped, she admitted. She walked slowly over to join the others at the table. "Going to eat it all without me, weren't you?" she teased.

"Oh, we would have saved you a couple carrots, maybe a leaf or two of lettuce," Larry said.

"I bet." She sat down and served herself from the plate of fish in the center of the table. "Hmmm, smells good."

They enjoyed the fresh cooked fish and the salad. Larry and Reed steered the conversation to nice, safe topics, discussing the local weather, how the fishing had been, whether the geese were as plentiful this year as last.

After several minutes of this Char threw her hands up. "Enough! You two are skirting around talking about everything but what Reed is here for. Now 'fess up and tell me what the deal is before you get me mad. You don't want any part of an angry, expectant mother, do you?" She glared at them, daring them to withhold information.

"Okay," Larry said. "I didn't want to upset you, but it's clear that you're going to be upset one way or another, so I might as well tell you." He paused, put a hand on hers to try to keep her calm. "I'm sure we're okay, but some people were in town asking questions about us."

"What men? What questions? Do they know we're here?"

"Settle down, Char," Larry said in a soothing voice. "It's like I said, I'm sure it's nothing. Nobody in town knows us. What little shopping we've done has been an hour's drive or more from here. We're okay, they won't find us here. Reed will keep an eye on things in town, just to keep tabs on the men asking questions. We're in the middle of nowhere, as far as they are concerned. We're safe here, I promise."

She sighed. "If you say so. It's still scary, knowing they are this close. How did they even know to look in this area?"

"I don't know. They knew we were headed south. We didn't stop using cards until we left Kentucky. Who knows how many places they are checking? As long as no one points them to Shenandoah Estates, we'll be fine."

Reed nodded his agreement. "And don't you worry about anyone pointing them this way. Like your dad said, no one but me knows you're out here, and I'm sure as heck not telling."

Char smiled at their reassurances. "All right. I'll just sit back and rest and let you two take care of all the little details like government men tearing up the country looking for us. In fact, I think I am going to bed for another nap."

Larry smiled, motioned for her to leave her dishes on the table. "I'll take care of that. You go on to bed."

She kissed him on the cheek. She looked at Reed. He's just like Dad, she thought; same kind, gentle strength, same feeling of good heartedness. She walked over to Reed and gave him a kiss on the cheek, too. "Thanks, Reed. I can see why Dad trusted you. You're a good person."

Reed placed his hand on the spot where she had pressed her lips and watched her walk into her bedroom. "You're right, Larry," he said after she had closed the door. "The spitting image of Amy."

Chapter Seventeen: Evolution

Inside the spacecraft, the collection of cells grew. Memory cells activated, driving the mutation of structure, adapting the growing organism to its environment. Its remarkable ability to morph its cellular characteristics, the functions and processes within its gelatinous body, enabled it to shift its essential composition.

It adopted properties inherent in the mixed heritage that made up the creature. Dual origins of its male progenitor, possessing the characteristics of Grant's father and the vaporous cloud that had merged with Grant in his infancy, coupled with the homo sapiens genetic material from the cells captured from Char Amberson It was a testimony to just how adaptable the inherited properties of the cloud had remained, even in this second generation of hybridization, that the being was able to successfully meld this mixed conglomeration of cells.

The controlling factor in the process remained those awakened memory cells that had been part of the outer layer of protection. These memories drove the merging into a human-like form, formed the new being into a sentient life form not vastly different from its parents. The love for Char had been strongly imprinted in Grant's bonding cells, and this drove it to shape itself into female form.

The new being continued to feed on the nutrients supplied by the tube it had attached itself to. It reached out with additional tendrils, exploring its small world inside the cockpit of the rocket ship. It sought the interface link with the ship's computer and after several attempts modified the properties of the tendril to successfully connect.

The ship's computer accepted the link. The characteristics were similar enough to Grant to communicate the desires of the being. The computer initiated the education programs it had first administered to Grant decades earlier, when he had begun his flight from his home world. The being, nourished both physically and mentally, grew, matured and learned, as the craft headed inward, toward the center of the solar system, the new trajectory given it by the same crash that had stirred the life within to growth.

Chapter Eighteen: The Search is Over

Major Atkins looked up from the report when the soldier rushed into his room. "Sir! We may have had a breakthrough!"

"What is it, Campbell?"

"We got an update from Davis. He cross-referenced the men in Larry Amberson's companies from his army stints with motor vehicle and county tax records in this region. Five hits came up. The first four were dead ends. But the last one – a Reed Saginaw – turned up some property that looks like it would be an ideal location to lay low."

"Get a team together. I want us en route in ten minutes." Major Atkins rubbed his hands together. Finally, some good luck. No, it wasn't luck, he thought, it was destiny. This was the result of hard work and planning. He knew it had been a matter of time before they found the Ambersons; his only fear was that it would be after the child was born, that they would seek new ground and prolong the search. He hoped that had not occurred.

The convoy sped from the hotel parking lot. It was thirty-seven miles over county roads to the Saginaw land. They reached it in less than an hour, bouncing over pot holes and pushing their four-wheel-drive vehicles to the limit on the winding roads. The trucks halted outside the small drive with the faded Shenandoah Estates sign.

Major Atkins sent a truck in either direction along the county road to seal off traffic. He and the remaining dozen men walked down the path. They got to the opening and spread out among the ramshackle cabins, searching each one. Upon finding them empty, a soldier pointed out the path leading up the hill. A couple soldiers remained on watch near the cabins while the rest followed the path.

After cresting the hill and seeing the manager's cabin, Major Atkins signaled his men to huddle up. "Listen, no matter what happens, Char Amberson must be captured alive. Do not under any circumstance harm her. Larry Amberson is expendable, although I would rather have him taken alive too. Now let's go do this."

They fanned out and surrounded the cabin. At Major Atkins signal they stormed the place, four men and Major Atkins going in the front door, the rest covering all directions of escape.

Larry and Char were sitting on the couch when the soldiers burst into the cabin. Before they could react they were surrounded. Larry slowly raised his arms as the guns were directed at them. Char clutched at her father, holding on to him, tears of fright falling.

"Good Lord," Larry said, "put those things away. You think you need machine guns to protect yourselves from an old man and a pregnant woman? You should be ashamed of yourselves."

Major Atkins motioned to his soldiers to stand down. They remained alert, two of them watching the Ambersons carefully, the other two spreading out to ensure no one entered the room without warning. "Good afternoon, Larry, Char. I'm sorry to barge in like this, but you've been very difficult to locate, and I simply had to find you. I was worried if I waited for an invitation I might never get a chance to see you –" he paused as he glanced intently at Char's swollen belly "—all of you – again. I must say I am very pleased to see just how much of you there is."

"What do you want?" Char asked. "Why can't you just leave us alone?"

"My dear, I'm afraid that is entirely out of the question. You are far too valuable, too special, to leave alone. I'm only doing what's best for you. Who knows what could happen to you – what could happen to that particularly unique child you carry – if you were left alone. I am offering the finest medical specialists in the United States. I am going to do whatever is necessary to ensure that your child is born alive. Surely you can see the sense in that?"

"Leave me and my baby alone! We don't need your help. Dad and I can handle everything just fine." Her face was red as she fought to keep control of her emotions.

Major Atkins shook his head. "That's a risk I am not prepared to take, Char. Larry may have experience with delivering cows, hell, he could be an obstetrician for all I care, but there is obviously a great chance for unforeseen developments with this birth."

He smiled at her. "Really, Char, this is for the best."

He motioned to the soldier guarding the front door. "Signal all clear. Get a couple men in here to pack up the place. I want a clean sweep – no trace left of us or them."

"What do you mean?" Larry asked. "What's going to happen to us?"

"We're moving to a more secure location, Larry. You and your daughter are going to be in good hands."

Major Atkins stepped into the kitchen area and flipped open his cell phone. He called his senior officer, Lieutenant Jenkins. "Jenkins, we got them. Operation Jettison is a go."

"Roger that, Major. We'll bag them and meet you at the bat cave."

Major Atkins smiled. It was all coming together. By midnight tonight they would be at the underground base. Lieutenant Jenkins would bring the rest of the men he had personally selected for his new world order, along with the three team members who had experience with the cloud and the alien hybrid. Those three would come around to his way of thinking eventually. If not, they would still do the work he commanded. They wouldn't have a choice, not if they wanted to live. He felt the heavy yoke of submission fall from his shoulders. His secession from the United States had begun.

Chapter Nineteen: The Bat Cave

It was ten o'clock at night when the trucks pulled off the highway and headed into the Arizona desert. They drove down unmarked roads to arrive at the location of the hidden base. Major Atkins keyed in the security code to his transmitter and large metal plates slid apart from under the sand, revealing a wide ramp leading beneath the desert surface. They drove down the ramp and the bay doors closed behind them.

The ramp led a hundred feet underground before it opened into a large chamber. They parked the trucks and got out, ushering the Ambersons into a freight elevator. After entering additional codes, the elevator descended further into the earth.

When it reached the bottom of the shaft they got out, entering a wide hallway, bright white on all surfaces, with florescent lighting along the ceiling at ten foot intervals. The group walked down the hallway until it ended at a large steel door. Larry looked at Char and rolled his eyes. "Let me guess, another secret code in case the last two secret codes were compromised."

Major Atkins glared at him. "Security is vital, Larry. If you had better security perhaps you wouldn't be here, hmmm?" He pressed his thumb against a pad on the wall next to the door. A clicking sound was audible as the lock released and the door opened.

They walked into a large chamber, the command center of the underground base. Several doors led to adjacent areas – sleeping quarters, conference rooms, bathrooms, kitchen and mess hall – but the primary functions were performed in this room. Various banks of computers lined one wall, with several cubicles set up for work areas.

"Okay men," Major Atkins said. "Operation Jettison is in progress. You know what you have to do."

His troops spread out in the large room, accessing computers and launching programs that were part of Major Atkins' plan. These efforts would effectively erase their tracks from the last six months, replacing them with false trails, planting fake reports so even were someone to investigate they would assume there had been nothing to the Amberson farm studies, that the results had been negative. The other main objective was to wipe the existence of this location from the military records. This would enable them to develop the weapons and build their organization without hindrance.

Major Atkins led Char and Larry to one of the sleeping rooms. "Once the doctors arrive, you'll be in the medical wing, Char. But for now you can stay here with your father."

He left the room and they heard the lock click into place. Char trembled, let out all the fear she had been holding in. Larry held her, rubbing her back with one hand, whispering that it would be all right. After a while she calmed down and they sat on the edge of one of the beds in the room.

"Char, I know this seems bad, but Major Atkins did have one point."

"What do you mean? That crazy Hitler wannabe kidnapped us!"

"I know that, and I sure as heck don't like being taken here against our will. But he said there will be really good doctors here, and that part makes me feel a little better. I'm sure everything is going to go smoothly with the delivery, please don't worry about that. But it's always good to have a doctor around, no matter how experienced I am with animal births at the farm. I didn't want to say it before, but I was a little scared at the prospect of handling this myself. We don't know what the baby is going to need – maybe an incubator, or transfusion – it's not like this has happened before. I couldn't stand the thought of not being to help it, of there being a problem we couldn't fix because we weren't in a hospital or didn't have the best doctors available."

She sniffed, wiping her nose on her sleeve. "I suppose having someone else clean up will be nice. And I can get something a little stronger than Tylenol if I need it."

He hugged her, brushed his hand through her hair. "See, it's not all bad getting kidnapped by crazy majors who want to take over the world."

She laughed, despite herself. "No, I guess not."

Major Atkins turned away from the monitor. "Don't forget, I want twenty-four hour video and audio on both of them, wherever they go. Bathroom, bedroom, closet – everywhere. Anything noteworthy happens, let me know ASAP, otherwise a synopsis every eight hours."

"Yes sir," the soldier said. He kept his eyes on the panel of screens that showed every movement either of the Ambersons made.

Major Atkins addressed the soldier on watch duty, monitoring the video and satellite feeds for the entrance area. "I'm going to my office. Send the new recruits in as soon as they get here."

He walked into the small room he had taken over as his own. It was stark, with a few maps and a whiteboard on the walls. He didn't want to waste his time decorating it, it was only a staging area. He would worry about making his room comfortable when he was in the Oval Office. He sat down behind the medium sized oak desk and entered his logon information into the terminal. He checked on the status of Operation Jettison. Everything was on schedule. Soon all real information regarding the cloud and the space man would reside only in the databases internal to this command center.

He frowned. He wasn't going to feel totally secure about the network security until they could sever the connections with the military servers. That had to wait until they had finished all their programs. Until then, there was a risk that someone could detect their activity and stop it. Or worse, backtrack and locate their base. Fortunately, the person most likely to notice any strange activity involving the cloud files would be delivered to the underground base within the hour. Without Allan Davis monitoring the network, the odds were against anyone discovering them in time to stop them.

Chapter Twenty: Impressed to the Cause

Allan Davis looked around the inside of the van. It seemed like Doctor Scott and Sid Eckham were as nervous as he was. None of them had any foreknowledge of the new mission they were on. He wondered if Grant had returned. He was pretty sure it had something to do with the alien - there was nothing else the three had in common. But Lieutenant Jenkins had been stone faced the whole trip, saying that Major Atkins would explain the mission when they arrived at their destination. Wherever that was. He wanted to be excited, wanted to hope that this really was another close encounter with an alien life form. But since Major Atkins had taken over, even that didn't hold the same attraction as before. Maybe it was because seeing how the experience had affected the Ambersons, had cast them out from their home, left him feeling mixed about the whole affair.

When Lieutenant Jenkins had told him they were leaving immediately, Allan had managed to convince him he needed to shut down the servers properly or the database would get corrupted. He used the extra thirty seconds that bought him to quickly post another message through his chat connection. He wasn't sure what was going on, and didn't even know if Jeff or Tia were checking for messages anymore, it had been so long since he had heard from either of them. But this seemed like something big was happening, and he didn't have anyone else to tell. He kept the window minimized while he typed the message, not wanting the lieutenant to suspect he was doing anything other than shutting down the servers. "BUGGING OUT. EPISODE 6?" he typed in and posted to the chat session. He closed the window, finished shutting down the servers and grabbed his laptop. The lieutenant had rushed him to the van where he found the others waiting for them. As soon as he and Lieutenant Jenkins were seated the van had sped off.

Sid Eckham and Doctor Scott were talking quietly, not eager to draw the attention of the soldiers riding in the van with them. "So you don't know what this is about either?" Sid asked Doctor Scott.

"No, they came and grabbed me out of my office without a minute's notice. Wouldn't even let me finish the e-mail I was writing. Said it could wait, that Major Atkins had ordered us on this mission without delay." He shrugged his shoulders. "What can you do? That's the life of a military scientist. You get great research opportunities but when they say jump, you jump."

"I hated to leave the farm, though," Sid said. "I think the last diffraction on the soil sample from the meadow had detected a modification in the cellular structure of some of the particles. It was very interesting; I was hoping to run a second trial tonight."

"Well, it will still be there when we get back," Doctor Scott said. "Trust me, the army is not going to let anyone step foot on that farm until we have put every last grain of dirt under the microscope."

They stopped the conversation as the van turned off the main road and onto a bumpy dirt road. The windows were tinted and they could not see where they were going, only knew that the surface of the road had changed dramatically.

In a few minutes the van slowed to a stop. After a moment it resumed and they could sense the slope as the van went down the ramp. It stopped again. The driver shut off the engine and the soldiers opened the doors. When they got out they saw the parking area and the elevator.

Lieutenant Jenkins punched in the codes and the group entered the elevator and descended down to the long white hallway. Jenkins used his thumbprint to open the final door and they all stepped through into the command center of the underground base.

A soldier walked up to them as soon as they entered. "Major Atkins wants them taken to his office right away," he told Lieutenant Jenkins.

The lieutenant nodded and escorted Davis, Eckham and Scott to the major's office. "No problems, sir," he reported. "Everything is on schedule."

"Thank you, Jenkins. Go check with the others – I want to have a moment with these three."

The lieutenant left the office, closing the door behind him. Major Atkins motioned for the newcomers to have a seat. He stood up, paced back and forth a couple times, before addressing them.

"I brought the three of you here for obvious reasons. You have the most direct knowledge of the alien cloud and the space man. There have been new developments in this matter, and it is imperative that things are handled correctly this time." He spun around, eyeing them almost manically. "We cannot repeat the mistakes of last August!"

He resumed pacing, his voice calmer but his tone still firm. "We never should have allowed the space man to leave. We never should have wasted our entire nuclear arsenal on a futile launch against a foe impervious to their effect. Those two events have essentially handcuffed the United States against the rest of the world. We no longer have a dominant force that no one can match. We lost our edge, and let the one thing that could have replaced it slip out of our grasp."

He stopped in front of the men, his voice growing louder with each statement, his passion evident in face and body posture. "This will not happen on my watch. I will not stand idly by while the leaders of this army, the leaders of this nation, let all we have fought for over the past two hundred years be pissed away into the wind. I will not stand for it!"

"I need each of you to make a decision. Think hard on this, for it is the single most important decision of your lives, but think fast, for we do not have time to waste." He sat back on the edge of his desk, looked each of them in the eyes for a full minute before he continued. "Are you willing to let this great nation fall victim to the rest of the world, to let her stumble because of the spineless leadership that has already brought her to her knees? Or are you willing to do something about it? Are you willing to stand with me as we show those jellyfish what real men can do, what real leadership can provide for this country? In short, gentlemen, are you with me?"

Allan and Sid looked to the senior member among them. Doctor Scott met Major Atkins' stare unblinkingly. He had faced Congressional hearings with irate Senators and countless belligerent military officers. Though the major's tone was a bit more obsessive than most, he felt it was still the usual rhetoric and nothing beyond that. "What exactly do you want us to do, Major Atkins?" he asked.

Major Atkins sighed. He got up from the desk, circled around the three men. Allan couldn't help craning his neck around to watch the major as he walked behind them, not sure if this scene was going to end up badly, with Major Atkins swinging a baseball bat at the back of their heads. Doctor Scott calmly faced forward, and Sid held his head down, wringing his hands in his lap.

"I was hoping that love for your country – rather, the ideals that made this country – would be enough to sway you to reason. I can see that additional encouragement must be supplied. Very well. As I mentioned earlier, there have been new developments in the alien situation."

Major Atkins went to his desk and sat down. He accessed his terminal and brought up part of the video that had been recorded in the sleeping quarters of the Ambersons. He paused the video and zoomed in on Char Amberson, a profile image that clearly showed her current condition. He turned his monitor around so the others could see the image. Only Allan with his prior knowledge was prepared for the sight.

"Who is that?" Sid asked. He squinted then answered his own question. "That's Char Amberson!"

"A very pregnant Char Amberson," Doctor Scott said. "Let me guess – just shy of nine months?"

Major Atkins nodded. The situation crystallized in their minds, what must have happened, what – as impossible as it could have been, as incredibly incomprehensible as it was – what the picture on the monitor so clearly indicated had truly occurred.

Sid jumped out of his chair, putting his nose almost against the monitor. "Not just different species, but different ecosystems, different genetic bases – it's impossible. There's no way two beings from different planets could produce a viable offspring. It's just not possible."

Doctor Scott pointed at the image. "Clearly, it is."

"How do we know that it was Grant?" Allan asked. It was a question he had not been willing to ask before, but with the others in the office he felt it was safe. "Isn't a more likely explanation Char just had a tumble in the hay with some hick from the next farm over?"

Major Atkins smiled at the three of them. "Well, based on all our research and reconnaissance, we are certain it was the space man that impregnated her. However, that is one of the reasons we brought you three in on this. You have more knowledge about this alien than anyone else. I want you to continue what we started on the Amberson farm. But this time, we will have a real live sample. No digging around in the dirt, hoping to get a speck of alien DNA, no running the same diagnostic programs again and again – you will be performing brand new experiments, leading science into undiscovered regions. You will be the forefathers of a brand new age."

He let those thoughts rest in their minds for a minute. Then he pressed a key on his terminal and the monitor went dark. He let them watch the blank screen for another minute, then another, until they got his point. He nodded at them. "That is what is at stake here. You choose to live in the old world, to follow those aimless leaders blindly, then you walk away from this. You walk away from ever having another chance to work on any project remotely approaching this one in importance, in groundbreaking opportunities, in relevance to the entire human race. But," he emphasized the point, pounding his fist on his desk, and then turning the monitor back on, their eyes inevitably drawn to the swollen belly on the screen, "if you choose to stand with me, then you participate in the greatest endeavor mankind has ever undertaken; you help shape the very future of this country. You will be instrumental in bringing control and order back to the world."

He turned the monitor off, stood up, walked behind the three. He put a hand on the shoulders of each man in turn, letting it rest there for a moment before moving on to the next, and then walking around in front of them again. He sat down on his desk, a confident, strong smile on his face. He knew their answer; he knew the only answer any vibrant, breathing man could make, given the choice of stagnancy or life.

Doctor Scott looked at Allan and Sid. He saw the general agreement in their eyes. He nodded to them. "We're in."

Major Atkins clapped his hands, rubbed them together. "Great. Let's get started."

Chapter Twenty-One: Preparation

The next several days were an endless series of tests. Two medical specialists were brought in and set up a complete maternity ward. The surgery room utilized state of the art diagnostic and operating equipment. Char was moved to an isolated room that was adjacent to the surgery room. Larry had been given an attached room to Char's, but his contact with his daughter was strictly limited by the doctors. They allowed them to share a few hours a day; the rest were taken up by naps and examinations.

Major Atkins considered taking action as Larry's protests became more boisterous. Not yet, he decided. There could still be use for him, as leverage to force Char to cooperate. He gave in to some of Larry's demands, allowing the Ambersons to share meals in addition to an hour in the morning and an hour in the evening. After talking with the doctors they assured him they could still get all their tests performed in the remaining time. It was important to keep her spirits up, they told him, and nothing did a better job of that than visiting with her father.

Doctor Scott and Sid Eckham were working closely with the two medical specialists. They were checking ultrasounds, testing fluids drawn from Char, discussing different options based on how the birth went. Allan supported them with processing the data and modifying programs to include new parameters outside those expected in human infants. Most of his work was in preparation for future tests, assuming a live birth.

Larry did his best to hide his frustration, fears and anger from Char during their visits. There was nothing he could do about their situation, anyway. They had kept him away from everyone else, other than the soldiers who brought their lunch and the doctors who came in to take readings and check on Char while he sat beside her bed and talked to her. None of them said anything to Larry, treating him as a necessary object in the room, good for the patient but of no direct use to them. If they came through this with a healthy mother, and a healthy child, then it did not matter what they went through now. He knew Major Atkins would do anything to ensure that; obviously he wanted the child alive, but of equal importance was Char's health, for no one knew if the child could survive without her. It might be only her body that could feed the child, that could sustain it on this planet which was only half of its heritage. Larry recognized equally that he was the expendable member of the Amberson family. He didn't believe that his government would kill him, though he wondered exactly what part of the government knew they were here. He wasn't sure if Major Atkins was working covertly, with plausible deniability, or had gone rogue. He had caught glimpses of Allan Davis, Sid Eckham and Doctor Scott, but had been unable to talk to them. They looked guilty and turned from his questioning gaze, hurrying away before he could say a word. That made him worry quite a bit as to what exactly was going on; the fact that General Crowell hadn't stopped in to reassure him also made him uneasy.

Char was too tired to wonder about Major Atkins' objectives. Her day consisted of getting poked and prodded, exposing most of her body to the medical specialists as they felt for unusual shapes or looked for blue skin or whatever they were seeking. The only good times were when she lay in bed, listening to her father tell her stories, talking about her mother, about the farm back when he was a little boy, about summer evenings at the fishing pond. She noticed, but chose to ignore, that he never mentioned what was going on around them, never speculated on what would happen after the birth. She tried to ask him once, but he brushed it aside and smiled. "We'll worry about that when the time comes, Char," he had said. She supposed that he was right. She couldn't deny the feeling of security these doctors and fancy medical equipment gave her. It wasn't the warm and fuzzy feeling she had when sitting with Dad by the fireplace in the log cabin, but a more studied, analytical sense that whatever complications might occur, these experts could handle it. Whatever the future held, at least this setting meant that all that could be done for her baby would be done. That was enough for today.

Doctor Scott knocked on the door to Major Atkins' office. "Sir? It's time."

"Everybody agrees. If the fetus gets any larger, it could cause complications. We recommend inducing labor now."

"All right – do it." Major Atkins got up from the desk and followed Doctor Scott back to the surgery room. He went through the door and into Char's bedroom, where Larry was watching her sleep.

"The doctors are going to induce labor," Major Atkins told him. "They decided it's the best thing, for her and the baby."

Larry nodded. He knew they would not do anything to jeopardize either of them. If the doctors thought it was for the best, then he trusted them, as far as this situation went, anyway. "I'd like to be there with her."

"Sorry, Larry, the surgery room is going to be doctors only. We don't want anyone in the way, should they have to react quickly in case the baby needs immediate attention. You can join me in the observation room – we'll be able to see everything that's going on."

Larry wasn't happy about being kept out of the operating room, but followed Major Atkins up to the observation room without protest. His hands were tied. He was lucky they were going to let him watch. Two soldiers were also in the observation room. Larry looked through the glass window down at the surgery room and saw the two medical specialists, along with Doctor Scott and Sid Eckham, standing below him. The four men had the operating table surrounded. Char lay flat on her back, eyes wide, looking frightened.

There was a microphone attached to the sill under the observation window. Larry pointed at it. "Can I talk to her?"

Major Atkins nodded. "Probably help her settle down."

Larry picked the microphone up and moved the switch to the on position. "Char, honey? Can you hear me?"

She looked around. "Dad?"

Larry heard her voice through a speaker in the wall of the observation room. "I'm up above you, Char. Keeping my germs out of the room." His tone was light, joking; he wanted to calm her down, to let her know he was watching over her.

She looked up and saw him through the glass window. "I'm scared, Dad. I'm not ready for this."

"Yes you are," he said. "You are going to be just fine. These are the best doctors in the country; they are going to take wonderful care of you and your baby; you pay attention to what they tell you and before you know it you are going to be holding a baby in your arms. You're going to be a wonderful mother, Char. Just like your mother."

She smiled at him, then grimaced as a contraction hit her. Larry lost eye contact with her as the doctors bent over her. A mix of medical commands and clanking of instruments came through the speaker.

Larry clicked the microphone off and replaced it on the sill. He bent his head and prayed to God for the lives of his little girl and her baby.

Chapter Twenty-Two: Demon and Angel

All the advanced medical equipment, the hyperbolic chamber, the blood transfusion area, the surgical preparations, were exactly what they had hoped they would be: precautions, just-in-cases that proved unnecessary. Three hours after the delivery process had begun, a screaming, fluid covered babe was lifted up from the table.

The doctor held the infant up, turning the child over to face Char. "Congratulations, you have a healthy baby boy."

Char cried, held out her hands, wanting to take her son and hold him against her body. She was tired, exhausted from the labor, but had never felt more alive than when she looked up and saw the issue of her and Grant's love. "Hugh," she said, "his name is Hugh."

She cried out when the doctor turned away, still carrying her son. The infant felt her call, felt the familiar essence that had cradled him for the past nine months fade as the doctor walked toward the side of the room, intending to clean the baby and check on his vital signs.

Hugh's tiny body had been reacting to the abrupt change in environments since Char's water broke. His body had formed in general human terms, relying on the latent characteristics within his genetic structure. He had coughed as he drew in the first breath of oxygen, modifying lungs slightly to adjust for the exact composition of the air, all by instinct, self-preservation and adaptation inherent in his body's abilities.

When the umbilical cord had been cut he felt the cessation of the direct connection with Char. It had been jolting enough to be forced out of the warm, safe chamber that had been his entire universe. But now the life force that bonded with him, the tie to the being that fed him, that grew him, was severed on the physical level. He still felt her warm essence, the life force bubbling in comforting waves near him, and this kept the babe from instinctive reactions to reconnect; this feeling was enough to give Hugh a sense of protection from his mother.

But when the doctor carried him away, when he felt the panic, the sense of loss emanating from Char, the infant's instincts took over. The only thing he could do was pull back toward that essence, to draw it to him so he could feel the love in his body, the warmth surround him. Char cried out in pain as she felt the hunger reach out to her. She felt cold as her very spirit began to drain from her body, as she felt her essence flow from her.

Larry watched in horror as Char's expression changed from wonder and awe at the sight of her child to pain and fright. He grabbed the microphone from the sill, clicked it on and shouted, "Give him to her! Give the baby to Char!"

Doctor Scott rushed to the doctor carrying Hugh and pushed him back toward the bed. He took the baby from him and placed it on Char's chest. The color returned to her face as the infant felt the nearness of her essence. He relaxed as he lay against her, the skin to skin contact reestablishing their physical bond, and as he calmed down the spiritual drain halted.

Doctor Scott looked up at the observation window. "She's all right. They're both all right." He turned to the other doctors. "Go ahead and clean them both up. Don't move them more than a foot apart until we figure this out. Remember to bag and label everything – all towels, all wipes; we will be analyzing all of it."

Hugh nestled in a blanket on top of Char's chest. They elevated the head end of the bed to enable her to sit up and hold him. She looked down at the sleeping infant. He looked like an angel, she thought. She pushed away the memory of how she had felt when he had sucked at her life force, how her body grew cold as he was carried away from her. It didn't matter, she thought. He'd never hurt her; even if he took her life, she would always love him. He would always be her baby, the love child that Grant had left her. She smiled as she realized that Major Atkins couldn't risk separating them. They were going to be forced to leave him with her. He needed her, she thought, and they knew it.

Chapter Twenty-Three: Suspicions

General Adam Crowell put down the phone in disgust. Another dead end. He had not heard from Larry Amberson for over a month now, and was getting worried. He knew the Ambersons were laying low, that it wasn't unfeasible that the delay was simply Larry being cautious. But his gut said otherwise, and that gut was something he had grown to trust through the years.

He looked over the reports he had ordered on the activities of the group controlling the Amberson farm project. There had been no activity on any of the accounts they had tracked. Larry and Char had obviously been careful in their dealings with the local merchants. In fact, they had halted the traces a week ago. Evidently they had given up on finding them through the database searches.

He slammed his hand flat against the top of his desk. That was it - that was what was fishy about the whole thing. They wouldn't have stopped those traces unless they didn't need them anymore. They would have kept looking for the Ambersons for years if necessary; no expense or length of time would have stood in the government's way given the potential prize at the end. They must have succeeded. He looked at the reports again. Somewhere in the mess of data they had accumulated, something had pointed them in the right direction. Major Atkins had the Ambersons, his churning gut told him.

He made more phone calls, requested additional reports and information on the Amberson project, as well as Major Atkins' military history. He was dumbfounded when he saw the dearth of concrete information about the project. There were essential details from the cloud incident that were missing from the reports. From what was included, it supported the idea that nothing out of the ordinary had happened last August. That it had been another false sighting with no evidence to corroborate the idea of extraterrestrial involvement.

Major Atkins' history was equally disturbing. Highly qualified, a career man who had resigned abruptly a week ago. General Crowell began investigating others related to the Amberson project and with Major Atkins' prior commands. He soon found that over a dozen men had either left the service or had been reported missing in the last week. Of particular interest were the three individuals he recognized from the cloud incident: Doctor Eugene Scott, biologist Sid Eckham and computer specialist Allan Davis.

The only figure involved in the episode last August who had not disappeared was Major Drake. It took a while to find him, but after several false trails he finally located the major where he had been reassigned. "Major Drake, this is General Adam Crowell; we met through the conference call last August," he said into the phone.

"General Crowell – of course I remember. What can I do for you?"

"I'm hoping you can help me find Larry and Char Amberson."

Major Drake sighed. "I'm sorry, I have been relieved of command of that project, General Crowell. Not my choice, but orders are orders."

"Well, Major, I have a new assignment for you. Effective immediately, you are on my personal staff. I want you here in Norfolk first thing tomorrow. Unless you would rather continue to sit on your butt while a rogue officer tries to create a new world order."

"No sir," Major Drake said. "I'm on my way. And sir? Thank you."

"Don't thank me until after I tell you what kind of a mess you're getting yourself into. See you tomorrow."

General Crowell hung up the phone. That was one member of the team, he thought. Major Drake should be able to help. But he was still going to need a break to find Atkins. It had taken nine months for the Ambersons to be uncovered. He knew he didn't have that much time. Who knew how long it would be before Larry and Char were dead? He knew someone willing to take the risks that Major Atkins was taking would not hesitate to injure either one of the Ambersons if it served his purpose. He shuddered as he thought of what could happen if Major Atkins actually succeeded in his quest to control extraterrestrial technology.

Major Drake was the first piece of the puzzle. He thought about where the next one would come from. The three members of Drake's team that had disappeared – Scott, Eckham, Davis – their profiles didn't match those of the other men that had apparently joined Major Atkins' clandestine organization. They had only worked with him for a few months, for one thing, and had always shown more interest in the science, the research aspects of their jobs rather than career advancement. His gut told him they were critical to his search for the Ambersons. If there was a chink in the armor, it would be through one of them.

He ordered additional reports on the three men, requesting associations, phone records and computer activity. He needed to find another contact, someone who one of the three might have reached, might even still be in touch with. There had to be a thread he could follow to the Ambersons.

Chapter Twenty-Four: First Days

The initial time for Char and her newborn son was not vastly different than the experience of any mother in any hospital in the country. It was more a matter of degree, than anything else. She was monitored closely, diagnostic tests were performed on her blood and urine, she was given expert medical care. Likewise, Hugh was under intense scrutiny twenty-four hours a day. With extreme care, tiny amounts of his blood were also taken for analysis.

Char felt an emotional, almost psychic bond with Hugh. It reminded her of the virtually complete merging she had experienced with Grant. She felt their spirits mingle when she held him to her breast. As he suckled, she felt he was giving her as much spiritual energy and love as she gave him milk.

She looked into his bright blue eyes, eyes that looked at her with the love that Grant had. That same intense stare, unblinking, locked on her own brown eyes. She thought she could look into those tiny eyes forever. She saw eternity in them, she saw endless possibilities. She saw hope and the stars and perpetual love and happiness.

She did not know what the future would bring them, but she was happy for the moment. She was determined to enjoy this time with her son, these moments that were filled with first events: his first smile, his first burp, everything he did was tinged with newness, held all the magic experienced by any mother with her first child. She was too intelligent to even pretend that it would stay this way forever; she knew that before too long Major Atkins would impose his will on their lives. But for now, they were left to bond together and she was as happy as she could be given the circumstances.

Larry kept to his own room for the most part. He would watch over his grandson when Char needed to sleep, but recognized Char's desire to spend all her moments focused on Hugh. She slept enough that he did not feel slighted in his own time with Hugh. Even under his watch, they remained in the same room as Char. Hugh still reacted with violent screams and tears if he was taken more than ten feet from his mother. No one was willing to risk his reaction at this point in time. Larry was glad of the uniqueness of their situation, if only for the cautious nature it gave their captors. Major Atkins wasn't willing to harm Hugh or Char with rash actions. Larry worried over the day when Hugh was less dependent on his mother. If this situation cost Larry his life, that was one thing; he prayed there would be a solution that would spare the lives of his daughter and grandson.

Hugh gradually became aware that the other presences in the room were also living beings. He was still most comfortable with Char, felt safest while in her arms; but as his perceptions grew, he realized these other beings also held life energy within their bodies. He sensed them walking around, various shapes and brightness, their life energies sometimes flowing freely throughout their bodies, sometimes curled in tight little balls that barely let the aura call to his senses.

The infant felt a pull from these life energies as they walked about the room. The open, flowing ones were especially attractive to him. As Larry sat by him during meals, watched over him while Char slept, he became familiar with the essence emanating from his grandfather. It was similar in many ways to his mother's essence. Hugh felt a consistent warmth, a sensation of love and safety, when he tentatively reached out to Larry's life force.

The others were not so warm or comforting to his senses. Some of them had an almost palpable coldness to them, and he shrank within his own body when they were in the room. It did not feel good when he curiously reached out to the muted curled balls of life energy of those beings. He contracted his energy quickly, reached back toward Char to warm his spirit up after the icy contact with the dark forces. Char felt a chill along her spine when he did this, as he drew warmth from her to replace the chill in his bones.

Still, something attracted him to the life energies of the others, whether they were bright and flowing or dark and balled up. Sometimes, it seemed the energy flowed both ways, that he felt a small surge of power as he attached to another life essence. The rush would make him dizzy and he would lose contact as he squirmed in the bed by his mother's side or in her arms. She would tickle his stomach and soon he forgot about what he had just experienced until the next time a life force walked by and his curiosity got the better of him.

The people walking by did not really notice these brief linkings with the child. The hairs on their arms might rise, or a chill go down their backs, but they attributed it to the nervousness they already felt when they entered the room. No one forgot the delivery, how it seemed that the baby was draining the very life out of Char. So whether Hugh was looking at them or at Char, whether he was awake or asleep, they felt strange around him, felt that the tiny babe might at any moment erupt into the monstrosity that was a quarter its heritage. They feared that this child would one day become another cloud, a potential annihilator of humanity. They feared this, and yet they also hoped that it might be true, in the manner of the strange attraction mankind has for disasters, for train wrecks and car crashes and category five hurricanes. They sought the hurricane, but at the same time they were apprehensive. They wanted to be able to unleash this power but only under their direction. Both biological and technological advances were their goals with this project. An alien designed spaceship would be one wonder to awe the world with; an alien cloud capable of absorbing an entire army, impervious to any counterattack would be quite another. The world, literally and figuratively, would be theirs with those powers under their command.

Chapter Twenty-Five: Impatience

Doctor Scott frowned. "I don't like it, Major Atkins. We don't know enough about their relationship. It could kill either one of them."

The major drummed his fingers on his desk. "Scott, we're going to have to try it sooner or later. I agreed with the initial decision to keep Hugh and Char together; it was clear from what happened after the birth that there was some kind of bond between them, that the boy needed to be near her to survive."

"That's why I think separating them now would be a mistake. It's only been a month; if anything, their bond is stronger now." Doctor Scott shook his head. "It's a needless risk."

"It's a risk I'm willing to take," Major Atkins said. "We need to be able to work with this child, to take it places without the mother. It must learn to exist without her. We have to wean it, and we need to start soon. The first few weeks, it might not have been able to handle it, but it's stronger now; it's used to spending some time outside Char's arms. I'm not saying rush this, but just carefully extend the range of separation. Place it in a crib to sleep, start moving that crib a couple inches further away each time."

"I don't disagree with that process, Major Atkins," Doctor Scott said. "It's the other proposal: the shock treatments, where we rush Hugh from the room completely for a brief period, then bring him back. Those are what I am concerned about."

"Those are most critical, Scott. Trust me, by doing that, Hugh won't even notice the little weaning steps we take the rest of the time. He won't feel a thing at being ten feet away from Char instead of eight, if between them he was taken completely out of sight of her. The shock separations are the splash of icy water to wake him up."

"I still think we should wait until the child is older, until he can understand what we're doing."

Major Atkins shook his head. "No, that will be too late. He'll be so imprinted on his mother that we'll never be able to sever the bond. He has to become a soldier, Scott. A weapon that is completely under our control. If we let him maintain the human mother-child relationship, there will always be a risk he could desert us. No, we have to start now to prevent his dependence on her."

Doctor Scott sighed. "If that's the way you want it. I'll get a schedule set up. We'll initiate the weaning process tomorrow morning."

"Excellent," Major Atkins said, rubbing his hands together. He looked up at Doctor Scott. "This is where it starts, Scott. This is where we begin to create the perfect soldier."

Doctor Scott nodded and left to prepare the schedule. Major Atkins remained seated behind his desk. He clasped his hands behind his head and leaned back, ruminating on the future, dreaming about a world which he held in firm check. He fantasized about sitting in the Oval Office, the presidential seal replaced with one of his own design, world leaders at his beck and call. Finally, the people of the world would know true justice, true leadership, he thought. There would be democracy everywhere, the principles of the original founding fathers of the United States carried out to the letter in all countries across the globe. And who knows, he thought, as he continued to think on the future, perhaps on other planets as well. Once Hugh matured, after they had gleaned every bit of alien technology from him and held him firmly in their control, there would be no limit to what they could accomplish.

Major Atkins let his hands slide from behind his head. Time enough for dreaming later, he thought. He bent over the reports on his desk that detailed the results from the past month's analysis of the tests performed on Hugh and Char. He frowned at the inconclusiveness of most of them. It was evident there were unknown characteristics and properties of the fluids taken from both of them; unfortunately, exactly what the nature of those differences was, the why and what and how to replicate them, had remained unanswered despite the scientists' best efforts. It was all well and good to have one perfect soldier in the making, but it would be years before Hugh was ready to use, and Major Atkins sorely wished to find a way to transfer some of the alien abilities to his own already trained men. He wanted a super-soldier formula, and so far they had been unable to create one. He sighed and pushed the reports aside. Tomorrow would be better, he thought. Once the weaning started, it would provide a boost to the morale as their control over the infant was demonstrated. Tomorrow would be better, he repeated.

He got up from the desk, walked around his office. He looked at the maps displayed on one of the walls. He had already sketched out initial battle plans for several different scenarios. He knew the ones involving use of Hugh would be redrawn, modified greatly, before Hugh would be old enough to undertake them. But that was no matter; the plans kept him sharp and focused on the ultimate goal. Other plans were drawn up to utilize his hand-picked crew, assuming the super-soldier formula was developed. One man equal to twenty, he thought. It would make conventional security plans obsolete overnight. A half-dozen men could take over an army base, if they were enhanced soldiers with alien abilities. That was what he hoped he could initiate within a year. He did not want to wait fifteen or twenty years to achieve his dreams. He was a man of action, and this patient waiting did not suit him. They would find the serum to transform his men. Then he could implement the plans that would lead to the unleashing of Hugh when the boy was ready, to deliver the final blow to the world governments and force them to fall in line under his control.

Chapter Twenty-Six: Experiment

Major Atkins had approved the schedule developed by Doctor Scott. It was nine o'clock in the morning, and the first experiment was ready to begin. Char was wheeled into the surgery room in her bed, with Hugh sleeping beside her. Larry was taken back to his own quarters and locked in. Major Atkins and Doctor Scott were in the observation room, looking down over the surgery room. One of the two staff medical specialists and Sid Eckham were in the surgery room along with two soldiers. The rest of the staff were either off duty in their own quarters or stationed in the command center.

The medical specialist walked over to the bed. "As we explained, this is just a normal, healthy process. We need to get Hugh comfortable with some separation, or he will become too dependent on you and that would slow down his development. It's just part of his maturation."

Char nodded but tears still fell down her cheeks as the doctor carefully lifted Hugh from the bed and placed him in a rolling bassinet beside the bed. The infant squirmed slightly at the movement but remained asleep.

Sid carefully observed both Hugh and Char, noting nothing of significance. He looked up to the observation window. Doctor Scott nodded at him, indicating to the biologist that they should continue.

Sid maintained watch on Char as the doctor slowly rolled the bassinet away from the bed. They kept looking at each other as they monitored the mother and child, to make sure nothing had changed in their normal readings. In addition, Doctor Scott was monitoring the readings from sensors attached to both the woman and baby. He noted Char's heart rate elevation, but it was still within acceptable range, attributable to normal stress from seeing her son rolled away from her.

Just after the distance reached five feet, Hugh awoke. His immediate reaction was evident to all as the baby erupted in loud cries of dismay, his face turning red as he wailed in protest at the unexpected separation from his mother. His readings vacillated wildly as the sensors tracked his bodily functions. He reached for her warm spirit as he had on the day of his birth. Char felt weakness as he began to drain her essence in his attempt to pull her to him. Doctor Scott noted the change in her vital signs at the same time that Sid saw the physical changes in her face and body, as the color left her and pain replaced the nervous anxiety that had present. Doctor Scott shouted into the microphone he had held at the ready, "Phase Two! Now!"

The doctor grabbed the bassinet handle firmly and sprinted to the wide double doors that lead to the connected post-op room, pulling the cart with its infant cargo behind him as the soldiers held the doors open. They were trying to create enough separation between Char and Hugh to prevent him from feeding on her life force, trying the first shock treatment that Major Atkins had ordered.

That part of the plan succeeded. Hugh was still operating on basic instincts ingrained in the genetics inherited from the cloud through Grant. He was still a newborn; his reach was limited to what he could sense in his immediate surroundings. As they crossed through to post-op and the doors swung shut behind them, the connecting bond between his life force and Char's was interrupted.

Char felt the relief immediately, felt her energy plateau as Hugh's feeding stopped. She was weak, but her vital signs stabilized quickly. At the same time, however, she felt a hollowness inside, an emptiness as she realized she did not feel the warm pulsating throb that had been near her, inside her, ever since his conception. She felt like part of her soul was gone; her reason for living had left the room, and she started to cry.

Hugh did not know what was happening. He had felt cold, frightened when he had awakened and the warm loving energy that he was tied to was distant. He had instinctively reached out and been reassured when he felt that energy flow to him, fill him again with warmth and security. His anguish and fear had multiplied a hundredfold when he had been whisked away out of the room and the renewed connection had been cut off completely, leaving him feeling abandoned, alone and cold – without the love that had comforted him since his very beginning.

He reached out and failed to find the familiar life force of his mother. There were three other essences in the room. They were not the bright and flowing ones that he had identified with Char and Larry. These were colder, duller balls of lukewarm energy. Still, he could not find his mother, and he reached desperately for these in her place. He drew them in, taking their life forces to sustain his own body against the dark isolation. As he pulled their essence into his, as he filled his tiny body with their energies, his senses expanded. The soldiers at the door and the medical doctor who still clutched the bassinet all collapsed as he took their life forces.

The lifeless bodies were but emaciated husks after their essences had been sucked into Hugh. The capture of their energies was somewhat modified from the process that both the cloud and Grant had performed; while he absorbed their energies in them, the essences were broken down, their spirits no longer intact as the life left their bodies. He did not have the same conflict that Grant had, did not have to overpower the will of those that were drained. His was a pure transfer of energy.

Sid looked at the double-wide doors, one of them propped open by a fallen soldier. He trembled as he walked over to the doors. He stepped over the body and looked into the bassinet. When he entered the room he felt Hugh latch on to him; sudden coldness overcame him as his energy was pulled away. He gave a brief cry as he fell, dead before his body hit the floor.

Just as quickly as it had started, it was over. Hugh no longer sensed any other life forces in the room. But he was no longer cold, did not feel as vulnerable as he had before, now that the energy he had absorbed filled his body. With a child's curiosity, he reached out with his questing tendrils of energy, finding that he could reach further than before after the influx of power. His wails lessened, fear and abandonment forgotten as he wondered at what his expanded senses detected. Now, with the surge of energy he had taken in, he was able to sense the twenty-five feet from this room, through the doors, to the next, where his mother was. He was able to feel her presence, and quieted down as he sent a thin tendril of energy to her, not to drain but to reconnect with her.

Char stopped sobbing as she felt the warmth fill her body. Hugh was with her again, she instantly knew that her baby was okay and that the love was still there between them. But then the hunger that had been awakened within Hugh took over. It was instinctual, the same feeding desire that had threatened to overwhelm his father, before Grant had sacrificed himself to stop it. Hugh had not matured enough, did not have the capacity yet to make that decision, to control the beast that once fed by the life essence of another would not be stilled. The connection sought for love and warmth turned into a sucking vacuum pulling all the life force of Char into him. It was almost immediate, as she was still weakened from the earlier drain, and before Major Atkins or Doctor Scott could react to the alarms from the sensors monitoring her vital signs, Char Amberson was gone.

The life force of his mother threatened to overwhelm him with its intensity. This was no dark muted lukewarm spirit like the others he had absorbed. Char's was a vibrant, glowing sun compared to them. His cells mutated, modified structure as it processed the huge influx of energy rapidly in order to avoid being consumed by it. His tiny body actually grew in mass as the energy was converted to physical form. The greatest change was in his brain, expanding greatly, reacting to latent memories still carried within its genetic heritage.

The time it took Hugh to react to the changes predicated by the life forces he had just absorbed allowed Major Atkins and Doctor Scott brief seconds to undergo their own metamorphoses, although their change was solely in their minds. Doctor Scott fully realized from the brief images he had seen of the bodies below that they had unleashed the very monster they had risked everything last August to stop. Major Atkins concluded that it was better to research alien technology from a dead specimen than to be dead himself. They both reached for the red safety switch on the panel next to the observation window.

Red lights flashed in the surgery and post-op rooms after the switch was flipped. Steel panels slid down over each of the entrances, slicing through the desiccated corpse of the soldier in the double doorway. Vents, electrical outlets and cable access points were all sealed off. The two rooms were turned into isolated gas chambers, and poisonous and acidic fumes were pumped into them.

The observation room was an elongated hallway, essentially, and they ran the fifteen feet to the next window. They looked down at the post-op room.

The bodies of the biologist and one and a half soldiers were sprawled out on the floor. They peered through the noxious vapors that filled the room, trying to see through it into the bassinet below them.

"I can't tell if he's moving or not," Doctor Scott said. "The sensors all went off-line when we sealed the room."

"It will clear in a moment," Major Atkins said.

They stood, sweating, as the mists slowly dissipated. "Oh my God," Doctor Scott said, when he caught his first glimpse of the transformed baby. Hugh was now twice his prior size, with an enlarged head.

Major Atkins blinked, stared hard through the vapors, until he too saw Hugh. "Jesus Christ, what the hell happened to it?"

Their curiosity vanished, replaced by horror as they saw it tilt its enormous head. "It's still alive!" Major Atkins cried.

Hugh's adaptive body had no difficulty in shifting the properties of his skin to repel the corrosive gases. Likewise, it filtered the poison from the air instantaneously as he breathed. The consumption of the life forces was complete; he had processed the energy and was now far advanced from his infantile guise of mere moments ago. His brain, energized and filled with awakened memories, was processing the new information from his heritage as well as what his heightened senses fed him about his surroundings. The hunger lay coiled within, and as those senses expanded, it prepared to strike.

Before either of the men could plan their next action, before the horror of the misshapen hybrid below them could fully register, they were struck down. Their life forces were pulled into Hugh, and the new world order so desired by Major Atkins had begun.

Larry was sitting on his bed, worried about Char when the feeling hit him. He felt his body growing cold and his strength sapped. As he fell to the floor, his final thoughts were for Char, praying that Hugh would spare her, that they would escape together.

Allan Davis had been at his computer when he heard the alarm. He opened a new window on his laptop. He connected to the external server that he had not dared to since he had been taken here. No time for regrets, he thought, as he transmitted a file containing everything he knew about the project to the server. The wave of energy from Hugh hit him as he closed the window, sucking his life force from him. As he fell forward in his chair, his body knocked the laptop to the floor, where it hit the hard tile with a loud crash, breaking into several pieces.

Within fifteen minutes Hugh had extended his senses throughout the underground base. The hunger was insatiable; with each new absorption it sought further, faster, expanding its range and its capacity to take in new energy. Hugh rapidly became the killing machine that the Major had envisioned – that very essence of what Grant had died to prevent.

Hugh spilled out of the bassinet. His body was the size of a child now, weighing in at nearly seventy pounds. He got to his hands and knees on the floor. His misshapen head, larger than a grown man's, was difficult to lift up. His body adapted, shortening the neck, strengthening the ligaments and muscles around it. He straightened up and rose to his feet. He stretched, relishing in the feeling of power flowing through his body. He sent his tendrils of energy hundreds of feet in all directions. There were minor creatures in the soil as he went beyond the confines of the base: worms, beetles, grubs; he drank their essences in without thought, as a plant pulled solar energy from the sun. When all was clear he sat down on the floor. The hunger was still there, though the vast feeding had satiated it for now. He concentrated on his internal processes, on understanding all that had been latent in his memory cells. He learned.

Chapter Twenty-Seven: The Break

Jeff had been depressed for months. He ignored the few friends that remained, after being abandoned by Tia. He couldn't believe she had led him on again only to disappear once more. He did not know that Tia had been victim to Grant's energy absorption, that she had died after she had attacked Grant and Char. He just knew that right after he fell back in love with her she had abandoned him in the corn field outside the Amberson farm.

Even the occasional e-mail from Allan had been unable to interest him. The usual cryptic messages, vague Star Wars references intended to invoke the old feelings from their days at Berkeley, did not raise his curiosity. Not until this last one. The attached file had blown his mind. Secret military experiments, kidnapping, alien babies – there was so much material it was overwhelming. But over and above all the data, all the incredible proof of alien life, secret military bases and rogue military officers, was the undeniable plea for help.

Allan was in serious trouble, and Jeff was his only hope. Jeff felt alive for the first time since Tia left. He remembered all the good times he had shared with Allan, how they had been best friends for years. They had not had the same opportunities to spend time with each other the last few years, as they both had gotten involved more with their work, but they had always stayed in touch, sharing information, spending an occasional technical conference together. Until he had fallen into this pool of self-pity, Jeff realized. Maybe Allan wouldn't be in this situation, if he had paid attention to those earlier messages.

No use crying over that, he thought. Only thing to do would be to follow up now and avoid repeating the mistakes of the past. He opened up search windows to locate the contact information for the person that most stood out from the information Allan had given him, the one name Allan indicated he could trust: General Adam Crowell.

Chapter Twenty-Eight: Maturation

Hugh continued to reach out automatically, absorbing whatever life forms came within his range. His mental abilities were almost fully formed. He soon determined how to shift his body structure and properties deliberately. This allowed him to shift forms and phase through the metal doors trapping him in the post-op room.

He explored the entire underground base with an insatiable curiosity. His mental hunger matched that of the beast within that fed upon life energies. He was able to figure out the procedures needed to connect with the command center's computer network. Soon he had absorbed all the information contained within the vast databases. He learned language, government systems, military procedures; he drank in every byte of data present in the vast storehouse of knowledge.

He learned of the plans that Major Atkins had stored on his personal computer. He assimilated the nuances of strategy, rules and power. He saw how Major Atkins had planned on controlling other beings, to use them for his own gain. He interpreted mankind's historical wars, of conquering and conquered, how the mighty ruled over the lowly, how the rich mandated the life of the poor. He contrasted his own abilities and powers against those of the human beings he studied. He realized they paled in comparison – that humans would be no match for him. He saw this, and was glad.

This was what he was here for, he thought. Hugh had learned of his mixed heritage, knew he was the inheritor of the cloud's destiny. He would utilize Major Atkins' plans, he decided. He would rule mankind as shepherds herd sheep. He would prepare them for his harvest.

But he wanted to learn more. He wanted to build his body up, and his mind, so he could come to them much as his father had first appeared to his mother. He would shift his mass, grow into the appearance of a man – no, a god. Large, bronzed, muscled, a figure that would inspire awe and fear. A god among mortals.

Chapter Twenty-Nine: Rescue Attempt

General Adam Crowell wasted no time after Jeff called him. He and Major Drake immediately met with Jeff and recognized the situation from the data files Allan had sent. General Crowell contacted the Pentagon and soon had authorization for his mission.

Allan had not been able to give the exact location of the base in his files, as he did not know it, but there was enough data present, coupled with what information was strangely missing from the military's databases, to locate it. By the next day, a strike force of special ops troops was assembled in the Arizona desert.

General Crowell addressed the soldiers before they turned down the rough road that led to the underground base. "Men, this mission is of vital importance to the security of our nation. Lethal force is authorized, but I must stress that there are at least two civilians – Char and Larry Amberson, you all have seen their pictures – that are being held captive. We're here to rescue them, not shoot them, okay? Additionally, three other personnel – Scott, Davis and Eckham – may not be there willingly. As far as we know, everyone else is down there in direct violation of the oaths they took when they joined the army. We prefer to capture as many alive as possible, but do not risk your own lives in doing so. One last reminder: if there is a baby down there, do not, I repeat do not take any action. Secure the area and contact me at once."

The military convoy drove down the road to the large bay doors hidden under the sand. They blew the doors open and raced down the ramp to the underground parking area and the elevator bay.

An electronics specialist had the elevator door open in two minutes. He and the rest of the first squad piled into the elevator and descended the hundred feet to the bottom of the shaft.

Hugh felt the life forces approaching, picking them up as they traveled downward in the elevator. The hunger uncurled within his body, lashing out like a cobra at the energies closing in. The soldiers did not even have a chance to radio General Crowell, so quickly was the life pulled from them. The elevator reached the bottom floor and stopped. The doors opened, but nothing moved inside, no stirring among the dozen uniformed men piled on top of one another on the floor of the elevator.

Hugh walked down the hall to the open elevator. He quickly assessed the situation, realized that someone on the outside must have found out about Major Atkins' operation. There would be more above, he thought. More energy. More importantly, there would be more to learn. He wasn't ready to take control, not yet. He removed the bodies, spreading them out in the hallway. He stripped one of them and donned the uniform, shaping his face and altering the pigment of his skin and hair to match that of the identification badge on the uniform. Private Ken Graves, he read on the badge. He scanned the other uniforms, picking up the last names of the rest of the fallen soldiers. He bent over the emaciated husk of Graves, sending some of his cells into the dead tissue, shifting its form, altering its appearance until it looked like a small child. Hugh unhooked the radio attached to his belt and knocked it hard against the floor before putting it back on the belt. He then took a grenade, pulled the pin and tossed it into the hallway. He entered the elevator and pressed the button to ascend. He sat down on the floor, leaning against one of the corners.

General Crowell swore when the doors opened and he saw a single soldier sitting on the floor against the wall. He rushed forward, closely followed by Major Drake, to check on the fallen man.

General Crowell leaned over Hugh. "Are you okay, son? What happened down there?"

Hugh was not sure how the voice of private Ken Graves sounded, so he kept his tone soft, his words paused, as if it hurt to speak. He looked up into General Crowell's face, let tears run down his battered face. "I'm not sure. It all happened so fast. We got out of the elevator, fanned out and then it hit us."

"What hit you, soldier?" Major Drake asked.

"Some kind of energy wave, it knocked us over and then it felt like everything was going cold. It sucked the life right out of us, I felt everything going numb. I was at the rear of the group; I saw Kirkpatrick and Johnson fall right in front of me. I tossed a grenade; when it exploded I fell backwards into the elevator. I looked out; no one was moving, my radio was busted. I knew I had to let you know what happened." He reached up, clutched General Crowell's arm. "I didn't want to leave them, sir, you got to believe me."

"I know, son; you did the right thing. We needed to hear what happened." General Crowell turned to the soldiers waiting in the parking area. "Get this man upstairs. I need a dozen men to go back down there. Who's in?"

Twenty troops stepped forward. He motioned at the twelve nearest. "Okay, let's go." He stepped into the elevator and they followed him in.

"Sir? You should stay up here. I'll go down with them," Major Drake said.

"I've got an army buddy down there that saved my skin a dozen times, Major Drake," the general said. "It's time I evened the score. You stay here; you're in charge – you know what to do if I don't come back."

"Yes sir. Blow the whole thing up."

"That's right. Now don't get too itchy on that trigger – give me a half hour."

Major Drake watched the elevators close on General Crowell and the dozen volunteers. He walked back to the van where they had taken the man he thought was Graves to check on him. Graves had been on the detail at the Amberson farm, back when he was in command.

"Graves," Major Drake said, leaning over the man.

Hugh was on a stretcher, being prepped for driving off and up to the rest of the convoy. He looked up at the officer addressing him. He peered to look at the rank and name tag, feigning an ache in his head as he reached his hand up to his forehead. "Major Drake," he said, slurring the words. "I'm afraid I don't feel so hot."

"That's understandable, that was quite a scene down there. Thank God you came out of it alive." Major Drake put a hand on the man's shoulder. "Don't blame yourself, Graves. It was a miracle that you survived."

"Yes, sir," Hugh said.

"Pretty strange trip we've been on this past year. Hopefully we'll get you some rest and things will be calm for a while."

He shouted up to the driver. "Okay, take him back to the base and get him checked into the infirmary."

Hugh closed his eyes to discourage conversation from the two soldiers who rode in the van with him. He instead concentrated on his senses. He felt their life energies, but held the hunger at bay. The men he had absorbed below ground still filled him with seemingly boundless energy; he was able to keep the hunger under control. His conscious efforts were in the forefront now, instincts held in check. Instead of absorbing the life forces in the van with him, he investigated them. He sent thin tendrils into the soldiers' essences, tasting the vibrant pulse of their energies. Each being was different, he was learning, in the sensations he received from them as he attached the gossamer-like webs of force from his own being to theirs.

He tried new things with his connections. He tried to interlay his energy with the soldier closest to him, and was rewarded with a rich bonding, almost reeling as the images and sensations flowed rapidly between Hugh and the soldier. He got impressions and visions from the soldier's mind, viewing the man's life in a flash of colors and sounds and emotions.

The soldier sat up with a start as he received the same flurry of memories from Hugh's mind. He turned to look at Hugh laying down in the stretcher, shock clear on his face as he realized that Hugh was not their comrade in arms, that Graves was as dead as the rest of the troops that had ventured down the elevator. He turned to shout a warning to the driver when Hugh shifted the direction of the energy connection and pulled the life from the soldier in an instant.

The soldier slumped over in his seat, and the driver, unaware of the events happening in the back of the van, continued on toward the base. Hugh maintained a vestigial connection to the driver and the soldier in the front seat, monitoring their energies but keeping it to a minimum level. He had learned what he needed to from the soldier beside him. There would be time to absorb these men later. When they arrived at the base, he would take their life forces, and then those of the any other army personnel present. He smiled as he thought of the power waiting for him. It was simple, to take the life forces of these humans. He would need new amusements soon. Even before he had established his reign, he thought feeding the hunger would become tiresome. He would not become bored with the feeling of elation he received as he felt another being's energy fill him, as he sucked the essence into his body, but his mind was at a higher level than that of the cloud which had passed this ability on to him through Grant. The joy of power flowing through his body was incredible, but his mind, too, needed stimulation. That would be how he could continue to enjoy his rule over such a primitive, vulnerable race. His mind would come up with pleasurable diversions using his subjects.

Chapter Thirty: Return to Base

General Crowell said little on the trip back to the base. Major Drake wanted to ask him about what had been discovered in the underground base, but the look on the general's face warned him off. The bodies brought up told enough of the story.

Technicians had reconnected the base's command center to central defense networks. All the information would be transferred and ready for their review by the time they returned to the base. Major Drake would wait until then, allow General Crowell some time to deal with the loss of his friend.

It seemed like it was over based on the body count. The Ambersons, the missing members of his own team, their soldiers and Major Atkins' troops had all been accounted for. The last body bag contained the deformed body of a child that they could only assume had been the alien being responsible for the deaths. They were fortunate that Kirkpatrick's grenade had killed it before it did any more harm.

They were all back to square one, it seemed, but the equilibrium was not restored entirely. They had lost some fine men, military and civilian; they had recovered the research performed by the clandestine operation of Major Atkins, as well as the body of an alien, perhaps, but no clear direction. Had they averted another all-consuming alien cloud? Was there another one looming just beyond the solar system? They did not know; they could not know.

They pulled into the base and it was clear that things were not as they should be. Bodies were strewn throughout the grounds: on sidewalks, in doorways, in the middle of the road. The emaciated corpses matched those in the body bags carried in the back of the vans in the convoy.

"Christ," General Crowell said. He picked up his radio. "Everyone, clear out of here ASAP. Get to the entrance road now!"

The drivers wheeled the vans around and headed back up the entry road to the front gates of the base. As they did so, a steak of light went over their heads. When they arrived at the front gates, a glowing figure hovered several feet off the ground in the center of the road. Hugh was a magnificent sight, the embodiment of the Greek gods personified; a golden aura shone from his body, his bronze skin glistened in the sunlight, his eyes blazed brightly, electric sparks coursed through his hair.

Hugh raised his hand to signal them to stop, and the drivers complied when he reinforced his gesture with a mental wave of energy that sapped any will to resist. He had learned much from his brief time at the army base. He had absorbed the life energies of the thousands of men and women stationed there. Moreover, he had not drained them instantaneously; rather he had pulled them one by one, attaching to them first so as to share their memories. He had not only taken their lives, but had learned their ways of living, their fears, loves, desires, secrets and truths. By taking in such a large quantity of information from the diverse people living at the base, he had learned much about how the human race functioned, although there was the obvious slant toward western ways and the culture of the United States. He was intelligent enough to discern this, to screen out prejudices and national sentiment, as he garnered from them the ways of this world.

He had pooled this vast energy inside his body, roaring in ecstasy as the life force from a thousand men and women filled him with raw power. He discovered he could channel this energy in myriad ways; could alter the very fields of energy surrounding him to propel his body along the forces of gravity. He picked the heroic imagery from the memories he had stolen, learned the ways of human idolatry, and modified his appearance accordingly. This altered appearance was what took the breaths away from General Crowell and Major Drake as their driver halted before the majestic figure floating in the air above the roadway.

Hugh amplified his voice, sending out his words in deafening tones that easily passed through the barriers of metal and glass before him. "Exit your vehicles and come before me. I would look on the faces of my servants."

General Crowell keyed his radio. "Hold positions. Rear unit, prepare grenade launchers."

Hugh watched the men squirm in the vans. He detected movement in the van at the back of the convoy. He permitted their actions to continue. If they wanted to perform a test of his godhood, of his invulnerability to their actions, he would allow it. Once. Should they dare it a second time then they would see the wrath of a god unleashed.

He hovered with his arms at his hips as the soldiers in the rear van crept forward alongside the vehicles lined up along the road. He smiled, spread his arms out to invite the attack when they reached the first vehicle. "I am Hugh Grant Amberson," he bellowed. "You cannot harm me; I am the child of the stars, the legacy of the cloud, the god destined to rule this mortal orb."

"Rule this," a soldier said, and fired a grenade at Hugh. The three other soldiers with him fired their launchers also, and the four grenades exploded as they hit the chest of their target.

When the smoke had cleared, Hugh hovered unchanged, not a hair moved from its prior location, not a visible trace of the grenades appearing on him. Hugh flew to the four soldiers who had fired the grenades over him. He raised his hand to them. "This is for the audacity to approach unbidden, to dare to assume you could do me harm." He extended four thin tendrils of energy to them, wrapped the gossamer strands around their bodies. He leached the energy from them, not completely, but took the core of their essence. He let them live, with but a shell of their former spirit, with wrinkled, decimated bodies that could barely perform the basic function of breathing. "You will remain with me always," Hugh said, "as symbols of what befalls those who defy me. I will keep your fragile shells intact, with just enough life to follow me, just enough sanity to know the living hell you inhabit."

Hugh waved his arm and the four men stumbled forward to stand behind him. He turned to address the remaining occupants of the vans. "Now, come out and kneel before your god, or be destroyed. There is no other option; there is nothing you can do to me. Your only choice is kneel or die."

Major Drake looked at General Crowell. "I don't see as we have a choice, General. If we surrender, at least some of the men might live."

"I'd rather die," General Crowell said. "I'm going to send the men out; I want you to go with them. I've had a long life. I'll be damned if I'm going to kneel before this alien bastard. It's just not in me."

"Sir, I can stay with you," Major Drake said.

"No, Major Drake. They need an officer with them. The men deserve that. If there is some way out of this, they'll need your leadership." He keyed the mike open. "Men, I know this is hard, but we have no choice. We have to hope reinforcements arrive to change the situation, but for now we have to comply with his demands. This is a direct order from your commanding officer: exit your vehicles and kneel to him."

General Crowell turned to Major Drake and the other soldiers in their vehicle. "Do it, now," he said.

Major Drake and the others left the van and slowly walked up to Hugh. Dejected, they hung their heads as they knelt before him. The soldiers in the other vehicles saw them and followed suit. Major Drake looked over his shoulder as the men approached. He saw one soldier lift his assault rifle up and aim it at Hugh.

"No!" he screamed, but it was too late. The soldier fired at Hugh, bullets ripping through the air toward the glowing figure.

Hugh raised a hand and the bullets stopped in mid air as he sent a wave of kinetic energy at them. Rage emanated from him as his face twisted, an evil mask of hate and anger transfiguring the angelic god-like figure floating above them to that of a demon. He pushed his hand forward and the bullets reversed flight and tore into the chest of the soldier who had fired them. He reached out and sucked the life force from the soldier before he expired from the bullet wounds.

Hugh turned on the men kneeling before him. He reached out and latched onto ten of them, manipulating his energy fields around them until they rose in the air above the rest. He caused them to turn and twist in unnatural convulsions. They screamed in agony, almost but not quite drowning out the sound of muscles tearing and bones breaking. He released the energy fields and their mangled forms fell hard to the road.

"Let this be a lesson for you: for every one that dares to act against me, ten will die with him. That is the price of defiance." He looked out over the kneeling men that remained, a dozen soldiers left of the thousands that had been at the base. He noticed one life force had stayed in a van. A bright, burning spirit that attracted his attention as a flame does a moth. "Come out," he commanded.

General Crowell sat still, breathing hard, trying to still his fears. He shook his head. No, let him do what he would. Death would be a release after all his hard years.

"Come out," Hugh repeated, "or I will kill these men."

General Crowell swore. Regardless of his own pride, he held his men's safety before it. Reluctantly, he got out of the van and approached Hugh. He looked up into the blazing eyes of the alien, trying to see if there was any trace of his human heritage in them. His gut told him what his vision confirmed: this being held no connection to this world, regardless of genetic make-up. This was a monster. No quarter could be asked, or given, with one such as this. He realized his men were doomed no matter what he did. Better to die than face life with Hugh as their master. Even if that death were painful, even if they were tortured as the first group had been, it would be better than living under this creature's control. He remained standing.

"Kneel," Hugh commanded.

He shook his head. "I will kneel before no man, no alien. The Lord is my God and my Shepherd; He alone will I kneel before."

Hugh ensnared General Crowell with a net of energy. "You will kneel before me," he said, pushing and pulling at the energy, forcing the general to his knees and locking his body in position.

"You may make my body kneel, but my mind is mine alone, and I will always picture you as the half-breed pretender who will always use force because no one would willingly follow you by choice."

Hugh was livid with rage at the defiant words. He contracted the energy fields around General Crowell, collapsing the man's chest, crushing his heart, killing him in an instant. His wrath unfulfilled, he turned to the others kneeling before him. He ripped into them with waves of energy, wrecking their bodies, draining the life forces from them. In seconds he was left alone, surrounded by the remains of the soldiers, feeling a white hot fire within his belly, having no one left to vent his rage on.

He let out a scream of frustration. The old man had caused him to lose control, had made him kill them all. Even the four soldiers who were to serve as an example to others lay on the ground behind him, drained of the last vestiges of their spirits.

Hugh rose in the air, elevating himself high above the base. He reached out his senses, detecting various life forms in all directions. This was a populous land, a populous world, he told himself. There would be others to enslave and force to do his bidding. There would be diversions as he compelled these people to perform for his amusements. He had gathered many different sensations, images and lusts as he had absorbed the personnel of the army base. He was eager to try many of them out, as well as to command others to act them out for his viewing pleasure. It would still be his world to play with as he would; no old man was going to take that from him. One old man's defiance meant nothing to him. He located the nearest city to him, detecting the large number of life forms within its boundaries, and flew to it.

Chapter Thirty-One: Crash Landing

The collision with the meteoroid had damaged the spacecraft's guidance systems. As it neared the blue-green orb, the systems failed completely. The computer alerted the inhabitant within of an impending crash.

As she grew rapidly within the cockpit of the ship, she unlocked the vast storehouse of recordings contained in the computer's database. Her cells, a mixture of cloud, Grant and Char, adapted quickly; her mental and physical growth occurred at an astounding rate. By the time the rocket ship passed Mars on its collision course with Earth, she had learned Grant's entire history. She knew her origin, she knew her heritage, but most of all she knew the love that had brought her to existence. She knew the love that Hugrant had for Grant, to send him out. She knew the love Grant had for Char, to sacrifice himself to keep her from harm, to love her so much he couldn't bear to destroy the tiny clutch of cells that had led to her birth.

Amy, she decided, would be her name, the name of her grandmother, a symbol of the love that had begotten her. She thought of what it would be like to meet her mother. Char would cry, she knew, when she told her of Grant's final fate. She would be destroying the faint hope her mother might have of him returning. She wiped a tear from her cheek as she thought of the pain that would bring to Char. But she would know how much he loved her, Amy thought. She would understand he did it so she would be safe from harm.

She was concerned that she might be bringing the very threat that Grant had died to prevent. She tested her body's abilities, tried reaching out with her senses as Grant had described in his logs. She felt nothing, did not sense anything beyond the normal sensations as described in the medical recordings. Whatever energy absorbing power had passed from the cloud to Grant, it did not carry forward in her genetic makeup, she was certain. She was able to manipulate her cellular structure, but had found no talent in detecting energy or reaching beyond her own body. It would be safe for her to return to Earth.

The guidance system had been damaged - it would fail before they got there. She had managed to alter their course just enough to ensure that they would be pulled in by Earth's gravity. Controlling their landing would be too much for the failing systems. There would be little left of the ship by the time it came to a stop. She concentrated, manipulating tissue, bones, muscles, transforming her physical containment to a soft gelatinous vessel. She surrounded her brain functions with several layers of hard shielding. The gelatin would absorb the impact, would serve as cushion for her vital functions. As long as the impact was lessened, the hard protective layers would protect her mind from the crash. With brain functions intact, she could survive virtually anything, would be able to mutate her physical form as needed. Once she was on the surface, Amy could reassume the female human form.

The entry was every bit as rough as Amy had imagined. Parts of the ship tore off where gashes in the hull from the earlier collision had left it less than streamlined. The exterior heated up tremendously as it rocketed through the atmosphere. The steep angle of entry did little to reduce the speed of the rocket; it did prevent the ship from bouncing off as it encountered the outer layers of the atmosphere.

The ship descended nearly straight down toward the ground at hundreds of thousands of miles per hour. The impact was akin to a nuclear warhead, creating tidal waves of sound, force and earth as it blasted into the earth. A huge crater was formed, and in the center, four hundred feet below the surface, the burned, broken remains of the craft smoldered, with naught but the inner shell of the cockpit having any visible form remaining.

An amorphous blob oozed out through the cracked hull of the shattered ship. Amy modified her outer layer as she poured over the hot surface of the impact crater. She maintained the shape until she had gotten out of the crater. She shifted her body to that of a human female, basing it on her memories of Grant's recordings of her mother. She recalled the memory Grant had stored in the database about his first encounter with Char and her embarrassment over his nakedness, and modified layers of cells to appear as clothes conventional to this world. When Amy was finished, no one who had known Char would have doubted for a second that the young woman in jeans and a sweatshirt was her daughter.

She walked away from the crash site. The descent had been too haphazard to ascertain the exact location of the landing. She had to find someone to tell her where she was; she needed assistance to get to the Amberson farm just outside of Kanapolis, Indiana.

She had walked for ten minutes when she heard the first sirens. Local police and county emergency crews were rushing to the scene. She knew authorities would not necessarily believe her story, that it might delay her reaching her mother. She determined that it would be best to stay out of their sight. She needed to find someone she could trust to assist her in her travels. She hid behind a tree as police cars, fire engines and ambulances raced past, heading toward the crash site. She ran along the edge of the road until she came upon a narrow lane that led back to a large house.

Amy followed the lane and walked up to the front door. She accessed appropriate greeting rituals from the recordings she had absorbed in her education, and knocked on the door.

An old woman answered her knock. "Hello," the woman said. "Aren't you a pretty young thing? What can I do for you?"

Amy smiled at the kindness evident in the old woman's face. "My name is Amy Amberson. Could you please tell me where I am? I need to get to Kanapolis, Indiana to see my mother."

"Oh, dear, you're five states away from Indiana! Come in, sit down and tell me all about it." The old woman took Amy's hand and led her to a small love seat in her front room. "You sit right there. I'm going to get us some tea and we can figure out what to do with you."

Amy looked around the room as she waited for the woman to return. It was clear the woman had lived here for a long time; the room was decorated with many knickknacks and yellowing photographs of family long since gone. It felt like a home, Amy thought, or what she had imagined a home would feel like. She was familiar with how the Ambersons' farm house looked from Grant's recordings, and while the style was different, the richness of furnishing was varied, she knew the sense it would give would be similar to this woman's sitting room.

The woman returned with a tray on which a kettle of hot water and two cups were balanced. She set the tray down on the coffee table in front of the love seat. She filled the cups with hot water and added tea bags. "There, let that soak a minute or two. Now, dear, I'm afraid I've been remiss. My name is Emily Barrister. This is my house, well, mine ever since dear Charles passed last year. You said your name was Amy? That's a lovely name."

"It was my grandmother's," Amy said. "I never met her, but from what I have learned she was a wonderful woman. I think you would have liked her."

"I'm sure I would have, dear. Now, tell me everything. I'm an old woman with nothing but time, and I'm sure after I hear your story I will be able to see what would be best for you."

"You'll help me get home?" Amy asked, tears brimming in her eyes as she thought of meeting her mother.

Emily smiled at her, patted her hand. She raised a laced handkerchief up and wiped the moistness from Amy's cheeks. "Yes, dear. If there's anything I can do to help, I will."

Amy smiled at Emily. This woman was kind; she felt she could trust her. She took a deep breath and told her all about what had happened. Told her everything, from cloud to space battles to meteoroid collisions, a tale of hunger and love, victory and defeat.

Emily sat still, the tea growing cold as it was forgotten, captivated by the Amy's story. She felt her heart racing, the blood rushing through her brittle veins as she was completely taken in with the story. The lace handkerchief was dabbing at her eyes as she heard of Grant's sacrifice, of the love so strong that he gave his life to protect humanity and the woman he would have been with forever.

Emily sat quietly after the tale was finished. This young woman, there was so much love radiating from her; she wanted to take her and hug her, make her forget about the losses, the pains, wanted to hold her and let her know that everything would be all right. But what an extraordinary story – what a fantastic tale Amy had told! It was clear she believed it, poor thing, Emily thought. She reached out and took Amy's hand. "Dear, I know you must have suffered, that something terrible must have happened to you. Please. Try to remember what really happened to your family."

Amy looked at Emily, smiled, letting her know it was okay that the old woman doubted her story. She recognized the warmth in Emily's soul and did not judge her for her disbelief. She lifted one of the cups with its tepid tea, dipped a finger in it. She shifted her cells, intermingling with the liquid, passing kinetic energy to the tea, heating it up nigh to boiling temperature.

Emily gasped as she saw the steam rise from the cup. "Land sakes, Amy, how did you do that?"

Amy smiled. "I can shift my cells – modify them to interact with my surroundings. I don't do this to startle or scare you; you have nothing to fear from me. I just wanted to let you know it was not a fabrication; that my story, as bizarre as it must seem to you, happened just as I described. My father did come from another planet; there was an alien cloud that threatened this planet, and he sacrificed himself in overcoming that danger and the danger inherent within his own body. My mother does live on a farm in Kanapolis, Indiana, and it is my heart's desire to be with her."

Emily watched the steam rising from the cup, looked back up into the angelic face of the young woman sitting beside her. The goodness that poured out from Amy in tangible waves could not be denied. She didn't care what planet her father was from; this was a good person, someone who cared about others, someone who loved her mother and someone that Emily was going to help.

"Dear, let's go get my road atlas. I'll show you how to get there."

Chapter Thirty-Two: March on Washington

Hugh had learned from the minds of the men and women he had scanned that the center of this country's government was in Washington, DC. As he flew over cities on the way to the seat of power he paused, taking in some of the life forces residing there to replenish the energy he spent in flight. He would wait until arriving at the White House before he started to command the citizens of this land. For now, he simply fed as he went, leaving a trail of emaciated bodies in his wake.

He flew at a leisurely place, exalting in his freedom from gravity, in his symbolic and literal rise above the simple human beings below. As more deaths were discovered, the path of destruction was apparent after local emergencies were reported up to the state level. Soon, federal agencies were notified that an unknown menace was headed towards the capitol, killing thousands indiscriminately as it passed.

Military alerts were sent and positions fortified along the expected route. Television crews set up as close to the cordoned off areas as allowed, eager to report on the unknown phenomenon that had elevated security levels to red, restricted air travel and caused mandatory evacuations to be issued for hundreds of thousands of civilians.

Live broadcasts were shown on the major networks as the military dispersed their forces. A battalion of soldiers, supported by jets and tanks, prepared defensive positions a hundred miles outside the capitol. Helicopters were on standby at the principle buildings; the President was already miles away aboard Air Force One.

Hugh sensed the gathered forces as he approached Washington. He smiled. This act of defiance did not irritate him or raise his wrath. No, this was the stand he had expected; this was the battle that would show them just how invulnerable he was and how hopeless it would be to defy him. The handful of men at the gates of the base had been a wasted effort, he realized. He needed their television cameras, their army at full force, to crystallize in their human minds his godliness. He slowed his flight, making sure that the army was ready, had fortified their positions, all arms at the ready. He did not want them to think any other outcome was possible after he had defeated them. He wanted to destroy them at full capacity.

When he sensed that their movements had stopped, that the men were hunkered behind their makeshift walls of sand bags and the tanks were aligned along the road, he picked up speed. He shifted his appearance so that gleaming white robes wrapped around him, the toga of the Greek gods. He swelled his physical body until it was an eight foot giant that rode the wind, a bronze Adonis of perfection.

He halted when he got within sight of the waiting forces. He hovered above them, letting them see his shining aura, the palpable power emanating from his body. He amplified his voice and challenged them. "Behold, mortal men, the god that is Hugh Grant Amberson. Do your worst, so that the rest of this world can see how futile it is to defy me!"

He hovered toward them, arms outstretched, inviting their attack. The invitation was quickly answered. Soldiers lifted grenade launchers to their shoulders and fired dozens of grenades at Hugh. Tanks aimed their long muzzles and shot mortar shells at the glowing figure. Fighter planes zoomed down from the skies and launched Tomahawk missiles. All available fire power was sent against Hugh.

He toyed with them. He would shift his form instantly, at one turn becoming intangible, a gaseous cloud that the bullets and grenades simply passed through, wreaking havoc on the ground beyond him where they landed. Other times he would form an impenetrable energy shield around him, and the force was turned outward where the missiles exploded against it.

He lifted his head to the sky and laughed, an earth-shattering howl that caused the soldiers to clap their hands over their ears, trying to drown out the sound. He lifted a hand and waved it in front of him, reaching out and draining the life from the soldiers on the front line. The soldiers behind them backed away in terror as the dried husks of their comrades in arms fell lifeless to the ground.

The commander called for a retreat and the forces pulled back. Hugh hovered, allowing them to regroup a half-mile away. He rose high enough and increased the shimmering aura about his body so they could see his glowing figure from their new position. He wanted to let the futility of their assault sink in completely before finishing them. He wanted the news to spread so that the entire world knew of Hugh Grant Amberson, and the extent of his power.

The President of the United States had watched the fight while aboard Air Force One. He answered the phone before the first ring had finished. "Permission to launch. Nuke the bastard." He hung up the phone and turned back to his screen.

Four jets wheeled in the sky, high above Washington. They flipped switches, arming the twin nuclear warheads they each carried. This was the last resort; the rest of the nuclear arsenal had gone off into space last August in the attempt to destroy the cloud. These eight missiles were not even supposed to exist; they had been manufactured in secret, in defiance of the United Nations Disarmament Pact signed after the incident with the cloud. The President had argued against their production; now he wished he had authorized more.

The jets aligned their formation. The glowing energy field was easy to find on their radar screens, and they adjusted course to intercept it. Hugh sensed the eight energy fields of the men and women aboard the jets, two aboard each jet. He rose to meet them.

"Hawk One locked on target," the squad leader radioed. The other three pilots confirmed that they, too, were locked in. The squad leader radioed that they were ready.

"Permission to launch," came the order.

"Fire on zero," the squad leader told the other pilots. "Three, two, one, zero."

Four hands pressed firing triggers on their first missile, and then the second. Eight nuclear warheads shot across the sky toward the eight-foot man hovering in the sky with arms outstretched and a smile on his face.

The jets veered away, needing to get out of the range of the concussive back blast from the detonation. The missiles raced unerringly toward their target. "I am your god!" Hugh shouted just as the missiles arrived.

The explosion knocked people to the ground, the backlash tearing through the air, wind ripping anything that wasn't heavy or tied down, sending it flying. The thunderous sound, louder than Hugh's shouts had been, deafened all within a mile. Clouds of billowing smoke poured out, sending plumes miles high and thousands of feet to all sides.

The President stared at his screen. "What happened?" he asked. "Can anyone see?"

The commander of the ground forces looked up at the slowly fading clouds. "Nothing yet, sir. It's still clearing up. Stand by."

Bit by bit the mists were carried away by wind. Finally, the commander was able to see clearly. The soldiers had gotten back up to their feet from the ground where the explosion had sent them, and they saw what the commander did: a clear sky, empty of all but a few lingering wisps of smoke. Cheers rang up throughout the forces, loud cries of joy at the apparent defeat of their enemy.

"Mr. President, we got him," the commander radioed.

"Thank God," the President answered. "Good job, commander."

Suddenly, the cries quieted, as soldiers pointed back up at the sky. A blurring, shifting shape, transparent, rippled up in the air. Hugh had toyed with them, shifting his particles so as to become transparent. The nuclear warheads had as little effect on him as they did on the cloud last August. He became visible again, slowly increasing his physical form and glowing aura until the shining giant, the god among mortals, was before them. He had shifted the spectrum of his robes: he was now garbed in bright blood-red robes.

"This is what will happen to all who oppose me!" He stretched out his hands, attaching tendrils of energy to all the life forms before him. He pulled the essence from the soldiers, draining them, letting their life force pour into him, filling him with power.

He permitted only those running the cameras to live. He wanted this to be witnessed. He flew down to one of the cameras. The cameraman tried to run, but with a wave of his hand Hugh forced him to halt. "You will live, if you do what I say. Defy me and you will die a thousand deaths. Understand?" The cameraman nodded, unable to speak from fright. "Good. Now broadcast this." Hugh waited until the cameraman indicated he was broadcasting.

"People of Earth, I have allowed this display of bravado by the armed forces of this land simply to show you how useless it is to defy me. If any of you are so foolish as to repeat this episode, I swear to you that a thousand innocents will be slain for every man who dares to raise arms against me. Ten thousand children will forfeit their lives for every tank or airplane that launches a shell or missile. I trust this demonstration has shown you how useless those attacks would be. It is not out of fear that I issue this mandate – it is out of the desire to be properly worshipped. It is out of respect for your god that you must follow it. You must obey me, utterly, without question. You exist to amuse me. The moment that is no longer true, your usefulness will have ended, and I will leave your world a lifeless desert."

Chapter Thirty-Three: Change in Destination

Amy waited while Emily retrieved the road atlas. She felt better, felt like she was going to make it home, thanks to the kindness of the old woman. She smiled as she dreamed about arriving at the farm, knocking on the door, having it open and then looking into the soft brown eyes of her mother.

Emily returned with the atlas. She sat down on the love seat next to Amy, opened up the soft bound book to a large double-page spread showing the continental United States. She pointed out Virginia on the map. "This is where you're at now, Amy." She traced a line heading west on the map, moving her finger until it rested on Indiana. "This is Indiana. Let's see, I think we'll have to go to the state page to find Kanapolis."

She turned the pages in the atlas. She paused as she saw thick black lines from a permanent marker following a path across Connecticut. "Charles and I followed this route," she said, showing the page to Amy. "We were going to visit Michelle. She was just about your age, maybe a little older. She was a freshman in college. That was the last time we saw her. She was so pretty, such a little angel. She died in a car crash later that same year. The other driver was drinking, but he got off on a technicality, something about his rights not being read." Emily turned to Amy, tears in her eyes, voice quaking as she remembered how the police captain had explained it to her. "His rights! As if he deserved any, after murdering our Michelle."

Amy leaned over and hugged the old woman. Emily felt the care and concern radiating from Amy fill her body, uplift her soul from the dark abyss she was treading the edge of, with these painful memories of her long lost daughter.

"Oh, dear, thank you," she said, tears spilling over. She clutched Amy tightly, drawing on her strength, knowing the love came to her not unlike a daughter's love for her mother. "Thank you, Amy."

Emily pulled away after a moment, dabbed her eyes again with the lace handkerchief. "I'm afraid I've about used this up," she said, trying to smile, to let Amy know that the sentimental old fool she was would be all right. She turned the page away from Connecticut, flipping through the Atlas until she came to the state map of Indiana. She looked through the index running alongside the edge of the page and found coordinates for Kanapolis. She found the small dot – indicating a population of less than a thousand but more than five hundred – northeast of Indianapolis. She tapped her finger at the spot on the map. "There it is, Amy. There's your mother's home town."

Amy peered at the map. She had absorbed geographical information, including the methods of cartography utilized by the people of Earth, and was able to understand the maps presented to her. She had noted the cities, roads, directions and scales on each of the pages that Emily turned to. She knew how to find her way home.

Amy took Emily's hand in hers. "Thank you, Emily. I will never forget you, or how you have helped me."

"Well, dear, I would feel better if you let me give you a little something to eat." She saw Amy's hesitation. "Please, humor an old woman. I could use the company. It will be fun; we'll watch Jeopardy while the stew heats up."

The desire for sharing a moment with another, Emily's need for companionship, reached Amy's heart. She nodded. Emily squealed with delight and rushed into the kitchen to put the stew on the stove.

Emily returned to the sitting room. She turned the television set on. "Jeopardy is just about ready to start. I bet you'll be great at this; you seem like you have a good head on your shoulders."

The television screen warmed up and the picture came on, displaying a far different scene than the setting of a game show. Footage of Hugh's total defeat of the United States army on the outskirts of Washington was being shown. A reporter recapped the events, telling about the strange glowing man who flew above the ground and had survived everything that the military could throw at him. "He declared himself our god," the reporter said. "He said his name was Hugh Grant Amberson before flying off toward the capitol. The latest word from the President is that we should remain calm, that everyone should stay indoors and await instructions as the military deals with this man – if indeed, Hugh Grant Amberson is a man. For now, we urge our listeners to follow the President's mandate. May God help us all in this dark hour."

Emily and Amy stared at the screen in shock. "Oh my stars, that man – the reporter said he was named –"

Amy nodded before Emily could finish the question. "Yes, that man – that person causing this death and destruction – he must be related to me somehow. He is not my father – he is not Grant – but from his face, from his name, obviously from his powers – I can't help but conclude that he is my brother." She put her head in her hands and cried, warm tears gushing forth, splashing against her palms.

Emily reached over, pulled Amy's head to her bosom. "There, there, dear. Don't be scared. I'm sure the President will figure out a way to stop him. That's what he's there for, after all."

Amy looked up, blinking away the tears. "I'm not scared, Emily. I'm just sad that all those people had to die. It's not right, Hugh killing them."

"Maybe he didn't know better," Emily suggested. "Maybe he's just confused about who he is, about why he is different from everyone else."

Amy shook her head. "That doesn't excuse his actions. He can't just be allowed to do that. If he doesn't understand, that's just a – a –." Amy remembered the story about Michelle. "That's just a technicality. It doesn't make it right."

"No, dear, I suppose it doesn't."

Amy stood up. "I've got to go see him. I have to explain what he is doing is wrong. I will have to wait to see my mother. She will understand." Amy leaned down, flipped through the atlas, memorizing all the data contained therein. "I cannot stay for dinner; I am going to Washington to talk to Hugh."

"How will you get there?" Emily asked. "I can take you, if you want. Charles' car is in the garage. It hasn't been driven anywhere in a year, but our handyman George starts it up once a month. George helps me out; comes by to make sure I'm not drowning in the bathtub or forgot where I put the can opener, does odd little tasks around the house. He wants me to sell the car, but I can't. It was Charles' car, I couldn't sell it. Oh, listen to me go on. All I mean is I can drive you, dear."

Amy smiled at the offer. "I don't think that will be necessary, Emily. Apparently, I can fly." She paused, frowned briefly. "That is, my brother can. Surely I will be able to, don't you think?"

Without waiting for an answer, Amy hugged Emily goodbye, thanked her again for her help, and walked out of the house. She thought about what she had seen on the footage, how Hugh had hovered in the air and then flew away with a simple wave of his hand. She concentrated on her body, trying to determine how to shift her structure in order to do as Hugh had. She shook her head. It wasn't coming to her. She already knew that Grant had possessed sensory powers that she had not been able to emulate. Apparently Hugh's flying abilities were also of a nature beyond her abilities.

She shrugged. She had learned of many creatures on this planet, of land and sea and air. She concentrated and shifted her form until large wings with snow-white feathers and nearly translucent membranes grew from her shoulders. She modified her bone structure, creating thin, hollow supports that were strong but light. She blew a kiss to Emily, stretched her wings out, and took off from the ground. She exhilarated in the feel of the wind in her face as she flapped her wings and flew towards the Capitol.

"An angel," Emily said. She stood on the front steps and watched Amy fly away. "I've just had tea with an angel."

Chapter Thirty-Four: Mile High Summit

The President took a deep breath and exhaled slowly. He stretched out his arms, resting them on the conference table. He was in a meeting room fifteen thousand feet in the air, aboard Air Force One as it flew holding patterns a hundred miles outside of Washington.

He nodded at the technician that he was ready to begin. Dozens of monitors were set in the wall, and as the communication link went live he was conferenced in with leaders throughout the world, east and west, democratic and autocratic alike.

"Thank you for joining me on such short notice, gentlemen and ladies. You have all heard by now what happened at our military base in Arizona, as well as what transpired outside of Washington."

One of the leaders commented, "We were rather surprised to see the use of nuclear warheads. We were under the impression that the United States had signed the United Nations Disarmament Pact last September."

The President dismissed the remarks with a wave of his hand. "Don't get started with me on that; those were all we had left, the missiles we couldn't retrofit for the attack in time. Besides, half of you already have resumed your missile production processes, don't even pretend you haven't."

Protests arose from most of the monitors. "Enough!" The President slammed his fist against the table. "It doesn't matter. Clearly, from the powers he has displayed and the name he has chosen, this Hugh Grant Amberson is akin to the space man that came to our world last August. Just as clear is the fact that he is not here to help but to conquer. You saw the outcome outside Washington. Mortar shells, bombs, nuclear warheads – they were as useless against him as our combined volley of a hundred nuclear missiles were against the cloud."

He hung his head. "I will make this brief, so you can meet with your own advisors. Hugh has issued an ultimatum: surrender or be destroyed. We must lay down all arms; senior political and military leaders must present themselves to him and swear oaths of fealty; we must order all our citizens to comply unquestioningly with all of his decrees. We must all accept Hugh as our world leader, or he will pass over each of our lands, annihilating all living creatures, leaving Earth nothing but a barren waste."

He looked up, eyes filled with despair and regret. "We have no choice. I have already informed my cabinet that the United States will comply with his ultimatum. I cannot force you to do as he says; force is the one option that has completely left us all. But I would rather put my people into subjection, with the hope that someday a savior will come to free them. I would rather give them slavery with a chance of redemption than certain death."

There was silence as the leaders took in his words. He waited, let them feel the weight as he had. "Hugh said you have until midnight, Easter Standard

Time, to make your decision. If any one of you chooses to defy him, we will all pay the price. May God be with us all."

He terminated the call. The President bowed his head. "God be with us all," he repeated softly. He locked up, eyes red, sorrow lining his face. "Where the hell is He?"

Chapter Thirty-Five: It's not Easy Being King

Hugh glared at the prancing fools performing tricks in the Oval Office. With a gesture, they acted out his every caprice. Hours since taking control of the White House, he was already growing bored with the amusements the humans could provide him.

He had at first been intrigued by the vast possibilities he had found while absorbing the memories of tens of thousands of people. Their lusts, their fears, seemed endless. But he soon discovered that playing puppeteer to these marionettes was less than satisfying. He could force them to live out fantasies and phobias, turn husband against wife, force lovers to betray one another, make sons murder their fathers in endless variations of tragedy and drama. It was hollow, though, leaving his own senses with no rush, no feeling of power as they were not worthy of it. They offered no resistance; it was all too easy to make them act out his whims.

He had tried to stimulate his senses by participating in the activities, but no human woman was desirable to him. It was no different than wasting his passions on an automaton. He had mated with dozens of women, and still had felt no true release, no true joy or ecstasy in the acts. He had killed the women for failing to bring him satisfaction.

Blood sport was no better at bringing him entertainment. Whether he killed a man by draining his life force or cleaving his head off with a sword, it barely stirred his emotions. Did a man feel anything when stepping on an ant hill? So was mankind to him. There was no challenge, no effort involved in conquering this world.

He sighed. He waved the room clear, permitting the entertainers to run from his presence rather than absorbing their life energy. He almost hoped that one or more of the nations would defy his ultimatum. It would be better to rise up in flight and destroy a country than to sit here idly waiting for them to comply with his orders.

He doubted there would be resistance; not on a national scale, anyway. He would perhaps find some pleasure in hunting out the little pockets of rebels that would be hiding all over the world, insignificant gnats planning assassination attempts and fantastical, impossible schemes to overthrow him. A simple swat would send them to their deaths. Still, they might provide diversion for a brief time.

Hugh was alone; he knew this, realized that with no equal to show his prize to, conquering the world meant little. He would go through the entire population, he resolved, to find a woman – young, beautiful, intelligent– who was worthy to sit by his side. Someone to be his consort, his confidant – to acknowledge the breadth of his power.

He would take the life of every being on this world. He would absorb their memories, measure their worth, and as they fell short of the honor of sitting at his right hand he would drink their essence, allow them to give him their life energy so he could continue his quest. Once he found the one he sought, he could allow the rest of the humans to live, to serve him and his mate. Together, they could enjoy ruling their subjects. With someone to validate his authority, to laugh as he forced the puppets to dance, to make love and to fight barehanded until one lived and one died – all these things would be better, would matter, were he to have a suitable mate beside him.

He smiled, a terrible sight were there anyone left in the room to see it. This was a good plan; this would make great adventure as he sought his queen.

Chapter Thirty-Six: Flight

Amy exalted in the feeling of the wind rushing through the snow white feathers on her wings. Despite the purpose of her mission, she could not help smiling and laughing with joy as she flew high above the land.

Her mind traveled on many paths as she winged her way toward Washington. She thought about Emily, how the old woman had been so kind to her, had been willing to sit and talk and help her even before she knew the truth about her. Amy's story had not necessarily been believed at first, but as bizarre as it must have been to Emily, the woman had still thought of how she could help Amy, her compassion coming to the forefront far ahead of fear or doubts at the young woman who had knocked on her door out of the blue.

Amy also thought about her mother, felt sorrow that she was delaying her meeting with Char. Still, it was more important to find her brother. Hugh needed to be corrected. She was sure that talking with him would let him understand the wrong that he had done. It did not even occur to her that his actions could have been intentional. She did not have the capacity to see or expect evil in others; she was a being of pure love, from her conception to her maturation, completely and wholly born from acts of love.

She wished she had her father's ability to sense the life forces around her. She drank in all that her senses could absorb: the smells, the sights, the tactile pressure of wind against her body as she soared. She took these in with biologically enhanced levels of perception, above the human scale, but they were still part of the basic human senses. She longed to feel the pulse of another's life force, to be so in tune with another being that their essences were intermingled, almost becoming one in body and soul.

Hers was not a possessive desire; she did not want to control anyone else or take life from them. She just wanted to share, to breathe together, to live in harmony. She just wanted to love.

Amy flapped her wings, thrilling in the physical motions, reveling in the joy of flying through the air. She grinned as she caught up to a flock of geese. She flew under them, slowing so as not to startle them, and then rose higher after she had passed the lead goose in the formation. She looked back as she outdistanced them. The geese continued in their 'V' pattern, undisturbed by her passage.

She looked back down at the ground. She recognized the pattern of roads from the maps she had memorized. She flew lower occasionally, investigating the smaller towns she passed over. She would increase her speed to avoid detection when she did this. She did not want to frighten the local residents anymore than the geese she had flown by. She thought it best if she remained unidentified, at least until she had a chance to talk with Hugh. And with her mother – she would not want to go public without her blessing, if at all. She did not want to be a curiosity to be studied or gawked at; she wanted to be with her family, to spend time with her mother, and now that she knew he existed, her brother.

She smiled as she thought of another family member. Larry Amberson, her grandfather – what a joy it would be to meet him! She knew he was kind and caring from Grant's memories of him. She imagined going fishing with her grandfather, sitting back on a bank, telling stories, casting lines – basking in the warmth she knew would be in his eyes.

She looked down at the ground again. The smile faded from her face as she passed over the battlefield outside of Washington. There were still hundreds of bodies strewn about the street and alleys of the site. She shook her head. Nothing could be done for them. She could only reach Hugh so it would not happen again.

She resumed her flight, leaving the remnants of the battle behind her. Her mind did not wander; the smile did not return to her face. Her eyes were clear but sad; sorrowful pools of beautiful blue orbs set in a face lined with compassion. A soft whoosh as she flapped her wings was the only sound to be heard; Washington was deserted but for the men and woman serving Hugh. Anyone who could leave the city had bolted.

Amy spread her wings out to slow her descent as she landed on the front lawn of the White House. She stood still, bright white wings spread out, glowing face of an angel, purity and innocence flowing out of her in an almost visible wave.

Chapter Thirty-Seven: Checkmate

Hugh felt Amy's presence, knew she was there before the grass bent beneath her feet on the White House lawn. From the bleak, muted atmosphere surrounding him had appeared a brilliant bright sphere of energy more powerful than any he had sensed.

He stood up, trembling as he reached out with his senses, exploring what was outside the building. It was an incredible, pure spirit: a sun shining so bright it blinded him to all other energies in the surrounding area. He stumbled across his office to the large window. He sent a wave of energy out with a wave of his hand and the extra-thick, bullet-proof glass shattered, sending thousands of tiny shards spilling out into the yard. He levitated his body, shifting the energy fields around his body and flew out through the window and to the front yard.

His robes retained the crimson hue of his demonic nature. He alit upon the grass, the blood red attire offering sharp contrast to the gleaming white apparel that Amy wore. He cocked his head at the vision standing before him. Snow white wings spread out to either side, poised delicately yet powerfully above each shoulder, crisp feathers fluttering slightly in the breeze. Amy turned her face to look at Hugh as he landed in front of her. He gasped when he saw the blue eyes, the angelic face. But more so than the exterior beauty, the wondrous majesty of wings and female perfection, the life force bursting within this lovely shell beckoned him. An essence of absolute glory, of pure bright energy beyond any he had imagined existed. This was his queen; this was the woman who would rule beside him. After sensing her energy, no one else could ever compare.

He took a step toward her and she smiled. She smiled, but the sorrow still tinged her look; there were tears in her eyes, glistening diamonds in a sea of blue. "Hugh," she said softly. "I am your sister, Amy."

He stopped, startled by her words. Sister? He looked again at her face, seeing layered in among the perfect features aspects of Char Amberson. He realized that it made sense, that no mere mortal, no human female, could have contained the life force he sensed burning within her. Sister? It did not matter. She was the only one worthy of being his queen. Human conventions were beneath them. He resumed his approach, walking up until they were but a foot apart. He looked her up and down, marveling in her form and at the spirit within.

Amy closed the final twelve inches of distance, folding the wings behind her as she stepped forward and embraced Hugh. She hugged him tightly, wanting him to feel her sisterly love, her gladness and joy at meeting her brother.

For a moment, Hugh simply accepted the embrace. Her arms around him, her cheek against his and the flow of energy from her body bringing him a warm, safe feeling without his even trying to draw it from her; it was easy to stay in her arms and experience these things. But he did not want to feel warm and safe. He did not want to feel as a brother might. He lifted one hand to her head and pulled it away from his shoulder, turned it so he could press his lips against hers in a lustful, possessive kiss.

She pushed against his chest, freeing her from his arms. "Hugh! I am your sister!"

Hugh laughed. "So what? We are above human morality. We are gods to these human cattle; we can do as we will. As I will. And I will have you as my queen. There is no one worthy among the humans, Amy; it is clear that you are destined to rule by my side, to share in my glorious achievements, to assist in making my reign a pleasurable one."

Amy shook her head. "Hugh, I am not here to rule with you. I'm here to explain how you have done wrong. I know it was not intentional; you could not have understood what you were doing, the harm you have caused innocents. Hugh, these humans – they are not cattle; they are not animals or insects to be ignored or ruled! They are living creatures, vibrant life forms capable of love and hope and they should be protected, not used or played with. We have been given tremendous abilities, wondrous powers, that we should be using to help them. No, Hugh, I am not here to be your queen. I am your sister, not your mate. I am here to stop this madness. I am here to take you home."

"Home? What home do you speak of? The lifeless planet of our father? The vacuum of space where the cloud once roamed? Or perhaps you mean the quaint farm outside Kanapolis, Indiana where our dear departed mother and grandfather once lived?"

The color left Amy's face, blood draining in an instant as his words hit her like hammers on a pane of glass. "No," she cried, "Char, Larry – they can't be dead! They can't be!"

For a brief second, Hugh felt a tinge of regret as Amy sank to her knees, head bent down in her arms, sobbing uncontrollably at the sudden loss of all that she had desired. Her body shook as she cried over the deaths of her mother and grandfather, over her never having the chance to meet them even a single time, to hug or laugh or smile with them, to share any part of their lives.

Hugh knelt beside her, put his arms around her and hugged her as she rocked back and forth. Her spirit shown just as bright beneath her skin, despite the darkness he had just injected in it. Even with grief wracking her body, he felt the goodness, the warmth, the love emanating from Amy's life force.

The hunger uncoiled within him. The sheer overpowering nature of Amy's life force, the heretofore unknown nature of the purity of her spirit, had kept it at bay, along with Hugh's own will that this was a spirit to be joined with, not absorbed. But the close contact, the strong emotions cascading over him from Amy's shaking body, were too much. The lust overcame his willpower; the need for her, for her body and her energy, was overwhelming and the hunger lashed out at the same time that he again lifted her head to his and forced his lips upon hers.

She pushed against his chest, trying to stop him, but this time he would not allow her to escape his hold. He circled his energy fields around her, trapping her next to him. He held her against his body, pushing his flesh against hers, keeping his lips pressed to hers.

Amy did not know how to respond to this brutal assault. She could not understand how her brother could do this to her, how he could even think of such wrongness, let alone commit it. Suddenly, she realized that all she had suspected was true: he truly did not understand the nature of his actions. Her fright at his relentless passions was replaced by her sorrow at his misunderstanding. Her spirit rekindled brighter than ever, her love and compassion pouring forth in an almost super-nova of energy.

Hugh was blindsided by the rush of love that exploded from Amy's spirit. It filled the tightly enclosed energy field he had wrapped around them, saturating his body, his mind and his spirit with the unconditional love that Amy had for her brother. Every cell was permeated with her essence.

His earliest memories were brought forth as he was inundated with love: Char singing to him while he was still growing within her womb, his first panic after the birth and Char's comforting presence that stilled his cries, drawing warmth and comfort from his mother. He saw the reflection of his mother in Amy's angelic features, in the characteristics of her warm, loving essence. He recoiled in agony as he understood for the first time what love was, and how far from it his every action had been.

He broke the shield but it did not matter. Amy's essence continued to wash over him in wave after wave of compassion and forgiveness. He closed his eyes, trying to block out the dual images before him, the angel and the sister, the mother and the daughter, but it was as useless as shutting down the energy field had been. The energy flowed through his body, and it burned as he recalled the evil he had done.

Hugh tried to shut out the light, to dwell again in darkness, but it was too bright, too pervasive. He fell to his knees, screamed his frustration, his pain, his regret to the world he had thought to rule. He looked up and saw Amy watching him, tears rolling down her cheeks. She held her hand outstretched to him, offering to take him to her, offering salvation and forgiveness. As a sister to a brother. The hunger coiled within him, still wanting to fulfill its destiny, to drink in the life force burning so bright before him.

Hugh realized he would never be equal to the power of her love. He accepted he had made the choices that led him to this crossroad. It was clear that Amy had selected the heritage she would honor, that of the love that their mother and father had shared. He had elected to follow that of the alien cloud, to become a destroyer of all he encountered. There was no forgiveness for that, no redemption possible for one who had absorbed the life energies of tens of thousands of sentient beings.

He looked at Amy and smiled faintly. He focused on her clear, pure energy, carefully letting the hunger within reach out toward it. Through force of will he kept it in check, easing it out bit by bit, letting it pull in the essence it sought. He shifted his cellular structures as he absorbed her spirit, removing the protective properties, letting the pure energy burn the cells away.

Amy felt cold as Hugh pulled energy from her. She watched Hugh fall from his knees to the ground, his own face glowing red, heat waves rising from his flesh as he burned his body from within.

Amy radiated stronger and brighter as her love and concern grew in intensity. Hugh pulled a final time from the bright soul before him, pushing the burning energy through his body in a wave of cleansing, purifying release. He shuddered, and then was still.

Amy cradled Hugh's body in her arms, crying for her lost brother. He understood what he had done, she realized, as she brushed his golden locks from his face. She kissed him on the forehead, gathered him in her arms and stood up. She stretched her wings and flew off with his body.

Chapter Thirty-Eight: Epilogue

Emily turned off the television set when she heard the knock on the door. She rose from the love seat and walked over to the door. She opened it up. Amy stood on her front steps, a disheartened young woman, eyes red from crying, face the picture of despair.

"Oh, dear, come here, Amy, come here," Emily said. She reached forward and hugged Amy tightly. "It's okay, honey, I've got you." She sniffled as she felt her heart go out to the poor girl. "Let's go sit down. I'll fix you a cup of tea and you can tell me all about it."

Amy sat silently on the love seat, hands in her lap, eyes blinking back tears that threatened to again spill down her pale face. She took the cup gratefully from Emily when the older woman came back from the kitchen.

After a few moments, Emily patted Amy on the arm. "All right, dear, why don't you tell Emily what happened. I know from the news that Hugh isn't in Washington anymore, but no one knows where he went."

Amy told her of the encounter with Hugh. She told Emily about the deaths of the Ambersons, how Hugh grabbed; she shook as she related how in the end he must have realized what he had done, and that he had chosen the same path of self-sacrifice as Grant. "I guess he couldn't forgive himself," Amy concluded. "I buried him so the government wouldn't try to do anything stupid like clone him and start this whole mess all over again."

Emily put her tea cup down. She dabbed her eyes with her lace handkerchief. "I'm so sorry, Amy. Sorry about your mother, your grandfather — even Hugh. I know he did a lot of bad things, but I'm sure he would have been so different if he had had a chance to know you. You're a very special young woman, Amy. You have such love, such compassion — that's your gift. It's not growing wings or changing shape or any of those other things. Your gift — what makes you an angel among us — is your love. That's what reached Hugh, that's what kept him from wanting to go on with his destructive ways."

Amy smiled at the old woman. "Thank you, Emily. After all that's happened, I didn't know what to do, where to go."

Emily hugged her again. "Dear, I'm glad you came here. You remind me so much of my Michelle, I swear it does a body good to see a young face, to talk with someone again." She sat back, brushed Amy's hair with one hand. "Amy, what are you going to do now?"

Amy shrugged. "I don't know. I really don't want to be a government experiment, or a world leader. I just wanted to be with my mother. I just wanted to go home. But now she's gone; they're all gone. There is no more home to go to."

Emily sniffled, trying to stifle the sadness brought to her heart by Amy's losses. She clasped the young woman's hands in hers, brought them up in an almost prayerful motion. "Dear, dear, child," she said, her eyes brimming wetly, "would you consider making this your home? Could you possibly stay here with me?"

Amy smiled and pulled Emily's hands up and gently kissed them. "I would love to, Emily."

Emily cried out in joy and hugged her new found daughter. "Welcome home, child," she whispered in Amy's ear as they embraced.